BORDER

THE SWEAT BOX
ISBN-10: 1-58790-106-4 / ISBN-13: 978-1-58790-106-5 / 216 pages / paperback / $16.95
A series of unsavory acts ties a rancher in Texas to old farming money in California. In this third Dalton Keys mystery, U.S. Marshal Keys wends his way through an entanglement of relationships to corner a barn burner and killer.

A fast-paced whodunit — you never know what to expect next.
— SACRAMENTO MYSTERY READERS

UNDER DRAGON HOUSE
ISBN-10: 1-58790-090-4 / ISBN-13: 978-1-58790-090-7 / 238 pages / paperback / $14.95
This fourth Dalton Keys mystery finds the illegal sale of firearms to insurgents leading to a statewide manhunt for the son of a priest turned tracker. Addie Marjoe has all the makings of a maverick cop except he's his own dungeon keeper in this novel on customs and abortion rights.

Full of complex, twisty suspense.
— David Doerrer, MYSTERY SCENE

BLUEPRINT
ISBN-10: 1-58790-157-9 / ISBN-13: 978-1-58790-157-7 / 170 pages / paperback / $22
Fifth and last Dalton Keys based on the actual 1951 New York subway bombing, leads to a suspected reunion of terrorists who commit a mine bombing in the California desert.

An excellent, well-portrayed loot book, fast paced, gripping action.
— MYSTERIES IN BRIEF

SNAPSHOT, COLLECTED STORIES
ISBN-10: 1-58790-158-4 / ISBN-13: 978-1-58790-158-4 / 170 pages / paperback / $20
A collection of compassionately told stories that include eight short works previously published in Ellery Queen Mystery Magazine under the author's pen name Lea Cash-Domingo.

Superb, substantive well-crafted puzzlers.
— Library Journal

One of the most notable features of Judy Koretsky's stories is the vivid depiction of setting. Judy brings her background so thoroughly to life that she seems to create a painting with words.
—ELLERY QUEEN MYSTERY MAGAZINE

CHERISHED MEMORY, POEMS & A PLAY

ISBN-10: 1-58790-152-8 / ISBN-13: 978-1-58790-152-2 / 92 pages / paperback / $18

Written in the style of Shakespearean sonnets, there are over two hundred poems in this book. This is Ms. Koretsky's first work of poetry. "How many days will it take to know you?/ When sweet designs their answers echo clear?/ Once agreed will you tumble fast and true/ And hold me close and always keep me near?/ Or will you fickle for sweet restraint/ Fall for some other woman's arduous complaint?"

ROPE

ISBN-10: 1-58790-171-4 / ISBN-13: 978-1-58790-171-3 / 344 pages / paperback / $27

Three novels-in-one book also featuring ROOM and DEATHMASK each about Criminal Intelligence Division investigations in Scotland and England. In ROPE three physicians-in-training and five nurse shipmates are murdered by rope hanging at their college of medicine in Edinburgh, Scotland after a day outing consisting of military exercises. In ROOM the controversial "no egg" case focuses on a team of divers whose bodies were found in opaque morgue bags after a locked room shooting death of a county planning commissioner. In DEATHMASK the famous Brughel murder of a young Backwalk girl who is brutally stabbed haunts forensic detectives in the Clough in Ireland.

Barnes & Noble gives ROPE a five star rating.

Tower Books ranks ROPE #1 in Fantasy-Historical

TROJAN PARK

ISBN-13: 978-1-58790-211-6 / 212 pages / paperback / $18.00

TROJAN PARK A California Mystery is a glimpse at the narcissist prone culture of the society noir which upper elite artists careers ascend as quickly as they recede. From ritzy Terra Linda to glitzy Montclair the social climb to wealth seduces a young socialite, whose flirtation with thrill-seeking and reckless danger leaves dead two husbands on the Fourth of July. A fast paced page turner, this novel sizzles with intrigue and tawdry motivation and a questionable cast of characters. Who stands to earn a killing on the senior Roark's life? Alameda County Deputy District Attorney Lenny Cliford tracks the desperate dealings of a family at war with its adolescent heir-son. Through tantalizing art and state-of-the-day security systems to protect a museum, a fail-safe chase takes this investigator-attorney to Paris to the Musee du Louvre, to the Los Osos coast and then Seattle to dragnet a diamond heist of staggering proportions.

BORDER

J. LEA KORETSKY

REGENT PRESS
BERKELEY, CA

paperback
ISBN 13: 978-1-58790-225-3
ISBN 10: 1-58790-225-7
Library of Congress Control Number: 2012939195
e-book
ISBN 13: 978-1-58790-226-0
ISBN 10: 1-58790-226-5

10 9 8 7 6 5 4 3 2 1

Manufactured in the U.S.A.
REGENT PRESS
www.regentpress.net

TABLE OF CONTENTS

HAVANA

1. A barge of stemmed sugar cane burned as a blazoning sunset the color of tequila settled into the crystalline waters in the inlet some forty kilometers off the untrammeled beach of Nassau. Through the night the plumed wraith rose like a path above emerald trees, flickers of sparks casting off evil spirits of succor in a nearby village. The archeological team had come and gone out to the cay island of sand, flowering trees and castle having identified a sunken vessel lying on a shelf at a hundred feet submerged, their red and white fishing boats scattered on the beach, nets abandoned with trowels and spades. In a lilting breeze tide poured over the flat sand of the beach until all one could see for a half mile was a lazy drifting silken sheen whose rich brown bottom moved in surface rivulets and periodically emerged glistening with shrinkage. On that small plateau of sand on the far side of the castle in a small white wooden hut with chartreuse roof and windows some twenty feet into the brush of spiny cholla and choking purple and pink wildflower a light burned distinct as any buoy throwing slanted light across the beach and azure water. By dawn Salvatore d'Atope, a handsome young man in the prime of his mid thirties, conveying but a studious, somewhat forlorn concentration, a shock of blond wavy hair, dark eyes, narrow shoulders, long legs, commonly found on the beaches to count the distance set by a recent tide of remaining damp sand, would have caught a few hours sleep, the computer on standby, sunlight flooding above the trees vanishing the now slanted amber light emanating from the window slats, a pier of rocks on a jetty visible.

In the good old days when teaching assistants were honest and languished on the beach in barely nude proud exhibition Salvatore d'Atope might agree that he was the hottest agent around. In the morning just as the sun was rising from the cleavaged mountains Jose took two camera shots of anything that stepped onto the beach whenever he arose for tea. Usually any half dozen sequences captured off the preferred mailbox camera were of aquamarine, vivid, icy stills of glimmering ocean, the farthest utter tranquility; each was accompanied by date, day, time and in a sea bearing entry log a description – cold blue, sunlight on aqua, cove low tide – hundreds, each their own distinct face, cresting waves, night blue, almost contra negro, horizon, water with pier lights. Amidst a school of gorgeous sleek marlin, he had been tracking an unusual species of shiny backed stingray for weeks – gold metal shapes traveling through jet cool waters at surface of the Caribbean. The nearest dateline city desk from whom to acquire information as to changes in ocean habitat was Miami and he sent a county gram once he identified the closest match in photo resembling the fleet at a horizontal distance.

Miami's off station was a small three story hotel on a posh velveteen green on the north tip of Nassau, a verdant setting with suites and balconies all facing the glittering ocean and stretch of white sand beach. Three swimming pools, four outdoor restaurants and bars, a nightclub open to the night air and twenty smoke lanterns alit with fire torches, the Avalon Beach Hotel aspired to the most celebrated attaché and the worst of indentured foreign office, both whose former role until the 1980's was to improve small harvest farms and build missions to educate children. In the twelve and a half years that followed their core task became a collaborative effort under Dr. Paul Farmer, Director of Harvard University Partners in Health Works, known to the lower Americas as Zanhi Lasante, to help businessmen establish lucrative hotels to encourage trade relations with United States officials, especially statesmen. With eastern bloc influence from the Rosa Luxemborg Platz and the Berlin Mite to the famed estates of Deibert and wife Elizabeth Eames Roebling, the PIX picture malls and color desk aided even the least scholarly chirper a focus in on clandestine security protected pictures, close-in on streets, close-in on a car, any in a vicinity would do the job. For example the report dated September 30, 2009, for 09:38am, gave the tsunami as having landed with California unscathed covered by NBC 13; in the Birmingham-Tuscaloosa News the quake was recorded with a 5.1 magnitude in central California at 2 .01am Thursday about 148 miles west of Las Vegas in the vicinity of Death Valley National Park.

"See what you make of this." The assignment manager, a man named Hilgarde Massey, often in stony silence, of a salty air disposition, aged well into his seventies, lines etched across his jowls, a weather beaten mangle of grey brown hair, rumpled tie worn daily, a crisp collar with rolled sleeves, negative black trousers, Mocktoes his only extravagance, several bourbons under his belt by seven at night, gave his man, a mild looking executive – pencil behind right ear, careful tweed professional who crossed his t's, black hair, trim, a duty port-bound guy, almost always upbeat, unmarried the essential – up for assignment rotation the coolpix photo.

Jones Baylor gave the item a distant glance-over. The photo appeared to be of a ship hull with a cabin on top, not unlike Florida magazine advertisements of Earth cosmopolitan leanings. "Straight navy scorcher, built to ring," he replied.

"Nope," Hil said. "Neither a stuffer nor a bell. Angle's

wrong for the docking."

Jones disagreed. "Color's tan, thin line blue and up white; it's Turkish. Who's waters is it in?"

"You tell me. Port says no ship in our waters for date given."

"Maybe it's a class line, a Nor stopper."

"No one knows, Equator thought a document runner."

Jones received the photo and placing it inside an insert into a notepad binder already filled with hundreds of tabulated articles, news clippings, bribed and borrowed photo insertions, other downloads and painstakingly researched notations, he asked,

"What are you inclined to reduce this for? Oil tankard lost at sea? Pilfered museum articles? Why not send it through to Military?"

"There's no presence of a uniform. Ocean appears to look resort."

"Alright, I'll see what I can drum up. How soon do you need the initial finding?"

"Stat."

A cool handshake job; Jones could see it taking anywhere between a month to a year, twelve hours a day researching on the computer. He'd pick up lunch first, as soon as he could arrange check with his man before he began the actual research, find out if the foreign correspondent had any idea where to look for an unmanned ship.

He donned his sticky brim hat and went for a stroll on the golfing green. The first clouds of the warm weather typhoon season were amassing, soon the light rains would pelt the small community with giant globs of inconsistent downpours, the violent winds would marshal over the ocean and grey skies would drench the vessels caught between the Keys and the Caribbean, storm warning lights shrieking at night.

The field staff had gone to lunch to write their bylines and soak up what remained of the final hours. Without an urgent notto, Jones spent his days in the evidence recovery unit running through a series of a hundred photo clips a week for identification, referring knowns to indexing which in any month might generate one to two articles on biosphere, wind technology or capable nomenclature. A sight processor for five years since retirement from OBISPO oceanography, he was approaching sixty-four, was tallish with a mawkish bedraggled mien, expressionless even under benign circumstances, a previous state university lecturer who stayed in the lab producing photographic evidence for test trials for the Agency. Despite four divorces, each derivative of one red haired beauty, he was usually to be found weekends at a downtown bar soaking a bourbon with his group or up to midnight on his beachfront patio grilling a steak shooting the breeze with an expert shaker from the office. Underwater scenes were his specialty from the Belize tidal basin to the filmy barrier of Jamaica, the scintillating surface to the innocuous cave with stairs. Forty years in a combination of the arctic to the moonlit grottos to the darkest dirty green slime off the islands to the sapphire depths of South America. His sons wound up leaving long before adulthood seeking the permanence their research mothers maintained.

He picked up a turkey and cranberry salad sandwich from the deli in the lobby and returned to his office on the third floor. His suite like the other seventy-five rooms contained a full port computer with telephones on a long desk with plenty of elbow room, a dining room set for six on an enormous dark scarlet Berber with thin black stripes, a kitchen big enough to turn around inside, a grey marble tiled counter, a living room fully furnished with two tropical paradise couches, leafy green on ultra black background, all on a parquet floor, a few lamps and through a short hallway a small bedroom and adequate bathroom with a walk in closet and peach tiled, open entrance shower, mirrors everywhere, one disappointingly tiny sink in alabaster.

Jones dialed his original dateline office in Houston, sent a copy of his working photo, typed in his byline. Then he set about to work. He placed the photo on his lab translator, waited for it to appear on the console, sectored the picture and quartered the top sections looking for any archival similarity. Within an hour Houston responded with a series of color matches for vessels on waterways – a capable large boat with seventy-two feet deck and cabin in South Carolina, several similar boats docked at Ft. Lauderdale, a road with torrential rain bent palms, Seven Mile Marker, a pier with sand off Long Key, a private dock with plenty of grass, trees obscuring a cabin or studio house and a small sleek cabin cruiser, family night on a beach with campfires and a game of volleyball, and rental outboards on the southern side of Haiti. In the subsequent series of photo clips there were men on the beach beside a lagoon, boat track under water, the tile interior of a building underwater, a diver in shorts in a swimming pool, a coastline of stunning beach and disturbed dark blue water, a brief news report from The Houston Chronicle titled, "After the Shock – Reality," a picture of Cuba on the Gulf of Mexico side in brown celestial tint, a series of newspaper shorts from Marine Science for Public Defender Reale, artist, city data, geology and a tycoon report on Randolph Corbusier, son and partner of a Florida mobile camera surveillance firm, a one distance lens shot of black film for the Bahamas and a chart of tide patterns found for the Gulf; all photos conveyed more or less that the darker blue upper sections of the photo depending upon the target of intensity of blue could as well be deep water trench, inlet, ocean directly above a cave or a coastal body of ocean, shallow in comparison. No river, it was a reality he had to deal with.

As he proceeded with each lineup, making notes as he went, Houston posted commentary with a sidebar, "Adjust Date/and Time," for which he established ten year by profile columns and reworked his groupings of photos. When he had completed that singular task he ran an inquiry through Reuters News Service; in minutes the high speed network shot back with a picture of a partially floundered yacht that read, "File: Ehime Mara, U.W.A. Jima found." He had been at it for over four hours, his half eaten sandwich no longer of interest, he got up to stretch his legs, rinsed the glass pot and emptied the used coffee filter in the kitchen and made a fresh brew. It was 11:42 pm and he had not yet covered three frames. Jones showered, put on pajamas of gentlemen's silk, creamy white with the initials ABH embossed in gold over a left pocket by the hotel, and towel drying his hair sauntered to his desk to check on any additional incoming status advice. In the lower right hand corner some news reporter had sent a frame-up of a building from the movie Citizen Kane with a notation, "Portland, OR street cover for rain drainage" and showed below the wording a yet tinier photo of a section of track leading underwater. It meant something absolutely convincing to someone, but hard lived years had earned his respect for the conscientious, meticulously hard driven statistician he often communicated with and never met, and he sent a query without any expectation of hearing back until later that week.

Diplomats and journalists among a few hundred tourists stood alongside the track their bodies straining with anticipation as the announcer's voice thundered overhead booming over loud speakers, twelve horses stamping up dust and flying dirt, they rounded the halfway mark, one bay taking the lead pulling far ahead of the others, sure to be the victor, the announcer producing jockey names and cup titles for each winner of the past season. One female in particular, lazy brunette hair twisted at the nape, wearing a black silk A-line dress with white polkas and a large red belt at the waist, heeled in black with white toes, strode from the field onlookers, her long legs carrying her at a brisk pace through the crowd past the concession stands. Once Desde stepped into the plaza she hailed a cab directing the driver to the rinky-dink district of pink and dark pink stucco houses with brown oak doors that lined cobblestone alleys in the high country of Havana's Matamoras district. She paid the man two pesos, heard him speed away, unlocked the gate to a brick laid garden with benches for the old men, set about the shortest path to her condominium, the glass entrance backed by dark stained wood blinds, let herself inside a foyer with polished brick tile, opened the door to the modest sized living room – white upholstered sofa and easy chair on a fur throw over sanded floors in front of a fireplace, light bluish grey photo set of three separately framed, flicked on a computer and went to change into relaxing red lounge pants and pink cashmere sweater with V-neck. The all-day operating tape recorder was turned off, she withdrew a prepared tape entering the race course chatter with the aid of a mixer, sent it to the man up the road for composite background for electronic surveillance, she placed the distribution in top of a picture of the ocean at dawn, filling a request from Houston; before getting down to the latest assignment of discerning a photo taken at dark, all a risk for anyone in Cuba. The bytes segregated easily into groupings of typical chatter, children at play on a school yard, voices gaily conversing off a deck upstairs above a calle, an argument from a working couple, two males presumably their down prints leaving little variation, tours walking through a town square appreciating church landmarks, a series of long telescope camera shots taken she guessed over a playa lawn from an upstairs hotel open air balcony. Because she was paid only to say where the black photo was taken, she had to break down sections of corresponding chatter in order to point fix likelihood of discourse. When she had broken apart the bytes as many times as possible, she typed, "The photo was taken on the beach at Southport, on a balcony at 3rd and Beach, three people on board a small motor craft, families with children leaving a park after a festivity on a Saturday afternoon beginning around four, identifiers include a homosexual couple had an argument after six-thirty, tour finished with a discussion at the beachfront of Playa Mayor celebrating Antonio Marquez Iglesia around six-forty under street lamp. Date of unveiling of Mayor's church October 6, 2000, date of festivity October 20, 2000."

Jones had completed the first section of definition, by meridian time of day was one hour after sunset which during the Nassau winter occurred in late September when the ocean turned a deeper hue, on the color chart it was a 90, a darker gradation of ocean blue, the waters at night were at least two feet high, astounding salty sands extending beneath turquoise clear water for a half mile, a craft making landfall would leave a wind driven churning front, with less sunlight or darker clouds but no rain there would be less visibility, hence merely the dark blue portion of one wave. He ate a meal of cornbread and chili beef stew shortly after midnight and went to bed. He dreamed no dreams, was not awakened as he usually was by the neighbor's cat running over the roof.

Sometime during the night before he awakened at eight to the shrill alarm, the Miami office had sent him a logotype, "It is a ghost." The reference was to Okinawa, U.S.S. Emmons which sank near Kouri Island, some two thousand meters off the north end to the bottom at a hundred and forty-seven feet, a war grave during which sixty United States sailors and five Japanese pilots were entombed. Jones opened a photo series on the tragedy and placed a color photo of a ship rail underwater beside his segment for color comparison of the blue ocean. His camera PIX gave the fingerprint as identical. He drew upon any photo clip for the area, the pictoral numbers showed in type 8482137 head gear lights only on two divers, very deep inside the depleted hull, at Cozumel a porthole window on a bottom ship matched to an underwater canyon, 8482144 down by cable to the ocean floor at the same depth the presence of a cavernous hull, actual ocean color a slime green, impossible to see through, the dark blue at the surface replaced by fern grotto caves underwater off Florida Keys, sunken ship with side bars off radio cabin, an article from The Miami Sun titled "Search for Sunken Treasure" with a net of gold artifacts, in Ocean Technology in the Hartley Library an article on the technology that gets a ship across ice, and in The College Fjord a series of articles on the Coast Guard.

Jones bleached the murky greenish water with a series of screens, regrouping his collection to distances until the gigantic shapes were reduced, eventually bright stunningly aqua blue light shone in to a top deck and through it to a visible enclosure immediately below. He cross-indexed to his secure database on seven lost cities retrieving additional similarities, deleting sunken archeology, cantilevering portions of sunken ships, surface light, currents of graduated depths at ten feet, twenty-five feet, fifty feet and a hundred feet, narrowing frames, chalking wave breakers; he removed the screens one at a time, reduced the portion of luminescence to stills before the image caught his eye and placing it in the surface above matched the underside of a boat.

2. Jones typed a hundred and thirty words per minute, for composure he sped up to a hundred and forty words, speed typing until he had a speed of a hundred and fifty to discern the exact image of the boat had been kicked about by a fierce wind, he'd guess during a flood, matching the boat to probable crime rendered him an activity report on ocean raqueteering. The FBI top national news listed a free wheeling drug cartel, drug trafficking of cocaine, immigration crimes and a bribery violation of the Hobbs Act. Broadcaster Pete Anslow reporting from Atherton, California steadied the thoroughfare of drugs with a release of police photographs – a walkway connecting a walking path to a driveway, traffic lights reflecting on a river, an aerial of a snow-doused stadium in Purdue, Washington state, bike lanes at UCSB, a door of a lab with a sky of clouds, ice with water on the floor, a reflection of the sky and door on a grayish floor. Through a close view of the blue sky with clouds, he decided the image was a column of blue underwater, that a grate of sunlight, each width of grey lines a demarcation of a reflection in the metal underside of the sunken boat.

He sent Houston Texas the logotype he had received from Miami before he left for his twice a week walk across the lawn to the beachfront garden poolside restaurant he infrequently took with the computer data consultant of the Agency. Normally Lewis Lewis would be found at the poolside bar at an umbrella drinking his way through a martini up comfortably attired in shorts and stylish tourist shirt displaying townhouses and postcard landmarks, buckle sandals, a nondescript baseball cap worn over a balding patch of blond red fuzz hair.

The air was consumptive, a breeze wafting a scent of wisteria. A few ladies lay on white plastic lounge recliners at the pool on the cement in bikinis, sun glasses, one with a turban. Jones had dressed down for the occasion in a light green silk shirt and dark green khakis, thong sandals, his sticky brim hat, his dark hair brushed back. An Agency man had emerged from a cab and waved, and Jones returned the gesture thinking the field agent was a middle aged bloke always on the move, a reportable byline in a day.

"Been wondering when you'd show," Lewis drawled in his favorite Ft. Lauderdale accent, his friendly face worsted by his martini. "Heard the old buzzer put you on rotation. Could be the one plantation you'll never locate."

"I've made a bit of progress. It's a sogg, that's for certain," and handed Lewis a reasonable download. "I'll have a whiskey neat," he told the waiter. Then to his friend, "What would you make of it?"

Lewis shrugged. "Definitely a ship. Are you sure that's a cabin on top?"

"Haven't gotten there yet. I'm still working my way through upper left. You can't see it by simply looking but it's medium deep with a sunken boat."

"You retrieved a date yet? That might be of help."

"I'm going by the book."

The waiter produced his drink and set it on the glass table between them. Sipping his drink, Jones made a baleful remark, "How about your lights?"

"Nothing in any entire series, dry remarks each. Some headlights, building lights, bridge lights at the base, car lanes in black and white, raised lights to motorways with blur of white streak converging on convention center blue glass reflecting terminal lights, months worth. Lines, patterns and colors, Art 70 stuff."

"What did the photo come in as?"

"Laboratory streaks, presumably city car lanes. Routine, one should imagine, FSX 100 camera, lab design − science technology, bio-imaging, research and design. Bright gold neon lights, razzle dazzle like at carnival, best guess it's the stadium at the races."

"We should have more on stick light."

"That's a suitable technical category." And took a sip, snapped his fingers for the waiter to serve the day's fresh catch. "It's all one carbon nanotube."

Jones smiled a wry salt. "Arena of light, brights, rush hour – what does Hil want? A crash site?"

"It's more complicated than that, my good man. Hil wants to know where to position the lights independent of the buildings. Such as Florida tall glass lit at night, top floor."

"Yours is complex," Jones said ironically.

Lunch was carried on a tray, a plate each of petrale sole buttered with herbs and lightly crusted with pecans, fluffy saffron rice, half a broiled apple and a square of Mexican corn pudding bread. Lewis Lewis who enjoyed the midday meal best bibbed himself and took a few spoonfuls of sole; Jones cleaned his plate of the rice, apple and pudding before he called it quits, he never ate fish except at dinner.

"I've even used zoom electric red with bright white to distinguish traffic from buildings," Lewis remarked, finishing up both his apple and rice with a final swig of his martini, before they ordered another round.

"Clouds are the damnedest," Jones said, and drank half the neat.

"Couldn't be more correct than that."

"Here's a toast."

They clinked their glasses and sipped, took a moment to bask in the warm sunlight, admired the ladies who had turned over onto their fronts and unhooked their bikinis.

"I'm thinking of taking a weekend in Cuba, far west," Lewis said.

"Love to. When?"

"Next week. I thought a little boating, snorkeling, a visit to see my exwife – it'd do you good. I'll book the boat if that's alright."

"Great idea. I'd like to see Rhonda. She still up to penguin habitats?"

"I'm told she has to check over all my work." He grinned

broadly, a sly old guy enjoying a private indulgence.

Jones felt a slight aspersion toward the command who with nothing better to do kept relationships going until spouses forgave each other over some indignity that had caused a separation. He remembered Lewis Lewis had a whirlwind affair while he was married to someone else, had promised Rhonda he would be a free man, took her to the altar and ten years later separated when the work became too demanding. There was no incentive for the wives, typing up their husband's summaries, keeping statistics and dashing off correspondence, doing almost everything but the comprehensive coordination of research which when Lewis joined the service in Puerto Rico began its issues on advertising over a much noticed scandalous obscenity when the then Democratic Underground halted ships to Antartica after the group posed nude on a glacier and their protest for the endangered penguin categorized as offensive.

There were all sorts of ludicrous projects that came and went as their sibling rival the State Department was exercising its talons in the industrialization of oil for trade with America. Public fear was sufficiently raised over greenhouse emissions and glacier melt emptying into the ocean, until James Holmes, Haiti's brain child, son of Reverand Robert Usher and mother Bertha Cook Holmes, came to breathe common sense into the reversal on state policy on trade.

Jones asked him, "Are you still wandering footloose to Puerto Rico beaches?"

"That stint's winding down. I was asked to build a village and few resorts to keep the nurses happy and you know how nine year projects are, what with the trade winds dumping hurricanes yearly, giving the coast a thorough smash, littering the beaches with cabin wood."

"Grieves me to recall she had not a cyclone on her in 1958. I guess the rice didn't warrant it."

"I had forgotten she didn't begin harvesting cane until 1963. The Puertoriquenos weren't particularly consentual to a group from Florida who came to grow coffee on their hillsides, although I will say it beats any other grower. No doubt I covered her early days, it made me my post – she was a port in 1920, a paradise for port captains in 1932 and a coffee bean plantation in 1943."

"She's completely date worthy."

"Oh, indeed, presumed bonny isle for survivors of shipwrecks – Norway in 1919 and Denmark in 1932, swam for safety, mind you. The Agency sent me to P.R. in 1942 to secure housing, plantations, missions, a full list of foreign service network. So, yes, I return at least yearly, see how the old schools are doing, a lively chat at the Habana Hotel, a good stiff drink with the cronies."

"Well, here's the item. In charting this new assignment when I pulled in a thread on dark green ocean my screen went black except for a blue square positioned to the upper right hand side. My observation was that although I'm researching the Gulf, the point is actually closer to Puerto Rico."

"Shouldn't be, blue square at upper right is the Florida Keys."

Jones replied, "Except the bottom ocean there is blue grey. Murky green is only southern side Puerto Rico. Shipwreck confirms."

"Yes, that is murky green, blue is an island, probably a header this side off Cayman. Do you have plank bottom or stairs down?"

"Cave has filled with rain but does not open to ocean."

Lewis' brow furrowed in thought. "Your only posit is an on-land cave, no matter the depth, the blue can only correspond to Mexico, there's no comparison to Gulfport or interior Everglades for that matter. This is the photo you showed me?"

Jones casually tossed the 9" millimeter photo with telescopic lens view on the table. "Same. I've checked my underwater excavation notes and it's no Cunard hit by torpedo; definitely no gigantic 17-story floating football field Bismaerck alleged to be sitting off Cork. My assumption is it's a sunken harbor and this cabin at the top in fact a train."

"If dateline won't give you a verify there's no conclusion

you can draw. That's just life. Have you found any depth that gives an ultraviolet match?"

"None show 110 color."

"Then you're out of luck, unless depth of bottom to pier is four stories, actual custom houses three and remaining stories up to ship liner height measuring ten stories on distance lens scale. So," Lewis continued, thinking aloud, "to qualify the actual question if you believe you have a decoupage of numerous crimes you may have to summarize by color alone assuming ship plans, log accounts, expedition journals, old maps, legal or business records contain no picture representations of any kind. I've always considered the description of the Bis as three stadium fields long to be misleading."

"Returning to the subject of Puerto Rico a minute, how many planks were you sent to?"

"Oh, for sure, there are a bunch, two ports about an hour apart by motorcoach, all on the southerly side."

"Any predominantly shallow beachline?" Jones drank the rest of his neat and lit an after-meal cigarette, a Havana special, one each for Lewis and himself, while Lewis flagged their waiter for another round.

Lewis relaxed with his first smoke. "One. The ships unload in water. It's the reason their piers extend far, could be your murky ocean rests a mile or so out at sea. The other is standard wharf, fairly deep." He picked up the photo, slipped on his bifocals, scrutinized the edges of the photo. "I agree, you're looking at deep blue, 100 color max., some aquamarine, possibly a ship and harbor, not likely it's the Liverpool Lusitania, but you're correct, even with dredging the ship would have been too damaged to have been raised with any intact hull, it would've come apart due to pressure in a month at the most."

"Why didn't the ship get raised the week it went down?"

Lewis shrugged, took the drinks with two fingers off the waiter's tray, handed Jones his. "Probably couldn't get to it."

"That's my point, there's more than one body of water here."

"Try a deep bottom river, they're usually murky green. If

all Hil wants tagged are the ship and cabin, he may not require the bays."

They tasted their liquor, it was obvious to Jones Lewis was on his way to a decent stagger. By this time at 0200 hours Jones would be winding down his afternoon for a nap on his balcony having shot a narrative to Miami and closed his desk until five. The boredom that settled the long term agent to his or her hotel suite was disreputedly referred to as midlife, accommodated by occasional golf, never a swim, taking a late lunch or stealing a nap by three when the air condition was certain to fail.

"I think the ship is typical White Star Line on account it's bow is gutted tin can opener, its engine exposed. It's not tax day, the Titanic collided with an iceberg in arctic weather April 15, 1912. The body can't be a discontinued star construction, I can't determine the cabin, it's unlike any ship line."

Lewis gave signs of final surrender to the sunshine to which Jones inquired if they should wrap up. Lewis waved a hand shaking his head no, he'd be fine despite an appearance to the contrary.

Jones set down his whiskey, pleased by the perfection of the drink.

"It's not on the U.S. seaboard," Lewis said, "doubtful your ship is in Hawaiian waters, you'd have sunbathers. You would have plenty of sand, beach restaurants, tour boats, you would get the pink hotel. Since you have none nor any evidence of property, nor green or divers, it's an off shore, somewhat shallow bay. If your murky waters is a river you'd see large ships at surface and you have none either. For the markers not to exist, this thing ought to be seen off an island, that's acceptable by anyone's standards. Slimy green, Rico, dark blue, Mexico, aqua probably an island, won't be the Pacific. That's the most astute I can give."

Long after evening had emblazoned the western sky with bright orange, yellow and pink Jones had slept off his lunch and begun to define the lateral color above the cabin and top deck. His best bet was to find any likeness for the ship rail. He consulted Artifacts, Ocean Technology, also an island travel section for starters. A ship deck came up off Taiwan, another with visible railing was marked for Lesser drifting into an underwater cave not far below surface. The cave was dark with heights of two hundred feet of dark rock, some bluish and white glassified stalactite pinnacles, surface water aqua blue, dazzling in clarity, much below the water took on the deep blue crystalline cold of ocean. Jones contrasted each sector with references finally matching his deck railing to similar ocean depth locations just below Long Key outside the Gulf and off the Belize coast. It took most of the night to obtain similarities around nearby islands, growth of trees, lithic landmarks, color of sky, sandy or rocky beach, when dateline responded they sent a photo of men lying on a beige sand beach, location undetermined as to shipwreck of a docking vessel, medium sized, hull blasted, having sailed from Puerto Rico face harbor for destination Cayman, reported sunk at sea below Meridian. Whether a crime had occurred involving deportation of illegals, cocaine manufacture and transportation, bootleg, weapons parts, or a vessel loaded with sinkables would become a target concern if the item he was assigned to establish identity of could be categorized as such. Many a vessel intending to enter Florida's waters was denied clearance if illegals were discovered and escorted to an island port for detention. Not so easily recognizable were vessels with previous entry documents which had returned for repair, repurchased by a less than reputable company, stripped down and utilized for ocean radio calls, which was illegal off any shore not monitored by its own government. United States required a vessel to dock at a first port for clearance of crew and products before it allowed sail in order to monitor tariff controls. Once a ship passed all inspections, usually through Panama for destinations in the Pacific, or headed for U.S. mainland through Bermuda or Havana, the last port being Veracruz, then the documents were passed through on a telex system to any of ten southern ports, none in Texas. In the early days of foreign service ports any number of illegals arrived in seemingly respectable vessels accompanying artifacts, statuary, copper goods, rum, cane – coffee was managed – additionally scuba gear, each transmission requiring hotel, Bureau office clearances, and extensive permissions for product acquisition, permits to sell and transport by sea, and release to a particular harbor. The men lying on the beach in Madras shirts and well made trousers might at best be off duty employees or seasonal harbor crew looking for a vacation on a nearby coast.

On the islands, from lesser Antilles as far southerly as Santo to the luxurious Cayman resorts, on down to Jamaica harbor, crew were identified by the wharf, dock or rail bay they worked. Of all products to be permitted trade into U.S. the declared items remained rum, pineapples, Rican brown sugar, Cayman banking bonds of certificate issued by Saudi Arabia, fishing bootle crab off the Keys, Mexican tile, turf by growers in Havana predominantly, lapis as well as attributable turquoise found in Yucatan and Columbian oil extract   destined for oil wells, one to twenty years on the laptop before utilization in refineries. Each county in twenty ports in Mexico and various islands shelved platforms of crates for a bevy of inspectors, Customs, Foreign Service, International Resort Corporation, marina districts and warehousing with tag destinations of Louisiana, Mississippi, Missouri and Florida with receipt rail assignments. Prior to resuming sail from Havana all bottles of a spill of rum were opened, tested by each of a dozen labs, certified for non toxic additives and repackaged, every food examined, turf and stone subjected to standards of acceptability before being approved, the FDA notified, any stray adherent releasing product to the underworld, stigmatized by a stamp on cellophane which even in water read for blackout with a top bar blue square code. Daily wharf crew underwent scrutiny through detectors, docking officials who boarded boats checked in with medical; all left thumb prints on listings to verify daily wage for warehousing.

With probable ocean location and depth surmised, he sent a preview summary to Miami – "Look for indeterminate depth, Art 70, 100+ on color scale, standards for ships lost at sea, rico products under lights interrogation, offshore island non resort, printing plates unlikely, cave snorkeling preferred. Evident cloudy sky, radio room, port deception, bright surface fifty feet up, deck cabin, white line, lighthouse." He set his bedroom clock for six-forty, took two aspirin, went to sleep with the sliding glass open, a wind buffeting the barely visible curtain.

He arrived to the city desk by 0730 hours, the floor buzzed with telephone conversation, all screens were on, the field operatives appeared haggard if not outright impatient. The two secretariats impressed the hell out of him as they downloaded from camera phones and desktops, in the legal department office the data clerks kept tabs to organize the collections, their one spy detective batched data questionnaires with resolved photos taken from assignments. Data transcript analysts summarized in narrative bands, file recorder administrative assistants, all male, placed classified advertisements in Gulfport newspapers, New Orleans had reported in with vessel specifications which Jones recognized at a glance, his own office of thirty-two investigator reporters were still where he had left them three days ago searching photo renewals for whatever Hilgarde assigned, news clippings, broker reports, researched stats lay upon his desk in no apparent order of response, photo series of docks sat in his "in" basket. Someone had turned on his computer and mail files chronicled several image documents in brown tint celestial, New Orleans ships, crab in Corpus Christi, rugby in Shreveport, and Cuba and the Gulf of Mexico in brown tint celestial demarcating the path of ruinous destruction of Hurricane Trina of houses, buildings and harbors.

3. The cabin cruiser sped across the silken water into the ocean at full throttle, the rented driver in a zesty spirit yelling above the commotion of the motor about the destination, fine food, tiny women, crazy benders, beautiful sunsets. Below

them white sand stretched for an infinity, dense emerald forests on peninsulas jutted over grey black rocks, the sun basked the nearly empty beaches with pure golden light flecking frothy white waves. Lewis and Jones stood at the railing sipping tequilas and pepsi chatting about a recent squirmish on the air ways concerning a street fight in downtown Haiti which left a man dead, discovered under a pile of garbage in full view of footloose barely clad children. The situation there had become deplorable, the once resplendent two story apartos built of such inferior stucco that painting their exteriors was forbidden because the steel based paint caused faster deterioration and crumbling. Steel base lacked the acetone quality that retained paint to surface, it typically made the paint become like wood and chip off like old wallpaper, with steel from Biloxi factories the paint caused too much sealant which in turn fractured the already depleted stucco into spindly lines eventually causing debris. Jones actually thought the stucco was inferior to begin with, it consisted of mixed gravel, powdered brick, sidewalk cement. The problem with Haiti were her burnt rubber mills, long shut down by court order of Havana, the sludge piled high onto the often marshy mud, today its own nemesis that left miles of stank rubbery garbage ready for burning, torched on a weekly basis the rubber had formed a river, trenched hills, unable to be stopped.

Havana had deployed troops to shovel a fire line, build a new village some ten miles away, placed individual adults with two children each as family units into new flats of four hundred square feet, kitchen, living area, bath and two bedrooms, and posted sentinels on the beach who daily collected the children for school and taught the adults literacy before pulling out after a year, then the adult females walked to the rubber pits to dig holes for garbage and the antiquated system of disposing rubbish returned to a dictatorship. Havana had her own troubles, her capital had become gutted after torrential rains, her vehicles barely operated and her once French splendor became appeased by dysfunctional teen males whose needs for social order were to establish lookouts for any Cajun or colored female

under the age of twelve for carloads of adult men who descended onto beaches for a week or less, these men arrived who the
hell knew from where, took a single room at a cheap hotel, took
over a bar and tried to set up wives and illegal papers. In the
days when illegals flocked from closed factories in the swamp
laden factories of the deep South, many scored a few rounds of
inferior cocaine, chanced an encounter with a young girl leaving her in the brush and making a dash for the first ship headed
for a little known U.S. port. The first of twelve Fidels, because
each man kept to the persuasion of a drug-free, modest society
with good port controls, came to oversee new villages, build
schools and small textile companies, and provide free meals
at the postal offices at the central unloading port. He was the
chief approval for a tobacco company that rolled cigars who
established his Castro Sentimento shops at duty free tourist
centers. After he opened pancerias, small lounges that served
a tortilla with baked cheese, chopped tomatoes and spicy peppers and a glass of milk to children and coffee to the adults, he
provided after school instruction for families who were under
served by employment. The second Fidel entered the gobierno
approximately five years later and put sidewalks in everywhere.

They enjoyed a few laughs and Lewis commented that Havana had looked its best when she was relatively uninhabited.
The morning wore on in the absence of anything important
as the boat entered the dark blue ocean, a dolphin surfaced,
and the two correspondents shot photographs and went to raid
the cold box for sandwiches and macaroni salad. Puerto Rico
was the place to be, she had everything in the way of luxury,
cruise ship meal platters, excellent TV reception from U.S.
and HBO, fancier swimming pools, the whitest beaches, the
best outdoor poolside bars, any magazine, freer women, call
forwarding, casinos and betting in international water, everything except work, the three-day vacation turnaround and the
sweepstakes.

The west side of Cuba, southerly of Havana, was itself the
paradise, Jones thought, comfortably situated in a lavish hotel

room on the top third floor with an end balcony overlooking an immense golf course of the greenest grass, tennis courts, five elegant pools of various shapes, round, square, one with a waterfall, a connecting pool tiled in sparkling gold with a narrow marble black walkway to an outdoor lounge with large upholstered chairs with square tables the same marble color, and an eternity pool with water even with the stunning turquoise ocean. His room apparently provided every amenity for the traveling exec, rate 5 dark peach carpet, a high king size bed, silk crème comforter with crème pillows embroidered with a cursive A, entertainment stand of dark cherry ebony wood with 36" console, a dark tan loveseat and matching chair, a fully stocked bar, a bathroom entirely of black and gold marble including the walk in shower with oversized soft black towels, each with a gold A emblem, and subdued ceiling light over the mirror and sink. He poured a brandy and opened a beef roll and carried them to the balcony where Lewis already sat, his opaque glass door ajar to his connecting room.

"Did you call Rhonda?" Jones inquired, sorely imbibed and still consciously irritable of the weather, a sticky stuffy warmth.

"She'll have us over tomorrow late, I suspect she has to bring in a maid."

"Does she have an elegant sort of place?"

"Like these suites, she's comfortable. I left her with a nest."

"Lawn?"

"Her duplex is in the best area, it has palm leaf, an upper cortisone, shutters, very American. We will stop into el capitolio for a bite, proceed with caution through the factory section and round out our tour on the beach, she's no pink stucco nor cement patio on a corner."

"Did she ever remarry?"

"What for? I give her everything she needs, a car that almost no one drives here, a beach club membership, a man for a catamaran rental, we have few pleasures in the world. How come you haven't married in twenty-four years?"

"Busy at work."

"Good grief, man, you wear the pants, that's your job."

"The women don't stick around these days, as I'm getting to feel good, they leave; only so far one can go when tied to a dateline. Had I come to a desk in my mid years armed with a realization that I would require a wife, which is a real impediment, I would have spent my youth with one female. It didn't occur to me. How'd you figure that out?"

"She was my good man's girl and I walked her to the altar in a bride's full attire."

"What happened to him?"

"He had some on the side, I'm almost positive; he hung around refusing to go away."

"Where is her place? I thought I might drop you off with her."

Lewis blanched at the idea. "What you say we bring her here?"

"We could, I s'pose. Does she like stepping out a bit?"

"She's always up for a long drive. Frankly, to get there, her place is through the San Cristobal, stunning poured castment with nymphs, small Moorish towers, grave sites, praying females of statues, quite domination."

"It seems a well thought through tour," Jones said, sipping his brandy that burned in his throat. "The Rhonda I remember was quite a mischief maker."

"She was a girl then, she has work under her belt, she's highly paid, she works a correspondence desk, we're old longtime friends by now, I might ask you to escort her dancing, she won't step with me. You know that one day she was upset at me, did she pour her heart out to you?"

"She did. I remember I put my arm around her."

"It's no big deal, I was a difficult husband in those days, as I recall we went for drinks that night, I'm apologetic we slept in the car."

Jones was more than aware he was sogged. It was a cheap trick for Lewis to have placed his young pretty fiancé between them in the car, to have driven to a wooded hill overlooking the twinkling lights of the new city, to have filled their glasses and then attempted seduction with Jones pressed up against the door. He ought to have bought a newspaper, sat on a green overlooking the sands and ocean, and read a late edition, but he had gone to defend Lewis against a girl who had written up his summaries.

It was little more than déjà vu when at noon he and Lewis rode to Havana, dropped off at the square of the memorial statue and sipped muddy caffee, smoked a non chalant cigarette and awaited plates draped with smothered scrambled egg, thyme, misted lemon and chilled kipper and garnish, hot buttered sesame light bread, fruit cup of mango, papaya and saro, with a second cup, leche and sucar. As described the taxi driver ascended a steep hillside planted with rosaries to a calle di mezzo filled with narrow alleys, cobble laid seambricks, several Puerto churches, their iron lace latticework more noteworthy than the seraph statues, some ten feet high, all alabaster, and fountains descending small steps through green tiers of blessed virgin stone. The apartos rose two story off the calles, iron lattice over round or square windows, stunning sash work, tan portice stucco, placement of separation dominant over the doorways of thick birch wood and semi fastened black copper, amidst tiles of every notation, blocks after blocks, until they reached a garden filled with sour orange trees, coppertine leaves, amber trunks, the ground a dusky dirt depleted either with age or with lack of watering. Through the six story apartos painted red, white, green or sometimes yellow, crowded, one aparto on top of another, the working class of tired, sometimes retired, populace, functioning at borderline payroll, here and there a furniture store of beds, desks, and marble topped drawers or a soda fountain and small bistro playing the last of the favorite Clerico Gable of some forty years past, at last they emerged down a long canal in the directivo of a walled in storm port to a small wooded, somewhat glass, rows of port assigned roof homes.

Rhonda stepped onto the porch facing the drive, shutters over two windows, a tarnished maple door slightly ajar, a plank's worth of grass and red leafed hedges bordering the house, she wore a brief skirt of black denim, a low cut cashmere blouse with a burgandy necklace of macramé twine with garnets, a set of matching bracelets, thong sandals, her curly blond hair tied back in a clasp. Jones hugged her and she pressed herself to him saying it had been awhile, then reached for her ex-husband and drew him into her embrace as though this moment might be their opportunity for intimacy. After a long moment in which she stifled tears of gratitude she took them inside, to a sitting area with tan and rose polished tile beneath dark tan berber, a dark crème couch, a black sitting chair, a long Mexican intricately carved table topped with malachite, a polished birch dining room table with high backed chairs in the adjoining space, then into a fully modern kitchen with dark green and black marble counters, an island with stove top, and a separate room with round yellow glass table to eat in, each looking onto a small garden of leafy palms, sand and grass and white plastic lounge chairs with the ocean beyond, up maple wood stairs to the second floor landing where a hall fed onto two bedrooms, each with entry to a large, all black tiled bathroom, two sinks, counter, mirrored walls, dressing room, toilet closet, Jacuzzi tub and shower.

She fed them outside in the garden grilled lamb that she had marinated during the night with orange glace and mint and herbs, saffron and tea with sprig of licorice, they sat at a very small oblong table with tablecloth, talked about her career, she was a lively friendly intimate and after she unclasped her hair and let her wavy, curly hair fall down her back Jones grew oddly still, Lewis had withdrawn from dialogue, his usually severe mien taking her in, Rhonda did all the talking, she was the essence of Cuba, a well doctored scholar of ocean breeding, their natural habitats, fish, birds, flower blossoms, erstwhile barked trees, beaches, ocean whaling, walls, small ports with docking privileges. She cleared the table, set out porcelain, white, saucers and demitasse and poured strong bitter Puerto Rico coffee with crumbling brown sugar and a baked lemon filled with custard. A breeze came in off the water, the sky glistened, Lewis disappeared into the house, Rhonda sat beside Jones, tousled his hair laughing, a youthful girlish delight, leaned against him, her soft breasts resting against his arm, took his hand in her lap, his fingers found their way on her skin beneath her skirt, he let her feed him, a heady exhilaration overcame him, she moved his leg towards her, when Lewis re-emerged, he sat down cheery and his mood lingering, she stood, leaned over the table, her leg pressing Jones and fed Lewis a spoonful of baked lemon, Lewis kissed her hand, then her arm and she sat next to Jones, let Lewis give her several spoonfuls, then entwined an arm through Jones' drawing Lewis to she, Lewis gave Jones a few spoonfuls, Lewis shot a picture of them, then asked her to stand in front of Jones and took a few photos and asked Jones to encircle his arms about her thighs, Lewis asked could Jones put her in his lap, Lewis discarded his shirt, poured an aperitif, asked them to kiss, shot their faces, asked her to strip to her bikini and took a handful of pictures, poured brandy, talked about the loft he had built where Jones would sleep, talked some about his new assignment at work, the tiny blue lights he converted from the orange, rambled on, wishing he were back in Porto he cried, and she rose taking his cue and led him inside her house.

Jones sat with the breeze angling in toward the grass feeling satisfactorily contented, sipping the brandy. He recognized a barely remembered theme when Lewis had insisted bringing a girl to Jones' pad and the three had gotten drunk, watched a game on the HBO and fallen asleep on the divan, Jones had awakened to find them having oral sex. She was a pretty girl of her twenties, Lewis had ignored the obvious. There were girls in and out of Lewis' place, Lewis' boredom always relinquished to sex, it was always a surprise to Jones that Lewis had lived at every port in the Rib, he was the only one who had at one time or another been expected to entertain every Egg sent to Havana. The evening had faded, the patio light cancelled out the dark, he ate a healthy portion of desert, washed it down with brandy, smoked a stick, dropped a pastel, the buzz hit him almost at once. Within minutes he felt loosened, he permitted himself to inspect the home, there was plenty of brandy in a rack, a good quarter baritome in the medicine cabinet, a massage deck at the rear of the glass enclosed linae off the dining hall, in a closet all sorts of terrycloth robes, Jones slid one on, walked upstairs, fell onto the bed beneath the skylight, listening until he fell asleep to Lewis and Rhonda make love behind the closed door.

They took the boat from Havana in the morning, Jones chatted with their captain while Lewis, a trim sailor-looking type stood with his gal on deck, Rhonda wore culots and a seersucker and styled trim band. More than a few times when Lewis ran his hands over her shoulders, Rhonda hugged him, kissed him, pressing him to the rail, fevering, without reluctance giving herself over, once retrieving Jones to join them for brandy. He followed her along the deck hall to where Lewis stood, reel line taking a beating in the silvery blue ocean.

"Honey, fix him up," Lewis told her.

She gave Lewis a throaty kiss, steered Jones to the table and prepared him a slice of rhubarb lamb meat pie with garden salad and glass of limon, sat beside him as he ate, put her hand on his thigh and leaned affectionately into him.

Jones was famished, had a second helping, Rhonda joined him for raspberry tea, they chatted about the last time she came to Lewis' hotel with luggage, she was going for a cruise to late Bahamas before she went out to Santiago, an end summer trip with stops to visit Lewis, on the return she brought a cabin mate, the three of them took in an American movie, dinner in port, played a night game of tether on the sand, went for a midnight swim. Every time was to be newly in love.

Lewis joined them for church land chess. Rhonda instructed Jones, although it was he who lost. Lewis took a nap in a recliner, the sun making him bead with perspiration, Jones put his hand on Rhonda's thigh to which she gave him a Lewis kiss.

"Any time," Jones said.

She put her arms around his neck kissing him longingly; then she said, "I'm supposed to seduce you. Lewis asked me to."

He smiled at her, removed a pastel and dropped the mint in her tea. "I'm certain he didn't mean it that way, Rhonda."

"That's what he said."

"He just wants you to have a good time. Try the sprite."

She gave her drink a few sips. "Will I know when I'm there?"

"Probably. I always know."

The cab dropped them off at their four story hotel on the beach in Cuba West, Lewis escorted them by way of the bar to show Rhonda the poolside and grounds, the tennis courts, spa and lounges, in a mirror-encased elevator he described the adjoining bedroom suites, the vista of the white sand beach, the evening tours if she wanted. Once inside their rooms Jones decided he was relieved to be out of Havana, he parked his bag, went along the balcony, drink in hand, to see what they were up to, Lewis sat in a comfy stuffed chair, Rhonda had showered and was dressed in a silk pink lounge gown, a turban towel on her head. The TV was on to the hotel channel, nightlife at the pool and cabana featured delicacies of stuffed mahi, caviar, petrale, sushi; a jazz singer at a mike, card tables being shuffled, die on the carpet, strip tease in the chorus lineup. Jones made himself at home on the divan, nursed his drink until Rhonda gave Lewis a half hour pampering on a massage table, when it was time for Rhonda to receive her massage, Lewis drew the curtains, flicked on a light, worked the tension out of her tired body, talking to Jones about his latest thoughts about his assignment, could be a yacht masting, a low wharf or repair shelf, Jones should try a two day stiller at a lab, objective a land shot maximizer, Lewis worked Rhonda Swedish-style, handed Jones a soaking cloth instructing him to wash off her copper tan lotion, talked non stop about his latest idea about his bleach out and getting in a game of racket ball before nightfall. He placed a five hundred bill between Rhonda's fingers, for the gambling he told her, started on her neck and upper torso, gave Jones the task of massaging her feet, talked about tints on negatives to better make accessible color print negatives.

Lewis opened the curtains, staged the suite with lights, took a handful of photo shots while Rhonda was naked, a solo of her coming out of the bathroom in her pink flowing gown, several of her and Jones, with drinks, her blond hair in ringlets, an arm around his neck, some kisses, hand on Jones' lap. Jones smiled throughout, debonair in his mildly tolerable good looks, studious in contemplation without involvement, Rhonda came off the couch, Lewis shot her for a window and balcony pose, then to Jones, first pausing to unbutton his shirt for a glimpse of skin, both standing, then of Jones with his hands on her arms, another shot of Jones with his arm around her waist, of her kissing him, staging Jones' hands on her shoulders, another kiss, a hand on her bosom, a candid of Jones kissing her neck, her collar, her waist, her knees. Lewis set the camera on a tripod, sat beside it, asked her to dim the lights, by gradual instructions Jones passed out the pastels, unzipped her gown, disrobed her to lace underwear and slip, removed his robe and shirt, posed as she kissed his neck, his chest, unclasped his belt, took down his trousers, ran her hands down his trim body, posing for the camera, Lewis went over, adjusted her slip over a peach lacy revealing body garment, unsnapped her garter, took a lip gloss and painted her mouth, turned her face to Jones, whispered in her ear, while she strained against him, when he gave in in absolute promise, the camera at the foot of the bed clicking frames per second.

When he awoke in the dark, she was slumped in Lewis' lap sleeping, Lewis hand across her stomach. Jones was seized by a realizable desire for her, by an assuredly deafening enlistment, the pastel most likely a poor idea, but in a continued burden of unrestrained passion he had to ask why Lewis wanted the ménage at all, in what essential fashion had his life grown too base, tedious or unembellished, had a marriage to Rhonda deadened an essence, it wouldn't be he, Jones had years ago said no to most intimate indulgences. He arose from bed, poured himself a brandy with water, imbibed a pastel, slipped on his robe, removed a blanket from the closet and draped it over them, turned up the heat and grabbing a cigarette from a pack on the desk was surprised to find Lewis clamped a hand on his wrist.

"Not embarrassed, Jones, are we?" Lewis asked him.

"Could become so, I s'pose. Not yet, haven't thought it through."

"Don't be, it's her pleasure. Stay awhile, I'll wake her."

"It's after nine, I should freshen up."

"Use our shower, be a sport, the moon's not up yet."

Jones walked into the bathroom, put the shower on. He was unaware as he soaped that Rhonda slid into the enclosure wearing only her lace see-through underwear and garter with one bare stocking, took the soap from his hand to lather him, he felt her kiss him, barely perceived her finger insert inside him, stood affixed by some heretofore unappreciated fleeting ecstacy, his body erect and throbbing, he awaited her next caress against his backside, her release of spoken desire, Lewis joined them, hands on her breasts in an impulsive frenzy, urging her into Jones' arms, Lewis kissing her breasts with longing tenderness, smothering her with his own wild caresses, backing her up to Jones, pressing her in motion at him, Jones holding her by the hips to steady himself, Lewis putting both together in urgent appeal, Lewis crying out, she was his soul love, Jones abandoning his own urgent necessity.

They slipped on towels, sipped drinks, watched television, finally dressed and went down to the poolside for a late dinner. In the morning they would boat out leaving Rhonda to stay the week. She was in a rare form doing all the talking, she intended to vacation in Capri the next summer, snorkel, having obtained a grant to track wild birds and nesting, she was getting on in life, she wanted at least a paid honorarium to Norway before she was seventy, steak strips on buttered corn arrived along with salad and they ate ravenously, dessert a sliver of pumpkin cheesecake, coffee demitasses, the patio crowded with barstool drinkers, piano and bass player putting forth lullabyes, they walked to a spa where Rhonda and Jones removed clothing, descended to their waists while Lewis smoked a stick occasionally passing it to them, a walk on the beach for a quarter mile after which they retired to the suite. Jones kissed Rhonda good night, told Lewis he'd be around in the morning and entered the solitude of his suite, oddly aware he hadn't spent much time in it.

He awakened at four to Rhonda slipping through the connecting door. She was naked, her body glistened with recent lovemaking. She opened the balcony door, crawling into the bed she said Lewis had gone to the bar to pick up a girl and had asked her to leave their room, Jones took her in his embrace, kissing her until he could rest his face just below her breasts, ran his hand up her leg, found her wanting him and moving onto her entered pausing a moment, heard a door open and close, a female's giggle, Lewis speaking in coarse vulgar language, Jones went deeper, softly, slowly, until her body took on an urgency of her own, Lewis' voice getting louder, the female becoming supplicant, urging him, his voice demanding, he was gasping, she was so young any man could come, whipped up like a lash; Rhonda gripped Jones and he canceled Lewis out, coming fast, then easy, fast, until Rhonda was crying, her body charging at his, until he was there, repeating to her, no girl like you, Rhonda, no one like you, like you.

Jones asked, "Has he ever done this to you before?"

"Time to time, but he usually comes home, we still have a good time."

"What caused you to divorce him?"

"He has a son. There's some other woman."

"He's a real bungler."

"I told you, he said he was going to get me to spend a night with you."

"That was this afternoon."

"He did it for me."

Except Lewis hadn't done it for her. He was a selfish, self-absorbed man who wasn't at peace with his soul.

The office was in an uproar, a clerk for the color lab had it on good authority numerous pictures had been grouped as classified after a test had identified wharves under repair, his being one of them. An envelope routed to his desk by unreadable initials contained twenty-five Sigmas, each a small 2"x 2", three Pentax sheets showing blurs underwater, a good Casio underwater shot, with a matching Block 5, a detailed night vision

PC and a chart for resonance: 100 pixel, 350 pixel, 1.3 million pixel; VGA, 10 to 30 frames per second. Using these standards Jones would arrange his priorities, establish his Pentax without blurs with use of a Holga, placing the scenes, evaluate the water depth for his assignment to place, compare other selections for disposition. He'd take some listings off high dimensional surveillance cameras, stillers submitted off an Olympus or a Nikon, obtain a nice traffic at 20 fps, a Lumix for movie extracts, before he would do as Lewis recommended – request a two day stiller on his best shots.

He gave each photo bearing a full workup, when he had the resolution perfected to 150 pixels at 10 frames per second he then compared, he saw the wharf right away, it was in a marina capable of tour vessels on a lake or in a bay, the under hull was a steel freeway, the top deck possibly a distant island such as Alcatraz or a jutting peninsula. He went after the blurs downloading through water taken from a Holga, diminishing each streak for a dark orange teaser showing a city of high rises and canals of river, perhaps Manhattan, New Orleans, China Basin San Francisco, Portland or Seattle bay. It might not be all that unusual for a mixer to duplicate a photo to a different angle to slow amount of light. At 20 frames he qualified for traffic on the road, the newer glass buildings surrounding the Kansas Convention Center popped into perspective, when he ran the various sites for a set of images he got a Lumix; he closed out immediately, he couldn't have a movie for analysis. He returned to the wharf photo, defined the steel freeway as a docking bay and the other as a charting navigational deck, not U.S. Navy, and submitted the two photos to the lab personnel who would run them for two days indexing for any photo and let him know what the light speed actually was.

4. Salvatore looked at the last stillers the lab had dispatched, the aquamarine bays of sparkling gold sand, the quiet stretches of white sand of shrinking bluish eggshell color and white calm waves, the ten or more fishing boats in the bay, their hulls stained tan, green or yellow, the emerald green peninsulas covered with ebony trees, the uprisings of grayish corral which under water were stunning red, orange and purple. He inserted these pictures as slides, copied them into his computer and assigned screens for the aquamarine turquoise color of the bay he daily took pictures of canvassing each in shallow water color to the definition per each island in the Rib. The segments took him an hour to wash, he caught hold the sparkling dancing elusive sand and upon enlarging the sun glints inherent for each frame tried to establish them for the mesmerizing current of gold metallic squares he had placed but again convened only for shiny swimming light as could be found in a pool. Schools of stingray appeared in Haitian waters periodically depending upon the warming closest to the equator, otherwise they grouped at surface above underwater caves in deep waters, an ironical nomenclature of fish whose sleek bodies were most often photographed as silvery blue, out of the ocean they were pale pinkish blue, anything but riveting. His bay was north at Nassau, far from submerged harbors of underwater archeology where recovery was difficult because hulls could not be excavated intact. Off theYucatan a hundred miles northeast of Veracruz lay yachts and small ships surrendered to the ocean, rooms looking up a blasted deck at bluish ocean, the underwater creatures dazzling, colorful and bright, unusual shapes.

The sparkling sand was on the hotel side of Puerto Rico, on the ship side were the deep waters, the equator line was situated at Nassau where most off stations such as his were grouped, only one remained in Havana. In order for shiny gold backs to have swum from Puerto Rico to Nassau seemed to suggest that the sort of activity for which gold stingrays presented rested somewhere along that shelf, Long Key was too far north, Mexico too far west, Guantanamo Province too far south, therefore the activity was situated off his bay and to the east on a route taken predominantly by ships anchoring to the hotel side of Puerto Rico. Therefore it made sense that in hotel waters a new problem lay that had not yet been historically encountered. Salvatore sent a telex to the Hotel Le Grand whose room doors opened onto gold sparkling sand beach for the names of any ships deplanking at sea.

Lewis was not where Jones was used to seeing him for their midweek lunch, he was instead on the tennis courts practicing his serve. Jones had ambled across the lush green gardens of the Avalon Beach Hotel, on the windward side of the three story hotel where he kept his suite, past several patios with fountains and benches, past a row of hotel businesses, a tour office nicely situated off a brick inlaid terrace, a men's shop offering linen sports jackets, sun glasses and newspapers, a small market that sold any sandwich and confection one could desire, a currency exchange and a library with a comfortable sitting room with four separate fireplaces. He had lingered at the market for a roasted Java cup of coffee with cream, talked to some of the port boys, before he took leave and rounded out his stroll at the tennis courts. Lewis wore all white, a shirt with boxer sleeves, cotton trousers, leather shoes, he made no effort to chase the ball but every so often raised his racket arm for an impossible return. Jones waited until the match was done, waving Lewis over, he stepped up to the rose bush corridor for Lewis to walk spritely toward him and arrived, they fell into step conversing about the latest decline at the Agency to preserve weeks of hard work when the mainframe was gutted.

"I thought we'd do lunch by motor car on the green," Jones said, a stigma of moodiness coming on with the thought of Rhonda.

"We can do a few irons if it'd raise the blood." Lewis was affable.

They moseyed across the upper green with wind bent palm trees, a pond, a stand of beets and a golf course at the top of the hill. They entered a small shop, chose their irons, a basket of balls, and walked to the first flag on the green.

"I'm reassigned," Lewis said, a short put placing the tee square down the aisle. "My photo landed a duck."

Jones thought this one through as he adjusted his stance, raised to the swing and sent the tee arcing high to the trees down to a few inches side of the hole. "Will Hil give you the detail?"

"I listed the last batch who worked the grave. It's a group of businessmen who made a killing on hotel leeward side designs. Not much anyone can do with them – they were sent to Galvaston just prior to Katrina, had the electricity knocked out of them, piles of termites laid to waste."

"This has to be bigger than hurricane outages." Jones resumed his put dead on center.

Lewis saddled his bag, parked it, swung low and fixed shy of the flag. "Golf's not my best cut. I'd say with all the parking lots the game is on the ports, several pool lights, a cave of clam dwellers."

"It'll be my crop, what do we do besides harvest beets?"

They strode to the second range, cloud shadow sitting low over the green, the skies looking as though rain were imminent. Jones had squeezed in a lead, he set the ball onto the tee, placed his aim and swung, always a reacher.

"I ran a two day stiller," he said, while Lewis bonked his ball at the sloping sand. "I've got a freeway, red the color of rust, no cement overlay, no ship grounded at bay."

"Could be damn near anywhere," Lewis said, a grouchy elbow at the failed distance to make the goalee.

They walked to Jones' ball, a neat tuck did the trick.

Lewis smacked his ball straight zinger to the prompt where it rested precariously. "The fact is whatever Hil was given, they're images that fly at one stop, how that came about could itself be a bumpo. Were it up to me I'd close down some hotels."

"That would be a giveaway, better to look for seekers."

They played two more sets, Jones flew the ball right to the pit both times, Lewis had one in, one lost to the pond for a score, no match.

"Want to talk about Rhonda?" Lewis asked on the walk back.

"Why do you shovel her that way? You were together a long time."

"It's my way of leaving a good time, or she's all over me, impossibly so."

"You told her you had a son. How could you?"

"I didn't tell her that, she must've gotten the wrong picture, I got a vasectomy before I met her."

"Oh, it must've been one of your girls. Well, you don't leave her with much."

Lewis shrugged. They had reached the golf shop.

"The work we do precludes a marriageable life," he said, in a dejected tone that implied Jones ought to know better.

They turned in their irons and tees and paid thirty-six apiece. On the way out they took a mint.

"You wait for the pictures to get developed," Lewis said.

"And then what?" Jones retorted.

"You're single. It won't amount to much, a mere fling. I on the other hand can't take the risk, in a photo I'm a duck. That's Havana."

In Havana's Matamoras district Desde Consuela corrected a line of chatter to match decibels on a recording sent her by the port district lab, only as the tones flattened out could she decipher an additional sound, one that did not belong in the congruence of pitch, a motor moving at five or six knots, a vessel in harbor waters approaching a speedway. She classified the item as a harbor tug, its outboard gaining headway on whatever ship it was turning, she ran it through her synthesizer and produced a name, Alouette, a Saudi midsize vessel with cable strings that received clearance to pass through Gibraltar when it sank off Canary in the late 1950's. She removed a orange pencil from her drawer, notated onto the sound thumbnail recording the fixed demarcations the ship signaled as it entered a previously undedicated harbor, then oddly began to retract removing the harbor dock with it. She zerox filed the recording to the district lab stationed at the Head Institute at both Cuba and Puerto Rico with a copy of each the sound track as well as the record photo under a file heading of World War ? Since she was not the one who could track vessels by surface or underwater – that was the entire privy of those Domain confluent officers who visited every port in the Caribbean ocean – she had to maintain her information by a difficult procedure of combining sound bars with port call entries and documented recordings registered with decibel, landings, strikethroughs for matching dates.

The shadow desk in Cabo Rojo, Puerto Rico listed the bars as soon as the report came in, for the next twenty hours all ocean fare would be grounded, vessels lined up at a docking column, boarding boats called to hotel ports. Officer Joseph Donovan tore the stat off the CPU, placed it beneath stripping, put on his eyeglasses, studied the waterfall, marked up his copy and sheeted the read-out with an overlay. Sure enough, the pitfall down the page looked to be identical, however the vessel's shadow was grossly inconsistent, displaying corruptions which could be damn anything from underwater erosion to a fleet of whales to a moving motor. He switched on all wall computers in the wash room checking for under surface cogitation from established feeds, then he typed in the various coordinates for which about two lines of telex were output and signified which canopy to send the registers if any produced.

At the Head Labs in Cuba, situated inside a small one story hotel with a garden roof, surrounded by acres of golfing greens, a discreet walkup and sightseeing marina, the light lab examined the pitfall photograph for actual image, amount of light speed, what part of the image was likely to have been used, seeing it receded to black page with a blue block and small white commentary block the lab officer compared it to a frontline analysis first obtaining the Gulf of Ceylon, once she had defined it for a peninsula she used this section to create the analysis for the assignment and redirected the photograph back to her supervisor who would subsequently match it to any set on file and assign for investigative routine, it consisted of all boat tours for photographers, any underwater pilings, ships at sea and in harbors, islands with buildings, surrounding ocean, and divisive imagery such as fake holograms, the lab unit would go for a ten day series to match to any light read off PC microscopes. Once they identified a vessel they were required to place planned chatter to arrive at actual sounds for the spills that were taken; from this discernment the tasks included photo profiles as to who had taken the photos, who brought them into a developer, and who assigned negatives with recommendation for use of blurs and light speed for use in offshore clandestine activity. The image came back as roiling ultra green ocean waves of frothy cresting sixty footers, each wave containing a tubular curl beneath its height, waves riding at a mile an hour, landfall to any of a small number of unregistered tiny rocky islands below Tobago above the excelsior cliffs and beaches of northern Brazil. Because the implication inherent in an image of ocean wilderness was that either a ship had wandered off course or an aircraft had gone down in that part of the ocean, the laboratory evaluation for a pitfall could necessarily take unceasingly tireless days to locate. Tracking a disaster put every rank on standby at radio and satellite communications on ships, mountain stations, harbor radio, or low lying land, in time feeders picked out unusual frequencies of illegal vessels not allowed to enter the triangulated area, frequencies were then translated to the language of the phantom vessel, spoon feeds reflected any dish on deck of such a vessel, when the frequencies were finally positioned to chart for degree and longitude, the command authority would receive a series of course and destination for the pitting.

Officer Donovan scooped in the final data which completed the pitfall for a healthy thumbnail, he gave it a cursory examination, realized a potential enemy tank lacking paint and attributes had rounded far beneath Puerto Rico and come down outside the normal shipping channels to northern Brazil and was intending to attempt an entry into the Panama Canal probably when officer staff would be low during deep night, sitting like a quarry on empty ocean, mimicking a frequently seen fishing type vessel. Immediately he posted a silent communiqué to all ocean-bearing vessels in open lanes, to all ship repair bays and product ports, alerting them to be on a lookout for an illegal docking bay with incorrectly painted sides and a deck tower which at a distance resembled a wharf and scorcher.

Jones uploaded from camera phone, desktop and dateline E-mail, grouped collections and tagged categories in order of organization of use, then rifled through photograph files looking for any description of vessel that might indicate the location the ghost had been constructed. Although it was extremely unlikely a group of detainees had escaped in a fishing stacker, he relegated his search to hidden villages where shrubbery, old fading boats lining a small beach, abandoned hotels and damaged stone docks had passed into dilapidated carnage. He gave special note to raised hulls erected by steel pier, to any inlet and cove that hauled to sandy waters parts of wreckages that had remained on the ocean bottom long enough for their hulls to have separated in whole or section, to communities of young teens who old enough to get it into their desires to float onto an affluent shoreline had rigged a capable steerage. He looked for any nearby islands that allowed illegal transportation of bootleg and emeralds, or production of communications predominantly by self-styled groups taking advantage of a hotel and village street wares. He evaluated New Orleans ships that had embarked to the Caribbean, crab boats out of Corpus Christi, boats carrying rugby players to Freeport, flooded train track on Bahamas coastline, tide patterns, tycoon reports for boating incidents, a cache of gold bar identified on Reuters News Service, album covers related to ships grounding, a building in the movie Citizen Kane, top news of the year involving a train blast in Mississippi and mapping a shipwreck off Long Key, he consulted the Agency's webcam for location, view and direct link, studied aerial photographs of photos made in the dark and telephone taps without wires, sheets of twenty-five photos apiece of gear lights beneath a harbor or of a reflection in water off land, a ship deck evident on bottom sand at fifty feet, still waters for shallow boating, small yachts with low berths, a ship ramming another ship, both having single deck towers for radio communications, Medivac ships that conducted ocean rescues, coffee ships that went down off Haiti, submerged harbors, several limnology studies from Scripps Institute in Mexico, demolished boat on sand off Trinidad, also a rotting pier at Tobago, last series of Montego Bay in Jamaica. He compiled an entire shelf of stats to study at his suite for the duration of the week, killing his desk light at midnight an hour after the last of the agency investigators and photo excavationists working under pressure of an alert deadline had left for the night.

He walked down the path leading from the rear entrance through the tennis courts passing the gymnasium, indoor pool and sauna, through the perfumed bougainvillea to the expansive rolling green overlooking the white sandy beach that extended a half mile on which his three story hotel of white marble and floor to ceiling glass balconies stood. The sky lit by the full moon gave no indication of any incoming storms, light poured over the gardens and hotel giving off a weakly silver luster, in the distance on the ocean he could barely discern a ship approaching the shore, its deck of Christmas lights making it seem like a festivity, garish gay red and orange lights reflected on the ocean like pillars of a palace.

He caught four hours sleep on the living room sofa awakening before dawn while the night was still grey. Jones poured himself a cup of coffee, fried up tamales and scrambled egg and salmon and took his meal onto the balcony eating in the warm sixty-eight degrees, alone to the world, the smoke torch at the poolside below sending sparks into the night causing him to think about the party dinner with Lewis and Rhonda. The fact that she was in her fifties, still a good looking woman to catch a man, made him wonder why she stayed the week on Lewis' ticket, why she wanted to be the researcher who checked over all his notes, why she submitted to the male domination thing at all. Lewis would never content to be held by her for long, he'd always wrestle against whatever was the net Life had cast him in, he'd always be trying to defy her as though she herself had unwillingly captured him, he had adopted a transference making her as much his mother as his wife, even in divorce he gave her reason to capitulate to him. Having eaten his meal, Jones sipped his coffee lingering with the thought that even if Rhonda clung to him in need, Jones couldn't really have her without Lewis calling the shots, looking in on them every so often, throwing it back in Rhonda's face.

Although he was of a mind to go for his usual six o'clock swim, he forewent it, entering yesterday's prototype, looking for groupings which by photo could become references for definition of ocean depth. In his segments he registered onto any convention joining them to buildings, hotels, harbors, mission schools or entertainment events. He was surprised to take in Lewis' caption and buildings which he had assumed were to be found in southern Florida at her tip and were instead plaza squares for Mobile or Biloxi, tags of blue lights inside the buildings and streaks of white and red lights on freeways on bridges, a straight shot north as the crow flies from Havana. It was on bridges that it was possible to obtain a watery reflection; he didn't download these, instead he searched for any similarity and finding only one in the Keys placed the image of a bridge at Seventh Key on his view. He sent a request for information to Miami dateline as follows, Any vessels tan, rust and blue resembling dock bay or deck trim beached on sand bar, history for fields and communications, years.

Dateline replied, The bridge connecting the Keys was built in 1961 to prohibit boats bringing in illegals who then entered Florida's cities without going through immigration, only 6th Key has the ship repair yards, Southwestern Florida was a swamp with small wood houses on stilts, industries that were placed off gulf coast were tobacco originally to Trinidad opening Wall Street, coffee bean to Haiti, tanning to Santiago Cuba, and peyote leaf to Lesser, six cities replaced these factory fields – Galveston, New Orleans, Biloxi, Mobile, Pensacola and Tallahassee – for lower glass rentals and inexpensive houses despite yearly seasonal hurricanes and monsoons which capsized ships, wreaked havoc laying flat suburbs, and smashing coastal buildings, communications has never been good on the Keys, even worse on Cuba, the most satisfactory reception is on Puerto Rico where sugar is harvested because the wet weather is most agreeable to cane which is a real soaker, the worst incident occurred in 1962 when a low berth vessel departing Puerto Rico headed to Dinner Key sank when it entered Galveston's windshield off the eastern seaboard below Florida, As you have described this phantom a similar descriptive ship entered above the windshield headed to Tampa and Tallahassee and was beached when it put into harbor and floundered on a low sand bar, subsequently a hotel was built on the point to prevent other beach heads.

Since there weren't any bridges in the islands, it meant the vessel in question had departed the Keys prior to sailing to Puerto Rico before entering the route that led to Antigua.

5. A balmy breeze lifted over the ocean scurrying low lying clouds in shadows up the green. Jones nursed his first tequila of the season between ladles of Cajun sausage, rice and blue oyster jambalaya stewed to perfection in a crab lathered broth, periodically taking a bite of garlic bread toasted under a grill. The teasers had come back with the late afternoon fax releasing all similar photos taken that spring of the vessel in question. Lewis supped at the table sipping a fresh clam stew smothered in melted butter, his chubby hand circling areas of Jones' photograph, his bifocals halfway down his nose.

Jones asked him, "How many boats make it past customs a year when entering US?"

"Almost none since off shore oil began being drilled on the Galveston coast in the mid 1990s."

"Have illegals been routinely deported?"

Lewis set down his pen. "Immigration quarantines them as well as their vessels, vessels are taken to booby shipping harbors where they are stripped, computers are assessed, all equipment on the ship tested including for sensors, hidden cameras, spy surveillance, recording instrumentation and matched to any vessel. Is this what the lab actually confirmed on your boat – tan sides, rust bottom line, blue deck, white deck tower, no split level, sensors at starboard?"

"Yes, without transportation papers, with the explanation if sensors were frequently utilized in illegal transportation, they would be captured by reflections in the water."

"We often see bright spotlights flash in the middle of nowhere sometimes on a cloudy night," Lewis said.

"I asked about types of ships that resemble dock bays. They told me there are several types, standard dock to build warehouses on a wharf, medium upsize to rescue a smaller vessel at sea, and large dock with road on it, usually these are longer; last category found almost entirely in Pensacola and Keys."

"There you have it. What course did the lab recommend?"

"They asked a determination be made from where the boat originated."

"Well," Lewis said, pulling off a clean bib of cloth napkin, "it could only be one place if what I've heard is true, that sunken ships hauled into the gulf are used for newer product lines all the time."

"The tower is the first item to pull away in the current," Jones replied.

"Tell yourself, the vessels leave the U.S. before they even enter island waters. The Bahamas are very tightly controlled, Cuba impossible to enter, I don't know where that leaves you. Have you determined where each ship of your camouflage is manufactured?"

"The length is substandard small oil tanker made in Bermuda, the docking bay, usually in southern Florida, it is that a tower without satellite can only be made in US, so that's the problem, not a single scorcher has ever gone down at sea."

"Some small towers have burned up," Lewis said. "Little rinky dink ones carrying stowaways."

"That's not the problem, that small vessels that transport

illegals are burned. The problem is the vessel in the photo was last seen in Cuban waters. Since it did not originate in American waters, the question is where was it built? There are of course other problems – illegals bring their own towels and sleep on beaches, where did they come from if not from movie companies that went to Puerto Rico, built a set of hotels and studios, made a movie, and left behind low paid employees."

"Well, that's always been a central argument, the role hotels play when illegals enter an affluent island if they couldn't land on Cuba, it was for detainees, Dominican was out because it was staffed for customs products clearance only, they obviously never made it to Jamaica."

"Hil has asked me to compare stillers for each type of camera with slowest number frames per second so as to reduce intensity of light, then to apply to photo density incapable of reading for camouflage, this is essentially the new task."

"His instructions for my set was to reduce all light to essential camera used for making blurs, that's how I got blue with a Casio and orange with Nikon. The Holga was necessary to define the streak blurs, it took a bit of work but it's defined. When I began I thought it was strictly freeway because there's no reflections, when I decreased light for the streaks I produced buildings, one which had a reflection of lights."

"Have you identified for location?"

"Not yet. I have to eliminate background, Hil's suspicion is the photos were shot at night of a harbor but not of sea-going vessels." Lewis added, "I asked whether the recent assignment matches a single incident but as usual he was reluctant to give an opinion. I can't but imagine a department of seventy-five service each working on some aspect of a problem, we haven't heard about a monsoon out of season."

Jones chased a wry smile down with a sip. "I'm nearly ready to send my image and summary to Edit. The comparisons will give me a better idea if there is no background."

"Far better than shooting them off to display to determine the brand names of the furniture."

"Full screen's never been much of a yield for me."

Lewis piled the remainder of clam stew in his bowl onto a piece of flat bread toast and ate it washing down his meal with his spritz, thinking as he ate. "The ground is tricky because while there's evidence of a freeway there's nothing to suggest it isn't a major city, except in the original there are nothing but these giant streaks. Removing them leaves almost nothing except faint light at the horizon. You can't get one image with the other, that must be how Hilliard arrived at his deduction. You on the other hand have blended images of sky and water."

"They look all water to me."

"No, not where the dock is. That's either an overlay or another photo or there'd be no sand, there's just too much sand for where the vessel would have to sit in water. Even if you calibrated for depth based upon color, the probable color is too light to be at the ocean bottom suggested, talk to any docking expert, they'll all tell you bright light in depth is out of the question, the sun just doesn't penetrate farther than a few feet."

The next time Jones looked at his material he segmented out all visible presumption of sky contextually positioning for where surface could be. By color the bottom had to be at least a hundred feet deep, by study the underwater landscape was neither sandy nor surface rock, the illumination gave off no indicators for slopes, walls or depth, therefore the photo looked up toward surface light. When he substituted sky for the upper slant of light blue chilling water he came upon a rather odd glimpse of sky peering between waves through the convention of a catamaran or a moving dock. When he put that area on his computer for sky he captured the underside of a ship's prow with sky juxtaposed above and the side of a piece of wharf with ships and rolling green hills. He had the same stupid oil tankard in view, a slight reduction of a hull.

Jones spoke to Havana's port rudimentary color shutter light incapable refractory specialist who had spent his entire career of forty years in Havana, a darkie whose tall willowy composure had on first meeting reminded Jones of a typical dominican.

"Who approves color of liquors?" Jones asked Malabi.

The sixty-five year old port officer usually in forest green uniform replied in a clipped accent, "Dominican Republic."

"What does Haiti do for her bean?"

"She merely grows, harvests, sends product to Dominican."

"Are there chemists for product color on any other island?"

"Yes, on Puerto Rico, for magazines."

"Are they approved?"

"No, they are required to send all galleys to Havana."

"How does Havana measure against deflection?"

"She uses primarily a Casio with a very slow land identifiable meter such as a Shadelands, not distributed in US, or a non digital compatible."

"Are these vessels built in the islands?"

"The hulls are taken from rusted tankers and sand blasted and painted a color which cannot streak, the deck is repaired with standard lumber, the wood tower is supposed to be built in Pensacola."

"Is there a connection between fast speed cameras and illegal entry of ships?"

"Do you mean, does the camera that aids the ship's view of the ocean have a faster light speed than what US law allows? It shouldn't."

Over the telephone the din of cargo being moved about on the cement dock could be heard, a commotion of voices penetrated Malabi's office.

"We received a late shipment," he explained. "Now we are in a hurry to review documents."

"Can I fax you a ship photo, see if you recognize it?"

"Certainly, Jones, I will be here until seven-thirty this afternoon."

"Then I'll do that now. May I hold?"

"Yes, no problem."

Jones sent the photo through.

"Ah, here we are, a good likeness I should say. We pulled over a few boats this last month, similar although painted differently. Why don't you fly out in the morning, take a look-see?

We haven't yet wrestled up papers on them."

"I s'pose I could. Shall we say around eleven?"

Jones flew in on the 6:38 and caught a cab to the dock. Malabi Sawali greeted him in the port room looking cheerful and harried at the same time, his still dark black hair wavy and curly, a yellow handkerchief in his breast pocket, his full name stitched above it onto his dark green uniform. Grabbing a logbook he patiently explained they would tour the dock to determine whether the shipment he had spoken of was ready before he took Jones to the quarantined area. A lengthy red ship rested alongside the dock, its boarding planks ready to load. They walked down the stairs to the dock, climbed into a golf cart and zipped through the loading zone to a large warehouse filled with several hundred barrels. Malabi disappeared inside with his logbook returning after ten minutes apologetic for having kept Jones waiting.

The quarantine dock contained four vessels more or less the size of Jones' photograph. The vessels were long, painted white and tan with a red bottom line resembling oil tankers, with wide decks and a small tower beside a normally revolving directional compass, all in all about five houses in length by approximately sixty feet across. Malabi explained the board took in the sound of bins rolling over the deck, helicopters, a man shouting something garbled, their radio sounded like static as if the telephone wires were wet, they could hear it for a good hour until the radio went dead, they still had the recording, as though the boats were caught in the rain, a loud burst of static meant someone was trying to get through, one quick sound meant whoever was trying established contact – might have been your ship, Malabi said with a broad smile – one gets the static when crew jumps ship, the erratic sound of the radio becomes loud as the port ship approaches, our screen readers jumped on and off indicating someone was in the area, the east board heard it in the fog and reported in a lost at sea, we went out on the coast guard, put a spotlight on the ocean, swells yea high, ten feet or so, greenest water you'd ever see above the Grenadines like detergent, these four vessels were adrift, we pulled in ten aged males, all wetbacks, brick layers, typical white Kingstown, we spent the night with a translator, they were making a run for Long Key, we got nothing on the board, just a lot of sound, it happens.

Jones walked with Malabi leading onto the largest of the four white vessels inside the radio room. The equipment had been gutted, all that remained was the chart room screen, the pilot's chair, three seats at what would have been the panel for signaling and brooming in coordinates of other vessels at sea.

"What was the status that night?" Jones asked.

"Very similar to the 1983 Grenada incident, we took a telephone call off Fancy on St. Vincent, call was intercepted at Nevis base, operation aborted by Havana. Map registered ants on Haiti, we've been working with anthropologists and epidemiologists from Kansas since 1986 since we suppressed."

They were looking at the bunks. Jones headed up the stairs to the tower, he cast a glance-about, all gear had been cut free, the sight of the quarantined dock, the warehouses of separate berths gave him plenty to consider.

"St. Vincent is remote," Jones said, thinking aloud. "Were you around for that invasion of St. Lucia?"

"Report was put in immediately to Miami, jets were sent straightaway. We towed their cargo to 3 Palms Island off Venezuela."

"Good deal of action to see. Must have had a man or two in the scuttlebutt."

Malabi laughed good humorously. "More than a few in the brink. We turned them loose all over, one to Mopion sand bar, a few to Kingstown, St. Vincent, we already had a good size population of scientists there, one to Trinidad Cuba as I recall, one to Ponce San Juan, several into Dominica, if I'm not mistaken," he answered, his English letter perfect.

"What must we be overlooking to have a flare up of the same trouble?"

"The group is bigger than we knew," Malabi said with a shrug.

"Do you know anyone who may have taken shorthand

when the radio was hooked back up on this incident?"

"An officer in Varadero, man by the name of Lively at the Xanadu, you won't worry he stays up all night translating, his phone doesn't work so well if he has the TV news on, he works with boat boxes, he knows everything, he used to sail the coffee ships to the Keys."

Jones rode the elevator up the side of the striped white and black glass hotel looking at the gold swimming pools and beyond, at the sparkling gold sand beach, scintillating azure green water, yachts tied to moorings bobbing in the evening breeze. William Lively was all of five feet four, a balding port officer dressed casually in silk dark blue lounge wear and terrycloth sandals, large spectacles taking up most of his skeleton face. Lively showed him to a sitting room at the edge of the suite, sleek ebony furniture, maroon sofas, glass cabinetry throughout an adjoining, fully loaded kitchen, shiny black marble tile with bright yellow and peach Turkish rugs, four stereos, one hooked up to a thin silver box which recorded decibels of static.

"The moment we plugged the sound in, they were dead," Lively said in a somber, capable of catching anything resonance. "It's all a matter of time to catch up to the windjammer that's still on the ocean."

"Where do you think the haul originated?" Jones asked.

"Possibly as far west as Grenada. Despite the number of tours we have there, it still remains a trouble spot. Erecting the Alhambra with that intricate gothic stone work we continue to place unit sea coordinates with unusual difficulty. We've put in every last type of syllable buster we can imagine, the caves, lighthouses, church bells, the El Malecon waterfront walkway, cobblestone streets, tree paths to the beaches, palacios on moored sand, nothing quite does the trick, they still on occasion get through to the Gulf."

"Here's a photo of a vessel I'm looking for."

"That's navy, docking bay, you see them at every port."

"That's exactly what I said two weeks ago, actually it's a composite meant to camouflage a vessel such as what you took in off the shoreline."

Lively gave the photo another look. "Length resembles an oil tanker with its ass cut loose, tower isn't part of the direction, insufficient to track for long, no gunnery, that's good, these the colors?"

"Yes, island boat blends."

"Maybe Old San Juan, but I'd guess too much tourism to sail without lots of notice. Probably set sail from some conveniently single resort, possibly one with divers, no one pays much attention nowadays to archeological sites, no matter what the draw, could be a tour itself that took off once they collected enough to make their trip."

"I'm interested to learn what the garble raised off your ear."

"A deckmate shouted – there's a rock, another voice said – the ship's taking in water, gasoline is floating about, a horn blare sounded, the same voice yelled they grounded."

"Oh, then my original photo was accurate."

Lively handed him his photo, asking, "Where did you pinpoint the water?"

"Anywhere between Puerto Rico and here. It's all a mixture of blue."

"They were arrested in sparkling green ocean."

"My sand rests on blue."

"Can't contradict facts, did you receive a green in any of your series?"

"One."

"It's green then, has to be consistent with gobs of gasoline pouring out all over the place, gasoline makes the ocean green. The party in question has a reason to eject gasoline."

"I see. Then it must be green if the voice was freaked out about losing too much gasoline."

"That's right. That's why these boats didn't sink, they weren't torpedoed, they didn't catch on fire – they may have tried a stunt like that before arriving at this particular plan – they didn't really have a problem until they spilled, then they were unable to steer, all except for yours. The last incident four caught on fire and they swam away somewhere or were washed up on shore."

"You can't help with anything else, like who might be on my vessel, where might it be?"

"I have a few telephone calls, all answerable to St. Maarten's."

"What's up there? Besides pretty beach hotels on Orient Bay?"

"Identities, they have call forwarding, license plates, medical clinics, at least one wooded bay, boat rentals, it's the place to go for weddings."

"Someone with money perhaps with a long distance cell phone."

Lively thought about it, stood, took a decanter of amber light off a wet bar, poured two Scotch neat drinks. "I'll tell you the point. The car is for the town, the telephone is for the bay, I doubt if your boat has even a radio phone."

It was a subtle put down, intended to inform Jones that the caller's ability to make contact was because he was on land communicating to the offshore line. "The operating base on land is a duck with the military post at Philips Ville."

"Philip never read in, so presumably your vessel picked up the other four closer into Cuba. The fact that he already has an identity suggests he could answer anywhere, any place."

"I think the camouflage gets rid of that sort of problem for the boaters."

"Could." Lively sipped his drink. "From a distance which might be all we ever have for a long time your sail resembles an oil cargo."

"Or a wharf and high tower ship."

"You have to ask why does this group want to make a secret cargo, possibly add something in a product that isn't listed in description."

"That's not my problem. I am required to identify it. If it's a painted white boat, then it's a probable. The prow of one like it was identified underwater."

Lively got noticeably bothered. "Here's the problem, we manufacture pharmaceuticals down here in St. Maarten. Who wants to put an ingredient in a Squibbs for example that isn't supposed to be there? That's one thing our chemists test for to curtail street drugs."

Jones took his drink in a swallow. "Can you tell me if the cello derives from a boat such as mine?"

"I told you, the cello is on land, not in the water. If he has a boat out there, we don't have a collectible. The fact that your vessel resembles a Turkish fishing jug found in the Grenadines is a minor interest but not reported, could be your photo is shot at such a distance the actual ship size and color are approximate to waning daylight."

"Did you map for each transmission?"

"All but one, those white vessels you saw in the berth loading dock."

"Okay, I'm clear. Can you match a boat like mine to a cello?"

"I suppose I could and send you photo draw. Do you have a wire cork?"

Jones supplied Lively with his adaptation telephone to Email, FAX, HBO, radio, dateline and permissions, and thanked him for his time.

6.

Jones met Rhonda in front of the elegant Capitolio Nacional. She arrived promptly at three driving a Rabbit coupe, her hair curled and teased, wearing a straight navy blue sheath with broad white collar and black bowtie. They kissed, Jones felt the odd tug of doing something unscrupulous, he proceeded to give her a report on his day. As she winded her way onto a main thoroughfare headed for the Bellamar Caves in Havana, he lit a cigarette for himself and one for her.

"I recollect that situation in 1982, a ship of insurgents showed up off Trinidad Cuba and shot the coastline up, the government went out in four ships and torpedoed it. Then the Grenada incident occurred. Where were you, do you remember?"

"Yes, I was on the other side across the strait from Cabo

right next to Acapulco getting the university document control program headed, it involved extensive interviews of Mexican straight shore officers, sight recognition of warrants, speedways, arrest and seizure boats, harbor pile dock procedure, a museum containing presumed status lost at sea which has since been resituated at Veracruz."

She inhaled, let out a stream of smoke, turned on her radio, and said, "Lewis was in Puerto Rico around that time. He was assigned not to product control but to verifying permissions, in those days a gigantic issue because of the attempt on Grenada. He stayed through every weekend, when he came home for a few days, it seemed like hours, he hustled us to a new hotel, he took me once to the Alhambra when the invasion was over and then told me, never again unless I wanted Fancy at Vincent which I didn't because who the heck wants to stay at a place while the husband is out on sea patrol."

"I wasn't aware he did duty in 1983. I remember the agency packed officers into the Caribe at San Juan."

"Right, the old fortress was shot at, I heard the island patrol units had to build a lighthouse at every major island town."

"That was the indicator we received when the university became a resort," Jones said, with a laugh ditching his partially smoked cigarette out the window.

Rhonda had pulled onto the sand lot of the Caves. She tied a pretty pink and white silk scarf over her head to protect her hair against the wind which kicked up quite a bit in the open.

He paid for the two of them. The guided tours departed on the half hour, the walk into the damp cave was alit with soft yellow light that revealed deep gold, striking dark blue, mesmerizing green stalactites and twelve foot long points that nearly touched a salt pond of aquamarine, greenish yellow and purple water. In a yet warmer area large stalagmites with clustered fool's gold, chunks of raw white amethyst and low grade corrupted emerald protruding, tiny pieces of shooting star formation. They exited through a narrow hallway into a gift shop in which Jones purchased a necklace of white amethyst strung together by thin gold plate.

They drove through a jumble of stucco colored houses all with square windows to the El Malecon where Rhonda took him to dinner at Malfea's. Over candlelight, white tablecloths covering very small formica tables, beneath rows of billboard lights, inside the azure blue room, they shared a conquistador meal served in Trini iglesias after mid morning mass made of squid – even expensive restaurants serving sour pickle were unable to afford lobster – oyster, delicious corn, a center of grilled polenta bread, red snapper, ocean fried chicken, shelled peas and broth. Jones was fascinated by the Madonna at the back with a small waterfall fountain into the pond where dinner patrons had placed silver coin, a tradition which begun had grown to folklore. They ate sweet caramel mole for dessert with bitter dark syrupy coffee. After, they walked down a cobblestone corridor amidst churning ocean waves, too low to give off either spray or mist passing high ceilinged, arching entrances, soft autumn color buildings with narrow windows.

Jones asked her to select a nightclub, she drove them to the Marquis Gran, a dance club with attached all night bar and small hotel, where they were seated at a table on a raised stage, Fillmore Philippines style, served iced melon champagne in a flute, listened to a band play Silver era, the trombone player got on his knees while in the spotlight, his jazzy suit of dark gold shirt, yellow trousers and purple jacket, an aging Cajun with frizzy fuzzy scalp hair, bleated soulful twangs of sex and desperation. He talked in a whisper about the green lights, the raised baby grand piano, the thin boned Haitian girl doing belly dance under a gradually lowered bar, the band played recognizable Fats Domino, Little Richard, a few Cuban sets; Jones agreed to the hotel, ten minutes from the aeropuerto, they enjoyed a spa, curled up in bed under a black comforter white six black pillows, he lay her on his stomach with her spine against him, his arms covering across her shoulders, kissed her neck, nibbled her ear, talking the entire time about the warmth of her body, her softly glowing nudity, she could have him anytime she wanted, he was always ready. She was as he expected, releasing, passionate, eager, comfortable, a good port to stay awhile, no tearful pleadings, no exhaustive complications either, he slept soundly, his hand on her arm.

In the morning she was gone. He showered, dressed, fixed himself a cup of coffee which by any standard tasted drab, and sat down at the hotel computer and typed an address to Dateline, Miami, "Fishing vessel in peril on ocean off presumed forest St. Maarten steering toward Gulf, no contraband, dunking oil, possibly soluble waste product, may intend to precede monsoon weather, identifier reading deck, no stacks, destination Pensacola or Ponchertrain. Reply."

The response returned swiftly. "St. Maarten puts into eastern seaboard only, Keys to Miami, Charleston, Boston, Pennsylvania; Galveston last stop for gulf sector, boats leave Puerto Rico, no deportation out of Haiti or Cuba. To reach Ponchertrain boats must embark from Veracruz. Corpus Christi tankards leave Santiago. Exception Galveston may deploy."

His vessel couldn't do any of it. If it left St. Maarten's green bays it had to be charting waters for the Atlantic, but because it resembled an oil tankard it made sense it was headed for an oil port, wrong direction for the Panama Canal, it had to be headed eventually to Texas.

It had the hull color of a small Turkish ship, these were almost never sent outside the Mediterranean unless for repair and then it was rare it would be as far west as the Caribbean, it could be a pirate ship in foreign waters, its off red tan color impossible to absorb a different paint, its usual high deck replaced for one easily mistaken for a Caribbean liner. Typical identifiers were prow, radio, length of deck and number of decks; if each of these departed from registrations the final determinant in the absence of crew and their known spoken language was where the vessel was capable of docking. Maybe instead of a repair dock building a high deck, a stack was made into a high deck.

Jones returned to Nassau by one o'clock relieved to be in his own suite where the view was second nature, the hotel schedule well accommodated to. In his printer tray was Lively's communication of photographs. Look alikes of his ship had a blue line between rusted tan and top white deck, question could it be a red line, from a distance on water the blue line held to horizon, it resembled a densely packed barge or low liner. Sometime before three Lewis called in to invite Jones to see a ship get raised off Antigua, another island surrounded by predominantly green ocean wave breakers; could prove to be a bust for their desks.

The hydro electric platform had the rusted tankard barely out of water when their cab set them on the long older constructed wharf, the tank was a good city block long, its rails affixed to the steel girders of the deck, all parts of the top deck gone, Lewis scouted the relic with binoculars, jotted down the ship's specifications, it was a U.S.S. series from the looks of it equal to any modern LHD4, built sturdy for rough ocean sail, stairs missing, doors eliminated, rooms mostly intact, it would make an honest weathered rebuilt taking some three years to sand-blast, paint, add a secure stage and halls.

Jones asked, "How's your assignment?"

Lewis said, "I'm still trying to achieve a correct dispo, my glass sits alongside a bridge, despite this I cannot determine how lights on a bridge are blurred while the reflecting image is of the street lights themselves."

"Sort of like the Lincoln Bridge Memorial."

"Oh, yeah, no kidding. I can't figure how the picture is taken."

"Obviously it's an incongruent shot, perhaps years older than the bridge."

"Looks to me to be severely flooded," Lewis said, perplexed, his mind elsewhere.

"It is during warm storm season. The question is how employees get inside, no way to do it."

"Well, that's the entire issue, why investigators make such a stir. Who remembered how much water there was, or when the bridge was built, or whether the library was abandoned, so on and so forth."

"I can't get my ship to port."

"Right, your picture. I gave it some thought, could be your

ship has an exclusion if its high deck is a part constructed for a special contract."

"It is not the correct kind of part to be repaired for a raised ship in dry dock, ships in general are not constructed in parts, damaged ships are rebuilt in their own frames."

The ship was levered onto a deck, the base of its hull securely wedged into the recessed portion of the dock some forty feet above the water in a separate berth. Two shipyard men climbed ladder stairs alongside the dock and could be seen examining their new repair task, one leaned against the side of railing and gave a thumb's up.

"Tell me," Lewis said, as they craned their heads up to the newly situated ship, "How's Rhonda?"

Jones was taken aback, it had been less than a day. "I'm surprised she told you."

Lewis cupped his hands to the wind to light a cigarette. "She tells me everything, old boy."

An acoustics machine was raised to the height of the dock and lowered onto it, testing would begin and proceed for several days to determine strength of hub, flexibility of interior steel carcass, solid weight, capacity to steer once a deck was trimmed for new height depending upon its assigned carrier function, and tested strength against a flounder.

"In her way she still needs me," Lewis said, "no matter the grief I give her."

"I'm no psychologist. If you ask me ---"

"No one's asking, Jones, just don't go helping yourself. She's no Madonna."

"You might try living without puddles in your pockets."

"I don't drink all so much," he said, as he accepted a hard hat and followed the jimson up the ladder.

That was why Lewis had dragged him out here, Jones thought, a sting of bitterness chill on a gust of wind, Lewis, who was an inveterate stale marital province, who had to mix love with ingratitude to firmly put Rhonda in as undemanding dependency as possible. He saw Lewis don the earphones, listen, raise his hat once or twice, this was the Lewis their agency tasked all active war to, the Lewis who could sink a sounder off any boat or coast to find last point of reference.

When Lewis came back down, he was fine, a hearty chuckle on his breath. "No Iwo Jima, that old rotten whaler, been down less than a two scale desert storm, even if the platform took off for coasts unknown, it didn't survive a strong gale, there's utterly no evidence of detonation, no chewed up steel bearing, she's as good to go in a few years."

It occurred to Jones rumor was correct, Lewis hadn't made it out of the ghost winds, whatever had caught and pinched his coattail had him still. If Lewis had been treated for hard lime, put on a ward in Mental, allowed to sweat the nightmares, there was an echo about.

"How does she look to you?" Jones asked him, when Lewis gave his hard hat to the first dock operator they walked up to.

"She took a right heave, a lifted swell must have got her, she'll blanch out alright, but she'll be dry a lot longer than they prefer, her wood is solid, her deck was torn asunder, were it me I'd have her painted first before they tip her galleon for sounding, they'll need to know the number of feet she took to dip."

"Any suspicion as to whether she was spotted by land first?"

"Not this one, she was hauled in under the wave, she was maybe a fathom deep, difficult to steer in, probably someone thinks your ship was bottom also by the looks of her sand beach."

"Could be," Jones replied, "my ship comes up for all sorts of ocean depth."

"This gal had to have been steered predominantly during night probably without radio room light, the crew in almost complete dark, for it to have not avoided a capsize, the call that got me out here is the ship captain couldn't explain how a reflection of the ship was produced in a waterway that had no other sighting of it before it set sail."

"Where was that?"

"Tallahassee ship repair, she had just been released after she rammed a floating dock."

"Assigned to Antigua, is that usual?"

"Who knows? Antigua docks between islands to assess buoyancy, it's her only grief. Half a dozen have taken a knockabout without any telling tear, since she plummeted after she was approved, it has to be depth that took her, that's what I will put in my status once I come into possession of her approvals based upon her startup, tags, vertical and codes."

They had arrived to the vehicle that would see them to the military airport. The drive to their escort airplane took fifteen minutes past hangars, a loading zone and employee parking, and let them out in front of a glass door beside a building marked Parcels, they checked in at the counter, then went to the bar for a drink. On the tar waited the plane, a small 747, and a hundred yards past it, the clouded over, choppy ocean, the one indicator their ride might be turbulent.

The bartender, an aging man from Trinidad, once handsome, now graying wavy hair, a bit of moustache, originally off the coast of Greece, named Jorgio, recognized Lewis by sight, fixed two dry martinis with spritz of orangine, served them up with toasted garlic bread, soggy with butter. Lewis started in with his catch of the day, the ship's radio had floated away, the case technically closed on the blip that put it into North Point harbor.

"Easy, walk right in," Jorgio said.

"Exactly, could've come charging at us." Lewis said, raising his wide angle glass in a salud.

"The airplane should have caught it," Jones interjected; "they never fly without a radio."

They regarded him casually for a moment.

Jorgio said, "No radio, too severe a storm. That's the only plausible explanation." Lewis said, "Search couldn't find it, dropped too deep."

"Not on Antigua," said Jones. "It must've gone down off Florida, must account for why it took so long to raise."

Lewis conceded, Jorgio went about his business rinsing glasses in suds.

"Can't imagine who was on board to do such a thing," Lewis said to be placating. "No use for a ship to be on the ocean."

Jones nodded. "Sheer stupidity. Kingston can't board, neither can the playas. Just don't see the point of a renegade."

"Is it your case?" Jorgio asked Lewis.

"All the glass come to me. They'll be searching for the glass deck direction until they locate it."

"Then there has to be a picture," Jones put in.

"A snafu," Jorgio said to be accommodating of Lewis' reputation. "Schedule didn't note if the communications was removed."

"Could be sitting on a dock for all anyone knows," was Lewis' quip.

They fished up their stems before they were served again, this time with lime, nursing their beverage while the fly boys entered the room and checked their flight schedule.

They boarded at 0833, seven people on an almost empty plane. The evening meal was served ten minutes after take-off, a lamb curry with a tiny garden and slice of cucumber, a square of cornbread with kernels showing, the ocean rippled beneath them, the last light of day swept over the waves, no cart with drinks on standby crew only.

They descended into Nassau after dark, the blue lights of the runway signaling safety of return.

"Was she what you thought?" Jones removed a cigarette from his three-pack inside his breast pocket.

"Long Key shot her as she proceeded past the call dock, yes, she fits her description."

"Destination was North Point?"

"Yup, no telling why she didn't land, she called in three times, one time she signaled, of course by that time without a radio she was sail to the sun."

"Maybe she collided with another ship, toppled her deck," Jones said.

Lewis agreed. "No telling Rhonda likes you, you're smart, but try this on for size, the radio was cut at its cable, you could see the trunk through the floor."

"Well, it's not as though she considers herself married, you did sign a divorce decree."

Lewis pulled out of the airport, he drove through the promenade, gave his ticket to the guard at the one room station house, took off down the central avenue headed for their hotel which could be seen, bright yellow and blue lights atop the roof. The heat filled Lewis' Cadillac, its sharp fins swerved at the speed of a bump in the road, Jones rolled down the window allowing for the warm night to breeze inside.

"I was a marine for the army before I met Rhonda," Lewis said, his voice tinged by self pity. "I was dating a friend of hers, I'd just returned from Ecuador when I was assigned her as a secretary, she kept all my document records, I couldn't correspond without her typing in notes of port transactions. Most of my work between '54 and '72 bears her shorthand."

"You should've had a child by her."

Lewis shrugged. "It didn't work out that way, the regrets are hers, I've nothing I can't look back on."

Jones hated the sense that he had been manipulated in a way he couldn't predict. He switched on the lights in his suite until the place blazed, fixed himself a stiff rye, his bottle had another day before he'd have to sprout ass it, flicked on the television to catch the news, placed a call to dateline Miami for a query on sightings of ships lost at sea resembling his tower by any base, land or harbor, and went to bed.

In the morning when he was thinking clearly he thought the military had knowingly put Lewis' ship on a single run as a quick finder intending it to chart course by direction, no radio, and to establish signal with a packaging eliminator solely to update fleet authority, if fleet had a towline available. Ships wandered in all the time from Meridian and wound up in a skirmish usually to extricate themselves without event. As big as the ocean was, his guess was the two ships were able to see one another, a horn probably sounded, the smaller of the two may not have been capable of getting out of the way especially if it were loaded with illegals.

He met Hil on the green outside the library for tea and salad, they took seats on the terrace overlooking the bay, Jones produced his portfolio of correspondence with the datelines and included the summary of the quarantine dock, all of which took his boss a good fifteen minutes to peruse.

"Grenada's hotels are all prisons," Hil Massey said, sliding the document across the table. "You'll want to tidy up an audit for all portage toVirgins, it's a task that requires a senior officer who has familiarity with brand approvals on food, could be coffee, preserved fruit, pineapple, mango, papaya."

"Routine controls?"

"All. Chemist stamped. Pre-shipment warranted. No tea, sugar, dyes."

"That's fine."

"You will assign Customs, return by ship."

"That could take a week. What am I looking for?"

"Three days by computer. You want to establish frequent cargo."

"You think you might have my ship floating about?"

"I gave each agent a stray dog, building plazas or vessels, no match, each wanted for clearing port when another vessel was being detained."

They talked about Jones' recent trip to the quarantine, the size of the boats detained, whether there were detainees, then onto the mumbo jumbo on the news, another typhoon out at sea, the anticipated wave breakers, at last Hil said he thought Lewis' glass reflected too much light for where the building was, the trouble with buildings these days was that the buildings added light at early evening, halfway through the meal Hil paid, gave Jones the requirements at each port. Jones had to warrant on any irregularity resulting from five thousand items, enter on computer each item by description, certificate with listed destination, and signature approval, and certify each by weight. It was to be a busy week.

7.
A wharf shelving involved a classification grouping of

distributable products by age or generic identification of shelf. For each product, shelf might consist of days prior to sail, could rely upon normal standards for itemization once they were received in stores, or could simply be stocked items in warehouse distribution centers; all but plants were subject to chemist approvals. Product penicillin for example, batched by refrigeration and approved by bacterial inhibitors, went out first; ampicillin was stored indefinitely and when aged past acceptable date was restricted for animals; food on the other hand stayed in warehouse coolers on ships until unloaded and had to be dumped after date approvals were reached, variances were sent back to warehouse containment storage centers usually located at headquartered stores, this generated listings of unusables which when subtracted from gross national product gave permission for replacement product. Jones had grouped the two hundred and fifty items by color and code and when they were neatly shelved by packaged crate resembled an opera seating arrangement with tiers to mark various related product for date and ship compartment, unloading off the ship was grouped by the station for which each product would be transported into American cities. For every tier in the placement of color photographs were taken at the wharf with any number of landmark references in a background so as to advance the finding of product if it were misplaced or lost; he came across an anomaly, an export building on a hillside on western Nassau that resembled a docking floor tower on a ship, seven windows across the top. From a photographic distance the ships resembled oil frigates with the long tankard, the hull a wharf, then the tower and a pair of stackers, giving the photographer the conveyance of a scorcher probably in a harbor it wasn't permitted. When he had disposed of a good twenty to thirty arenas he had what would very likely turn into a tough old bug of a snag, how to tell with reliability whether the tower in his photograph was part of a ship or an actual building, despite the metal container crates, the apparently frenetic activity of a loading dock, even the swing lift of placing crates onto a correctly identified ship, with or without a long telephoto lens with intricate resonance if what the camera identified was a position of ship to tower, it was almost impossible to discern by photograph alone.

He dragged the flap for a close up magnifier and scanned the shoreline and hill. In terms of perspective besides a wharf, there were red steel underpinnings of a freeway before a road is put in, assuming one could find a point of advantage, the dock shelf was the best reliable mechanism to determine a ship from a building, although the approximately two stories with tower, often found with stackers in the background passing by wells situated on a hill confused any draw of the photo bucket. A laboratory with a gawker, eight cameras of varying capabilities simultaneously, could differentiate the floor from the wharf, the radio telescope from the smaller version of ship with merely navigational capability for signaling land, or allow several retrievable images to be reported at the same time. The fact that the lab with the gawker had selected out a wharf instead of a floor for a ship, but had not identified a tower from a building when it could have, stayed with Jones as a question, possibly because the lab was stymied by another photograph.
So, of course, the only real problem with a floating cavern was its designated function on the ocean apart from trade; aside from moving products from clearances to warehouses for distribution, there were oil – gasoline was not supposed to move – refuse for ocean burial, transportation and movie making. It was unthinkable that to make a movie required a pristine beach of an untrammeled beach with no hotels or towns in order to create a private industry, but this often occurred especially as industrial retirees desired a change in their surroundings and endeavors. Thus a relatively small tankard relied upon as a desert prop on a distant island might be granted permissions to be torched and later ride the bays for sightseeing, no one the wiser for its continued unauthorized status.

After he finished his approvals in two and a half days, although he had routed all deportation photos to Miami for verification, he thoughtfully placed a communiqué to Aricebo observatory in the Puerto Rican forested canyons for the predisposition of warm green sea as it pertained to transatlantic shipping. They replied by camera telex saying the green under-water color was essential because only in green could a camera read people or objects, explained a baseball diamond of neatly secured props of cameras on steel frames attached to rock or to disposed ships could take pictures of any ships floating over-head and at intervals send pictographs to any tele-dot-com by automatic descension and then restore the display to blue ocean. That had to be a big deal, who outside a floating ship casino could attribute access to such a replay system, includ-ing an advance notification to a destination, could explain why the phantom ship disappeared, it could be sitting right there, it could be long gone, it could even be entering a port it was expected to arrive after it was posted for an earlier day.

He took a departure from resuming work on his photo as-signment, having concluded the meticulous classification of Hil's product list, before he sat down to the task of examining match-ing chatter to port activity on and off the ship. Jones strolled down the expansive rolling green, his mind never tiring of the luxuriating setting, to the four pools, grabbing a towel as he let himself inside a gate, the stripling beach and greenish blue water just below the end of the pavement of the last pool, removed his shirt and sandals and went for a swim, the pool refreshing, silky to the skin, twenty strident strokes before he got out and lay on a white lounge recliner, soaking in the warm sun, thinking he might squeeze in a tennis set later in the day, take a spin into town to his favorite bar, a steak well grilled, all three reports would be sent to Hil before nine, a mood stabilizer before bed. Tomorrow he'd be back at his desk with a photo ruler to measure any offsets, evaluate high edges, prominent color shading, pop the photo by sections through a watercolor rate, finalize the print jacket, send the whole goddamn thing to a felt tip pen analyst for variation from overlays, stack by dimension for definite to pre-sumptive status, and then for another telex run, this time more hopeful than the last the ship could finally be declared.

The morning had gotten off to a good start, the chatter gave note of an early bloom that had carried inland off a shore breeze situated at a waterfront plaza on his photo mid left and the desultory heat of the week had vanished, when he zeroed in on his photo in the upper left it showed nasty blur streaks in an inlet canal, he looked up the reflection to the building to the western side of the island, and positioning for color decided it contained both a new freeway under construction and the barest shell offshore of a boat the same colors anchored, he estimated the streaks at 0455 pm, consulted a harbor master schedule, opted for a ship by description, brought it up on computer. It took him a half hour to make the drive across town to the far end of the peninsula to the harbor there, barely a traffic wharf extending from a three story, all black glass hotel with a revolving crown bar, integrated by emerald green golf courses, white sand beaches surrounding the plaza it stood on, at the far eastern side was a thin mantle of cement that wrapped around a bunker of warehouses, a short main station in the road, the guard took one look at his photo, removed a pen and slashed through the top section, pointing to a building in clear view on the hill, Jones photographed the point, photographed the ships alongside the pier, still no match, but enough to at least give him the underside of his alleged docking bay and his top route along with probable ports because his ship would be dependent upon them for its look, now he could search for every same stupid port in the world.

He found Lewis on the green snacking up a lobster bisque drinking his way through the afternoon punch served on the terrace. Jones pulled up a chair, let Lewis put a lunch spread together for him from the buffet, crab omelet with a dash of mole, a piece of bass with crushed lemon, a piece of lime Jell-O with peach and a dollop of mayonnaise, described his big find as he typed in a summary onto his laptop, smoking a cigarette, downing a glass of the goofy punch. Lewis had made headway also, his building plaza was located on Dinner Key, it had a gliding tourist yacht tour every Monday, and he was comparing evening lights up and down the riverfront in a successful attempt to clear which building actually reflected the blur of lights on one of two cross town highways and having marked the suites he now was ready to take notes on the businessmen who leased those condominiums.

"Here's my best surrender," Lewis said about their assignments, "the glass reflected one thing not found in evidence anywhere in the jurisdiction, then yours is not what it looks like, Roberto in the cubicle next to mine had to track yellow brights off piers, Mick opposite Hil's office had to isolate motor boats, that no good self righteous prig who flirts with the secretaries was given golden sands of Puerto Rico, I should have been assigned everything to do with P.R., Hil says he gave most tear sheets to the green horns, Catrianna says she has been up to her eyeballs in sewer gunk and has to identify by ship and route for time of year, Gay was assigned burning oil pipes in Haiti, I thought that assignment ought to have been yours, you see, don't you, the implications?"

"No, what are they?" Jones asked, feeling to exuberant to be miffed.

"No one who knows anything about the lay of the land could receive what they know."

"Could be we're dealing with a port problem."

"Yes, minor understatement, we can't even make telephone inquiries, okay to send us to some neck of the woods that will take us months to figure out."

"You're getting pissy, Lewis, let's not have an argument."

"So here's my guess, it's a port stable affair, whoever identifies the problem for whatever it must be can't have done something in life, God knows what."

"Can't ever have chased after an aircraft that went down in the Rib?"

Lewis remarked, "Well, of course that leaves us all out, but this is no Army Air problem."

"Could be an easy item, an illegal trapping device for entry of boats into Key harbors," Jones said. "We haven't seen those in a long time."

"Except yours isn't a boat and my glass doesn't show a boat or a ship. My guess would be everyone jumped over board."

"What would be the point?"

"All the lights were left on, the captain wanted a full deck with brights."

Jones said, "Could explain all the blurs if these renegades wanted a docu-proof of their landing. Where would they be headed, do you suppose?"

"Anywhere. They obviously don't want their ship in a picture, so they're committing a repeat act."

"That's an island that has allowed transportation of illegals, swimming for Florida."

"It goes with press art and count, could be the methodology that gets used to smuggle in aliens," was Lewis' satirical summary. "I've invited Rhonda up, just so you know."

"Things could get out of hand."

"Oh, well, old fellow, we'll drop in and have drinks."

"Will she be arriving early?"

"First thing in the morning, don't worry, we won't get you out of bed."

"I'll look for you for lunch."

"Sure, do that, we'll just be getting started."

Jones stirred his punch and drank it all, thinking of his work to give himself an emotional distance from the idea he would have to see Rhonda quite so soon with Lewis lurking about, he'd have to dye out his picture to determine the color the ship put to port and most likely the variation in color to be seen on the ocean, in all probability land lent a variance in perception of color, perhaps the separate colors of the bay or ocean did the rest.

"I'll be tied to my computer," he said.

"All day? Oh, c'mon, it won't be as bad as that," Lewis replied.

Although he had no right to complain, Lewis' rivalry irritated like an open sore, even if Jones wasn't one to hold a grudge, there was no where to go to avoid a scene, he was certain Lewis would insist upon his hour, a public display, glitzy as the twinkling twilight of dim lights seen in the suites of the high rise.

Lewis stood with Jones embracing his shoulders in a compatriotic gesture. "Give it some thought, if you would, a superficial fulfillment between chums. I didn't say, did I, my array of tiny lights are the lights of the waterway from the first speed pole into the ocean, it's the height of the reflection that bewilders, you know the closest landmark is the highway, off to the exit is the bridge, every way to say December 21 with year, time or day clocked into every clock there, 12/21, 9:50 pm, Thursday 21 December, so on and so forth, twenty clocks, on the bridge, in the clock tower, in the plaza, on the garden square, at the city hall and courts, on closed circuit, all times identical, no offset, but then again no clock landmark reflects."

"Bravo," Jones said, "no clock, no boat."

"Ah, well, can't keep it all, sad to say, at 2033 the waterway turns down the yacht harbor lights, the vehicles don't actually produce blurs, coming near the ramp the traffic is at a crawl, the tiny lights are reflected until 0612 when the lights are shut off."

"That's a lot of time measurement you were put to, what gave you the idea to do it?"

Lewis steered Jones toward the lobby. "That's my specialty, fellow, if you have to know, always obtain a clock count down to the seconds, after all if the lights are the same every day of every year depending upon daylight then they have to be verified as to where they are seen for each light."

"Excellent work, Lewis, you astound me, call me in the morning," Jones said.

"Will do," Lewis replied happily, left, once outside the sliding glass doors he waved.

Jones waved back.

Oh, heck, what was he to do, Lewis had his lights figured out down to the dock by estimation of nautical charting which had to mean that any boat entering the ocean could be reflected at evening or night, if Jones' vessel had shown up in a reflection it would have been clocked, had it then traveled on the ocean, it would have been seen. The problem for Jones was he had a freeway, a wharf and a tower building and a ship and no finding yet for the ship. Because the radio had in every probability been chopped, whereas he'd have to look for reflection for departure, determining arrival was likely to be a needle in a haystack, best time of day to look was while there was almost no reflection of building light, around 3 pm and again as evening fell. At his desk he grouped by selected tug and trucking activity for usual sound prints, next by segregated photographs of new highways, any type wharf in case the ship put into a non dock inlet, and distance of high tower to measure one inch one eighth across, this task would take a good day of searching. The next best was to match for any repair or part, less time to compare for flat ships in shipyards. To avoid overlooking any repair of non-intact hulls he requested a white line on all ocean liners.

His white line came home first, the primary vessel leaving Havana to set sail to the lower Keys to their shipyards were docking bays. Two left the islands, one left St. Maarten's green bay every five months for a partial reconstruct of floundered ships weathered inside the Gulf states between Pensacola and Mobile and Galveston and New Orleans.

When he found a good likeness to his ship the starboard color was brown, not the red classification of oil tankard viewed on the ocean docked in Havana, the top blue line misleading because on scrutiny it was actually a deck with an exterior hall.

He had two days remaining to finish his assignment. The only thing he hadn't yet considered was his ship might go with a docking bay in which event the vessel that would show up on photograph was a docking bay itself. He placed an inquiry to dateline Miami and another to logotype New Orleans asking for any port at which a photograph of a flat ship would give a view of buildings with windows like a dock for control assigned to inappropriate deck authority and asked them to return to Havana. Then he booked his flight.

8.

He arrived after midnight. The maid's quarters had gone

to bed and the porter who had deposited his bag in the hall had gone to fetch a limo to drive him to his hotel flat at the Vacarro above the restaurant. The dogged nights whipped up a windy gale, four fathoms above. Finally when the sedan came around he stepped into the seat, picked up the newspaper to the first page and read the top bar, Too much weather abroad, astern. The flat was lit, one of few along the waterfront walk. He set the clock for eight, set up his computer, took a shower and called for a secretary in the morning, he went to sleep listening to the sound of the ocean, a window open. One thing for certain, he wouldn't be found in the daylight by Lewis. By all appearances Lewis was impotent, probably had been for years since his days in Rico when five islands had to suppress fire in the booty off Tahiti, the windstorm in Cubana province, all hands on deck, a ship firing into the rotund, the fortress secure, Vincent coming round the pass full clock thrust. Lewis had been a first to jump ship into the soup when less than a mile up the strait the flash went off in the water, a ship taking the plunger into the monsoon, the radios down for seconds. The story was heard forever in every bar and cleaver room in the islands, how when they hauled their men out of the sea they were sweat fatigued for a year.

Jones slept soundly as never before awakening to the jangling alarm, shot wide awake to a full shock of sunlight. A runner on the beach gave him low, low tide; the shopkeepers were setting up tables and parasols in the street. He checked his computer, found nothing, freshened up and went downstairs to the walled in garden, all rose pink walls, cast iron style, faint yellow patio and roses in planter boxes, bougainvillea hanging off trellises. He ordered mole cafe with ambrosia cream, a full box of eggs, baked, taters, and off border bacon and sauce. Lewis had broken vows to undesirables, come of age to Latin music, somehow was protected from his own field sojourns, granted amnesty. Jones settled into the weekend peace of having arrived early for a season when hotels cleaned right before their late Saturday onslaught. A shipmate in an outdated uniform was shown to a table, given a menu and a cup of brewed sistern ale with custard. Jones finished his meal, paid a red sieta and got the hell out of there, his comfort upset by a realization the hiding ship might come and go to St. Maarten and from there home to some smallish city desiring a bootleg permit for restaurants. He went for a stroll to the park, got a bag of popcorn and fed the pigeons before he walked the distance back.

The message was on his computer. It read, Supplies, fuel and sod for air operations, heavy rainfall for fuel, command, no orders in ready, island schedule puts in with ship that has wandered off course.

BOQUERON, PUERTZO RICO

Dupres had spent all morning watching for developments of the week long squall. Three dark green spots 20 West by 38 Longitude coveted the radio R-NAV, marine reported the trinity off shore forty miles. He fed the printer for an AIS reading, double checked on navigation – it showed three hundred feet to bottom, rocky. He turned on the blip for T-NAV, ten EKG-like segments surfaced, seven cold spots, bad weather; the vessels had to be big, two to three decks maximum to eliminate the possibility of sinking.

His programs flashed on screen, first LORAN-C to signify the reading reported only two big boats, then the check list to describe incorrect radio reported unverification, then the schoolmaster voice detection analysis, finally Boqueron shut down. Dupres plugged in for hostilities alert to Havana, a weather immersion showed as a ship. AIS gave two vessels astern within hundreds of feet of destination like lightning on the horizon, the appearance of a bar meant shallow water, two flat peninsulas showed available landings were a fishing dock with a market and a boat jetty in a canal, both in rivers. "Squall line sinkable," the storm would send them into a rough water port. At a dock someone might see them, at a jetty they could land at night but a canal meant they could get read, thus chances were destination point was a shoreline. Dupres looked for a harbor, his best bet was a jetty, he checked AIS for central Florida, but weather reported too much turbulence. Close-in off shore, all towns were on one half foot deep ocean. The warning came up, fishing vessel at risk, hurricane likely, Rhonda at sea. He called it in, put up the map of Florida, based upon steerage radio landing probably would be Jacksonville at Duval County.

He waited, attention riveted to the T-NAV. When telltale signs of cities lined the striated lines at the top and bottom, definitely a river, Dupres checked again for docks, minimum a hundred foot depth. He looked up at destination plank reading, striated lines through the center which was a low lying trench indicating a speedway, Nassau River marsh in northern Florida or St. John's River, docks, harbor, they would have to change onto a small boat or pick up a car, hit 95 South to Daytona Beach.

Miami

In Miami the central AIS monitor was just getting caught up on his sleep when the alarm went off. James flew off his bunk, ran into the hit room, studied all six computers, looked at the splashes and screenshots, took a sip of day old cold coffee, sat at his swivel chair, switched on the radio Cuba, removed a high point flash, and began to take readings for ocean depth. There were two large boats, one with a high deck, thirty-eight miles off shore, moving at approximately a hundred knots an hour.

He radioed Dinner Key. "Deep, no cold spots."

The return voice was broken up with weather. "We're looking for tie-ups for cabin cruisers, a walk down to level dock for boats on Daytona."

"When did you finish reading?"

"We took a shot at noon when there were no shadows. One vessel apparition."

"You are taking in two captures. Did you capture for voice analysis?"

Dinner Key answered, "Captain, map man, helm, maybe twenty men."

"I'm winding them to Indian River Harbor, interior is mostly marsh and bog, live there to learn actual channel in, there's a good landing at a small resort, good ocean flow, deep sixty-five feet, I'll need a few hours to get my first pics."

James backed up the instamatic schedule for clear body shots. Daytona Beach, one shot a week, dish satellite, if a walk-in it stays on, check harbor readings for reflection of a ship, harpoon, net, speed, small bite shark. Gulf Stream remains calm, Nassau River must be marked. He intended to knock off at noon, sit outside, enjoy the sun, catch up on some reading when the next advisory reported in, all black screen, average blue cube at the shallow fall.

There would be a few hours before any telescope would ID. He'd be watching for rudder on the T for days, if there were no indication of needing to fuel up prior to landfall.

Havana

The time clocked in at 9:42 pm.

The Lulu came singing round the bend toward Big Pine, Lower Keys, header reading for Islamorada, 80.6 West, the ship following was read to destination into Key Largo, 80.4 West. Lewis Lewis showed nothing but green bays, a maze of canals. Maximum velocity current, the image libraries opened to The Strand. At the moment the Gulf Stream under Haiti beneath Cuba reported; past Mexico above Havana to the Keys also reported, sailed right past him, an escort shark was reported moving at ten to twelve knots up Florida past Sarasota Bay having made radio contact with a fishing vessel from Myrtle Grove, Delaware, Carolina Beach Cape River entrance at Long Beach, nailed at 33.8 North by 78.03 West, headed through crystal blue for muddy waters. He closed all headers and relayed to Miami North, pulled up any program with descriptive profiles for board heads, beach bums, catamaran repair, e-faxed a brief memo that read, Stinker on its way in.

Holguin City
Thunderhead Bay

The assignment photo lay on Jones' desk, the clip-on read, "Stat – need at least ten identifiers by end day" and gave the final print sheet for grid square, photo number, image classification, date taken, subject location. He posted for the escort cabin; sure enough he placed to a docking bay, floating wharf, Detention Beach, Daytona, at The Carnegie, golf course package, all beige beachhead, expansive shallow water, sparkling coral reefs, nothing colonial, plenty of food if his touristas brought in cans or live catch. Jones looked for photos a weekend prior to date of ID in a boat or a charter. It was winter, bad time of year for anyone, he'd have to hope, if they were a relationship, they were struck by cabin fever.

In the spool were a matching set. A mid aging male, silver blond, blue eyes, pounder face, colorful blue, green, yellow short sleeved shirt over doper khaki pants, sandals; a female, dark tan, very thin, passionate reddish brown hair, no hat, sleeveless tight terricloth dress, unusually bright orange and tan, cut above the knees, orange cloth heels, yellow and alligator skin shoulder bag, dark shades. During the drenching storm they had driven down the Old Dixie Highway to Funky Town, North Key Largo for dinner of King Crab with fresh made pasta and white wine, no dessert. Well after ten o'clock at night, the gale doing major damage to the ocean front, hurling young palm trees, crashing tile roof tops, splashing ocean as high as second story balconies, they checked into a small harbor hotel cabin boarded with storm windows, lit a string of lights inside a living room with a linoleum floor and proceeded to get plastered on wine purchased in town at a small colonial market that sat on the wharf surrounded by low lying shrubs, palms, outboard stealths, the wind producing a slanted reflection of color in the rain. He was listed as John Somers, 5'10", Saudi, his primary occupation was removing grime from gelcoat boats; she was Irina Erata, also Saudi descent, a shrimpy fortyish; together they had cocktails at Sloppy's on Park West, sailed on the Key West Charter every few months, forty knots an hour, on the arches bridge taking photos, roller skating in the Carib section by the salons. Beach Patrol had spotted them at JB's Fish Camp at the red lighthouse at Ponce inlet the previous spring, at New Smyrna Beach that summer in a cabin boat, seventy-two footer tied to a pier dock raised on pilings fronting a bird sanctuary. Last fall they had taken a highrise condo amidst concession stands on the sand, scintillating damp white beach shining like abalone luster, gone surf fishing, strong poles bent in a silkscreen glow of foot high ocean. Most years they were among the jet set of trendy boaters who took the gulf stream to one of the Keys and by the time the boat returned at sunset the place would be alit with gas lanterns in jars, a low elbow living.

It was a whole different society in a vacation rental – a rum and jack card trade, a bit of light arts palate, a few soakers on the beach. Young people if they were in love had love; if not they went out and made money. For likable latitude they found a cozy place on the windless side where prices were higher up from $800 a week, but it meant they never went out except to enjoy a rare sunset beach grill. Jones would be at the shelf non stop to catch this pair, easy to look at, easy to find was what he hoped for, boozed snorkels lying on a beach, carefree in daylight. An occasional easterly at dusk would keep the two indoors hanging strands of lights the gale wouldn't douse. A magnolia style plant hotel wasn't their style despite their reservation ticket, they were loose garden kids. Before Jones rented an up deck, he had to have a week receipt. He'd place five on the bar to know he was even likely to find them, but the Keys were small, not invisible, a dive to many of jangling color straight off a canvas. Storm shutters permanently over screen porches, houses to let off season, pimento tuna spread in a cup with a grease stick and a margarita pitcher. The Keys were all about the after hours, wind coming up around the stream with a ruffle of breeze, tepid water temperature, the ocean a pale green, the marlin on the rise on a good sail day, a garland of daffodils cast off a gliding yacht as it charted a course to a snorkel bay, white veranda coffee bars, hair trim on a second story high table nook, deck hotels on the ocean, green mar across the alley a pool for the Women's Health and Counseling travel agency, amenities, pool, sailing, grill, Southpaw Fishing Charter at Kings Point.

Jones sent a report to San Juan by late afternoon. Overseas highway – paved, Mile Marker 101 rental, Whistle Bar on the corner with popcorn cart, shallow blue, white sand painted boats with motors, blue lawn chairs, striped red and orange brick antique shop in town of eight blocks by seven blocks close to warehousing marina district, very flat, everything is salty dog including key lime martini, frothy on top, beachcomber, two car trolley train runs four blocks.

Havana

Lewis Lewis caught the little pimp swimming off the ship, heading for the mile marker at Islamorada, making good time, a frothy on top moustache exactly per Jones' print-out, headed for a cement dock, boarded up houses and pebbly white sand, the sort of beach bum found in Everglades at Lost man's River. They showed signs of being loners, staying clear of densely populated wave runners, the type who liked to gaze out at clear blue water, scrape barnacles off a thrashed motorboat in low tide while standing in murky water, a pagoda boat rack a half mile on the road, weekenders to Medical Biscayne standing in spotlight cruisers waiting for port authorities at Higher Bridge at Fifth Street, Miami River, to approve passage for their arrivals on one of the two ships.

It would never happen; by the time the ships made North Key the crew would be floating debris, corks bobbing in the mouth of Coconut Grove, soon to be snapper, hooked and straitjacketed to pole houses standing on pilings on submerged farmland downriver of South Beach, Miami.

It was time to download – a brief interruption to local computer subscribers, he switched to NAV/com, traded one set of fourteen hour spools for fishing nets. Surf was up, he reported; he picked up some nibbles on his line which meant these station pimps had voice-over equipment. He switched to Dinner Key marina, a picture of a tripod on the sand off a yacht club, within seconds he had dots appearing over his pictures by location like punched out holes from a three ring notebook puncher. He typed in FLORIDA, BISCAYNE, SPANISH CAY, STRAND, THE GABLES BY THE SEA HOUSES ON FARM TRACT. He took a break, stepped outside onto the dock, and smoked a Charlton cigarette. It was a constant battle – put mud down and then tide blew in. With this upsurge of weather all ships would be docked, cable strong lines tying them to both sides of a dock, it was insanity for any size boat to make a dash through international lines for U.S., even a mayday hell bent for a cove breaker. It'd be weeks per man overboard to find the fish in the kettle, keep them at an original site, without an assignment of fifty or more beach patrol agents, one for each crew, then another group of ten to cover ramps, rope off stairs to boat landings, identify from storm service photos and photo verify, hundreds of man hours to scour shipping docks, ride ferries, board tugs, and securing them away from avenue docks, shipyard bays, canal junctions and used car lots.

Lewis Lewis alerted U.S. Coast Guard to patrol estates. Two crews meant forty-eight men, sponge divers were instructed to detain in cell houses on beaches or wooded areas, "Only to the bottom, then by dragline." He radioed Jones he'd fly in on the first flight at dawn.

Jones tracked verifiable boarding passes to photo circuitry to a small off shore floating dock construction. The owner offered seasonal professional work to any youthful male good with a boat rope and a screw driver and punch. After two years in the Caicos illicit arrangements were made to transport these illegals without benefit of work Visas, passports, permanent addresses, proof of U.S. citizenship and permit to dock. Sightseers who boarded a boat in Central America, Mexico or the islands who got as far as the Keys were ruthlessly pursued, only those who skirted Customs by hitching a ride to El Paso into Texas were tracked by Central custom agents. A hundred a year attempted the same stunt aboard cruise boats. The few who succeeded in obtaining shared residences obtained boat forfeitures, scarce low wages, infiltrating county and state boundaries and could wind up virtually anywhere, often married to citizens who were when found deported with their illegal mates. Illegals were U.S. government's single biggest problem, without steady labor they became forest fire arsonists, hunted bombers, murderers, vagabonds. Jones reported – fresh catch, illegals deporting, big boats, average fare $200 U.S. If these destitutes commit a crime, there was no way to track the crime.

By late night beach patrol would be crawling the beaches, the warning adviso to conduct a house by house search, look for points of contact, obscure exotic kitchen ware packed as product, probable hide-outs included secluded docks, none closed in by land; two identifiers – large weight divorced women and very young females with teenage daughters.

Pappy had resided in Islamorada since his father began working for the U.S. fishing industry taking fishing vessels with cranes and nets for shrimping in the gulf stream. A short man with fiery red tiny curly hair who dressed in grease overalls, a flannel long sleeved shirt, rubber boots, he awakened by three-thirty mornings, lit the kerosene lamps on the wharf, had scrubbed down the boat deck by five and started up the engine to be in international waters by nine. He would say that after fifty years on the channel leaving the Cape of Head Island he had observed every final fallacy a captain could encounter from nesting terns on the bow, to boobies in the hatch, new deltas where water had flowed into in a storm, to bright lights at night in marsh bird land, to walk-in cabins without doors or solid floor boards, to finding boats perched on top of a hill at low tide, relentless stories of ghosts and goblins on wharfs and boats and barnacles that had put in a solid gash into a boat's underside. Pappy had avoided marriage the way all mariners worth their pint at the wheel are kept faithful by their mistress, the ocean. Not without intention he had traveled every port and town on any water way and knew down to the minute how long it took to dock any size boat, yacht or canoe. He was also a keen observer of birds, had drawn pictures of every last red tail and spruce wing in the estuaries, could identify by warble and season, and could hear the damned thing coming across the radio frequencies despite any other background sound including drilling for off station rigs. At one minute before midnight when only a spotted yellow dove cries for ten minutes in concert with jumping fish, the relation to a black-brown winged hawk to be seen in the Indian River, Pappy recorded an odd far-off sound of water being sloshed out of an outboard by what he thought was a lone hand. He strapped on leg weights and waded into the marsh hoping to identify the looks of the man by pier light but instead saw a set of four canoes without people inside drifting peaceably on the tide as it left the basin, the sound of someone scooping out water now unquestionably distinct.

He left a message on radio call for Islamorada Vice, "boat winded, one minute to midnight, caught by yellow warbler, probable male with stern or engine room advice."

A light spilled on from a dockside cabin as the Vice officer took down the call. The person listening was sent periodically into Miami for docks, he was an expert in moving them.

Jones picked up Lewis Lewis at the San Juan airfield at six. To

Jones' way of thinking his long time associate whom he hadn't seen in weeks since this gulf crisis began was thinning out at the waistline where stress took its longest indenture. They hugged with the sanity that at least for the several days when Lewis would be stationed reviewing identifications they would have some intellectually satisfying discussion, a few meals at the Concierge and a handful of more or less pleasant evening strolls on the waterfront.

Jones said, "Good to see you."

"Likewise, good to get out of the storm."

"Technically Puerto is a U.S. base, I don't know how these boats made it all the way into Florida without alerting Immigrations."

"Port Authority was under the impression they were a day charter."

"They'd need a fishing permit."

"They may have one, we don't know yet why they jumped ship."

"You must have received tips by now."

"We placed a shaver on a tip Miami logotype received this morning, a real beaut," Lewis was the first to start filling in details at his end, as they dashed across the parking lot in near darkness to Jones' van. "Man identified a group of sleepers in canoe croppers while a radio ensign for one of these boats was baling out his getaway."

"That's what I like to hear." Jones tossed Lewis' bag into the luggage rear compartment, and they got underway. "We've found their walk out plank, a little dinghy start point west of Ponce."

He kicked the van motor onto full power, spun out of the field passing the lighthouse which was without its rotating beam for the hour, and fell alongside the bold lines marking the single lane road to town. Old faded orange stucco houses grew visible beneath the gradually emerging silvery sunlight, their brown tiled roofs like church tower tops, a harmonious church with three bell towers rising above the town populace in the distance.

Jones said, when the traffic became sparse after the second exit, "The boats were manufactured Miller Freeman with Inmarsat-R in the radio room as backup for voice, fax data and telex. The larger of the two boats, the second one, also had Iridium phone to shore which may account for the immersion apparition we recorded."

"What a goof," Lewis said. "Any idea who provided the equipment?"

"Not at the moment, but we're examining the feasibility of removing the engines on a remaining fleet."

"Accessible wharf?"

"Their boats sit on a long dockside, wood plank with road, probably won't take much to lock it up, de license their permits. Almost all are 72 feet, enclosed cabin window, power throttle."

"How many?"

"A good twenty. Our concern with all these petrols is their binary code interface; it comes up resembling a blue fence until you have it on a single screen and then it is a series of very small print of serial numbers."

"Obviously that's what the two boats did to project an apparition, probably combined with R and Iridium, be relatively easy if you knew how to program it."

"We've checked our findings against incidents; that's the concern, they've used this sort of thing to hide actual documents, if you don't recognize language, it doesn't necessarily occur to you numbering is interfaced."

"What sort of documents do they adhere to?"

"Shipping regulations, home control clearances, batching for year end products."

"Those dirty fucking bastards, I'd kill them. Who in hell are they?"

"At the moment a group that transports illegals."

"Have you brought in a pro-junk man?"

"You're the pro. You'll like to know the first situation we came across was we thought we had a ship in distress out at Bermudas, the furthest isle heard a whistle but when they went to verify, they had eighty radios coming in at once and the ship vanished."

"Advise Bermuda to leave stations on just for speed. With that, they may not get estimated arrival time but they can fix course. It's always hectic out here, the radio sounds as bad in the weather room as it does at sea."

Jones parked beneath a banyan tree up on the sidewalk. A series of three houses colored mustard with sturdy slate rooftops had hidden cameras, false recorder link hook-ups, ten to thirty stems feeding a murky pool and statue in the adjoining shared garden, each house had interior pink, brick tile floors throughout, walnut wood, ceiling beams, French doors off living room and a bedroom, a handsome balcony off three rooms on a top floor overlooking a narrow cobblestone alley, each an office, desks, chairs, tables, telephone and computers the only furniture besides a king size bed in the downstairs bedroom off the kitchen. Jones flickered on all ten computers in the far room, two showed their AIS dilemma, three were actual replays of the channels at sea, one listed all radio calls received up to the hour, and the other four were for tracking visuals to identifiable data. There were two computer telephones but at any time during a busy season there was a capacity for eight or nine telephones.

"Better put up the binary batches you've detected," Lewis said. He felt dead on his feet but sleep would have to wait.

Jones eliminated in-house coding and went to island to island, off shore inter systems long distance fax data capability. The electric blue data looked to be a wall at the end of which was unusual brightness that appeared haze like. It was similar to parts of the gulf stream during which at various hours of daylight around eleven in the summer months the water took on a dimension of imperceptible light. This condition was mimicked at North Carolina near its northernmost boundary where water stretched ensconced by absolutely calm crystal blue horizon.

Lewis put on eye glasses, studied the screens for visible distinction. "Here," he said, marking the numbering sequence, "you can break it up without producing a rearrangement of data by delaying the numerical output. It will take at least twenty-four hours to put in relay stop bytes."

"Fine, I'll take a snooze. After what I've been through, taking in reports solely by radio without dish, I'm exhausted."

Lewis ran two sets of frequency gambits per line of code. He sorted through sequences with the aid of a computer graphic database to assess for which system was extrapolated most often; he batched pairs of fax data in order to interrupt an automatic sequence using AIS; he gave each start word an abbreviated combined use so that field operatives could swim a fax to another station without appearing to go blind to eliminate the haze. When he finished, he had spent thirty hours at the job. He went to sleep on the floor pad, the shutters drawn shut.

They set out while it was still pre-dawn dark, the drive to Ponce in rain and bleary hail took all of an hour. A frontage highway deposited them in a modest city with modern stone, colonnaded bank in a city plaza, around the corner was the red and black striped stone Parque, behind it the white Ponce Cathedral with two towers in a plaza, its front curb lined with cars, the Playa Ponce along the waterfront, all white sand beach extending out a quarter of a mile beneath sparkling clear blue ocean, two story, white adobe Spanish style houses with red tile roof tops and crimson and pink peonies hanging on trellises dotting the city and last, the deep water port into which cruise ships and commerce ships of every size arrived daily. The U.S. Coast Guard had arrived during the night and sat in a nice harbor, actual cement marina dock opposite a club, lazy palms, tour boats, a large patio deck and restaurant looking out onto the wide winding channel. They parked in front of a long salmon orange customs building with aquamarine warehouse doors on a side street where city buses left every ten minutes to take port personnel to their offices on the hill and to the port again to receive new cargo. Inside they walked to Customs, entered a small office with three men at desks next to three windows, announced themselves and were led to the Manager's office, a separate room with white shutters over impossibly old floor to ceiling arced windows with a tiny opera balcony, a ceiling fan the long, wooden ebony blades which rotated slowly and kept the air cool, an opulent large desk made of sandalwood from the El Salvador rain forest, behind which sat a tall, thin elderly Puerto Rican consulate dressed in white uniform with gold arm stripes and a white captain's hat.

"We're docking every ship that enters from Las Viejes, boarding and conducting inspections," the consulate informed them in a distinct clipped accent that gave him away as French Latin. "We have run satellite surveillance on their hardware, referenced their passports for all port entries, given their crew fingerprinting, voice prints and measured shoe soles by laser; it's a very serious infraction that those two large boats passed the island without so much as a command notice."

"Your policy sounds excellent," Lewis said. "Those thugs weren't on a real vessel."

"Technically the scope read them in as Miller Freeman built."

"It's true their equipment was modern. Have you deported any population recently?"

He shook his head. "Not from here. The Coast Guard handles matters of non viable dismissals. Now, these big boats were found to be carrying detainees?"

Jones replied, saying, "That's what we suspect. These illegal workers are presumed to have boarded fully knowing they might wind up deported or imprisoned; not only that, they appear to have a network of associates capable of hiding them for months, maybe longer. The immediate concern is to reduce their fleet down to boats without fax data primarily."

The Ponce manager appeared to give the matter its full weight. He removed a file, withdrawing a form from it, stood to produce a Xerox on a flat copier at the window, and then handed Jones a docu-copy. It listed serial number of vessel, type of industry, dates of sail, intent to carry additional mates, destination port, person authorizing and days of trip. On this particular document the names of some added crew stood out, other names he suspected were conjured. The vessel name was listed as Storm Petulant, its destination Plantation Keys, estimated arrival 1850 hours, dock No. 10, anticipated return on February 7th for a stay of three and a half weeks, initials of customs officer, purpose of trip to build docks alongside parks, construction crew fifteen males, age 22 to 53, the foreman listed as Roger Edgerton, Real Estate, 52 years old, who specialized in floating docks, tie-ups, outboard posts, aluminum walk ways, fenced piers, and estuary king docks at city marinas for big boats with nets, large cabin cruisers and tall mast pole ships, everything for the modern fishing tackle with lockers. Attached C.V. gave Edgerton's recent job for Delaware state parks on the Indian River and showed a photographic print of a winding all wood rail less dock through a marsh, partially forested terrain with wilderness groves and bird look-outs, all on the up-and-up.

"Did his credentials match?" Lewis asked.

"We detained him for that job, kept his entire crew in a Ponce d'Leon Hotel for two days, clearing every man, matching prints, licenses, medicals, thorough, not so much as a prior on any."

Jones betrayed no sentiment, but he was thinking the Delaware trip had netted the real estate mogul a ton of useful information. "Was that boat equipped with fax data and voice?"

"No, it was a comfortable Rude-type large boat, had made numerous diving expeditions to corral reefs, under ocean caves, had gone once to Antartica."

"Are you familiar with either a Somers or Erata?" Jones queried.

"No. Were their voices picked up as part of the crew?"

"They appear to be sponsors for them, they're a beachcomber jet set newly arrived from Delaware."

"No, I don't know them. If Edgerton arranged to visit the couple while his crew built for the state park, it's not known."

"Is there a possibility you can get Edgerton's fleet location?"

"His boathouse is not difficult to find, it's down wind, a small dock marina called Diver's Locker, a turquoise and red market and tackle bait shop near a concrete foundry."

"Do you have a picture of him?"

"The Kingdoc is a tall, frizzy short blond hair, moustache, good physique, surfer type."

Key lime frothy martini came to Jones' mind. If he was also a skillful artist of blue binary code imagery painting blue or green oils of distorted curving or bending shapes and high-lighted codes in white contrast, it was uncertain why he needed to be at Head Island Beach at this time of year.

"What did you make of that?" Jones asked Lewis on their way back to the street.

Lewis said, "Customs has their hands tied, it'll be all they can do to contain a problem that actually isn't their jurisdiction. It's not Navy's authority either if these folks can build their own boats, technically equipment capability belongs to the manufacturer. I doubt if when we talk to whoever is minding the store, Customs will view those magnetic scopes as their problem."

"It's a trade wind route problem not to be able to have authority over their sight NAV capability as to who enters."

"Trade winds are not a difficult problem if the boats are registered to begin with, but if this crew has obtained docking permits in the recent year, my guess is they slipped through on a technicality."

"Good thinking," Jones answered. "Possibly this Edgerton declared to a Delaware address for this job also."

"If they don't have permission to be in Florida or they discovered they had to receive pending applications for work in advance and failed to do so, they can be swiftly disposed of. However, if they have time limited promised work, they may have counted on their pre-approved status. It's the fact that the crew jumped overboard before the boat's entry at High Bridge that makes them all suspects."

"And none have visas, making it open and closed."

They drove out in the morning to the dock, a long wooden ramp with handrails to a harbor of shipyard houses all painted vivid green and blue, on an adjacent calle made of blue cobble a Sandpiper Hotel stood beside a pink and brown tile customs house. The boats inside were standard top decks used for sailing Nov to May in a trade wind easterly when a warm ocean breeze in the tropics would swiftly move boats from one island to another, a male clearly not a Detention and Deportations Officer emerged through a door from a green and blue shipyard building, a medium height tanned scrawny male with dark wavy hair and matching moustache in workman's overalls with a cloth wiping his hands of boat petrol, when he spotted them he broke into a run, darting down the alley, making his get away, Lewis out-thought him and headed along the wharf along the protective high ocean wall, Jones climbed a fence and dashed atop roofs, jumping onto a nearby repair building like a cat on its feet, flying off with admirable agility throwing himself onto the scrawny man as he ran up a stairway down a higher street.

Jones muscled the man to the ground. "A donde esta su hombre?"

"No esta aqui, esta en la bota en Caribbean."

"Porque? Quanto dinero hacere?"

"Yo no se, no es mi problema?"

"Que es su dificil?"

"Mi esposa quiere mi chica."

Always a man being sought for questioning in the U.S. Puerto considered the best tactic to shout divorce, child custody, Lewis had arrived, yanked the man to his feet, fired a half dozen languages at him, asked him a few questions and threw him away from them.

"Mexican, not even Latin," Lewis said. "I can't detain him, he knows nothing of illegal radios on the boats, says they're handled off Old. That's where they have to net wire the ocean wall to hold back the moss so inland residents don't have ocean flowing down their streets. I let him go because there's no where he can get to to do sufficient damage. If they turn out to be combining fax data with telex to shore at a Vieques dock, we can bust them but we shouldn't beat them up."

Jones thought the motor repair man deserved at least a pair of cuffs, but Lewis was decided.

"It could explain why the boats don't get certified. We'll drop in, take a look."

Jones said, "They took advantage of the storm."

"Probably the only realistic times they wind up getting into Head Island."

He persisted. "It was the appearance of a third large boat with a deck that threw us off, they had a way to dock control our visors."

"A dish mechanism, it's only on one type of ship, a floating dock out in the middle of the ocean to warn of hurricanes."

"There was no one to go out beyond the three-mile to board them, check permits, detain or deport."

"There you have it." Lewis helped Jones to his feet. "Not much one can do in the face of a spitting gale. Here's my guess, once the crew was voice printed they didn't screen for the usual; no illicit drugs, no organized crime, no currency violation, no porn or obscenity, no importation of stolen vehicles, no mail fraud, no weapons and therefore no question. FBI's not going to want them, DEA won't either, if they aren't crime-bound there's no Secret Service involvement either. We just want them on deliberate evasion of immigration and customs laws."

At Cabo Rojos they checked into government rental flats in a governor hotel across the road from a sea wall and the ocean. They each took a suite which let onto a porch overlooking seven pools, tennis courts, rolling golf greens and lounge recliners on the sand beneath coconut palms. Jones hooked up his laptop, poured himself a dark, one shot whiskey and got to work.

San Juan, windy blue gray cobblestone, narrow alleys, brightly painted decorous yellow, blue, rust, real painted green sashes, San Juan Batista hides none of the recent mail fraud or vanished ninos despite extensive sand beach, shallow blue, docks of every kind, sea wall fortress; efforts to deter barrier reef coral gathering by non registered oyster divers has been effective in the prevention of substandard child labor and United States port authorities. DATELINE, DINNER.

The advantage of having taken a boat to Las Vieques Isle was seeing the proliferation of endless warehouses, racked berths, stackers of outboard cabin decks, boathouse shelves of kayaks, crowded gray docks, easily well over a hundred ramps, squeezed tightly with small motors, open cabins, cruiser power throttle, average, comfortable, large sleepers. Impossible to know how many computer businesses had a hand in the money. If the number of boats and people indicated a control system in which no one was allowed to get any idea of what data systems might actually be available, it should be available on federal registrar, otherwise it would take a hundred Immigration agents on the spot, between the two of them they bought out the markets of every picture slide available. This proved to be no world of turf or surf, nor of happy honeymooners on their first Caribbean trip, docks had foot lockers of every kind imaginable, every type cabin cruiser, walk-ins, single deck, captain's chair, out deck sleeper, bunks, kitchens, including the nets and topsails, lined the canals, small harbors, topsides, buoy cans, radios blasting, motors running, no one dock slot not filled, a veritable jungle. On any day Florida cleared her wide channels of boats and set her Boat Patrol on her waters, the sight from her high rise condominiums was of crystal blue, placid, unrippled ocean bays, everything tied up, in a single draw not a boat escaped detection, therefore an illegal entry had to take into account ditching the entry boat and having another method for getting about.

Jones scanned the slides for suggestive fare as to where large boats might be outfitted with hardware which while they were U.S. approved by manufacturer were not approved for various boats. He looked at island creeks, marsh land, cypress trees standing knee depth in passable waters, lakeside coves, arteries of waterways, speed courses, inlets for estate coves, under bridge golfing resort houses, dock landings off tiny restaurants, Viking golf moats, dock planks, yachts, murky weather water; he looked for and found Rude cabin cruisers, deep inland channel city boats, fully marooned with radio equipment, a sea shell city rimmed with boats, in bays, tied to posts, alongside fancy wood raft type docks, Kelmar Real Estate docks with single family size high tops, docks grouped by average size boats, some fronting art museums with warehouse entry and stairs to a street, directly on the ocean waves could get predictably high and capsize – they left the radio on day and night, every last boat packed into any dock had a radio, vessels with nets stood always at the ready, like dozens of East coast city marinas, Las Vieques was no exception for paint and gelcoat or for four story condominium flats with balcony, walk to the dock, post lights, ship at far wharf. Among private docks there were clear water terraces with car ports and boat tie-ups; well built planks on nude beige beaches, hedges, boats moored at the end near a boat marine shed with boats in deep blue water, and decks on top of cabins, distribution warehousing, and cabin boats with three visors.

"They were day divers," Jones shouted through the open connecting door.

"Looks that way to me," Lewis shouted back, "A real zoo, a sailable shop for any rental including a dockland filled with artist media in eighteen rooms in one warehouse."

They stopped for lunch, ordered in two menus of beef teriyaki, rice bowl, eggrolls, miso soup. Jones poured liberal doses of whiskey, dropped in several cubes, a sprig of mint.

Lewis said, entirely sardonic tone, "State of Florida has its Department of Business and Professional Regulation, a marine contractor can't enter without their knowledge, the state radio would have picked them up, long before now their names are listed in Navigator News."

"When we are done taking down descriptions we'll have to obtain every radio permit."

"That will be a big item because those come with names, which come with updated addresses, ports of call, entry, vacation cruises."

"How do you suppose they did it? Entered in a binary lapse?"

"Either they purchased a boat, they wouldn't have stolen a boat – those are reported right in, or they had a friend with full passage, because if they rented a boat, they would also have been reported to Detention and Deportation operatives."

Lunch arrived on an elegant tray wheeled onto the porch on a pink and green tablecloth. Lewis served, removing the silver covers, dishing out eggrolls, pineapple chunks, orange slices and ambrosia lime jello. They were silent for half a minute sampling the hot meal.

Finally Lewis took a sip of his whiskey. "Excellent. Let's give this some play, this group stayed at numerous beaches, most the same, right on the water, still blue, forty feet depth, in single family dwelling beach houses or in two story houses behind a stone wall to a quay with a road, sometimes a tug, small boats on a rocky beach strewn with wood or at a road dock end. Very rarely on a strand, even seldom near a pebble bottom, but occasionally at a bridge walk, no yachts, against their religion, often tile roof, stone dock, new mortar."

Jones slept with the door to the porch open. A breeze circulated in the warm heated room. After three o'clock in the morning his printer hammered out a response to his earlier message. Flicking on a small bed overhead light, he got out of bed, tired, and put on his reading eyeglasses. The report from DATELINE PUERTO read:

> *The problem with the storm entry is that an unidentified toronado vessel fully equipped by radio to air transmittal reconnoitered a landing through a visually goverened cape and in doing so was found to have acquired relief transmittal destination mode/frequency capability. This significant radio deterrent gave two large boats formerly able to detect stranded vessels on open sea outside the gulf stream but established in an easterly trade wind zone an index with which to reclassify incoming ship mechanisms.*

They had an Internal Affairs leak. Jones rustled Lewis out of bed shoving the computer print sheet at him, Lewis slipped on his eye glasses and read it, moodily he got up, slipped a velveteen grey robe over white and grey striped pajamas and removed a notepad with slanted writing.

Lewis spoke. "My advice tells me that there is a couple who came down from Delaware to arrange a boat firm to refurbish older boats in Islamorada, also a work team out of South Carolina who likely will complete the remainder of a previous year's contract for docks into an estuary there. My question quite understandably lends itself to the degree of assistance these boat runners had to have in order to pull their little stunt. We're obligated to make certain their crew is not illegal."

"This latest memo says they received a retrofit to a communications hookup that allowed them the weird appearance of flying a flag. It wouldn't have been us, that leaves
port entry."

"Let's walk through this. Higher Bridge is internal to Florida but not anything to do with port entry, it's just there; then there's beach patrol that has been assigned. Technically a false duplicate walk-in is not considered a priority although if Detention was sitting down on the job then the matter goes to IA. However if there's any concern prior to departure regarding applications for port permissions then it winds up in National Security, but only if there's documents already in question."

"Technically Detention only boards ships in port, the agents are not allowed onto the ocean; only Deportation can enter international waters and they have rights to board as well as to fire on any illegal vessel, but they weren't out there."

"Since there is a question as to how these boats came to possess a verifying instrument, we have to track that here, although Las Vieques is considered part of Puerto which is still retained as a U.S. base. My thought on this is that an engineer with full certified approvals may have left the device at an installation shop or called in ill and was replaced. We should be able to pull it up on screen."

They sat at Lewis' computer while Lewis attempted entry into the section that contained names of naval contractors approved by the Immigration Division of U.S. Customs, when the employee listing came up Lewis cross-indexed for any person who worked on the Storm Petulant. He was transferred to Documents.

Jones interjected, saying, "Try Security."

Lewis Lewis typed it in and received three avenues of entry: gulf stream police, coast guard police, and navigation police. "Which one?" he queried.

"It is probably navigation or gulf."

"Are these police trained to be engineers?"

"I wouldn't know. Take your pick."

Lewis data entered, "Navigation." The Index capability produced one name, Tim Stiles, age 62, an out-of-date photograph, an employee start date address, and a federal identification number. He tagged the data sheet to a fax to National Security.

"It'll take the entire day for a locator response," Lewis said, adding, "We may as well order breakfast."

They ate on the porch, showered and dressed habitually, sipped coffee, read a newspaper, the air although chilly was clear, the tide washed up on shore, hotel grooms swept the sand, a few golfers could be seen in ready go-carts, a sailboat on the water prepared to do a little pole fishing. Lewis lit a cigarette halfway through his meal, while Jones poured himself a second espresso from the shiny pot.

Jones said, "It would be no issue of obtaining medical, everything is legal in Puerto."

Lewis Lewis agreed. "If they attempted to fire upon the image and that's when these crews jumped, then they abandoned their boats, which would have been towed in, and crew assigned to hotels."

"Possibility the boats were quarantined."

"Who inspects them – that's going to be a major issue if we're looking for a bad agent who took a bribe," Lewis injected.

"Neither detention or deportation, at that point it's possession of an unauthorized use, in islands it is them who inspect, in Florida it would be FBI," Jones replied.

"Last time I came out it was for drugs, all sorts of places, chasing after art dealers who were into child porn as a way to get old guys who were experts at shooting movies, the two day filming stint, easy money."

"We'll need photos of them at unidentified docks to match up their whereabouts to actual places," Jones said.

"Goes without saying we know we have to track photos, preferably off shore at discreet locale, means they had to leave San Juan or Cuba, have to look for where these people do business, " Lewis said.

"If they tagged after larger ships, they were looked for high and low."

"Then it may be they were looking to get rid of their boat, it's far too big a liability, it's long served its purpose of identifying depth of rivers, this would net them seasonal trade wind info, the primary concern would be why did these guys enter Florida? Other matter would be why were they needed? What other capabilities does the device have, for instance, on land?"

"I am under the impression that it is from land they could have signaled out to sea."

Lewis stubbed out his cigarette. "That's the issue, what made it important for them to get to Florida? If getting rid of their boat was the only point, why are they still there?"

"Could be Florida is not as patrolled as Mexico, could be it was the only direction available or could be they notified someone by entering," Jones speculated. "It's just possible that over the years Florida has grown more lenient in her dealings with deportation."

"It could be whatever their dealings are, they exchange for periodic resort houses and that's the motive for them, a bunch of beach bums."

"Then it would make a difference what they can get their hands on and whether the U.S. knows they are there," Jones said.

By afternoon the response came in.

*Document, source undeclared, S.O.S. retrieved, We tried
radio contact, we got dead silence, Detention boarded
one vessel and fired on the other — agents decided to take*

into custody all students and to sink officers from foreign areas on the sole basis these two types would not travel together for the purpose of their declarations. All had work permits, all had appropriate entry papers, letters of promise of a job, length of time, dock contractor, hotel stay, telephone, None were found to have served in prison or to be wanted on federal extradition, each had attended a university and held a copy of their credential, they were expert divers or someone was in the water to rescue them, typist/engraver Jim John wanted on warrant for forgery,Were they tipped off or was it their practice to wear wetsuits?

Jones attached a copy of the docu-serve and sent a new message.

Suspect they may change names at every place they go, keep an open mind as to how they get about relatively undetected. CABO ROJO/PUERTO.

The sole responsibility of Border was to protect the country from having people enter who intended to commit an act of damage or sabotage. For the Border official the necessity to deter entry was of the utmost importance; once it was determined an illegal had entered smuggling human cargo it became essential to find and deport the entire group. San Juan, Puerto Rico detained ships in order to seize contraband and any illegal activity, while Ponce kept any size boat at any of her nine docks for the same purpose. He presumed San Juan detained the merry weather boat because it departed Old and assumed it might seek entry without getting stopped. Therefore, since Ponce knew it was sailing it also checked and found out San Juan had already approved for destination. The apparent problem turned out to be a control system on smugglers entering from the Keys in a vehicle, thus Border had been interested in determining why the group entered.

Rule of thumb for Customs Border was a practice of

inspecting boats particularly the fuel tank for illegal dough often wrapped in tar and cellophane; not all people who answered for strategic know-how information were cleared, once suspects had an arrest record, CB tried to establish intent of entry and tossed them back and not to Nogales, usually it was to Cuba Detention for a full scale inquiry, if the product they were bringing in was not already in U.S., Border did not bring it in, typical smuggling consisted of drugs, gun ammo, teen-agers; for art, often there was a buyer outside U.S., Border checked for type of paint, colors had to be on U.S. market, a stash specialist was brought into analyze artistic intent and files were established.

With a captain and crew who had attempted illegal entry during a hurricane, in order to get rid of a boat that had become too great a liability in a harbor dock over crowded with hundreds of similar looking boats – all which had a top open deck, curtained windows over the cabin, was seventy-two feet in length – there were tons of these boats that had to be registered which meant the one wardrobe malfunction was now identifiable and therefore the illegal traffic had become known. Chances were the Border Disrupt Teams had monitored the smugglers possibly for heroin or marijuana, but art suggested knowledgeable crossings, gobs of paint used with illegal fertilizer to obscure whatever was underneath. Radio rooms in houses perched on hilly overlooks to the Gulf Stream with the aid of Blackhawk helicopters whose traffickers were on an Omaha 423 radio would spot human cargo from a distance, the scarce problem were illegal response units, usually out after dark claiming to be Air and Marine Assault, something no one had as a military, they started in U.S. and got deported, no one bothered them because they looked stitched up right, but all U.S. law enforcement were required to report daily to work and technically none left U.S. for any reason.

Jones went through the first twenty minutes of every HBO film looking for any evidence of a Keys or Florida based film company that could have produced a flick in two days and had it on the air within a week for obvious short term cash. He watched Seagal, Rocky films, rain sequences, Bare Knuckles, Basic Training, Bucktown, Bug, Futureworld, Lover's Knot, Madhouse, Near Death, Unearthed, Vampire on Beach, Wild Country, distinctly artistic, unusual juxtaposition of color in opening scenes, gifted talent, peekers, gore, females in severe distress, being stalked, touting madness, being sliced, brutalized, young males capable merely of sadistic intimidation, a plethora of isolated, scary, limited intelligence, sixty movies in twelve and a half hours. A partial list of intentional viewer barrage, madness without escape, loss of personal freedoms, acquiescence, monster horror, way too bright desolation, profound rejection, lack of salvation in despair, morose greedy singling out of individual creativity for the goal of mass destruction. He lit a cigarette and poured a Bourbon and drank it down, a bitter tasting acrimony. Then he proceeded onto the matters of the investigation, the first set of photographs were of the hours immediately following the divers emerging onto land.

He studied the first series of photographs taken in the first ten hours of planking, Series 1 to 100, he stayed to docks along the coast and rivers. Long wooden planks, handrails down to harbors, dinghys tied to posts, yachts forty feet, houseboats, looked meticulously at tourists entering and leaving marina markets, isolated matching pictures, obtained normal data, fingerprints, recorded registrations for anything, boat and hotel rentals, cabins and houses, indexed to banks, clubs, churches, children, bars, pick ups, one night lovemaking. Covered ramps, stairs to boat landings, one man who had jumped overboard baling fish, a day later building a new dock, in a sailboat on the canal, registered to a rinky dink hotel off the beach a few blocks. Jones scoured dozens of pictures of hotels, docks secured by floater ramps with handrails, no store stairs, green water, kayak dock where the same man picked up a young girl, purchased stir fry Chinese food and ate it on the beach, each with sun shades on. He found three men on a houseboat tied to a pier bar, blue shallow water with expansive sand below, all dressed in long blue jeans, flowered shirts, straw brim hats, nursing cokes, looking as though they had waited hours for a drug connection. By the time he was done with his arduous task requiring minute concentration he hoped to have established a trail with a lengthy list of AKA's for hotel registrations and rentals, a vehicle or two, determined amount of cash on hand, run a counterfeit check on the transactions and obtained voice prints.

Despite a need to know most could be placed at resorts; once every crewmate was accounted for, although there were a remaining three who were at large, they had run for rivers in what was predominantly marshland. Because the crew of the boat that was not bombed jumped prior to the other boat being bombed, the crew who were not yet placed escaped detection somehow, like a swift deer stalking through high grass. Lewis Lewis had the only tip, four canoes floating downstream without people in them, some poor boat owner who had to pour water out of a flooded boat. Border had correctly positioned two points of entry, both off the Gulf Stream, one at Islamorada, the second up near Jacksonville. The case was on its way to completion, they had to track these men to their latest whereabouts, one a forger, one a dock builder, the final one a fake agent in green, no such uniform on the planet, frothy moustache, the dock builder.

Mid afternoon before the news report of a squall produced rain Jones and Lewis Lewis went strolling across the green to an oceanside restaurant for tequila and broiled steak. They were winding down their research, preparing for a trip to the Mainland, arranging their part of the manhunt into notebook files, sending for photos, boat registrations, duplicates of forgery black market business registrations cropping up from market suppliers.

The air was balmy, the beach pristine, beige and unmarred. From the deck of tables and green umbrellas, the seven pools behind them seen through large windows, the occasional ocean spray against a distant cove of high rocks gave an otherwise frequented bay a secluded feel. The laid back Lewis together with Jones' sprightly observance produced their usual camaraderie as they began napkin baskets of corn, fried sweet potato strips and molasses grilled prawns.

"One remains unaccounted for," Jones said, dipping a fry in hot mustard. "Forger, dock builder, both found; it is a talent scout probably for I & N because I can't find a match through Deportation. No question they are pro diving but not together. There is a likelihood your canoes and boat sinking are standard diversion for the boat docker, also their preference for docks are small resorts with a market, seasonal occupancy. The noticeable problem at the moment are the two couples who came in by car when the crew baled overboard, someone maybe their talent gets them into tourist vacancies where they fade in with the beach combers."

Lewis was staring at a female on the sand, skimpy bikini, fabulous breasts, long thin legs. "This group has already been identified, probably can't dock without getting posted, careers are on their way to being over, at least one of them, and it's not a Naturalization agent who probably is to be found at his desk in Miami South, brings in a small hurricane. He's going to be the one they want. The game was up when all boats could be registered and permits issued, my guess is they smuggle bad Americans back into U.S."

Jones said, taking a sip of straight tequila, "The Delaware couple made like a shot for Bermuda Island to an older ownership, downsized the place, rebuilt on stilts, hung a light inside the dockside room. What's that for?"

"They all do it, doesn't really matter only New Orleans Bayou and Virginia marsh have those types of homes, predominantly accessible by small boat. How many resorts does our groupies own?"

"Eight, built entirely by them."

"That's the profile. When are we leaving?"

"Tomorrow, late evening, I scheduled on the last flight out into Islamorada to a neighboring hotel to a cabin on the beach."

"We'll need to take a profile of every dock they've ever erected."

"I've done that. Every resort, aluminum shelf, king dock, market canal, estuary, media room, single tie-up, posts, all

their style, trade a boat, skim the waterways to a job, chip paint
for gel coat, houseboat fishing, crab and stingray – it's all they
do up and down the eastern rivers, they know every last rental, they've built most small grocery, they live like sun bums
who periodically supply food, bait and bangle, day outboards,
surfboard runners, paint signs, tweak engines, carry in icebox,
keep a little real estate, shine fiber board, sell grilled sausage
with pita, take romantic pictures on cruisers, keep a shined up
Caddy for evening outings, reside off a single road that leads
to the beach. They're a reasonably smaller outfit, getting on in
age, no longer desiring to travel a love boat, no longer any use
of a travel agency."

Lewis polished off his meal, an unheard of activity for
him, lit a french cigarette, spooned a bit of jello truffle, sipped
a bit of espresso. "Your Immigration and Naturalization man
must stamp papers for a job although I can't figure out what
he's doing on a boat from Old; technically their desk forbids
leaving Florida even onto the bays, even for a vacation, something gets him out there, can't be a wife, sibling, child or trade,
so if he hasn't broken any law, I don't know what it could be,
even Deportation can't leave." He moodily ate the truffle, left
any espresso untouched, smoked the fag to its cotton, thinking
what aspects of this crime might be overlooked.

Through the windbreaker line of palms Jones spied a pretty blonde, adequate, voluptuous in a blue silk swimsuit who
waved. "That's Rhonda," he said, with sudden amusement.

"Where?" Lewis craned his head. "I called her three days
ago, she took her sweet time,"and then spotting her motioned
her to join them.

Within the five minutes it took her to arrive to the deck,
Lewis had had deposited a waiter order of three glasses of tequila, one dessert plate of burnt chocolate cake pudding, a strawberry shortcake soaked in rum and a small tre of battered jumbo
shrimp. Rhonda wore a green polished cotton smock over her
swimsuit, small backless heels, and carried a sharkskin button
snap purse. She sat between them, planted a long kiss on Lewis'
mouth, squeezed Jones' upper arm, and took her shot glass in a

long gulp, took a second glass and began sipping it generously, ate a shrimp, sampled several strawberries, spooned up a good medium portion of pudding, and finished Jones' prawns and fries, started on the third glass of tequila, forked up a bite of shortcake and took a French fag off her husband.

She told them, "I've flown to Havana twice this month to sort arts of oil, some in frames, some still mounted, most got damp when a warehouse in Ponce had a roof leak, I've sent for registrations, categorized sets, rolled markings where labels used to be, labeled on the back side of each in paint and created metal warehouse numbers, it's bound to be months of further investigation simply because the galleries in Delaware can't receive prior to showings."

"Maybe Florida should be warehousing media art," Lewis said. "Seems the district is awfully fussy."

"That's Florida shelf law," Jones said.

"It's more than that," Rhonda replied. "Shelf law applies only to current art, whereas District of Columbia requires art produced twenty-five or more years ago be stored outside U.S. One corporation is located in Old, the other in Philippines, both yield to fine art standards of artists residing in usually Philippines, Java, Guam, Borneo but who cannot ever have lived in Laos, upper district Cambodia or Hawaii."

Lewis reached over, ran his hand over her leg.

"Any dye tests?" Jones inquired.

"Only one set permitted when the color orange is American made." She picked up the last drink and gave it her best. "There is an exception to that rule, if an artist appraiser at Old has available that particular orange, then only he tests."

"That's big money," Lewis said, "almost as big as these illegal NAVs we're chasing."

They paid the tab, walked arm in arm the three of them picking up a few magazines on the way to the hotel, Lewis bought her a lily corsage for the freezer, in Lewis' suite they ordered in two bottles of Bourbon, turned on the television, sat altogether on the long sofa, several packs of fags on the table, cubes of ice in a bucket, the drapes closed, a small container of liquid powder brought by Rhonda. Although Lewis would give her his smallest notepad to translate and send to his contact in interior Rojo as he had forever since their unwilling divorce, it was Lewis' preferred style he would give her a party where she was the sole desire.

Lewis poured the first round, Rhonda put a tiny portion in their glasses, they argued about the channel, Rhonda amended the disagreement by giving Jones a massage, and Lewis got chatty talking about all the botched art Ponce had to send despite their concerns. They sipped their drinks sparingly, Lewis asked her to dance for them, in her one piece shimmering swimsuit she donned long gloves, scarves and danced striptease, first discarding a glove at a time, then her hair unpinned came down, Lewis lowered the lights, Rhonda made unbuttoning her smock an enticing affair, she stepped out of her heels, her swimsuit came off as an over blouse to a bikini, she pulled Lewis off the couch, removed his trousers, tie, shoes, danced slow with him leading, before he had Jones take off his shoes, shirt and cufflinks, Lewis broke down, cried, said the last time they were in Rojo he kicked her out because he was drunk, he asked Jones to slow waltz her and she told Lewis he was still the one man she truly loved. The music from the television was slow slow eclectic rhumba, tobango, sweet salty, tender. She released Jones, encircled Lewis, kissed him tenderly, grabbed his mildly curly hair, placed her hand against his soft stem, walked him into the bedroom and could be heard closing the door. Jones found himself far gone, too disoriented to walk through the connecting door to his room, stretched out on the couch listening for sounds of her and Lewis, Lewis was crying, balling his heart out, he was unable to forgive himself but he wanted her again to love him as she once had, Cuba may not be in flames but Grenada was everywhere, banditos with curved knives, officers in shadows, prisons which once a tourist got lost inside an arabesque hotel never surfaced. Eventually Jones could hear their sounds of lovemaking, no girl for me, you are my familiar most clandestine allowance, it's only you Rhonda, but without my most careful friend I could not find you, say you will, any gratitude will do, any way to succumb, I never know who might want my life still, break for me sweetest girl, tumble the way you used to. It was a dim awareness for Jones to realize there was no way he would shake this stupor, Rhonda would emerge in an hour or so after Lewis had fallen blissfully asleep, and despite their friendship Jones would be powerless. As he fell drowsy he heard Lewis tell Rhonda it was a child he ought never to have given her, some dreams were to keep, some just for dreaming. Lewis was the best field agent anywhere, a devoutly honest man in his heart, but an enigma.

Jones awoke to Rhonda in the nude. He reached for her and she came down to him easily, seemingly willing, a woman who would do anything her husband asked, and he too drugged to protest asked why she thought Lewis wanted him to need her, upon which she mounted him and he no longer able to protect himself went with her, his entire being snagged by her apparent insatiable desire, holding her at the thighs he submitted, a cry unrestrained by common sense. She bent to him, her nipples sweeping his chest, to which he kissed them, holding her breasts he quickened inside her, he crested her until breathless he came out of her and digitally penetrated her until she came.

"Oh, Jones, you are sensational, if I didn't think he required a shadow, you know I wouldn't dare."

"Do you remember that night?" he asked about their affair in Havana.

She barely smiled. "In my own way I love you also, but I was a teenager when I first had sex with him."

Jones looked dreamily up into her angelic face. "Why does he want this? Has he asked you to love others?"

"There have been a few, none I trust as I trust you." She held him then and he knew he would come again, this time in but her grasp. She said, then, perhaps thinking he himself needed words he could define himself by, "You are like a young Lewis, excellent at that degree of life I may never see, but he trusts you and because he does, I am not untrue to him."

Jones asked her to put him in his bed. Rhonda helped

him stand and he all but slumped onto her, against his verbal protests she took him to his room Lewis snored out cold, she placed him on the large bed, got on him, seducing him again and as he became erect, he thought it was the bitch of the drug.

They took breakfast on the pool patio. The morning was shaping up to be a humid cloudy atmosphere with a salty wind blowing in from the sea. Rhonda ate eggs hollandaise ravenously as if nourishment was wanting, Lewis Lewis took caviar with a boiled egg, and Jones sipped a date shake and had hot oats with brown sugar, espressos all, broiled bear claws and sliced salmon and cream cheese on warm halved scones. A helicopter could be heard somewhere off in the distance.

"Lewis told me about your boat escapees," Rhonda said, shades on, her hair tossed about, sipping her espresso, her swimsuit strap easing down her arm.

Jones assented. "They work as retirees or are in resort construction, make tile, doors or decks."

"They would've had to have a presence in U.S. for five years in order to be naturalized," Rhonda said. "It must indicate that Americans are posing as family."

"Smart girl," Lewis said.

"They must look like the people who are defecting," she said.

"Doubt they'd have anything to defect over," Jones stated. "More likely they have to flee Old."

"What do you think went on there?" she asked him.

"I think whatever Lewis thinks."

She laughed gaily. "He doesn't think anything, do you sweetie?"

Jones thought that was quite impossible, Lewis had an opinion about everything.

Rhonda asked, "Were you aware there's an Immigration Deportation detention site for illegals in general?"

"Of course, honey," Lewis replied, putting his palm on her upper arm. "Jones knows that, the locked facility is a hospital, the staff are nurses from Boqueron, the next best thing to freedom is an inlet on several ships in Ponce."

"The detention ward runs its own boot camp, that much I do know," Rhonda said.

"It's no boot for prisoners," Lewis explained; "it's a twelve mile run through empty mud pails including a stretch of disease-infested swamp and crawling through pipes. The bastards who get there deserve the entire program."

"Why on earth are these people squatting?" Rhonda asked.

"They probably built the resorts, honey."

"Down to the estuary docks," Jones said facetiously; "the art and artifacts are worth it, after all if they get a gallery, they sell any damn thing they want."

"Maybe they're smuggling signatures for people who can't afford to be visible," she proposed.

Lewis snapped his fingers for the waitress and ordered tequila and lit a cigarette for each of them. Rhonda asked Jones to apply tanning lotion on her back and shoulders, to do this Jones unzipped her sleeveless windbreaker and slipped it off as the pitcher of tequila arrived and the breakfast china cleared. Jones swept Rhonda's hair into a hairnet and pulled it tight, then he began applying the rich tan oil, beginning with her back, then her shoulders; when she turned to face him lowering the other strap, he smoothed his hands across her chest and as she leaned forward to kiss him, he eyed Lewis who was eye balling some girl in a tight strapless bikini. Rhonda placed her hands on Jones' thighs and elongated her neck while Jones poured more oil and applied it to her exposed breast top, collarbone and neck.

"Painless," Jones announced.

"You're the best," Rhonda said, and started in on her tequila and cigarette.

Lewis said, without envy, "I said the same thing last night, did you have an enjoyable night, old buddy?"

"It was a sensation," he answered trying to appear nonchalant, although it was growing clear to him they were becoming an agreeable three-some.

Lewis said, "Truth is I'm not up for a strictly couple thing, if you're in this work past seventy-five, you have to put the work ahead of everything."

"It's the new day I worry about," Jones told him. "I don't as a rule compromise a friendship."

"I've compromised you," Lewis said, "don't ever forget that; I have needs no one understands."

Rhonda touseled Jones' hair. "I like you a lot, Jones, you're fun to be with."

"I'm becoming fond of you," he told her.

"Then there's no disagreement," Lewis said. "I've said, don't leave out Jones, make him happy." He took a long satisfying drink, smoked, squeezed Rhonda's leg, said, "You'll have the suite for two days same as usual but this time we'll return."

"I guessed as much," she said, removing her shades to have a long look at him. "I've got my own assignment to complete, you know."

He chuckled. "You're a busy researcher, I realize that, honey. Will you be flying into Havana?"

"Nope. I'm driving to Boqueron late in the day."

Lewis Lewis gave her matter some thought. "I didn't realize the Grenada boys traveled these days."

"They don't leave their castle. This is just Puerto biz."

Lewis suggested they go for a swim and then sit on the porch veranda. Rhonda wasn't up to swimming, citing the air temperature was too cold, and Jones said he would accompany her upstairs, but Lewis insisted he needed a dive.

Jones and Rhonda left as Lewis sauntered over to the girl in the pool, on a garden path behind the complex they were staying in, Jones helped Rhonda with her windbreaker, zipping it as she pressed against him, kissing him hard on the mouth. He kissed her in response placing his hands around her back holding her to him.

"The fact is I adore you, Rhonda."

She kissed him on the neck, whispering, "You're so willing."

"Is that bad?"

"No, Jones, that's good."

They entered the lobby, stepped inside an elevator, he

unzipped her vest and reached inside her swimsuit cupping her breast. She ran a hand to his groin and squeezed him. When the elevator opened she led him to Lewis' suite, poured two drinks, slipped in a drop from a vial she kept in her purse, and disrobed. Within minutes he was heady, feeling the pulsating sensation of the drug, he kissed her nipples longingly and she removed his shoes, unbuckled his trousers, caressing him until in a throbbing, aching moment he made love to her, she consensually limp, he breathing hard, thrusting until he felt he could fly. She rolled onto him, raised his leg and rubbed him, asked him to hold her legs beneath her bottom and came, orgiastic and crying.

Toward six they were awakened by the sound of Lewis stumbling in the dark He was drunk, speech slurred, reeking of the smell of a woman's jasmine perfume, lipstick planted like a jealous confession on his jowls. He confessed he had slept with two lesbians all day and all he thought about was her. Talking about nothing else other than his remorse and guilt, Lewis said he had slept almost none at all, he kept getting awakened by regret, he had lived through this scene a half dozen times and it still turned out the same.

The plane lifted into the air at nine o'clock at night, the runway lights sparkling like sapphires. Beside him, Lewis slept peaceably, the tension of his life evenly dissipated, although temporarily. Jones flipped through a few nudie magazines Lewis purchased at the airport for the four hour flight into Islamorada. Over the gulf stream the air turned turbulent, another header putting into land certain to uproot trees, fly sand and smash city lights; inside the airplane the lights doused, the cabin rocked like a boat on a tilter at sea. At the island fourth key, the wheels made a touchdown, wings tipping precariously, speed its own sanctum along the tiny strip bordered on both sides by wild tobacco plant. They disembarked into a gale of darkness, a cab ushered them to the outskirts of town, through the jet ink black night only lights – pole glass lit tinted brownish, warm yellow, silver bright – illuminated alleys, gardens, the wharf front, and for hotels dark blue candescent lights with silver lightning. The mansion they were disposed to had replaced lights with glass covered candles, a male bag man carried their bags up an elevator ensconced in mirrors to a third floor suite with all glass, balcony, modern kitchenette, three sofas of exquisite art, beige, dark yellow, black and violet abstract, and two king size beds in an L-shaped enclosure. Their studio overlooked a Far Isle home with a second story patio and private dock with a high speed boat and not even a half city block away a cabin on the sand strung by multi-color lights around the roof and inside. Lewis set up both telescope tripods, spools and dusters with capability up to a quarter mile for an all month listening voice recorder and ten monitors fully enhanced by camera transponder that interfaced with the telescopes. They were on their own now, no Puerto communications, no HBO satellite to the Keys, no station to station border to radio room. Jones showered, walked around in a white terrycloth robe, poured two bourbons, prepared a stirfry of hash browns, sliced tomato and scrambled eggs and dished out two plates with English muffins saturated with butter and currants.

By morning Jones had taken a walk, reported a flood on the front, twisted trees, a vehicle in water, their quarry in the cabin, making small talk with the two in Miami South; Lewis had slept a few hours and now ate his dinner and had begun his starter, he had produced voice prints, matched them to I&N which had a warrant posted, and was starting his usual room by room camera profile on the clay and tile house – a big surprise to find each room was thrashed completely, windows open, no furniture spared, wood torque twisted like ocean debris, expensive paintings ripped, glassware smashed, lights crashed, sand and water an inch deep covering the entire first floor, he transferred every image onto hard copy celluloid, framed and taped all. Proving what had occurred would take a few days, they'd have to download street lights assuming those had not first been shot at by a rifle, then look for any file from any other camera nearby, hotel, pool, pedestrian shops, construction, high rise, boat dock, any shadow capable of reaching beneath a closed door.

Jones had already begun an arduous task of taking night

stills for every rental and non American ownership to identify who lay asleep together in each bed, who their sexual callout partners were, basic shapes and tidbits of identities thrown into a jigsaw out of which the computer matched likeness to anyone from the keys to Virginia. Nightgowns showed as ghostly visitations, men's galoshes as boater weather ware, wedding rings were duplicated all over the eastern coastal U.S., beds and bedroom sets were in resorts, on boats, on movie sets, on nuptials in department stores. It would be up to Lewis to match any similar destruction to major store, shops, docks and boats, to assure he overlooked nothing he would read for all insurance claims as they were listed. Any artwork that had arrived since getting receipted through San Juan, Puerto or Ponce would send the liaison home through Deportation, but for the moment the insidious task was to determine what activities the group that had jumped off ship was doing. Because Jones and Lewis could not be seen in public together, couldn't take a swim or eat out, Lewis went on their first day to buy wigs, red curly, black straight, grey blonde short, blond greaser look and two brown long; he also purchased glassy beads, fake fur jackets, leather trousers, platform shoes, movie-style T-shirts, leg high boots, flashy men's shirts with avangarde ties.

They left their promising suite at noon dressed in long brown hair to their blades, Lewis in a body fitting, sleeveless shiny silver shirt and black leather tight pants with high black boots looking the part of an aged affluent hippie, Jones wore a short sleeved, silk black shirt with yellow breast pocket, a bright yellow and orange tie, tweed off yellow trousers and boots; together they were two older men long caught up in the glitz of beach living without a car, a pair of whiskey drinkers making small talk at a local pub frequented by summer residents. They looked distinct, they could be ID'd. They spent twelve hours watching the door for sign of the group, sipping seventy proof alcohol, snacking a corned beef sandwich and German sauerkraut and red skin potato salad until after midnight when they tossed three twenties as a tip, and headed out. They walked past the private dock, through the private garden, on their way back to the suite faking a good stagger, boisterous laughter, leaning into one another as though each step might be their final one, only once getting the dock owner to peer at them off a balcony. The other peering eye looked to be a gardener and he they recognized as the errant forger, he was medium height, thin, brown wavy hair, brown eyes, wary of anyone, a Hispanic islander. If they resided with females they were in bed or in a spa or smashing the place to hell.

Jones was relieved to return to their mechanical eye, Lewis made notes, swilled up, grilled up several burgers and zucchinis, left them in the dining area for whenever they got hungry. In their respective jobs neither could attract attention, which meant no females, no television or radio, no lights usually, no orders out for food, definitely no chats with neighbors, no moronic arguments, no telephone use, the suite paid in advance by a third party. They sat by the telescopes, ran the sound, downloaded for voice demarcation and established profiles; the conversationalists at the target proved hourly to be the same quartet – the forger, a stringer who fired at rotating cameras and street lamps whenever he went outside, an identities man who was establishing resort entertainment, boat tours and hired help, and some female who was nearly always sloshed and slept all day. The duo at the cabin spent their time sweeping the floors of in swept sand, drinking and snoozing it off; one time they took a call from the Cape Fear, Virginia couple who reported needing another boat but so far no one had made a move on it.

By dead night of their second night they were awakened by the sound of gun shots spraying over a lone shelf on the beach, Lewis repositioned a lens scanning the area for a culprit while Jones down sped any activity that came within view. On the consoles the stringer had stepped out under a clouded, moonless sky and fired buckshot at four dinghies on the beach which two males loaded inside an unlabeled van. Jones breached their security sending the camera activity sheet to the Immigration office in Indian River, he closed down that particular shutter for the remainder of their stay, a shutdown by any listed agent would register in for that investigation by international number.

The problem of youngsters residing with old men was consumptive at Plantation Keys as well; Lewis thought the moment the colony was closed, it wasn't long before a party returned with a group of underage tunas for a few months before the movie got busted and the gents sent home. The red eye flight took them into San Juan and there, they picked up a transfer flight to Nassau to a strip at the base near their permanent hotel residence. First thing once they were back, Lewis showered and ordered in a steak rare, Jones poured himself a neat clear, ran his computer for all intercepts, lit a French cigarette, and opened the drapes admiring the view of the expansive blue blue ocean.

Jones was a bit taken aback to find that in their absence Rhonda had wired from the Cabo hotel to Havana the brief message,

> *Forger declared. Stop. Captain most appreciated. Stop.*
> *Has to be in a black trade, tourism. Stop. Crime is shot-*
> *gun to boat hulls. Stop. Docks provide convenience,*
> *7-11, Thrifty's, Seagrams. Stop. PUERTO.*

He hadn't realized Rhonda was Lewis' information out nor that Lewis had determined in advance who the kingpin had to be nor that South Seas had outfitted him. He typed his report and sent it to his boss with a notation he would come to the office Monday bright and early.

SOUTHAMPTON

On Tuesday April 3rd Jones Baylor and Lewis Lewis flew into the flat pancake that made northern Bermuda a stretch of sand on top of the ocean into Saint George International Airport at 0600 hours. Their month-long task was to handle an assignment which called for two agents familiar with insurance briefs to prepare itemization for return of restored wreckage of the tall ship Monsoon to shipyard, with comment to the britch water, the area below deck that filters water after a smash-up; scallion, kitchen, usually first to explode from pressure in pipes; armory, money; hard castle, valued carriage; billet, crew quarters; and soame, captain's cabin. They hailed a cab from the baggage carousel and were driven to the elegant, stately Saint George resort, the chosen venue for the British agent, its dark walnut stained cherry wood interior, handsome lobby, softly muted red carpets in the three large sitting rooms, lit beige stone hearths, collector's vases with sleek red and pink gladiolas, a suite and balcony, two dark brown loveseats surrounding a dark salmon stone hearth, an elongated modern kitchen with long island containing stove and Formica, stairs to a library loft and two work stations with the works; two bedrooms with separate peach tiled bathrooms, shower and pampered vanity awaited their arrival, cane beds propped by puffed pillows and gold and dark red striped comforters, a bar, telephones, HBO, Jacuzzi, closets, small alcoves with desks and comfy chairs, overlooking the light blue ocean.

Bermuda lay north off the coast of North Carolina, pink sands, velveteen golf courses, all amenities, tennis courses, spa, pools, dining, striped dark and light blue parasols on beach, warm breezy low surf, afternoon trade wind, humid in summer, nine parishes connected by three roads, North Shore, Middle and South; its location, an archipelago of two hundred and fifteen miles in length and a mile wide on a nautical chart at 32, 20, created by a flash on the wave, on the Atlantic, from the air looked like a term of humpback whales, sparkling aquamarine waters, occasional gray rock jutting out of the ocean, a hundred and forty tiny islands, eight had five resorts, small clinics, a dockyard harbor and prison for thirty day detention, buildings everywhere were all white except for Southampton's predominant superscript light green and crème stucco with balconies, the eight major islands linked by bridges as follows, Ireland Island North, Ireland Island South, Boaz Island, Watford Island, Somerset Island, all on Port Royal Bay on the Great Sound; Bermuda Island with its tourist attractions the towns of Hamilton Beach and Flatts below the large Harrington Sound, Saint George with the international airport and Saint David, both sitting on Castle Harbor.

All subsequent medicals revealed the crew suffered TNB at drowning, the ship was carrying illegal rum, pharmaceutical drugs, crazy pills for heifer tranks, barbiturates for fish. On the airplane flying in from Nassau, discussing what line of inquiry should be first, they had already decided for starters they would visit the haulage and then run out to the Bermuda Underwater Institute in Hamilton to collect measurements for seawater, salinity, and corkage before they analyzed comparative tests.

The windjammer Monsoon sat in a dry dock gallery, wood scraped clean of paint, deck smooth, its keel laid, exterior hull unremarkable except for the bow, rotted and carbuncled, steel strip gone. Despite that the assembly of its deck port was not yet completed, it looked a good eighteen thousand feet in length, a remaining solid sea worthy, previously a fourteen mast ship, its ship lenses gone, its deck house deficient, cannon missing. An elevator took them up the equivalent of three floors to a ramp where they planked. The first observable correction was the tower being lifted high would replace the deteriorated deck house, the small cramped radio room of its day would in time become the communications room with a new scope, panels, hard chair. Below, deck cabins were still without walls, doors, metal casing warped. The engine room although preserved would have to be retrofitted with modern enhancements as would all instrumentation, satellite, data recorder and electronics.

Jones discussed the haulage problems with a skip master inside the Institute, a retired crony whose expertise rested in dating any part of any wreckage. It had taken fifty years for sailors to go down for the clamored Monsoon and haul it to harbor, the spout in the Atlantic at burial proving too dangerous to approach or to navigate from the depths, almost another twenty to dry sections and list bin applications. After a review of the historical documents, armed with copies to study inside their hotel, they went for dinner, took in the sights, rode out to the gothic gray cathedral ruin, stopped at a bar for a few lagers of Black Seal rum, picked up the Gibbs Hill chatter, and returned by night for the Carson show. Lewis Lewis was in a dark mood having spent a previous twenty hours downloading and reviewing all cut ables, Bermuda was an insurance-only industry, no one could live here year round, it was too small to be lived on, one couldn't get to it between mid September to March due to the floodwater off the spout of monsoons, one rainy season in Bermuda trained any stalwartly agent to work border deportation in the U.S. gulf from Florida's Sable up through Everglades into Texas; he had made up his mind he wouldn't spend much time dangling, he'd give a brief perusal as to cause, the ship per insurance was worth more than the damn fleet of eight ships altogether, each section from britch to soame was rated at $410,000 but more realistically would appraise at $319,000; a new one million total for the crew for life-saving procedures – the exact amount long ago paid with periodic cost-of-living adjustments – the fair, usual, standard categories for occupation, steerage, compartments, lost possessions, and sent communications would be denied, any complications would necessitate ongoing weather and infraction satellite to the southerly winds to offset the singing bird effect of the spout requiring about a hundred and twenty years.

For his part Jones felt agreeable now that they had seen the ship. The night air was warming up, a mild desultory breather. He'd lie on the beach or at the pool a few evenings, pour a few salt shakers, feel good as new. To his thinking Bermuda was primarily a medical stock with a modest government of several senators and a Premier who might or might not be signature captains all. He and Lewis had already studied the entire series of compiled photos first including those taken off station showing the stern pitching, then they took significant data by page, Jones' main concern was, did the ship take a default; all storage for additional satellite had originally netted into Old Tahiti in 1943, photos from the recon deck were mostly streamed out, too few identifiers to qualify deck rust and hull, his own belief was it was a strike of a match lit by torpedo off another ship, two knocks at the bench locker, tilted on runner's skids placed in the ocean, sinking it instantly, on the sheer fact the British didn't do tidal breakers.

Island living meant waking at five with daylight, taking a light fare and toasting a bauble at one-fifteen, beach at three or four, resuming at seven, the late edition on the setee at ten along with a hot chocolate. Jones stayed up all night cataloguing photos, Lewis was into his routine spending the afternoon on the patio sipping Bourbon listing objections to necessary equipment bids on a notepad. When Jones by early evening had sifted through enough to obtain a real default issue, had a hurricane assaulted the ship, had bridge orders been changed, were indicator readings severely off, they would begin taking apart the gray areas, defining them.

Institute files showered a newer series of photographs, staff having spent countless hours to raise clean images off the dirty water imprints, the lugging hull of the deck on its side floor down, bales of relics photo imaged as lockers were swept over ceilings, their key locks disrupted. Their final radio call, "the floor's giving way, Wyndam is plunging," reprinted for posterity in a closed document as the vessel lunged stern first into a great swell and plummeted, her bow showing fire, her amount she was supposed to carry, two hundred and twenty red newly minted guineas, a hundred packaged marks destined for Aruba and the Venezuelan crown, lost at sea, her name reconnoitered, her crew having surfaced a half mile west, found floating in three wide-berth canoes.

Lewis bellowed from his bedroom, "Look at hull line, did it take above or below the red line?"

"Below."

"What about the deck?"

"No straight line pin, all damage done to the hull under the ocean."

"Did radio room dislodge, chances are it did after plummeting, most of them do. Last thing I'd look for is where it blew into, usually into dining hall or berths, if it was somewhere else it had too close a range."

"No way to tell if ship's position and course was radioed," Jones replied, rising from his computer in the loft to spy Lewis walk into the living room below and pour himself a neat rye, "or whether there was radio interruption; without it, default is presumed to be non existent with a bomb."

"It should be easy enough to discern."

"What are you going to look for?"

"If two ships set sail together, then the skidded ship should have reported "Steel line or hull gone awry," if it was just the one ship the call should have been, "She's been hit," with map coordinates," Lewis said, up to Jones.

"If the only station capable of receiving was a far away

station, then the default is presumed to be an engineering glitch in the radio and there's no payout until Engineering can find it, assuming it is intact and it often isn't, they are metal and metal reacts poorly to underwater activity," Jones said. "The problem is the Atlantic doesn't have tilts and a ship wouldn't have sailed into the wrong wind."

Lewis remarked, "Replacement for Dutch marks listing reported actual drop line as "Steel... gone without notice, could mean just about anything."

As he walked down the stairs to the sitting room, Jones said, "Could be either the ship was hit or steel bearing gave way, unless engineers think it could only have been cause in which case we are here until we can make a determination. A treatment was performed to the wood once it dried."

"Is this a required procedure?"

"Yes, done in all circumstances of enemy fire."

"What was the analysis?"

"Report doesn't give an opinion."

"What would they have suspected was used in those days?"

Jones replied, "Lager with gunpowder."

"Be an awfully big sound."

"Not unless it was detonated during bad weather or in a crisis."

"There may have been some other relevant pertinence, for example," Lewis said, thinking it through, "a docking officer may have been added to the crew if weather and sea conditions turned ugly, there was an accident or a hazardous occurrence. Best to check accuracy of chart information system."

Jones checked the Bermuda Institute's document exhibits for Monsoon, as follows: notations for barometer, barograph, psychrometer and voyage data recorder. When he found actual description, he read aloud, "Distress monitor, freezing air temperature, unusually high waves and ice, ship locked into a bottle, dragged into long swell, gale force fifty knots."

"Dead. No one survives that. They may have fired their own torpedo. It's a miracle they got off the ship," Lewis said, shaking his head.

"I agree. Tragic. All we can do is to establish ship's position and course up to that point to determine if instruments were reliable."

They took dinner out on the concourse patio, beach torches alit, white tablecloths, small glass floating candles, the sea shimmering in the sunset, the sky vividly pink. Behind them rose two wings of the three storied pink hotel, balcony glass doors reflecting the shades of sky. Jones had ordered steak tribeca, grilled corn and lobster bisque, Lewis settled for beer battered bass and fries. Chardonnay was served in a decanter, for which Lewis poured two servings.

Lewis took a sip, put down his glass, slipped on his eyeglasses, and from his notepad he read. "Here's what I came across. 'TTT Storm, heavy rain squalls, conditions indicate cyclone, course 030, seven knots.'"

"Yes, I came across that also," Jones said. "Actually there is consistent radio early on. I found a call for compass deviations."

"Reported by whom?"

"Deck Officer, Master. He's the one who sent a diver down who found rudder was on skids. It was the diver who put flares in the iceberg to dislodge the keel."

"How much of a variance were the deviations?"

"Erratic, although they readjusted."

"Due to winds?"

"I presume so," Jones replied. "I came across the report that says nine hours before departure steering gear was checked and tested."

"That's tight running. It was a good crew."

"Every last one a good bell above the line."

"Here's the way it looks," Jones explained, as they tackled their meals. The sun finally set and the darkness accentuated the torches. "There's a question as to when the navigation bridge lost visibility. The standards call for the upper edge of bridge front windows must allow a forward view of horizon for height of eye of 1,800 millimeters."

"Sure, when ship is at conning position. But our poor

windjammer was pitching in a charging bull. For all we can guess the captain was staring down steep altitude reverses with technically plenty of gale visibility."

"Then does it matter how the ship is retrofitted?"

Lewis nodded. "Technically, yes, it would depend not so much on the aft so much as on the type of light. Could they see it through a lens before they broke wave?"

"Their radar was good, they thought initially when they encountered ice, a change of direction could avoid collision risk."

"Who manufactured port and starboard lights?"

"Chesapeake. They were red and green nautical lights with a masthead white light double lens, 18 ¾" by 8". "

"And the lens itself?"

Jones said, "A 360 degree clear Fresnel lens. I was told excellent photo clam."

"Yes, none better, but my problem for lens will be the spool line, it'd be good if you can feed me how many photos the lens is capable of taking at any single two minutes. Otherwise I'd ask the specialists for advice on a newer time and tide clock, maybe a Weems and Plath would give a more precise Atlantic tide cycle for barometer, you will need the newest temperature compensated aneroid movement, ask for a compass with higher lag error. Keep the barograph – that all by itself saved their lives. What sort of mission was it?"

"Standard transport." Jones consulted his notes. "Seal of Deliverance – 220 minted guinea, 100 Dutch notes, relic hard castle, 50 Norwegian crown notes, 8 signature ink syringes, 90 port authority notes for Bermuda, Suriname, Antilles and Aruba, cleansing medicinal hard rum, 50 spectacles of varying strengths, each guinea valued at $350, each Dutch note at $183, relic gold bar at $979 each, crown notes at $482 each, signature notaries up to $5,000; port authority notes to prove any food, shelf and medicinal; all reissued under surrender of actual portage; documents declared – bench shelf, artillery; armory, 43 vaults."

"Any prisoners?"

"Records don't say, although I did attempt to track the entry of shipped coin in stamped, labeled, rust colored paper per series of evidentiary photographs, our vessel intended to anchor at the Dockyard where artillery was usually brought with bank draft notes to the clock tower fortress and entered through five interlocking stations, each with impenetrable time piece locks, into a grand vault secured underground."

"Any other planned stops?"

"On all twenty previous voyages the Wyndam put into Flatts on a sheltered cove, eight feet deep canal with wharf wall, through a secured stone passage inside an armory plaza, unseen by any public landmark, to a four foot steel door containing a combination lock timed by sound into a safe without windows, and then at the Port Royal Fort, secured below ground in a gated, prison barred, safe room.
All amenities were seen to by presentation of a voucher stamped with a seal and logged into a registrar of description."

"I didn't realize she was a relatively new ship for her day. Do we know why?"

"The Merriweather went down two years prior and the Charles Morgan was lost at sea. That's why she was requisitioned."

Lewis jotted down a short summary. "Well, here's a thing or two to consider. The ship shooter lens for the docking pilot might do well to omit a curved field of the ocean but should have a short throw zoom lens, Whelen might offer a fair alternate opinion as to requirements for a lens, most measure 6 ½ " by 7", perhaps there will be offsets against design."

"The next size longer tall ship of the Forties today carries a 9000 series 9M LFL lens. It records passing ships, ocean waves, boats and small crafts, entries, ports and precipitation, motion of rain, usual advisories. "

Lewis threw a twenty on the table to cover the tab and they began their stroll across the green to their suite. "Once we are apprised what we can have, we will have a chief shipping consultant write in final approvals," he said. "We'll be looking at standard capabilities as for tall ships on the Great Lakes, lower

Mississippi and Puerto Rico. Primary to our summaries will have to begin with area radar, surface, temperature changes, trade winds and hurricane warnings."

A group of females scantily clad flashed smiles at them, Jones slowed down to exchange a few pleasantries, but it was Lewis Lewis who told them to run along, saying that they were too old for them and drew Jones by the elbow, pulling him into the weave of the night.

Lewis resumed, saying, "We have plenty of hard material to give us proof of navigational hazards and adverse weather to account for the ship moving through an ice region in ice season. When did we set sail on the final voyage?"

"Not until mid May, 1943. The logbook confirms it."

"It is ice season February 15th to July 1st."

"Not below 040. Below Maine there wasn't supposed to be unusual risk far past early May."

"It still bothers me that after they altered direction they may have traveled too close to Greenland's crash breakers. Perhaps they required some sort of automatic radar plotting and heading control when the first storm warning hit."

They rode an elevator inside the pink building to their floor and walked almost to the end where their suite was located. Jones opened the door, switched on the lights. A maid had come while they were at dinner, washed off their glasses, stocked the refrigerator with cereal, fruit, bananas, berries, mango and papaya, cheddar, brie and Swiss cheese, tri-tip steaks, lettuce, vegetables, milk, yogurt, cottage cheese, and New York cheesecake.

"This should keep us busy during the day," Jones remarked.

"That's for you, I live on the salty air."

"At least we'll have a solid breakfast."

"I never eat before noon, it's against my principles. I'm going to order in a masseuse, do you want one too?"

"You go right ahead, I'll pass."

"Those girls were just too young, probably not even out of their twenties. You can't afford a commitment."

Jones cut a slice of cake and poured himself a shot of

Scotch, while Lewis called for a female massage, fifties or slightly older ideal. Jones had his day's work spread out on the dining room table when the woman arrived. She proved to be a shapely blonde, long hair wrapped into a French braid, definitely a seductive mid fifty type, dreamy hazel eyes, wearing a tight silk black skirt that showed off good legs, a cotton short-sleeved top, a broad green belt and slip-on sandals. Lewis explained Jones had to work through the night and took her upstairs to his bedroom across the loft containing the two computer, printer, fax, copier work stations. Jones paid little attention to the sound of the shower, the slightly insistent commands of Lewis, more to the fact that by one in the morning the masseuse had not left. Jones spent hours batching the photos of the windjammer's fatal voyage, marking all significant weather readings and times by camera tape over the top right corner, giving notations in shorthand at the bottom of all bridge orders, focusing on high sea map conditions, then back over his notes for the information off the voyage data recorder, distress monitor, the chart computer display, barometer, gyrocompasses and automatic identification system, until he had an initial series to comprise a spool line, which the hotel camera lab could easily make into a video in a day. At four o'clock he turned in, aware Lewis was still engaged.

Jones awoke at seven. The sunlight streamed in through the window, a breeze wafting inside. Remembering the female, he showered and dressed fully in jocks, brown linen trousers, a white sleeveless button down shirt, a short tan scarf knotted, brown socks and trim shoes. He went downstairs to discover Lewis already up, hair combed through, khaki pants, a light weight polo yellow shirt, sandals. He sipped a cup of freshly brewed coffee from the sandwich shop, as he penciled in blue strike lines over weather charting for the forty mile by three mile ocean spout.

"Have a good time?" Jones asked politely, stirring chopped fruit left on a cutting board into a bowl of cottage cheese and sprinkling in a few cashews.

"I asked if you wanted one." Lewis was light hearted. "I'll

advance the tab, if you'd like."

"She stayed all night."

"Yes."

"I would have to think it over."

"We are here for a month, you might enjoy an evening and show."

Jones said, "Leave it alone, Lewis. I'm fine by myself. What are you working on?"

"An indication the barometer fell rapidly before they hit that section of ocean and then anything to suggest why it wasn't recorded."

"I've put together a draft for your perusal, but I have to get it on video."

"I'm certain a spool will address my basic questions."

"I noticed you set up your computer for a barograph."

"It's probably premature, I'll be ready to insert information as to passage of way points, weather and sea conditions, changes in speed in a few days," Lewis said. "I've manipulated barographs so I know when they spill for changes."

"I agree there should have been a control header but it's not mentioned although almost everything else that ought to have turned up is on a handful of read. Are you having your girl return?"

"Stella will be by at six for dinner."

Jones looked at photographs taken from the ship's system that predicted weather forecasts, storm headings, southerlies, directionals, pipelines in order to add to the culled information about when the captain anticipated crossing through these fronts. It was an unforgiving, treacherous sea not to know what lay ahead. Although inspections over twenty trips showed her to be a cautious crew given over to meticulous charting, these reports had not been matched with actual voyage difficulties. Thus, whereas the spool when it was finished would describe quickness of that ship lens to record entry of the crisis, Jones wanted to learn about any variance which had it been time-computed more quickly might have saved the ship.

Thus, the recorded conditions were essential to understand especially for the equipment the ship had relied upon; next the necessary testing before the voyage was confirmed as were bridge visibility and steerage; the fact that he still had to track number of compass deviations would be indexed also by Lewis. The chart display and information system had to be matched to any forecast for each 72 hour and 48 hour tropical winds read especially for hurricanes. As it became conclusive what occurred to navigation, the ship lens had to be evaluated as to accuracy and finally they had to access the sound reception system for its echo-sound equipment in water to determine if it recorded onto the graph accurately.

For seven tedious hours Jones poured over the task of studying series of bars produced by various ship equipment. The bars were set by function and date and time. There were bars for position; for weather conditions; and for sound under the surface. What sounded like a ball dribbling down pavement was a fish eating; or another frequently heard taped sound of objects crashing or bumping was due to normal passage of ship's starboard leaning far onto one side; no one could figure out how to get rid of these annoying sounds so they couldn't interfere with understanding what was there; the bars and graphs confirmed actual below surface condition. A mariner had to go out to sea many times before he could accurately learn to hear whatever was under water.

It often took eighty hours for the sea to calm down after a hurricane had receded. Prior to the aftermath during the first fifty hours waves could rise as high as sixty to seventy feet measuring ten across. For a windjammer that large, her deck would get doused but her fourteen masts would keep her keel straight, she'd be like a wave cutter, one could sail around the world in all seasons without mishap, easy. If there were the presence of another ship, the bar would show it, if there was a passing block which indicated a presence, he could measure it. With this they would ask for a reinforced keel and dark line as the ship was rebuilt, all it would take on a graph was to show too great a block on the light area, if it remained bar to bar it was probably an aggressing ship, couldn't see it by name, he would have to evaluate type of ship by sound itself, the sound made a distinctive funneling noise as it fired which lasted maybe all of ten minutes, if sound dropped through the belt it would leave a disconcerting noise but not a bang. This never showed on a graph, at this point the alarms went on and the bar fed only to surface. Each series of bars corresponded to a 72 hour segment and the voyage destined to take three and a half weeks felled in the second week. Shaded areas represented collision risk, degrees of light gave course and relative position for each segment; interruptions between segments could account for hazardous weather or heavy rainfall, clouding showed rate of turn indicator, staggered dark bars on a single frame revealed steady speed forward, it would be anywhere between fifty bars to several thousand bars to complete analysis for, before he could send the lot to an analyst, about forty hours to study, sufficient for recognition as a weather bar analyst.

He grilled up a steak hibachi style on the stove, threw in some diced peppers and ginger marinated mango and ate dinner. He was alone, the evening had come and gone and Lewis had taken off looking every bit the jet set, flashy gray silk, pink shirt, and stylish hat. After cleaning up the kitchen, Jones sipped coffee on the balcony, admiring the ladies below on their patio.

Jones awoke at dawn, grabbed a tennis racket, walked the concourse path that wound above the hotel on the bluff to the courts. Stepping through the wire gate, he entered onto the backgammon sets, took a few balls out of a wire basket, tossed one in the air, slammed it hard at the stone wall, on every return delivered it back until he volleyed the ball about fifty times. A tough attractive brunette, her blond streaked hair coiffed in a French braid, in a short white skirt and tight matching blouse took the board adjacent to him, dancing on her feet kept a strong serve going, the ball ricocheted until she matched his speed. Never one to not take up on a lead, he asked whether she wanted to try her hand at a tennis match to which she readily assented.

"Name's Jones," he said, extending a toned ivy league hand.

Her grasp, while brisk and somewhat distant, showed a friendly confidence upon withdrawal. "Lisa."

"Where are you from?"

"Jamaica. I grew up there."

"Near the beach?"

"In a hotel which my dad manages."

"Did you follow in his shoes?"

"Yes, I operate two myself."

They were lucky to find the courts all to themselves. She began the serve, arm raised, her body elongating through the ribcage, he crouched, whipped a return, satisfied it flew right to her feet, she quickly side stepped and with a powerful arm sent the ball at eye level, straight shot into his square, a polite repartee. They played a full set until she beat him, her last swing in a series of thirty non competitive returns a powerful juggernaut that smashed the ball over the net stop putting it, giving the ball not enough the send-off to land a birdie. With that, his initial instinct having determined her bloodthirsty need to win, he called it quits.

He showered, dressed and went for coffee at the magazine shop before he returned to work thinking the match over, he could've saved his game had he thought it through, his first impression was after all usually reliable but he often conceded on his instincts, nevertheless as he retraced the path he wrapped up the morning as a productive energetic start, a fine restitution for the tasks that lay ahead. He began the task of breaking down width in centimeters per each graph, each graph being a bar enlarged to detect weather problems. The task would take him ten hours, the isometrics of what got chosen for evaluation when the analyst had to confirm or deny alleged ship position as stated on data. Lewis had left him a bar of a grayish mass apparition which hung inside the frame and had circled it as a query queque, Jones couldn't put it on the magnifier until he had an isolated image, he thought it could be another ship, equally as long, a masthead. He examined how many bars it looked like had proofed in to decide which other systems gave the shipmaster the needed information for a change in starboard heading. He checked against data, sure enough Lewis' eye had caught something hazy, there was a passage of way call to starboard, a rate of turn demarcation, a few shouts of "Ship ahoy!" into the fog, with no responding cries, he measured the clearest image on the bar fractioning out for speed and set aside for Lewis a dark gyro-dot, a subsequent bar for speed of under two knots, despite this limitation the identification system listed a question for a ten mast, predominantly harbor bound, prisoner carryall which meant a cannon. Had the ship slowed down because a person was not at their station? That was the frightening situation on the Charles Morgan, the deck officer called out, "Bodies on the main," and nothing further, the Morgan never found, determined not likely to have sunk. Vanished.

He worked out rate of turn, position and course for the identification of the apparition, a grueling hour of prior day measurements projected against the known voyage plan. If the crew went up on deck more than twice which is likely, then if they still weren't able to see it, it meant the phantom was out of casting range, probably non verifiable. In order to make a determinant from so much sketchy information, he went over his calculations, even looked over Lewis' discernments as to his weather estimations to see if Lewis had surmised off-course complications. He had measured little else; he had four ships in the same quadrant all reporting in rough seas in the same week. Jones returned to the dining room table where his graphs lay and re-calculated for rate of turn, position and course logging by day and by night for a week. Lewis would require this information attached to his spool to proof line as to when it became absolutely necessary for the crew to abandon ship. After another few hours of reviewing echo-sound barographs Jones was certain that when the ship skidded into ice, she was fired upon. He provided in order of day and hour a list of headers along with bar designations – this precise data evaluation was the single procedure that defined how the systems collectively grouped every needed consideration of course.

The hour was late when he stopped working. He postponed the upcoming task to obtain color variables for his light bluish to slightly yellow and brown sediment-like cloudy photos of bar or graph, because the resonant translation could easily take another ten hours. He took a swim and spa at the poolhouse and was in bed when a boisterous Lewis entered with his date, loud, thoroughly giddy, they grabbed a few beers and proceeded to come upstairs, Lewis could be heard playfully fondling her as she disrobed, they kissed rather sloppily and Lewis made a remark which caused her raucous laughter, there was breathless passion and quick greedy supplications. Jones could only but guess Lewis was making love to her standing in the loft against the wall fronting Lewis' room and bath.

When Jones came to a little after three the suite was absolutely quiet. He drew the curtains and opened the doors to the balcony. Lewis' balcony doors were open, the curtains billowing out into the night breeze. Jones set up his laptop at the desk in the bedroom and began reviewing nautical maps of the charted region and photos of the ocean as that expanse of sea looked in that week. He looked for certain types of information, ship and vessel, ocean determinant color or variation for surface and depth by fifty feet. At 32,30 the sea was gemstone blue in icy regions, nearest Greenland's shelf it was ice and emerald green; at sea anywhere in northern Atlantic about eight hundred miles due south it became gray or gray blue, from a distance sapphire, a few miles off the Bermuda Islands at 32,60 the sea spread out in relative calm aquamarine, daily changes occurred in ocean straits, below depths of forty feet dark blackish waters dominated, a dark blue line became evident at the three-mile horizon of the Bermudas, light blue sparkling shallow sandy inlets surrounding all beaches. Once he obtained these distinctions he then sparred out zones of ocean in ship lens photo shots for better approximation with given data for ship position and speed alone.

Hours later around eight he began the weary chore to estimate noise level at listening posts underwater. With each capable filter droid, neglecting bar or graph, he positioned by coordinate any seismic or sliding plate activity, calculating for length of activity in seconds, then placing the ship in the correct color photograph, simulated staging to constancy of wave, and making necessary reductions in speed for each thirty hours of sail.

Someone banged loudly on the door downstairs, probably a delivery boy from the camera lab with the spool line video. He continued chart plotting by photo engineering, absorbed. Jones sipped his coffee as he carefully relayed signs of activity, timed them by computer, and made notes of changes in sea variations. The ocean rose in seventy foot swells, all bluish gray tinged with dark brownish green, sounds of sudden depth followed by severe storm lashing, seconds later a brief absence of dragging during which the ship lost all drop-line equipment on one side, interior-located sound equipment were meant primarily to read activity up close, he could not find any mention of sonar, ships could have been torpedoing undersea ice left and right with lots of motion resulting, he deduced this was when ice was grabbing the ship, a loud sound was produced that gave ballast swaying superceded by clanging sounds, he looked at his simulcast, there were sounds on deck and sounds of lowering boats. Now he had it. The sea looked to be in an uproar, more decibels, more dragging sounds, the stern went low, it gave off an identifiable plummet, then the unmistakable hard thud.

He refocused attention back to the ocean depth sounds prior to the seventy foot swells. The time was noon. He reversed the collection instrumentation by a day. The sea was a high plateau of small waves, no swells or bursts. The ship crested high, one side in the wake. Several minutes of large ice pieces underwater gave a wheezing intonation, the wake lasted a good two hours before it subsided at all, from the far depths rose a high pitched steady release of sound. Jones zeroed in for it as he imagined the master had done, his photos reassembled for identification, an avalanche of crashing rocks. The half turn was made, the bow relieved.

He found Lewis dressed for a day inside in dark green, polished cotton trousers and his undershirt busy downstairs watching the spool line trying to calculate rapidity of received images to correspond with recorded data on the predicting graphs for course plotting. The camera lab had set a running time by hour, minute and second for each photo. Photos requiring close-up and distance took over a minute; most shots numbered three a minute.

"What I really hope for," Lewis said, "is a capability in crisis coordination for clearer pictures with as many as ten or more photos a minute. The problem of changing course while explained by the voyage data does not predict as early as it probably might have."

Jones said, "I isolated water depth and points for passage up to the iceberg. There were high seas and underwater crashing."

"I have been speaking to the Institute about how much the ship veered off voyage plan, the replacement deck house pilot ordered a half turn within minutes before it ran on a skid with submerged ice. My concern is the rationale for the turn."

"There were substantial dragging sounds to indicate considerable activity below."

"But no photos of waves."

"Could the crew have used several anchors?"

"Moby Dick style? To use several anchors to prevent capsize?"

"Yes, but the problem is the same, they needed to readily identify any rock in ocean once they read for sound, sharper listening posts would have greatly facilitated."

"What about Loran-C?"

Lewis replied, "I am not sure the ability to measure the rate of speed of a hurricane by Loran-C is the best way to go about plotting course, course is indicated by height of sea, a short throw camera could be as effective, it would give actual wave length and height as opposed to imaging, the problem of Loran-C is it shows something that is not there."

"What will you recommend?"

"Whelen Edge Lens kit, Short Throw Zoom Lens, 360 degree clear Fresnel lens or double lens with increased capability."

"They will only go for the clear ones," Jones said, laughing.

"What about a Masthead White Light lens?"

"If our ship had one on it, it was doomed. It creates a satellite view of a massive breach for a flood. It does not allow any ability to distinguish between landmark and ocean. Technically in ice regions it builds up water mass."

"What else have you worked on?"

"I was at the Institute all day yesterday testing out the ship's capability. Some guy gave me his desk so I was able to correlate radar reflector imaging, charting deviations off magnetic compass wires, the same for daylight signaling lamps and the turn style mast lens camera. I took from descriptions any lag in emergency engine power, failure alarms, quit-emit recording devices, recorded error and readjusted compass coordinate points. Two other ships had lit up on the board at equal distance to the Monsoon, the problem was where could the fourth ship have been, had Monsoon over corrected her course?"

Jones said, "Maybe that's why the other ships weren't confronted by the steep incline on surface immediately prior to distress call?"

"Or was it they had left ports at later times?"

"For how long was she in fog ice?"

"The question you're asking is not whether all equipment could have been reliable against the limitation of the circumstances; you are really at the exact dilemma I've been pondering, why did her voyage plan take her into the vicinity of the spout?"

"It looks as though when she skidded on an ice bottle, the iceberg drifted taking her to it."

"Well, that's my point. The other ships managed to veer away despite the fact they each remained on their previously set voyage plan."

"The ship can't be faulted because they changed direction," Jones said. "The rationale can be supported despite the outcome."

"In my estimation they should not have replaced their pilot. The first one didn't sweat the ice."

"I wouldn't hold it against him. It was touch and go for at least a day."

Lewis shrugged to indicate how strongly he disagreed.

"It's not for us to decide."

"They'll want an opinion."

Jones picked up his key chain. "You want to stroll out on the beach?"

"I'll join you later, I have to complete this project."

"I will probably take a sandwich at the patio."

"Oh, fine, I'll see you around three."

Jones made it to the door, when Lewis asked, "Been around to see Rhonda lately?"

He turned to face Lewis. "I took her out one time."

"She told me it was intimate."

"No, you're confused. She spent that last night with me crying when you brought that broad to your room. She said she felt abandoned."

Lewis held his gaze.

"I just can't understand you."

"She is talking about splitting up permanent this time."

"She'll probably never quit you. For some reason she continues to stay in love with you no matter what you do."

"She said you two went to Rojo Beach."

"You have some sort of problem with control, Lewis, you have to make her crawl. Why don't you try talking to her?" he asked, not having intended to bring the subject up.

"Will you tell about last night?"

"It's your life, I have no right to say anything."

"Have a good stroll," Lewis said dismissively.

Jones went on his way. The air temperature had to be at least eighty-five. There was a breeze off the sea blowing sand about, flapping the parasols, leaning the slender palms. He walked the entire beach, eventually removed his shoes and socks, enjoying the warm bit of sand. Lewis had his guilt, it didn't cause Jones to admire or rely on the man any less. Jones still felt a bit of sorrow for Rhonda and knew there wasn't a thing he could do or say for her. He came across the young woman he had seen the other day on the green and decided she was too young for him, likely forty years younger. She waved at him, he waved also.

Eventually he tracked his way to the patio where he ordered lunch, an exquisitely dressed artichoke salad with lacy cucumber strips, horseradish root, diced cooked beet and delicate teriyaki beef with a side of hot starchy white rice, a dish he had seen on some other meal plate when he last dined. Good to his word, Lewis Lewis walked across the green in grey knits, a bluish sweater, Mocktoes and a green jacket on his arm. At brief Lewis seated himself, ordering up a dish of potato leek soup with cheese and a Scotch neat. He apologized for his remarks, said he knew better, and the moment his drink arrived he contented his misery in it. The meals came after, Lewis dipped a thick garlic toast garnish in his soup savoring it, embarrassment obvious, Jones tasted his teriyaki and gave an agreeable praise.

"How's yours?" Jones asked, deciding he would have to guard against asking Lewis for a more thorough, psychologically oriented explanation.

"Can't complain, spicy ginger, a thin flavor of herb."

"Are you going out tonight?"

"She can't make it, she has classes this evening and tomorrow, she's studying for an analyst post."

"Really. I wouldn't have thought a career change at fifty would be sought."

"She's raised children and one set of grandchildren, she says she's ready."

"Is she married?"

"He's dead. He used to work the Dockyard. I told myself no firm commitments."

"Well, ask the hotel to send another girl."

"Hell no! I can hang on for a few nights."

Jones took several bites more, tried the quarter of artichoke with dressing, and pleased with the tangy tangerine taste set down his fork.

"I've gone through the spool. The lens saw some problem with light, the photos are poor image retention, although sound measured in. I've been to the ship twice, there's no way the hole is not a direct hit, as a result I'm asking for a high speed video remake."

"Oh, that's an idea. We can compare, mine is a presumption of where on the ocean they have to be."

"No way to give weather a good likeness."

"Do you expect to see a torpedo?"

"Yup, a dug-out maybe."

"You'd have to get a close-in of the hull to detect shrapnel."

"Here's the fix, the photos display too much cloudy light under the surface. I'm taking bets on it."

"Smart."

"Yeah, I caught it straight away. I'll be sure to give your idea that there were ice obstacles about in the water at depth some work."

"Are you planning to prove the captain's pilot should have stayed with the original path plan?"

"Already have, open and shut."

"I would like to know how you derived your proof."

"I tested for sound bites over volume and can prove ice everywhere underwater freezing, thawing or re-cementing. I've arranged for a final risk analyst to take a look at the overall composure of complications."

In the morning Jones went in search of Lisa, finding her out near the old battalion practicing crochet bending to a strained concentration to aim the wooden ball through the loop from a distance of two yards, wearing a trendy one-piece white tennis dress, good soled tennis shoes, her shoulder length hair loose.

"Let's go get a bite to eat after a few serves."

She straightened up, her face suffused with intense effort. "Just this one," she said, bending, and gave the ball a firm whack. It angled through the loop in a quick rebuttal.

"I've been taught every game there is at our hotels," she remarked, pausing to light a cigarette, "and despite hours at them, the ones I come out ahead on are precious tedious."

"I play a mean golf, if you'd like to join me this weekend."

"I suppose, tennis is really my best."

They walked up the grass toward the courts, the wind level a furious half knot.

"So," she began in precise interview tone, "what brings you out to our building? You don't strike me much as a business type."

"A friend and I are looking over the ship that was dragged into Dockyard."

"You're an appraiser?"

"Yes. I have to make a quick down and dirty as to what conditions of sea sank her and then what it will cost to restore her."

"You're going to put new turbines in her engine room, an electronic chart display, some red and green zoom lens, like that?"

He laughed. "Just like that."

"The Whelen was the first brought to Dock in pieces when I was barely four. It caused a gigantic commotion."

"Do you remember much about it? I'd love to talk to you about it."

"Oh sure, I even have pictures that my dad took."

They entered the courts, Lisa removed grip gloves from her pocket, stretched each half finger, then slipped her fingers inside, grabbed a few balls turning on the automatic serve which would take a minute, they walked to their places opposite the wrung net, she served a typical lead beginning with a wide side delivery. He ran for it, tucked his racket, carried it three steps and returned the ball pyramid style which caused her to step away fast and backhand return sending it well into his upper court with maximum speed. They ran and killed, jumped and quashed, the automatic spit out a ball every three minutes into his court, he thought after a few he should claim a tournament but she was better and she won three out of four, having an ability to see weak places in his returns.

He treated her to breakfast at the poolside, ordered a buttered up dish of over medium egg on bacon and blue cheese English muffin, with Breakfast tea in rum glasses. The place was full by eight, chatter was full tip astern and the waiters tucked out in bibbed shirts and black suits hurried about with trays, setting dishes on tables with adroit quickness of early bird expertise.

"My father taught me to identify land mass by stars at all hours of the day," he told her, his gaze at her clean wide blue-eyed expressive countenance. "Because of that, I can enlist to any ship lost at sea and work out actual course for position and speed."

"Impressive," she replied, as two waiters swooped over them setting down hot plates with silver captain's domes, removing each dome to let stand steaming ensconced truffled cheese-dressed egg. She took a first bite, nodded, a sip of tea, poured in cream to her liking, sipped again, a smile of approval curved her lips.

Lots of breeding here, he'd finally have to acknowledge, questioning his own motives for pursuing her, after all she was not the wind swept look he went for. "I recollect the Whelen sank at latitude to Virginia and longitude to the North Sea."

"Technically it fell directly west of Bermuda South Beach, it was rumored to carry the prince jewels destined for Santiago, which unpleasantly were never recovered."

"What sort of masthead was she outfitted with?"

"Black ship lens. She was one of two ships of her era to sight under sea swells as they rolled into a beach head, she also had a separate torpedo drawer, a room between the first two captains' quarters and the dispatch room that contained a second radio predominantly for out-calls, and she had the first video signal of its kind. She carried a hawk box to detect sound from the deck, she had high deck trim to prevent waves washing onto deck, fittings that you'd never have thought to reinforce another less ocean advancing vessel with, and then she often lowered her masts in straits to obscure her bale wharf."

"Wow! I'd heard she had a printmaker on her."

"Neither for forfeit or replacement currency, as far as rumor went she was alleged to have stored blood red ink in drums for the purpose of seals and nothing like that was introduced. My dad's interest was her human cargo, but she's said to have arrived to harbor with none but French barons on board."

"Did your dad build prisons?"

"No, but he was told, at least that is what he has said, the kind of ship she was was to carry semi-legal forgers to the islands for dunth which means they go into detention cells until they are cleared of criminal allegations."

"Was she rebuilt?"

"No. Shipmasters recommended against it, their belief was never put a replacement back to sea."

He cut his dish into six neat pieces and ate one, tasted his tea, and added cream as she had done. "Might I see your photographs? You could drop by my place this evening, or do you have a husband who will object?"

"I'm not married, I suppose we could arrange a time."

"Seven-thirty? I'll cook dinner."

She removed a tiny cotillion-type writing pad and with a tiny pencil wrote in the assignment along with directions to his suite which he described. When she had finished, she asked, "Are you married?"

"No, I'm a veritable bachelor, no woman's ever kept me."

He swept into the suite feeling quite snappish. Lewis Lewis was on the tram line discussing with his friend at the Dockyard Institute their perceptions of which builders ought to take initial bidding and which should do piecework. The engines would receive priority as would gearbox, the standard kitchen would take nothing but the usual, berths could be retrofitted by double sealed compartments and constituted to resemble upgrades on container or sea salvage ships, then they were ready to go to draft – that meant that prior to a bid for proposal for which this bidding advisory group would have to approved manufacturers there had to be a list as to what failed, Lewis would compile costs, the barograph stays, his advice, apparently agreed to, was to junk all other systems that predicted tide, keep lens to what must be relied upon, no expedition liberal spending, then the two defaults, the prediction calendar based upon low accuracy of plotting, second the need for maximum capability lens with an advise committee just for that, finally fleshing out details as to interface systems for complications of steerage.

Jones invited Lewis to dinner at six but Lewis declined saying he was spending two days in Flatts and Jones would have the place to himself, they talked about what there was to do, Lewis said nothing much except he planned to treat himself, if he felt the sea breeze he'd take a yacht ride out to sea, although he thought he should fly down to Hamilton at which the government had secured the navigation saddle to check his findings against actual plot points, he also received a alternate route finder latitude marker for the anchor winch system which he expected to test on base out at Boaz, he left Jones a listing on his computer of major controls he could speak to his consultant at Saint David about, Lewis eventually left to go take in the sunshine at one of five bars.

Jones checked Lewis' main monitor and found the list, rudder, anchor, emergency, machine telegraph, bridge, wing, blackbox, internal comm., TV and navigation lights, Jones put in a lam to Harrington Sound, was given a number and put through, he asked mean tide or moonrise for Wyndam, Station Manager looked it up, sent by radio coordinate that fateful night's read,

Mean tide, 7:22 AM EST, April 24, 1943, .32 kts, offset .34; Sunrise, 7:20 AM EST, Sunset, 5:41 PM EST, Moonrise, 12:54 AM EST, Moonset, 11:19 PM, EST.

Jones got him on the horn again saying, Tell me, which time did Wyndam get taken by, station manager answered, Sunset. Only.

Lisa arrived promptly at six, wearing a black sheath that glimmered, a horn blower in her hair pulled back so tightly it strained her forehead, a banglet of silvery jangling fake stones, her face made up precisely. Because she had dressed for a formal sit down, the elaboration of a candlelight dinner not altogether lost on him, he found himself surprised to discover when the contents of her slim purse opened a pair of underwear and a small as yet unopened shampoo bottle. While thinking his decision to start a slow kindling affair, Jones removed her shawl, took her sequined charcoal purse, placed them close to the door on a long green marble cabinet usually reserved for outgoing mail and taking her by the hand he showed her the suite, took her onto the balcony where champagne uncorked in a bucket he poured two swan stem glasses.

The sparkling sea, fading sunset, changing color of the sandy beach from pink to beige, each enhanced the evening with gradual promise. She sat relaxed, a female of adept adaptation to social situations, she seemed uninvolved, or rather unaware of any awkwardness, quite capable of instantly fitting into a new armor without the usual signs of breaking the ice or normal tension of imagining herself a part of the décor. They sat without speaking a good minute, assuming a comfort he wasn't sure of, no doubt her skill matched years of living in hotels her father and she managed, she was born to the life, despite the captivating exhilaration he felt at the notion she might be consensual, he contained his pleasure to a mild discernment of her proximity.

"I bet you've seen many a sunset from a balcony."

"This is as pretty as they come," she answered, unaffected by either their closeness or distance of the lounge chairs and glass table between them. "I'm used to standing on a beach to watch a sunset."

"This is one of the best," he said, agreeing, "although we control agents have spent more than thirty years at places like this one."

"If you have the time, I'd like to take you to South to show you my newest cabin keeper. It's small for the standard of the industry but it has private patios on a superfluous green overlooking a mile of wind swept beach."

"How did you get it?"

"I stayed at a house there, average accommodations, and told a friend of my dad's that a hotel curved to fit the road from that vantage point would give any traveler unfamiliar with the beach at one's doorstep a view of the most stunning parcel in all Bermuda. After all, it's not what one thinks flying in, a scruffy landscape chock full of white stucco and salted fading grass."

He smiled. "The sand is everywhere, just walking across the concourse at this place I end with sand in my socks."

They sipped their champagne, he experienced a sudden tipsy release, she let her lips part on the edge of the glass staining it with red lipstick.

"I suppose it was your mother who handled general accounts."

"My mother despised hotel living and she left when I was five."

"That ought to have been difficult to tolerate."

"It was for several years, but my dad took me everywhere with him. By nine I answered his office telephone, at ten I handled billing, by eleven I was asked to compute measurements on additions, and by twelve I was given a small salary to inventory supplies."

This time he laughed. "There are worse upbringings. I, for one, left my family in England to join up with the Queen's Service as soon as I completed my nurse training. My mother didn't want me involved with the islands, my father, a Home Office agent, thought the salty wind would do me good. I was one of three male nurses to end up in Field."

"I've seen many of you stay at my hotels, you're a wind-defined organization. The men who reside here are generally speaking retired and many years older."

As soon as night fell, he set his glass on the table and invited her to come downstairs. He stood aside to let her pass into his bedroom ahead of him. She placed her hand on his back, coming close in, her shoulder brushing his, and once inside the room waited until he had closed the screen and was very nearly to her. He put his hands on her shoulders and let his hands move down her arms, thinking she possessed an exquisite nape, her skin soft, her perfume a trace of Chanel No. 17, no minor output of one's casually earned dollar, it sold at a hundred and twenty American for one ounce. When she moved slowly from him, he followed, a gambit that created a rise in him. They started downstairs, she took each stair deliberately, halfway down she paused for long enough for him to want her, before she proceeded to the dining room. He had set the table for a six piece candelabra with china, silver and flowered blue and orange napkins, prepared bubbling fondue. Serving a burgundy in chilled glasses, he dished out cheesecloth Caesar salad with anchovy, did the honors of lighting the candles and of supplying a thin plate with pickled sauerkraut and sliced salami. The candles flickered over the walls emitting long shadows of themselves. They talked about the original news of the Whelen, her missing crew, the bottom salvage, the catastrophe that had by all logic to have torn her apart, the attempts at underwater discovery, the collection of wood brought in on several barges. Lisa was a mere kid, she overheard the rumors at Gibb's Lighthouse and in town at the Dockyard, that she had been surrendered to the deep in a frightening succumbing wave some hundred feet high, which looked on a station monitor like a streaming wall of liquid glass that appeared off her starboard, that she was an instant goner. Three hundred men from the Dockyard left for sea in the hour, many boats returned with nearly drowned deck hands, the worst had died when he hit the water, the poor ship was scheduled to land not even by nightfall. She had given herself over to a belief since that day that it was best not to leave the safety of the ground, and she never had taken so much as a boat trip.

She helped clear the table saying the meal was a romantically persuasive endeavor and satisfied all her needs of the year, he put his arms around her as she rinsed off the dinnerware and stacked them in the Rubbermaid holder. He kissed her neck when she was done. For dessert he put out his specialty, vanilla wafers with banana nut cream custard on clear red plates. She barely ate hers, she had been taught while in her teens by a chef two or three bites. They talked into the late hour, at length he lit the fireplace and they spread out on the large tan rust rug, he ran a hand across her body feeling her slender, firm breasts, her jutting hip bones, running his hand up her thin tapered legs beneath her underwear. She lay passively, not directing or helping, her gaze remained unwavering as he moved on top of her. This woman was not Rhonda, Lisa wouldn't be one to entice nor draw him, his desire would do more of the buildup, but when he shook off his trousers, raised her dress high up her body and entered her, her readiness was like silk, she was all contained passion and as he rose on her she melted to his motion. Hours later, after he walked her to her door, he wondered what she was accustomed to, since she had not wanted to sleep over or leave the living room to his bedroom. She didn't invite him into her apartment or refuse him entirely for while they kissed lingeringly she moved her hand onto his hip and pressed against him and said she could do another night out.

Jones lay awake through the night. It had been years since he had pursued anyone. Looking back on the evening he thought it had come and gone too quickly. He would have preferred delaying love for a few weeks right up to the conclusion of his job. His sense of Lisa would be she could not be available enough, emotionally, he enjoyed the surge of lust that cropped up with Rhonda, as suddenly as it began it was over, with an understanding that was all it was, and if something grew out of those romantic incidents he couldn't be drawn out of himself past the limitation they represented. Although he gave everything he could capably produce to his work, he did so out of an honestly persuaded thinking that to give less was somehow an incorrect posture, and thus relationships, which almost no agent seemed to want, went unanswered. He for one had often elected to sacrifice if only because the women who worked in Nassau were neither commitment-oriented nor indulged in occasional stepping out. The structure of the agency did not correspond to residences for marrieds, couples who were deeply cherished or devout remained in the service at home.

In the morning he found her on the tennis court, racket in hand, the volley machine spitting out a ball every ten seconds, her lean elegance reformed into a sleeveless shirt and short skirt, thick soled shoes showing her ruthless ambition to the sport. He turned off the machine, graced his lithe body into an arched serve and delivered a flying ball that saved her no alternative except to step out of the ball's way to send a return. They found their instinct to a hard game, each self-composing for a win, he conserving his steps, she busting her back hand, the one ball zinging back and forth. In the past three days he learned not to play for an opponent's advantage, kick the ball, swing the racket. Their game lasted twenty-eight minutes, when Lisa caught the ball in her hand and bouncing it suggested they retreat to her flat for the start of the day.

They ran across the green to her studio. It was large, an open spacious sitting room with balcony, the French doors open to an enclosed fenced patio with garden trim, a separate long kitchen, all modern, a breakfast nook, and through a door a short hall to a nice sized bedroom and bath. They showered, she washed his back, he shampooed her hair, then they took a sauna and dried out.

"Remember last night in your bedroom?" she asked.

"Yes, I do."

"You're the first to decline an invitation."

"I debated, I like to discuss an important item first. Otherwise it's too fast for me."

"Is this too fast for you?" She stood, drew him to her and together they fell onto her bed, she becoming seemingly absent of drive.

"I can do this." He kissed her on the mouth, then on the neck, breasts. When he gazed up at her, she had closed her eyes, she lay unintruded upon. He kissed her underside of the swell of her breast, pretending she was Rhonda he drew her against him, mounted her, wondered whether he ought to ask her if he could have her, as he made love to her it occurred to him she had discovered men who responded to passivity and he paused, as she had done on the stairs. She opened her eyes, for an instant surprised, she moved up on him a few times, before he continued, suddenly infatuated.

He had no way of asking her what he feared might be heard as an uninvited question. He crashed against her driving himself, thinking only of himself, when she pinned herself to him as if willing him to become part of her.

"You're so completely beautiful, Lisa. I haven't stopped thinking about you since that first hour."

She gazed longingly into his eyes, touched his cheek, let herself look at him, until she had told herself something essential and drew him down to her, whispering, "think of me as the only one who won't demand."

Had he comprehended the ambiguity of her, he could have responded; instead he put his face against her breasts, ran his hand up the back of her leg and said, as if confessing, "you have the most beautiful body I've seen, you are ravishing, even if I wanted you for all time I'd never get enough." He drew his hand between her legs talking the entire time, about her sculpted features, her strength, her blondish brown streaks of hair, her corseted thighs, her arrested breath, softly whispering until she came, trembling against him.

He whispered, "You see, I wouldn't have had the temerity to have said no."

She said, "All the men I've had act fast. It's what I'm used to."

At lunch, the appraiser analyst says that's adequate for internal upgrades, each system on its own backup, his supervisor's stat was for ROVs, they recommended a zoom 10, the time and tide clock that measures from any source of sea where high waves would be originally was a Windmaster which nowadays sold for $8,000 a unit, then a blast of opinion, saying, The Whelen was shot down, the Wyndam was taken from below into a whirlpool, only the Trinity made it to Aruba carrying only the harbor box. The fact that any steer nav gets two high tides and two low tides per twenty-five hours in a very calculateable fashion which can be adjusted weekly if tides are irregular wasn't the essential item, the facts were the times were incorrect by two hours, two traces were made an hour prior to the time Wyndam struck ice, both ships reported in, the transferring bridge pilot wanted to get ahead of the trade winds, they thought there was a difficulty with the slide graph inside the barometer, whatever got entered got left off the plate –

"No," Lewis hollered; "That's tampering! We should be asking for an internal clock without a slide."

"Could switch to the Dunmore," the risk man said, "the Dun is equally reliable; as to the engines, you'll want the same Steelplate, your list will be relatively uncomplicated, turbines, for a windjammer that's eighty; brackets, steel plates, and steam whistle, that's what moves the ship. "

"Could the bridge have missed incoming information?"

"Not a chance if they were still on deck, inside the bridge as the information channels in it sounds like a disk being loaded to play, then all the charts appear on screen."

The box man said, "As to your gearbox, it's all electronic, it takes a half year to build, it is half the size of a standard size bedroom, inside are hundreds of connecting wires – "

Risk said, "Any manufacturer can do it, Dockyard can do it, it will take about seventy men. What'd they tell you, Lew, about your Raythoon cathode?"

"That the alternate route finder recorded another ship already had gone off the chart in a forceful gale that called in at 68 knots."

Risk said, "That spout is forty miles across by three miles wide. It was probably the reason Wyndam asked for another, more advanced pilot."

Jones said, "Damn good pilot, even you will have to agree, Lewis, cyclone at sea registers as early as 56 knots."

They all agreed raising their mugs of tea in salute. "Hear ye, hear ye," they said in unison.

The box man said, "Did you say the route finder gauge was stopped to 68?"

"Yes," Lewis said.

"That's indeed conclusive. If the ship went down by cyclone, the computation would have locked into the final read. How many times did information register?"

"At least twenty times. The first few were responded to, then the twelfth, the rest were ignored. Other screens appeared."

Risk gave a quick assent. "The other ships would have

received Wyn's status, their messages could have locked in as well if those ships hoped for a distress return."

Lewis inquired, "What about a bulbous bow?"

Box replied, "We've had plenty of time to rethink 1942 when the spout appeared after a gigantic cataclysm. ROVs are an absolute necessity just to know what's under the water. That sort of large bow is for front driving exactly like a car. The windjammer already has a wide berth keel giving it maximum stability, so I'm not sure about a pronounced bow at read level."

Jones, who wanted to cover all fronts of discussion, asked, "Could it prevent a skid?"

"The bow such as what you're describing is meant to facilitate speed for ships with canons that already ride high. The Wyndam actually is capable of conveying for depth since it is wide and you can't have that sort of weight exposed for depth."

"What about a ballast system?"

Box said, "No. Not with a balclutha."

The wind current on the Sound at Tucker's Town was a speedy low breeze. The greens stretched out, emerald velvet in a luxuriant descent to the rocks and beach, a hundred cabins the finest in condominium living for the relaxing golfer. Whatever had given the architect his first gaze the abundance of shimmering ponds and stately mansion clubs had done the job to provide a wealthy American's offshore elegance. Boats tied up inside a small harbor bobbed on a scintillating clear aquamarine surface. Jones and Lewis Lewis steered across the moorings to the southerly most point where the original piece of wreckage was discovered, the underside of half the hull, its very own mastern. When dredged it came up in a single trevelan of wood, even its deck plank dismissed to some far off region of ocean complaint. The two men cruised to the point where she had lain in water until an unsuspecting officer on a spring day rode out to do a little fishing and snapped a photograph. The site lay seven hundred miles due south, seemingly impossible to have drifted this far, but the sail fleet of many a down ship had come inexplicably to rest here.

At the approximate coordinates they photographed the surface, sent a sea photo container below to bottom and took four dozen shots, gave another container a shovel worth of sand, and took current readings. The five hour laborious task left them with red sun burnt complexions and weathery tough skin, despite the continual application of suntan lotion. Originally the Greek mariner expedition that monitored wind and drift for ships lost at sea derived from a simple fact that vessels gone down in quick turbulence proceed to drift over sand finding a resting place at a certain depth. With five expeditions reporting in, a rough and dirty calculation placed all pieces in various parts of the Atlantic. At this sea point, the air strained like high mountain altitude, the ocean, utterly peaceful, recorded in an odd hullabaloo of mincing sound. The cabin including the radio and spectrograph room was sealed, its gigantic instrumentation although rusted, still clamped onto the floor and the wall. The Greek team had followed an underwater path of recordings for six weeks recording underwater turbulence from a depth of two thousand feet. The continuous retching of wood which could be heard as a muffled presence stocked their computers with gradations of currents which as they passed above were graphed giving reads of 800, 950, an old barometer. Thus, the Wyndam, the fastest ship in the world, slid across the plateaus of the undersea to arrive at her farthest most landing, her gleaming buckle sprinting a gleam about fifty feet from surface.

When they sat down with their information, they compared to the point of furlough, mast steerage, wind element and harbord and realized rather oddly, the ship moved without incident for four hundred yards before it toppled down a steep canyon of unestimable depth. Its first shark fin would years later bob to the surface and like a restless ski knock into a minor sized vessel, knarking it in the rough well. Its other shark fin never to be identified lost its crude edge onto sand at Sand Dollar Point, a small beach head not posted to any map. Jones took the photos to use as comparison to all compiled information; Lewis's task was to put together ocean readings. After a tedious ninety hours, they left their cabin to play a game of golf, wile away an afternoon at the nines, run the cart through a vale around two ponds. They joked over their inconsistent findings, the bark read, the longitudinals never precise, the echo sounder spooling backwards, all the problems they'd have to fill in once the essential task was completed.

"If both hulls were found in different shelves, but both were conjured out of clear blue water, we might deduce they moved toward warmer seas," Lewis said, picking up a ball and placing it on the tee.

"The curious thing is the hull dragged in from the deep was completely shark finned," Jones said.

"It's not really going to get readily explained that our hull slipped through a current header, then must have been pummeled by an avalanche of mud according to path finds. Not only that but as she slid, she photographed a galleon and its masts resting on bottom."

"Crazy if no one could get to it for years, especially if it was hard fixed to the bottom."

Lewis swung bucking the ball high into a nice rounder. "Thar she goes."

Jones stepped up to the green, placed his mark, took a swing, sending it to its placement.

"Nice."

They got into the cart and zoomed off to the next green. Lewis's bub had landed in the sand, Jones had evened on the circle. Lewis complained as he swung his steer with a smack of flying sand onto the green, the next rolled the andie. Jones took a mild low placing the stupid game at the edge. They filled out their score cards and began a new shot. As they bounced along in the cart Lewis complained that this section of green was the worst, Jones never having visited Southampton put out a sympathetic field.

They drew up to a land filled lake of hedges and flowering gardenias and plumeria. Lewis found his ball designated by his square resting on a swath of ditch and swung the teddy onto the green, Jones who often laughed at where his marjories landed took a crook swing aiming through a stand of fir trees.

Pushing along the bag they set out for their mile stroll to the next course chatting about the printed estuary. A neat breeze was up fluffing sand onto broad palm plants and mimosa which although sturdy plants wilted in the hot sun.

"It's odd our hull made it past the blue line," Jones reported.

"The shallow narrows are covered with sand. Just look at Florida."

"Yeah, it's straight beach line."

Lewis said, "The problem is not going to be to count the number of holes, it's the various depths it fell into, that's going to be the predominant way we determine external hull. For one it's not all exterior wood on all of the ships that sailed, nor do they all come with dispatch rooms; in order to decide whether she should return to sea fully masted, we need to know roughly how often the ships of its kind require all masts for speed."

"We could put out two."

They chuckled over that one.

"At any rate with modern harbors and number of rocky ports, if she's not likely to sail Gibraltar, there might not be much need for a full masthead," Lewis said.

"There's also the question as to how often she may settle to sea on high seas," Jones added.

"So the concern of plank top is answered, always a best plan."

"The lift ceiling may have to be bid separately. Then, again, there is the inside deck, the chart room, concourse, sail map, gunnery, steam, and knockabout."

They walked up the gliding isle of sand, rock and stream onto a luscious table green. Their balls lay within a few feet of each other, each at cistern pleth. Lewis bent straight over his, gave the putt a bit of encouragement, it dived straight shot. Jones gave it a mild swing, his too went right for the goalie. Jones recorded for both, next they steered round toward the seventh hole and walked back to fetch the cart. By the end of the day, played out and exhausted, the score read in Jones' favor.

Until 1943 there was one other spout off the mid section of the coast of France, after a ship went down in 1403. The capable rudder had failed to steer leaving the underneath wooden sail to turn without completing its direction. After it sank it was thought the spout was the result of the turn tide, a system that drew all points as the ship moved forward over surface.

Jones and Lewis Lewis took dinner out on the patio beneath a deck of palms, multi-colored rocks and waterfalls. The sultry sea breeze came in off the Sound, stirring up the trees, gardens and herbaceous hedges. They had ordered lobster and tri-tip steak and their meal sat barely eaten on the table, their Scotch neat mostly drunk.

Lewis Lewis said, "Here's the smaller of the problems as evidenced by our findings of the points at sea. The Seal Rudder Indicator worked as well as it should, gave the steering a wide berth, the fin with a turbulence reducing structure came along perfectly, and whereas no one should have been put to the creative task of roll stabilization, the sad fact is no ship can take a planar without major damage. That year alone we had major shipping lost at sea due to collision with both another ship and a whale fleet, a ship ran aground and broke apart, one struck an uncharted rock and sank, an engine room caught on fire, a ship beached and was scrapped, and several struck piers. Only ours may have sustained structural failure. Once we take new indicator readings and measure by the statistics you found, we will know whether we have capable rudder steerage problems which I doubt or some semblance of harder in the ballast rolling pin of a centerboard which could then account for additional weight bearing gains."

"I don't think it's that complex. Sails were adequate size, their bearing ropes the needed lengths, no one fell off the mast foreafts nor was there rudder adjustment difficulty, otherwise when the ship reported in we'd have it documented by forward. The device that controlled the sails, the lert, was still attached to its winch."

"The difficulty is not borne out by ice breaker ships possibly due to their double hull, they can rock on giant waves without so much as a roll, but as we both know the Whelen sank while reporting in that despite six men to unfurl her ropes, they were washing across the deck in top speed. Even an ice breaker's single hull gives her more flexibility than our fastest ship, thus the speed has to be accounted for in her demise."

Jones gave the matter some thought, finally rejecting the notion of speed defining any disaster, saying rather impatiently, "Nope, I shouldn't think her eighteen thousand foot length which allows her to travel at five hundred knots could have failed to stop her. Look at the K-219 that sank in the Hatteras, not a damned thing wrong with her roll stabilization."

Lewis took a sip, screwed up his visor expression, flippantly agreed with, "It was all hands on deck, no more complete objective, there was no fault in the finder's direction, it certainly wasn't inoperable, but the reason that half of the ship took the course it did could be due to its direction set course."

They would fly on the early bird, collect the reports and recommendations from the experts and submit a cost prepared report. Jones would not wonder long when if the Wyndam had waited sixty years for restoration how many verifiable crustaceans lay sitting unapproved for even scavenger haul. He thought perhaps the dockyards were filled with analyses by men anxiously awaiting an end resolution to a personal tragedy.

"First thing upon return," he said, "I'm going to hire a vehicle to take me to Hamilton, get a little sightseeing in at the cathedral, Dock plaza and grotto."

Lewis replied, "I have a meeting lined up with the Dockyard with a man who tags whales, he has several reads on whale fleets that read in when the first of that Wyndam group went down."

"That's a good idea, how did it come up?"

"I had the idea while I was studying the capable rudder item, the Exxon Valdez was wrecked by a whale that was so gigantic no one realized it was there, the entire bay all but rose out of the water."

"Yes, I remember. Oceanography began tagging whales with sonar so they'd know where they were and wouldn't run into them," Jones said.

"Right, well, there's all sorts of limitations to the issue, how they respond to light, snow, rain, oil slicks, aside from steerage they run tremendous risks all by themselves. I'd like an inexpensive system which could give a man at a glance how many and in what direction."

"Like blips on a radio."

"Right, something simple. Rhonda often says, keep the wind at sea but the targets where you will find them."

"Rhonda should know. Any possibility she will have to submit our findings?"

"Not this time. The amounts will go straight to administration."

"Sails too?"

"The entire kit and caboodle."

Eventually they digressed to chatting about the last time Lewis came to Tucker's, the beachfront condo he stayed in and the casino he spent his waking hours in, Jones talked about a dinner held in his honor down at Boaz, the cute little telegraph mounted wall piece he was awarded, finally they got down to the messy business of prying apart the lobster, dipping strips of steak in butter, slopping on steak sauce on their rolls, and ordering fine grainy graham cracker crusted meringue cake.

First thing, Jones took in a game of tennis with a complete stranger, a young Panamanian man who told him his girlfriend had flown down to Ireland North Island to get a hurricane forecast. They played a set after which Jones went for a swim and spa, thereafter Jones was inside their suite the bulk of the week designated to cost itemization and manufacturer bids. KONE submitted a bevel on elevators and low speed dumbwaiters, valued at $24K, Weems and Plath on an Atlantic lunar tide cycle clock, with temperature compensated aneroid movement, valued at $8K, Loran gyro-compass with accuracy of indicator of lag error less than one degree, valued at $320K, Sea Source Lens with a zoom video that readjusted image, valued at $11K, Dunmore for a high synchronicity barometer without adjustable slide graph, valued at $16K, Nav Bridge at $2 million and Steelplate Lapier for engines, brackets, steel plates and steam whistles, another ungodly figure of $200K. Even with special improvements, the ship's overall cost was expected to top twenty million. The keel all by itself would wind up costing a half million – it had to be measured, corked, it required side bars for balance, it had to be weighed in for port or starboard, a highly competently administered keel ran upward of ten months on the block. Then it would be to Lewis for the better part of two weeks or greater to put the math for each component, once completed the starboard would have to get rate increased for insurance by an administrator, all ludicrously detailed precise accounting. The resulting statistic book, fully compiled, listed a hundred pages in final form.

An hour after the project closed Jones and Lewis were on a Corcoran flying home to their condominium flats in Nassau.

YUCATAN

The office was a blur of motion, at this time of year in late September the entire staff of thirty-two island Field agents preparing for a new budget year's contract for transportation and isolation monitoring of pharmaceutical and packaged food products. Jones studied the document given him by his supervisor for investigation. During early September Nassau agents had seized a ship that put into a Texas port at the border and redirected it under escort to Yucatan. Once there in chemist controlled warehouses the shipment would be tested taking one to three months maximum before being sent to Cuba for labels. Jones himself would depart for the peninsula as soon as the control agent checked the bills of lading against the product.

Tampering cases were given emergency status necessitating investigation to assure public use safety. He suspected either the product was inferior manufactured by a competitive deregulated outfit or that encased with the actual product there was also a pharmaceutical non leniency for a drug not classed, possibly with false billing arrangements. The document in question was ten pages with generic drug listings specifying product name, color of pill or tablet, insignia of manufacturer, grain, weight and retail cost as well as planned future distribution in Texas. Technically no pharmaceutical shipment was allowed to be shipped direct as resale into Texas or Louisiana, drugs were manufactured in China, Australia and Africa and all followed the same route to Cuba and from Cuba into Florida by way of South Miami, or through Panama to Pacific ports, duty paid on a drug category only if the shipment entered the United States. If these shipments were placed on the incorrect ship they had to be seized and put onto the correct ship, from Florida the product was put on ship vans and sent north, if the shipments were distributed to the gulf states they went by air or cargo, in California they were sent to Vallejo, Fortuna and Tahoe for distribution to county pharmacies. Inside the United States there were three thousand two hundred pharmacies, in Canada approximately one thousand nine hundred and for England three thousand four hundred worldwide.

Tracking illegal distribution of pharmaceuticals was taken up by inland ports with wharfs. Port controls operated for numerous products for which there were fewer than ten inland wharfs in the world – Seattle, Sausalito whose ships docked across the bay at the oil wells, Hampshire, Sydney, Auckland Point, Kingston Jamaica, Port of Aden in Yemen and nineteen piers in Stockholm. Most islands were descriptive to ports without their having wharfs, only docks or piers. Even England had no ocean ports, she had a river through which ships entered. Destined for the eastern coastal cliffs of a newly formed country of deed title, the wharf constructed almost entirely of wood was intended to allow for product shelving to assess for product and food tampering. All wharfs were the property and seizure capability of a navy. Technically island officers could determine for England the use of every port.

The modern day wharf grew from a practice of surrendering malaised victims to offshore small hospitals closest to a wharf usually situated along a river. Up until the late 19th century when post war era wharf control agents undertook to identify a group of savage underwater suspect counter harbor espionage rifle beach agents, the wharf changed its purpose to designate port controls for products. This was to immediately precede a control of a newly adjudicated country known as Industrial York with given precedent map coordinates as 32, 10 all the way south to 41, 15 and on the other side 30, 18 down to 47, 20. A crime committed in the then- wharf trade occurred in late 1940 in what was then a small camping town known as Port Wynn, California, up a northern strait bordered by what is commonly referred to as Sugar town in Hercules up to the only inland port of Vallejo, where at Jointville the tankards deplanked. At the wharf twice a month the Estuary, a bay masthead, refueled after having dispensed medicinals and sponge for seven small hospitals. Here physician officers were rated for readiness to sea, as to two weeks shore duty – for TABs, ENT, chart X ray, swab, and sling, leaving for doctors at wharf hospitals podiatry, chronic, disease, and surgery including OB. Chief of staff would see fifteen patients a day for job fatigue, endurance training, stress usually seen with alcohol and drugs, promotions, transfers – no to schizo, children, marital, truancy.

Jones referenced each product listing to be certain it did not contain too many ingredient names before he would contact the Yucatan storage yard to find out whether the bulk net was matched by inventory description. The inventory listed Film-tab, a hundred thousand chewable tablets, packaged in plastic coated sheets of twelve tablets, two per item; Codeine Sedative, a syrup, in red cherry flavored liquid pints, five thousand bottles in clear plastic bottles; Baby Cough, a syrup, in green, mint flavored liquid in four fluid ounce bottles, five thousand clear plastic bottles; Sleep Easy, ten thousand tablets, packaged in sealant proofed white plastic of forty each, wording missing on the reverse side for registered lot number and expiration date; and forty thousand unidentified peach orange elongated tablets presumed to be a laetrile product usually marketed as Elixir, 1-gram tablets, film coated, apricot flavored, in packages of ten, subsequently replaced by Tryptofan, a dietary supplement, for ease of mood. He looked up categories for usual standard types of drugs that passed through Havana every month into Florida, automatically found that codeine usually came in green liquid and cough medicines in red and yellow liquid; for which he tabbed the description on each page. It was presumed because they were in batches if one random selection tested bad, the entire shipment was bad; chemist analyzers would test any amount to establish ingredients for product identification until they made determinations on use of drug.

Jones requested samples with analyst signatures sent, he consulted a docu¬-proof to determine if the shipment was formerly seized and the products shipped for resale, at his desk he tracked the wharf in San Juan where the ship loaded, all items in accordance with shipping requirements into U.S. He concluded the individual items arrived in net storage-maintained large containers counting twenty-five thousand tablets each, that all warnings were followed, the items protected from strong light, stored at room temperature 59' to 72', an expiration date was printed on container labels accompanying documents, placed inside packaging and sealants applied, that the newly repackaged products carried product identification description, were packaged for shipment, no damage detected. Despite these procedures, the control document did not match the product descriptions, the product names were unapproved, use was not clearly indicated and the shipping order listed the incorrect destination.

The drugs described were determined as indicated –

Filmtab, GERIPLEX, Adult Vitamin-Mineral Formula,
    manufacturer Abbott
Codeine Sedative, A.P.C. with Codeine, each tablet contains aspirin 227
mg, phenacetin 162 mg, caffeine 32 mg. plus codeine phosphate,
    by Burroughs Wellcome, imitated by
GENERICS
Baby Cough, AMBENYL Expectorant, manufactured by Marion
Sleep Easy, QUAALUDE-150, Methaqualone
Unidentified product, AMPHETAMINE, ½ grain, for weight reduction

Five analysts tested random samplings as follows, gently rinsed smear of buffer in distilled water, stained with 1.0 milliliter of filtered elution on the smear for two minutes, scanned the smear for five minutes under high power (30X) magnification, count number of eluted adult ghost cells and calculate number as to drug description. Packaging, tablet is supplied in a product controlled for light, temperature, taste and non broken sealant containing one single dose, patient product control description giving active ingredients, inactive ingredients, indications, adverse reactions, dosage, precautions; or 100 single dose tablets. The unidentified product tablets tested for legal amphetamine, not a street product or methamphetamine. Medication placed in a freezer and examined afterward at a later date not to exceed three days and found to test for same resultants as earlier found.

Identifying the warehouses where the products were originally packaged was for some inexplicable reason difficult to determine where it ought to have been routine. Aside from Aden from which the K-line consisting of hauls and sheds were cleared for cargo forwarding, drug products manufactured in China progressed from Dalian Wharf where the product was classified generically and then shipped into Brisbane Port where products awaiting destination were wrapped and crated. There, the pill quantities sat in large bins on shelves for color dye chemists to appraise random samplings, a process which would take about one week. Despite a frequent shipping schedule for coal from China into Auckland New Zealand and twelve ships per week carrying industrial chemicals, potash, sulfur and wheat into Vigsnes and Callipe, Australia and Greenheart timber piles with a sturdy resistance to termites and decay for making docks into Darling at Sydney Cove, the container shipments for pharmacological product made rounds to Vigsnes, Callipe and Darling before being sent in smaller quantities to numerous ports for consumer packaging in different languages. Sometimes the shipments were lost, sometimes the incorrect brand name sent into a city centre that imported solely generic lines of various types of medicinals. It took the plants in Dalian about five weeks to manufacture two thousand containment crates. It was impossible to lose a shipment that size while it was inside bins containing either raw product or fifty thousand tabs, therefore the only thing that made sense was that the shipment sat at an unknown warehouse for weeks without its bills of lading while other crates were cleared out, before finally being shipped through Yemen onto Corporal, Texas at which the shipment was turned back to undergo final tests for clearance and was sent to deepwater port Vera Cruz to a cargo site in Tulum. Normally the initial pharmacological powder shipments out of Dalian sent to Australia accompanied stone meant for castles and churches at which point goods were separated out to special warehouses, stone subsequently shipped by Hapaag Lloyd to Kirkwall, Aberdeen or Kinsale for export along with marine dredged sand and gravel to predominantly active wharves in Portsmouth, Fareham and Little Hampton to unload soil; the drug listings went to Port Curtis and Cattledown for distribution into northern Europe and Switzerland or to the Puerto Rico ports before entering South Miami Florida. In the event of tropical cyclones, shipments waited for up to a month, setting sail on a dry day.

With the help of his staff point's product analyst supervisor, Jones was able to designate four potential ports that could have signed in the container crates and broken tablets down for inferior use. They were Darling Harbor which had unofficially closed in 2008 to put in parks and a commercial waterfront, which the primary trade was manufacturing crane ships for sand and gravel from Angerstein Wharf of St. Alban's, Darwin Wharf in Sydney into which iron ore ships usually stayed three to four days, Fort Hill Wharf also in Queensland into which the outbound ship destined for Jamaica arrived eighteen times a year, and Port Chalmers Wharf in New Zealand where the Customs House for surveyors of the New Auckland Land Corporation was unusually lax. He pulled documents for each wharf on his sections computer under an assumption the pill shipments came in powder and were shelved up until the last possible date due to understaffing and busy schedules kept by

batchers and toxicologists alike. Somewhere along the line the
buffered powder were stamped with legal aspirin compound
or large doses of amphetamine before being encapsulated and
gel coated; feed for animal slaughter, husbandry and the like
was often mixed with sufficient amounts of tranquilizer or legal
Ritalin. No exposes meant everything technically bore a pre-
approved ingredient and therefore when the lab coats arrived to
the Basins on the last few days of every month the beleaguered
shipments of non refined product passed inspection and were
sent on their way.

The Corporal shipment had been delivered with forty thousand
tons of sand on a ship weighing 14, 760 tons, measuring 161.9
meters long which originated out of Fort Sydney three days
before it would otherwise had it traveled its usual and customary route through Kingston and gone up the Gulf Stream to
South Miami where at the docks it would have been taken on
the Birmingham, Alabama train line bound for the New Orleans to Brenham, Texas or north on a Nashville line or a Cotton Belt to Illinois and into Chicago for standard prescription
before entering Toronto. The minerals and waste core needed
for wharf and rail throughout the southern coastal towns was
received with hundreds of hospital shipments, a typical storage
shed might contain a thousand containers in any given week,
thus increasing a likelihood that illegal product could get in
under someone's tired gaze, especially if the bill had come in
when a thunderstorm was on Sirius and the shipment had to go
to Port Everglades for encoding instructions. Then of course
there were the medicinals for the cruiseships, a hundred and
forty a year. He honed in on the well trafficked Howard Smith
wharves beneath the Story Bridge in Brisbane that made stops
at Fort Hill and Port Chalmers and looked up every dispensary destination trying to determine any weakness in costs that
might suggest an unconventional transaction. Whereas the
usual ocean liner pulled up curbside to any of three wharves
in full camera view of ships with cabins, he kept to the wharf
buildings on the landings that crane operated containers a full

twelve hours a day looking at each shipment and tracking it by camera back to its warehouse and from there back to its bootle and bog. Mini-cams worth of pictures of granite and sandstone, of gravel and sand, of ore, sulfur and dolomite from Tingwall wharf, archeology from Finstown graveyard, sea walls, Broch of Gurness packed slate country fence, stone tunnels, Skara Brae and Clestrain, here and there document proof photo film of boxes stacked on a wharf in the freezing cold of a remote cove, decorated Marischool College with spire tops and delivery vans depositing boxes of pharmaceuticals, each with its own photo series numbering some ten photo files apiece, some with defaults to evidence files, taking a day's time just to verify. In the past he had taken up to two years to track an unauthorized warehouse lab, necessitating matching pictures of any clandestine port building by target area and year to a legitimate operation. As near as he could make out, the building stood in Port Sydney directly beneath the bridge in a plant formerly used by United Aspirin Distributors.

"Usually Miami takes everything," Jones said to Lewis as they reclined on blue lounge bathing chairs at the poolside of their five-tier cruiseship into Havana.

Each man sipped an icy draft ale, as they chatted comfortably about their new assignment in the forested wiles of Tulum, south east of the Boca del Rio. The Kentucky University had recently opened a branch in the archeologically reknown area on natural, shallow water caves, sunken buildings and the Mayan stone jungles of massive stair cutaways into ancient pyramids that dwarfed even the fox trail of trees to the windward side of the ocean. Lewis was the bean counter capable of executing any document for tiny items without error. Jones on the other hand had to prove his case for an intended document infraction. As the remodeled stingy cabin worthy liner did battle with powerful splashing waves, the deck seemed to tilt a bit too much borrowing from the pleasure of the late afternoon.

"Only if the ship docks in upper Miami," Lewis said without his usual need to stand on ceremony. Today was technically his first work day of the week and he hadn't spent much tension yet. "If the documents prove to be false billing arrangements, then technically Jamaica has first dibs unless Havana sent her to another port, which she did."

"The deportation officials are likely to be all over the warehouse."

"They'll close the warehouse with the product if they come out for any reason."

"Three out of four of these tabs began in powder form from the Dalian harbor," Jones said.

"It's a respectable port, so are the manufacturers there," Lewis added. "Who was the first standby?"

"Auckland, two days, responsive port."

"Well, they're either busier than heck or under persistence orders."

"I've been chasing after primary purchasers for art imports into U.S., most from Venezuela."

"You and everyone else," Lewis said. "Who is the physician purchaser here?"

"A Dr. Lastran in Texas, his name used to be tagged to that laetrile scam in the seventies. Now he's up for speed and blow."

"These bone marrow weight clinics are fly-by-day operations. Where's he situated?"

"Galveston on the beach, it's likely he's seen it all."

Lewis asked, "In what quantities does he purchase?"

"By the seventy load yearly."

"That's gigantic. How many clinics does he operate?"

"Ten, each several floors. He makes out nicely to the tune of two hundred thousand a year."

"Probably all prescription for over-the-border illegal trade."

"He has four physicians at each location, it's a lot of mouths to feed." Jones replied.

"Perhaps he also takes in cosmetic surgery, four a month would about do it. Is he going to be hugely affected if his shipments are permanently detained?"

"Hard to know. He abandoned group practice only once before over the laetrile clampdown. He has suppliers in Chicago,

Maryland and Utah also."

"Wonder what he needs with this aggravation then?"
They caught some shuteye before they had to dress and their
paperwork examined at Customs, always an arduous complicated situation, but the official in charge called them a taxi which
arrived in fifteen minutes. They were driven to the calle several
boulevards past the De Los Muertos grave site and past a bevy
of pink apartments with green shutters and fancy wrought iron
balustrades and coveted interior gardens to Rhonda's modern
condominium building, wood paneled stucco home with lots
of windows, balconies and opaque glass entrances. She was up
to her elbows in paperwork obtaining permits to files listed by
Nassau under a research contract, she set them up in separate
rooms which looked out onto grass and the ocean and suggested they amuse themselves at work for an hour while she
prepared to close her files. Toward nightfall she grilled burgers with marinated mango and served them with chutney and
homemade chunky applesauce and sweet yam fries. They ate
inside the dining room watching the news on television, a set
of apple pie frothy rum drinks topped with thick cream, a bis-
cuit and raw sugar on the side. After dinner they watched a
movie, wound up the visit with a stroll on the beach.

Rhonda brought Jones several extra blankets as he was
shaving and getting ready for bed.

"We didn't really have a chance to talk over dinner. How're
things going?" Jones asked her.

"I got a promotion, I handle all island port entries for lading and warehousing. Technically I'm no longer reviewing
Lewis' summaries."

"What does Lewis think about it?"

"He'll gradually accept the fact, why it should matter when
he didn't want me in charge to begin with is baffling."

"These jobs aren't straight forward for what is called for.
He must have relied on you."

"He may have, but there has always been a tug of war with
him, it's not like I could openly make suggestions, with him
he's the bull."

"Who gives him his advance notices these days, do you know?"

She didn't, hadn't given it any thought since Mr. Wonderful walked into her life. Whatever had existed between her and Lewis could be ended without admonishment but Jones wasn't altogether convinced Lewis would take it well.

Jones fell asleep peaceably wondering whether Rhonda ever thought about himself. There had been touch-and-go dinners, a few consolation prizes after Lewis brought a prostitute home; Rhonda had made the right decision to go after a man who knew none of Lewis or the Agency.

Late in the night Jones awoke to the sound of Lewis' and Rhonda's voices wafting on a breeze from the patio.

Lewis was saying, "It's not as if I've asked for much, a few hours of your time when I travel into Cuba. This new friend of yours, just put the romance to bed."

"He respects me, Lewis, he doesn't play around behind my back.

"You've cut me off, I should've had your analyses in on my Bermuda assignment."

"I don't have anything to do with plummeted ships, I'm costs all the way, you know that."

"I need a man who can look at my runners and cost out."

"You should know by now I'm not a man."

Jones listened to as much as he could hear without an objection, Lewis' demands were predictable, in a year or so when the newness of romance had begun a routine, Rhonda would bow out, she would call Lewis up, put him on the chain again, and he'd wind down his sympathetic endurances, take her to the beaches, pay for another studio condo and they'd start over their familiar, somewhat cyclical yet stymied pattern of affection.

The postal flight over the greenery of islands and smooth sapphire ocean took a little under two hours to reach the stone Itzas that stood like prominent triangular temples off the flat green landscape. Inside his briefcase Jones carried the letters of the case that contained correct document microfiche labels that would correspond with actual lading bills to identify the ship's pharmaceutical medicines. The plane put down on the small runway and careened to a stop, inside the terminal they awaited their luggage at one of two carousels, then walked outside and hailed a taxi to the industrial port where they were shown to a two-story hotel. A man from the warehouse section telephoned with a few port-call identification numbers and gave Jones a funny celebrated discussion as to the route the Turkish ship had taken into Corporal, Texas upon where the shipment had been seized, port-authority denied.

Jones and Lewis took lunch at the commissary amidst port officers and border patrol who were in charge of the entire mess. Five warehouses had unloaded all the goods, the border agents had in the past twenty hours read every port bill into their office files by tag onto computers and determined the goods could not be shipped anyways because the actual generic demarcations were as yet unidentified. The chemists had been brought in again, ten per eight hours, in three groupings, working round the clock and were testing by counter each tablet container shipment. After they were finished in two weeks, the pharmacologists would come down to correctly label the batches, correctly stamp authorize any quantity that could be released and request a closure to the plant overseas, wherever it was, to assure standardized controls.

The warehouses constituted a pithy grouping, the building which contained the testing filtration apparatus connected through a corridor on the other side of which were seventy various compartmentalized units of some one or two senior chemists who day to day tested by random sampling any questionable seizure. Had the building undergone several cyclones, its weathered condition could be more readily explained, but the deterioration of the port building owed simply to a fact that a four story, inferior stucco building was outstripped by rain. The two Field agents were shown to a large room inside which packaged drugs had already been examined on a table, injections inserted into numerous sealed tablets and product identification cross matched. The manufacture although quasi-legal was considered substandard.

Jones produced the name list for bufferin ingredients that usually were shipped through the same ports for eventual proof if the tablets were found to be adequate for commercial dispensation. He also supplied the disclosure information for range of docufiable use per description. Thus far, tested tablets for Filmtab did not match to the ingredients determined to be in a multi-vitamin; these tablets were legal methamphetamine combined with starches often used for both weight reduction or tanning. A single sheet of eighteen tablets had tested in for FDA unapproved Nor-estrin, not birth control, for weight reduction prior to pregnancy. This one test by itself negated the entire shipment. As each crate was confirmed, Jones had to verify the chemist findings and the storage labeled products before he was able to reauthorize release into Miami. Verifications would then be mailed ahead to the logotype tray. It would be a good week before Lewis could tabulate number of irregular items.

That evening of their arrival a torrential storm rained complete with a dust-thick cloud cover that billowed across the entire peninsula. They kept to a fireplace at a grill and sipped bourbons into the wee hours of morning conversing with a bartender who was retired from border deportation. A Search and Rescue crew had returned from Cancun where a fishing vessel had barely survived a lashing at sea. The bar turned into a relegated cabin quarters with chatter that drifted from booths at the rear to the jukebox near the entrance. They took in the latest on the ocean climate, loose containers, evidence permanently stored and half dozen complaints on U.S. changes on ocean shipment, designated ports had been changed, Galveston was out as a port, Texas goods had to come in by either ship van or train, Everglades was recently only for passenger disembarking, the reins for border patrol were getting pulled in tight.

By two in the morning, when they returned to their two room, cramped suite and checked their computers, the information transmitted showed two batches approved for Filmtab

Vitamins, docketed as proofed by the manufacturer, by the end of the week these would be cased and sent to another warehouse for a late month shipping. From another building on the outskirts of town, Codeine A.P.C. had been approved for release under the Burroughs Wellcome trademark and was to be encased in plastic sealant only to Chicago for distribution to Texas. The entire staging after a ship was brought to another port to have its entire cargo appraised was as follows: wharf controls were designated by berth house numbers,
postal houses were also given warehouse numbers, by site warehouses were for materials brought to any designated area and were accompanied once a ship had been declared for denial by citation, once a shipment was redesignated it got selectively broken into maximum quantities and forwarded first by ship to areas receiving type of packaging and repackaged at that area and distributed by aero-van to the appropriate city.

Early their second day they were brought to a spired churchlike building where Lewis was sent to the encoding room to match ingredient listings and Jones to the verification office to check on original shipment slips from the wharfs which packed the powdered medicines as pills and tablets. His first task took the better part of a day – he had to match a hundred E-mails with what each manufacturer listed as having shipped from each wharf warehouse. The E-mails marched across the screens of five computers with unmanageable regularity. At least half the product slips had originated from Sydney Wharf adjacent to the five story hospital with the high stone sea wall at Walsh Bay. An asterisk noted recent changes on overseas routing instructions. Changes as of 1998 were: Pencillin was shipped only to army clinics, Ampicillin shipped to city center health or hospital dispensaries, Codeine and any derivative to any clinic, hospital or approved free standing pharmacy, Nembutabs only to hospitals, Debuterol, like dexadrine, to hospitals and some Rite Aids, and vitamins without iron supplements containing dioxin authorized for wide non prescription use. Prescription batch codes were FDA approved to any pharmacy and physician including prescription by triplicate.

Further shipment instructions affected eight U.S.A. port wharf hospitals – Hummels Wharf in Pennsylvania, the hospital network which practiced predominantly rare cancers discovered in children; Davis Wharf in Virginia which specialized in orthopedic and aerospace medicine at hospitals in Newport, Norfolk, Roanoke and Chesapeake for radiology, pathology and hematology and hired a hundred and ten surgeons; Long Wharf in Boston with a naval medical center and specialized in mental health modalities; and four other wharf hospital city centers including Chicago, Salt Lake City, UCLA and Vacaville, California. One other at Battles Wharf, Alabama, on U.S. 98 Alternate route, off Woodland Drive and Battles Road, shrouded in winter in mist on the ocean about Point Clear on the eastern shore of Mobile Bay handled all ship-returning naval and marine petty warrant officers at the garden and gun. Wharves with captain houses on each separate wharf had the sole responsibility of receipt of medicine after which the navy had to distribute to all naval hospitals. A wharf without any building had obligation only to port for automobiles and materials such as concrete, sand and gravel, or sandstone, oil, coal or other such non food. Foods were manufactured domestically except in the Keys, Bahamas, Nassau and Bermuda, these islands were prohibited from commercial kitchens although certain individual hotels had grills. Every island had shipped in food for dispensary utilization.

The complete verification procedure along with noticing the various Australian and New Zealand ports of detained and seized batched authorizations by designation of final destination through wharf hospital centers took a full two days, at the end of which had to follow an alert list of harbors for audit and temporary closure, Darling Harbor in its art deco Victorian housing establishment and bubble busker in a main square on its wharf. Also the west Circular where bridge climbers trekked at Dawes Station and a formerly private wharf at Campbell's Cove which began in 1799 for the British East India Company shipping raw sugar, teas, herbs and medicines; and Pyrmont Old Wharf on Jones Bay and its School of Medicine on John Street, a beautiful Victorian-Italia building and warehouses. Pending citations and authorization of pill packaging, these ports would with beefed up numbers of port officials reopen in the fall.

Original wharf hospitals for the Army in Benicia-Vallejo with four ports, Port Sacramento including billing costs, Port San Diego with allied services in Orange and Yellow counties, and on the east coast in Pennsylvania and Boston, at that time all positioned on the water, primary industrial ports in Chicago on the Great Lakes fed by shipping and train, essential shipyards in the Gulf of Mexico at Corpus, Mobile and Tallahassee, and on the Mississippi River at Orleans, Louisiana, north into Biloxi, Mississippi and Low Water, Tennessee, grain shipments left Chicago to Toronto, prison yards in 1955 in California at Vacaville and San Rafael, Illinois in Detroit, Pennsylvania in Stetley, Maryland in the District, Texas in El Paso, New Mexico at Guadalajara, and Utah in Salt Lake City, and two navy bases in Fort Lauderdale, Florida and in Precidio, San Francisco, California. In the same time in Canada there were three naval ports, one which was now closed, in Port Richard outside Gustavus, Port Tinglet near Victoria Island and Scandia on the Lakes, none which had hospitals; in Australia the main port in Sydney Cove had a hospital, in Africa there were two navy bench wharves, for ship repair, in Aswan, Egypt and at Port Elizabeth on the Cape, and in the Puerto Rico Islands five wharf hospital zones in San Juan, P.R., Havana, Cuba, Freeport, Nassau, South Road, Bermuda and Spanish Cay, Grenadines. Hospitals came with the turf of industry in the event of injury be it train ports on a river, stove manufacturers, usually twelve at least – ale, grain, chili, applesauce, tomato paste, soup barley, et cetera – steel and tin, prisons, industrial shipping, and education, fifteen universities, each different training and job placement.

They took a cab out to the caves and went snorkeling in fresh shallow aquamarine ocean exploring orange, red and pink coral reefs, colorful fish, and underwater tabernacles. By sunset they were rid of the long endless tedium of correcting and counting itemized cost lines and a plethora of untidy details that an illegal shipment conjured up, the least was an aching back and sore calloused fingers. A stroll on the windward downs on the cliffs, a serious discussion as to whether they would put in for retirement in South Cairns, Australia to work at troubleshooting or reside in Battles, Alabama, a fear that past assignments might one day catch up on a windy current out in a skiff, they angled to a small salsa joint for barbequed lamb and corn on the cob, soda pop, and sweetened baked squash. When the ristorante closed promptly at nine, they grabbed their windbreakers and headed along the cobble calles to the main port road past docked ships, warehouse berths and Customs Retention warehouses to their small palacio. Ten-thirty had come and gone when Lewis Lewis fixed their toddies and they sat in comfortable white painted wooden chairs high on a stone piedras plaza overlooking the intense darkness of ocean alit only along the docking bays. In the distance the leafy tops of trees were visible, at the northwestern city sector the large beige columns of a church stood in opposition to slanted slate roofs of two story tan, yellow and faded pink apartment buildings.

Lewis Lewis remarked, "I'll have you know I've received divorce papers. After thirty-two years I can't comprehend why she wants to separate now."

"Maybe her beau has popped the question."

"I asked, he didn't. It's this new promotion."

"Must be quite a bit more money."

"She'll end up depressed."

"Perhaps she's been offered a relocation to the Mainland," Jones suggested.

"She said in confidence that she plans to run the San Juan part of the agency."

Then Lewis could be at war, Jones surmised; instead he said, "That's a gigantic promotion for any evaluative risk budget analyst. Why not put in for advancement yourself, apply for a wharf network of ports, they'd give you a post."

"Wharf medicine's not for me, I'm an analyst, my work will always be behind a desk. I've thought this through and I've decided not to sign."

"What if she hires counsel?"

Lewis shrugged. "Technically if you agree to a separated status for thirty-one years, if the party at sea refuses, the wife usually won't obtain. That is sea faring law."

"I don't think that is a polite course to assume."

"She's my wife."

They remained there, drinking in peaceable quiet, Jones contemplating the messy divorces of friends who had divorced over job complications, usually office affairs. Here Lewis had an unconcealed reality to ditch all the uncertainties his marriage and legal separation had posed all this time, and he didn't want it? He wasn't the capable Lewis that Jones thought he knew for forty-four years.

After an interminable lack of conversation, Lewis said, less to Jones than to some internal piece of himself, "I've always given her half of everything I'd thought to give myself, other men, parties, jealousy, her own place, all without a legal return. Who will be there to warm up to when this other guy has to travel?"

The morning arrived in a summation of cloudburst which extended across the sky in a density of rapidly collecting drizzle. Adhering to it, forcing a churning gale that spilled out drops, a periodic downpour gave the soil a good drenching that within a half hour had dissipated leaving not a trace. Lewis Lewis had lost his acrimonious mood having risen upon the first peal of thunder to prepare a pot of coffee, opened the windows and taken a phone call on his computer from the port to stand by for further orders; now that testing and counts were completed, and all the confirmations received and tabulated, the office was tracking down patient prescription use for the previous nine months, a task that could only be done by the wharf products manager in Vera Cruz County.

Jones had awakened to the presence of wind and gone to discover what was going on. He found the windows stern wide, wind escaping the rain, in the kitchen sat Lewis who had chopped off his hair to a fuzz, dressed in fatigues he looked the part of a deeply weathered man who did not find his encounter on any narrow ridge in time for a depression which in a fortnight kicked in his gut.

"Stayed up late?" Jones asked, pouring a cup of coffee, taking it to the table, lit a cigarette.

"Gave it my best to determine realistically why the shipper tried to move goods direct without pre-ship authorization."

"Could be a laetrile dose question again for a physician with many port affiliations," Jones replied.

Lewis said, giving up his discernment of the incident, "It isn't that these drugs in any dose amount can be deciphered under a treatment of such as weight reduction for estrogen regrouping. Thus the lack of frequency of an illegal precursor suggests unavailability in quantity."

"If this is considered the idea of shipment, question is has he pre-ordered from every possible link for brand name or generic?"

"That's easy, if it contains no-ephrine, the drug name gets sent right through."

"For these folks to say even generic base drugs can't go through anymore suggests too much drug has already entered the mainland."

"Could be it was an essential to the drug that it was trimmed and cut back, if too much drug is already entered the country it stands to reason he doesn't go to another distributor because he's exhausted those avenues."

Jones sipped his coffee and stared at the rain pounding the slate. "It's hard to say who this physician is trying to put himself out as, whereas for a base this might be customary practice."

"We are no longer living in the same day and era, even if he has to supply new centers that used to be exclusively navy, then there are standards and he's not navy enough."

"Even base physicians are audited, the issue must be quantity that contradicts usual standards."

"It might be under a year's supply anyhow."

"What was going on with him prior to laetrile?"

"He's the same physician who had the problem on the east coast in the early Sixties with the hilly hill that descended down onto his clinic in Jazz Town, North Carolina. Authorities traced his problem to an excavation that caused such a number of beetles the houses swayed, those tiny monstrosity sang for an instant, but if not for the calamity of bugs to keep one afloat, those who were swept downriver could have lost their lives, not just their clinics."

"Poor guy, no sense in his supplying all these places unless he's continued as physician of record."

"His primary nurse stayed on through reconstruction, she was driving to the hospital when the hill came down, apparently the river washed in in a few minutes, sank everything but his clinic. Boats, lerts still attached to their winch, barges, sea walls, jettys, cargo, grain elevators, ramps, conveyor belts, all to breakwaters, a van in back of the library was under water in a second. "

"I would've thought their squadrons would have dealt with that, Douglas Field at Charlotte or Pope at Fayette."

"They probably did, I wouldn't know. Apparently this Dr. Lastran lost a captain's house in that flood."

"Was it situated on the coast or on a river?"

"On the coast, I would think."

"That could be more or less the barnacle, if he warehoused a full supply for his practice, was his captain's house at the end of a wharf for shipping or on land as a clinic?"

"Good question, I assumed it was on land."

"It could've been for shipping, a disembark plan."

Jones asked, "Would that make a difference in light of this situation?"

"It could justify the pains border has had to deal with, it would mean he has always had access to quasi-legal shipments that enter to an otherwise legitimate port. It's just remotely possible he goes to Battle if he can, when he can't he arranges for other facilities to justify the import cost."

"It had a slight cove with a wharf, convenience of unloading, there was a state building that was put underwater as well, the clinic was several blocks away, a library between them, some warehousing, a ship carrying 3539 blew up alongside the wharf and loading house, those flooded a few feet, the town went under, it's understood someone made a quick getaway."

"I seem to recollect a ship blew, no doubt it came from unfriendly waters bringing with it numerous malcontents," Lewis remarked, and finished his first cup of coffee. "It seems that in a restricted area there were two houses on a summit recording weather conditions and a group of ambitious mountain climbers came upon them and moved in, four females in one, three young men in the other, someone planted lightning trees such as what is in the Arizona desert to prevent a strike to the houses, all sorts of people went up there to cut them down when it was discovered that in horror the new inhabitants buried the weather-calculating machines causing the early formation of a volcano by lightning."

"It must be the inhabitants left and entered the North Carolina port to find the people who discovered them."

"Agreed," Lewis concluded.

The day proceeded slowly, reading three newspapers, checking data ports for the video library on a handful of new shipments, ten cups of coffee to pass the time as they waited for word, an English afternoon tea on a pond with gardens on an island, a few hours at a men's swim club with beach towels and chairs, before they returned ready for a late nap, as yet no word from the chemist or controller.

They were awakened at seven-forty and told the interdomestic handling authorities had adjourned. After extensive back and forth inquiries the port officials in Walsh Bay had asked that all triplicate prescriptions be handled out of Hummels Wharf in Pennsylvania and all expectorant for children under age 8 be limited through local pharmacy purchase from domestic suppliers. The drug Methaqualone was permitted for reduction primarily, it was also approved for use to bring under control hyper-anxiety, an inverted pharmacology control for limited periods. Walsh Bay was restricting from further shipping of medicine only at Darling Harbor, Dawes Station, Campbell's Wharf and plaza and Pyrmont Old Wharf. Orders were thorough probably to accommodate an undeniable historical pre-emptive that physician had come up for scrutiny in at least one medical crime, his circumstances defaulted as to complications of location, Lastran had over time become a falling star, no one but Hill investigators knew what any of it meant, especially if he had kept carbon monoxide on his premises, were he involved, he was up a creek, the worst of all questions being that he had begun medicine with Aqualone for tympanic tests, the noteworthy commentary arising long after the flood, a mere question that he had an apparatus that could have caused a tidal barrier to acquire water, although there was no evidence he was involved, did an unknown assailant gain entry to his captain's house or another nearby facility. The suppressed discovery was that all parties interested in the weather-lit houses were incapable of hearing according to normal scoring ranges and at least a couple sought treatment in Bridgewater, the nurse who could have testified when the female left the hospital transferred out of the state, a bell synchronizer that helped ships saddle into port to the wharf having dislodged and presumably carried away by force of tide, a chip, two reversing insulated wires, both attached through the synchronizer to the call port, a series of grid like metal attached to a spool, the device used to signal to a ship, spill water lime used for attaching needed wires to a ceiling to keep life-saving machines operative during a flood in a basement unit. For the inferences that had arisen since that unholy era, added by the laetrile-bile accusations, any peculiar request was looked upon with unusual caution, thus the port staff had been ordered to retest batch items for temperature inside packaging, use in the human body, and date expiration controls; they had to group the drugs under corrective name brands, analyze for capacity to be stored and packaging evaluated or recommended, before tab crates would be shipped for labeling in Cuba and a re-examination of accurate tabs for affixed label.

Jones and Lewis were shown to a large warehouse where

they then had to recount the newly repackaged tablets and bottles of expectorant per table and list by brand name the number
per sheet. Jones counted out loud, Lewis' quick computer skills
gave the total medicine content, despite this they switched
tasks every hour. They worked as a team, counting each table
for batch totals of three thousand tablets per box, ten boxes
per crate, a total of four hours to count one shipment; then
onto the bottles, one-half fluid ounce, repoured, twenty-five
per cardboard box, a hundred boxes, two hours to verify the
Ambeynl for readiness to ship; a total of nine hours to verify all
tables including the 150 and amphetamine. At four-thirty they
stopped and returned to their hotel, a return flight to Nassau
already booked for noon.

They caught five hours sleep, awakened around ten to write
summaries, submit reports through their totem bylines, and
order in scrambled eggs, hash browns, toast and jam, and coffee. A hasty retreat to the outlying airport gave them no time
to read the mid run newspaper or buy a martini. Lewis sipped
coffee on the airplane, worry had become part of pain, the days
were too long, the years too short; Jones relaxed in an opposite
aisle flirting with an aging short top brown haired, archeology
student from Cancun in a tight fitting polyester, khakis, and
Whole Earth sandals imported from Italy, his sole objective to
put as much distance on the tedium of the past week, maybe
burn up a bit of frustrated energy, if luck would have it, a date
for the evening.

MONTSERRAT

A low berth ship was docked inside a large covered dock, huge wooden crates lifted onto cement flooring and hauled during the night, absent of light inside rooms meant for legal warehousing of art. Jones took one glance inside several crates at the encased metal art of some four thousand original paintings, all canvas, not cloth or wood, all backed, the metal slips were used for sliding canvases in between, during winter months of rain color appeared tainted onto metal. On sticker label first name, immediately below appeared the rest of the name; no art was permitted in the islands, usually shipped direct by plane from origination to large city as office document under P-09, once on display a full screen and zoom were formed for printed watermark, windows made for splits. The essential task was to remake paintings once they were placed in a monastery museum basement of working art, each artist set had been shipped with paints stirred to eliminate white, artists would be required to reproduce originals of each painting before shipping on – at some time all paintings had sat in water, most up to a third of each painting, several up to a half,

others had already been reproduced; the only objective for reproductions was to find the originals, they would have to send
through customs a photo on disk to determine state of originals, some were sent to conventions, others archived, yet others
personal collections, all had printed documents that declared,
if those were gone one had to create files based upon countries, sometimes cities, where paints were made, requiring five
artists who were capable of recognizing origination of color,
conservative storage of categories of elastic binding for canvas
on anything such as impact, aria black and papyrus, none were
in frames even when the paintings hung. The Belgiums didn't
produce color, the following countries created paints, England,
Norway, Poland, Romania, India, Afghanistan, Tibet, Venezuela, Sweden, Greece, Vietnam, Russia, Australia, Canada,
and Africa continent; Africa made only crèmes, Afghanistan
predominantly shadow, Romania and Australia mostly red,
Poland white, India, mostly light yellow and orange yellow
and Vietnam, usually pigment based, darker yellow, Sweden
green, England blue, Romania ochre, Russia pink, an only non
white base that existed and accounted for twenty percent of her
income, all paints combined in Vietnam, Venezuela, Afghanistan, interior vats were made of non injurious glass, vat workers
could handle it all day, paintings handled with white paper,
10 weight, produced solely for this purpose. If artists thought
paintings were incorrectly mixed – would be only in Africa
– then painters could never be publicly recognized, had to be
painted with approved mixer paint, could never combine food
in producing paint such as coconut, papaya, crushed pome-
granate, ground nuts which often appeared on canvas, imple-
ments had to be ground up soil from the earth and could not be
an non restorative product such as brick, sodalite, or tapir, and
was required to match ratings established for control properties
by each country that manufactured paint, investigation was entered into acceptance by The Harmful Product Association for
the reason that non soil derivatives were used in latex. During
testing painting had to stay the same, it could not run or be affected, only blue, made with anti-resin, did not allow any other

colors use to run and was manufactured in all colors.

It was presumed when anchor docked prior to unloading there was water seepage, the shipper would end up paying millions of dollars, unless it could be proven water damage occurred at any time earlier. A quick finder searcher database allowed him to access documents regarding shippers which had sent the various paintings, there were the maximum allowed four – Sweden Covinger, Lusitan out of Norway, Daiger from Poland and Graffert from Romania, all but one had insured originals created under correct conditions, no heat, no unnatural light or stainless steel sudsing of brush. The one Lusitan had authorized three reproductions of originals which were also in evidence listed under an artist no longer thought to be alive, Jones who was assigned to research the majority of tasks so that Lewis' handling would not be priced by the insurers pulled a tabular capable of rendering him all original photographic proofs listed by author, date released, finding number or catalogue, this produced 4,218 listings suggesting collaboration and legal reproductions, he would have to decide if any artist's work was imitated under copying to deny them or why wasn't bulk of order released upon artist's death; if painting was created and dated prior or during commission of a crime it could never be released such as Pecano at the bombing of the Damme in Norway out on a far west peninsula within visible access to the smothering snows of the Norwegian twilight.

Dye solution that tested for red, yellow, orange, blue, green and under rare and unusual circumstances for gesso or pigment base determined mixture combinations at Montserrat, a small orthodoxy island tucked against tubular rocks of decided natural stone which could be powdered to form color base, damaged paintings were brought to air secure rooms within the teaching monastery there, architecturally resin-warp-free wood and white stone, red tile roofs, ochre fresco treated walls, a conundrum of buildings combined with flat stone patios and walkways, deplete of choir, master priest sanctums, a reveled city apart from corporation and university, open air passages that looked onto snow sprinkled heights in winter, a visage of stone cut stairways, the cloisters filled with thirty-two world reknown artists whose talent commingled with the worst habitual worries, incessant smoking, spilled wine, showers filled with emergence of wondrous art dripped by water, week old food before the maids were permitted entry, pots of fish ladle brimming with steam, cold wet cloths thrown onto sinisterly varnished work tainted by exposure to too much artificial light, the age of discoloration having long since faded all worthy brilliance, clandestine quarters for sketch and paint alike whose artists had stepped over a threshold of industrial cluttered living into utter peace for as lengthy a period that was necessary to restore fine art, all arsenic-based painted canvases shipped north to snow glazed cavernous tunnels far under ice to await conviction of scheduled infiltrations of momentary light to shine, glow, dazzle, capably ensconce, dapple or otherwise mesmerize the long muted colorful paint, awakening on the canvas at it were some godlike, formerly imperceptible strands which might be felt to stalk a new observant student of the arts in an airy chamber of a historic museo. Those paintings that slept in those entombed rooms with gigantic ice buds crystallizing at their entrances were carefully wrapped within celluloid, already stained and processed for white, shiny packaging which retained color against becoming bleached, the stark blues succeeding where red and orange sometimes had been found to mute, electric heat maintaining rooms at a mild 70 degrees that safe guarded against possible unpreventative damp and mildew at a slightly lesser, recommended 68 degrees for moderate climate storage, whenever the rooms began to decline in baseline warmth, a telephone rang, and a meter restored to its slightly elevated warmth, these measures were particularly essential for originals which almost always didn't use white color and had black painted canvases onto which other color was painted, especially Jack Venttriano's Dancing on the Beach with two butlers holding opened umbrellas to shield against the sun above a female and her partner, she dressed in a tight fitting upper body, floor length red dress and heels, the artist's typical use of blue never accentuated instead of his use of pigment as a color; or Stan Johnson's Albany Hill of bluff like trees on an inlet isle of sand on a yellow marsh, the sky blazoningly eclectic yet his choice of palate was often pastel violet rather than a deceivingly apparent pastel pink.

The problem with numerous artists was that they entered for them foreign countries under American names coming to the new address after they gained fame, making them border traffic problems, once they were determined by Immigration and Portage to enter using an alias they were prescripted to Haiti and Barbados to live under their god-given name producing their art for twenty-seven years, then they would go public under their correct name, Scandinavian born, Barbados legal resident after twenty-two years Leif Nilsson's famous portrayal of boat scene in a canal, seemingly a partial in vivid blue, green and yellow – his ten paintings had been water damaged oddly below the painted reflection in water; and often presumed to have lived in Bermudas but was factually a Bohemian from Jamaica transplanted to Romania at five, Angelina George, her eight 40 x 40 pictures of tan and crimson rock strata landscape had incomprehensibly survived unscathed; not so fortunate Jill David's two paintings of Cactus, linseed oil created for light green and blue, a noteworthy compassionist from Finland whose very first full exhibit brought her the mentionable worth of clairvoyant, Bob Dorsey's four paintings of sparse towns with a single perspective blue road through snow all the route to muted pink grey trees, three houses tossed about, had succumbed with no visible distortion, his paintings alone verified the length of three hours all paintings had stayed submerged.

If the protective valves opened sometime during a long voyage, any release of natural sealant should have been substantial to ward off against much damaging discoloration, Lucas Hill whose five paintings had miraculously withstood any taint, all flowers in bowls painted on silk, a German artist of considerable finding who learned his pliable trade in Russia, would have felt crushed to depths of his soul had a single silk even become torn; Bob Patterson, British scenic color abstractionist with a one image color blue on dark linograph had miserably between pauper and sensationist rendered an entire work to spotting as a result of loss due to water; then again Randy Wellborn, originally Welsh who took up a noteworthy canvas trial of studied climates while living on the Guadalcanal, his red red brick and Olds on a wet street titled Gay Line Teatro took a splash over the awning leaving the yellow lights permanently smeared, even with damage his two paintings could readily earn as much as five times the $150,000 chart price; Irish-raised Jeane MacKenzie, a favorite on the New York billboard scene, three white birch trees in grass of softly muted appearance would be sent to cloisters first light of morning. Evangela La Pune, Greek or Mediterranean, the listing preferred sale bill surmised by a handful of sales under a slightly changed honest name, whose Paris café scenes seemed etched with dabs of old Roman color, tarnished seed yellow, charcoal mixed red awning, darkish blue consignor building on background horizon, snow evident on sidewalk, could have authorized release yet never did, and hers also would accompany the skinny birch society in tall grass.

The restorers could take as long as a year to paint any number of size, authority and qualifier of the giant reputations, Renoir, Thornton Jones, and twenty-eight paintings of mother and child by Vermeer, Cassatt, Ruebens and Titian, the last best approved for sale as Marcos, his in notice were deceased estates, cultural gifts or conservation. Although Renoir's sole three paintings, created around 1703, of a mother in black with a low petticoat seated on a divan with two fair haired girls dressed in striped blue dresses and large black and white Asia mutt, in one painting there was no dog; only no dog survived without incident, rumored to have been attached to board and post-wire. Cezanne, pool and house and reflection of house, marble gate, flowers and trees, painted in heavy pastels was an obvious reproduction since it had been often researched that his works never had water, on close scrutiny palm leaves were gashes of black, brown and green, the sky blue grey with a white tinge, actually yellow, close looks usually gave no indication of separation of color; Ellen K.'s work – all eighty paintings in method blue watercolor of an antennae forest on water set against coastal mountains had been thrashed unforgivably the worst. It was the nature of oil to survive indeed far better than water but in situations of ruin oil went deplorably also. The one dim painting obviously affected by a thin veil of marijuana smoke of a Henry Raeburn of a pessimist male in a chair, condensed green, mixed gray, his featured art usually black trousers, seldom rouge, where red appeared it was dismally protracted would be reproduced by a smoker whose penchant was neither resin-stain nor marijuana but red wine, Raeburn himself palatially imbibed; Ken Bushe's Millpond, accentuated in blue and gold, had taken a cloud of water to its landscape thus falsely showing two ponds, H.A. Emini's radiant abstract in blue, tan and pink, slotted sideways had transgressed of half its paint; loose and flaking Janis Miglavs' orchard, fences and yellow squares of saturated dense fields, paintings neither representative of her Hungarian husband's homeland or of her Austrian mother's fascination with southern France; Ramin Rahimian, a desultory archivist who painted blood shot sunsets on icy lakes, technically Norwegian but found in Iran, and usually paired with painting scenes of underwater roots in mud slime by Adam Barker, the only Seventh Day Adventist to paint for another country outside Germany, both men lost over a fortress-showing of some hundred originals in Scotland to menacing mould.

A retirement predisposed Lewis Lewis had appraised art in the Puerto Rico Islands over twenty years whenever a shipment arrived, which was seldom. He could accurately define age, collaboration based often on preference of gesso paint and brush stroke, amount of sunlight inside a studio when a painting was made, culture and adaptation, all in three sentences of description placed on the backside of the work. Despite the fact that each work would have to be seen by a document of arts examiner for authenticity before it was brought usually by van to a restorer residing in the monastery, Lewis had a second task to perform to test for type of paint prior to the restoring priest applying it. To do this, Lewis went through an arduous comparison for color with original colors on a text base computer. Over the years he had mixed each paint with turpentine in a vat to wash the color letting it settle prior to pouring it into a funnel into half gallon glass wine bottles sipping the recorded amount of wine equivalent to the amount of paint needed to produce the exact match of tinniness the artist had used, Windsor blue, dense blue added to heavily diluted dense gray gave him a similarity for an Ellen K.; repeated wash outs of oil of Indian yellow applied to an already soaked paper mixed with dilutions of Indian red took him into the approximate range of a Randy Wellborn, his heavy paints for the rain wet asphalt street were easier to simulate than barely visible pastel or mixed, his mixtures took forever to precisely define percent, Barker's mud, so convincingly intrinsic, required black, permanent rose, raw sienna, cadmium yellow, a touch of yellow ochre. The ephemeral transitory quality of MacKenzie, her green grass nothing substantially green when he figured out her mixture of cadmium yellow, cerulean blue with a smarting welt of permanent green required of him fourteen hours of dry white wine.

For Vermeer, Ruebens and Renoir paintings having to get shipped to an ice field, every knowable feature had to be given so a painting could age, if restorers used different colors for aging, it depended what the colors were, whether figures were outlined or embossed, stylized by varnish, held inside plastic or cans in a freezer or beneath a house in a cellar, Ruebens enjoys a lacquered look but this style is accomplished by him by under painting what is ultimately black as brown or deep rudd, colors which in time lose quality of tint upon distance of perspective, requiring the effect of age to be softened. For a Renoir the guess was reproduction restorers dabbled because those paints no longer were used and a portion of color was greatly varied by direct sunlight accounting for hard color variations, by distilled paint combining mixture and oil, and on occasion adding features in order to replace tears; because Renior had used magenta and ochre for brown, base cerulean with tarnished red for rosette, Emerald Kelly with Sorrowful tan for blended green, and lacquered crimson and beleaguered beige for soft orange, his mixtures were considered too variegated to reproduce in a modern era. Although Lewis would not be able to obtain exact blends, he had experimented with unusual colors to derive closely matching colors which when aged were similar – Laurentan crimson with Finite red, Davenport light green mixed barely with Indistinguishable gray that came out blackish, soft Raspberry with orange Tangerine, the Brazilian off beat blends less responsive to making traditional colors by virtue of being combined with rich dark blue paste.

La Pune was rumored to have mixed base with a blend of plaster rendering her snow a thin film of white. For Lewis the prescribed combination required numerous wash outs taking well into two hours until the color spread almost as transparent.

The dubious effects of spending thirty hours straight without sleep measuring and stirring paints and comparing them to their alleged composition on the damaged art had left Lewis incapable of concentration, for which he slept in a restless non resonant dreamless weariness. Palpable exhaustion gave him no further assessment when he awakened, echoes of wind cast about in unending dogged pursuit, a tumult through halls banging half closed doors, insinuating against the walls and floorboards. He sipped a glass of day old coffee and took a cold shower, threw on a garden smock and trousers and went looking for the brethren who would by now have begun the painstaking task of restoration of landscapes, stills, and abstracts. The deserted campus of Montserrat, not in the least imposed upon by a range of tube spires of odd rock formation, struck him as long enduring, a promise that the magnificence of Time would invariably arrange the indefatigueable goals of Men, harnessing their inabilities to overcome that which had to be made sense of, a mildly rewarding relief that he would soon fly home done with the capitulations of the human creative experience put to rest. As he rode the elevator to the rooms of working art in the underground basement, he perceived a sting of resentment at having had to hand hold one of Jones' cases, not withstanding that there were at least two other appraisers, each younger, he decided that the agency had wrapped him about Jones, as if out of a symbiosis, a practicality seemingly borne of a helpless sentiment that two good friends who fit well together should be tossed in round the globe, a hapless stead that left scarcely room to step beyond the limitations of living in the islands, a shut-in sort of existence with few openings, a repetition of reviewing Jones' reports to identify the information he himself required. When he stepped into the corridor Lewis was at once aware he was inside a windowless chamber, to which he refused to capitulate, and although it winded through restrictive space much like a square walled tunnel, he felt the unadministered pressure of hurry as though the artists, however many there were, had to focus intently on a scarcely obtainable task. After walking through a dismal three sets of corridors, entering inside a large elongated room with small windows to foot traffic along a garden walk, fully aware he had dismissed any idea of restoring originals, he found three artists gleaning the washed over canvases with restoring equipment capable of drying the distressed imagery to a varnished dark brown surface that might allow repainting that would bring any of the originals to purchase-worthy status. Through a tint covered door window at the far northern end of the room a metallurgist using similar equipment emitted a volume of light sparks like a shower of welded sparks.

"How many plaster moulds did we bring in?" Lewis asked Brother DiCirn.

Gondezio DiCirn was in his late seventies, a priest who had been imprisoned at a Marque Di Sjad hospital for the damned during the occupation of southern Pi'lot in the advance of a ship crew having fled Normandy to seek any shelter they might find; a dark bluish man of stature whose avid capability had been trained as a result of having lived in a small island prison called Papillion on Montclaric with a handful of statuary artists who painted on marble surfaces. "Sixty, all told. The majority are marble encased and ought not to take more than a day to break; once broken we will restore a painted likeness to any painting by either a Dutch or Scandinavian painter. That we feel will remove all engine oil leakage because they had to be kept warm while in transport. There would have been oil leakage eventually, the ship was older."

Lewis took a green glass filled to the brim with tea, the floating leaves forming a nutmeg surface, lit a cigarette and enjoyed a mint pistachio flavor. "Will your sparker attempt to preserve oil smudges on any Rouselette? Those works have long been praised for their sienna."

"We won't know straight away. It could depend on how encrusted the moulds became."

"Are you attempting an orange sienna look?"

"Probably more toward greenish, they apparently found suds in the oil."

"Those rate higher."

"Yes, they do, a fetching cast of Peter may net this small group a tidy five thousand half notes and that won't be all; we will be listed as restorers."

"Is that usually how it goes for greenish?"

"Green and bluish, it's not up to us to determine outcome, it entirely relies on what tincture winds up as a fixative. Turpenoid on marble has been said to leave a black gold residual which prices art very high, the highest being red or crimson because the color suggests blood, even blood itself does not stain. So, when do you leave us?"

Lewis replied, "When the art is shipped out."

"That could be in a few weeks. What will you do with yourself? No visitor carries Time to advantage well here, there's literally nothing to amuse oneself at."

He took a long thoughtful smoke, issuing out a stream of wispy breath. "I expect to read some of your Latin, take a stroll about, write a letter or more before I am required to make a final rate qualifier as to improvements and loss adjustment."

"You'll take meals with us, we discuss the world's affairs, perhaps you will leave this century for a sip of Barcelona sherry."

"Certainly, look forward to it. Have you gone to other islands?"

"We are permitted storage on altitudinal formations in the Virgins where we have all of ten sites, but they are for wood backed 50 x 100 canvases and then they receive no daylight. We travel there by air which naturally shows us the greenery of unmarked coastlines, that, you know, feeds the mind with peace."

"Could one of you take me?"

"If we require storing. Rules are highly restrictive."

"Great, that would be a restive point in all this."

Jones had gone in search of Lewis, after climbing a hill above the narrow city, the strong current at his back, he sat to have lunch from a lunchbox put aside for him and admire the steep incline of surrounding hills, the collection of red roof tops in the center. He would have liked to confer on Lewis his somewhat conflicted findings that certain art had managed to have magazine tear sheets adhered to the surface for a rather unusual collage. Because he had handled over two hundred canvases dusting for arsenic treated sealant and for dust itself, his fingers felt metallic in the upper joints causing him to retreat for exercise. The brothers who did little more than paint a handful of hours each morning complained of numb index finger tips, metal splint fingers, stiff shoulders, no rumatoid, even the ankles felt as though bandaged. It would take numerous salt baths to feel as he should, but he had a thousand paintings to evaluate before the end of the week, a tendency to sit perfectly upright sipping brewed wine all day seemed to be a preferred resolution for most of the fifty resident priests. Unwrapping a sandwich he picked out the honey suckle flowers from the chopped avocado and papaya and took a bite, savoring the sweet unobserved presence of pickle and spicy curry mustard. He ate like a man contented by a simple meal, momentarily sampling coconut cookie drops in a package, a few sips from a small carafe of sweet red wine.

The age of the eighty buildings that made up the campus city looked to be about fifty years, similar to any white colored structure found in Lisbon, they were from his distance powdered by a granulation of chalk, a well established cultivation of two and three stories of priest quarters, instruction and preservation classrooms, windows were long and narrow, several roofs opened from gabled balconies, the entire impression was of cloistered containment enjoined by dispassionate surroundings, not a tree evident, the rough wooded hills below the city gave no sense of aestheticism along a dusty road that gave four miles to a tiny landing strip and average size harbor where at most one ship anchored. Even though he was certain life for the aged priest conformed to periodic sexual pleasure if not occasional partaking of cocaine and marijuana hash, he had to acknowledge all security was more than adequately monitored, each authorized task labored to without exception, all duties husbanded as to documents, verifications by watermark insignia, not without mention any technology capable of declaring an honest proven artistic hand, Customs instated for all, detection of black market trade revealed down to stains of crushed cranberries or powder blue laboratory testing to commiserate intention to package drugs or small transistor devices within backing of art. If not for an aircraft landing, he knew of no means for smuggling into and off this island, certainly not for art that was carefully encased within tubing that contained water infused by short amounts of dye which when broken, if the enclosed painting contained any irregularity such as a micro technological computer resistor or a type of restorative if when placed over museum entry glass, whether undetected, could never-the-less produce a vapor to release an alarm prematurely, the original work became entirely tainted by pink surface dye. When Jones had eaten his entire lunchbox meal leaving but half the container of hot wine, satisfied he had supped at the hand of a master chef, he denounced what remained of his clear thinking by enjoying a found marijuana cigarette with his drink. The sudden exultation of unreasonable relaxation derived a stunning sense of indecency, claimed probably by not any member of the Order, but instead by a profound idea that the most talented modern art had been touched by him, he thought of the young female in the kitchen, her agile hands for some unexplained reason unaffected by the miserable failings of the body of the priests, a pretty smile, long red hair to her waist, if not for an idea of her he knew he had fallen inescapably for Rhonda who, while she had clearly left her former male tryst of a year's duration, had continued to put him off over any notion of marital status. Not yet Lewis' newest fashionable desire allowed any permanent refraction from Rhonda, Lewis' stunningly enticing beauty was never as tender to him as Rhonda remained, drawn perhaps through an unsatisfied instinct to be intuitively adored, his only love in his heart, he realized he had surrendered through his conscious portal for desire to affectionate encounters, a newer thirst to be touched and thus known as intimacy-fulfilled. He had cause to find himself concerned over the now released identity of the first man who Lewis led to Rhonda some fifteen years ago, a man well known to the agency, a senior agent roughly the same seventy years as Lewis himself, the man the agency sent into Baja Canal just prior to shipping him for a reconnaissance over Guinea when war broke out in Tahiti, a male of fine snobbery, elegant, handsome in a classical way in that he had retained his looks, tall, warm blond haired, somewhat longer shag, flirty with the secretaries, rumored to have spent a night in a conference room on the carpet with two females. Jones surmised he was the individual who gave Lewis his pass-key to sex with more than one other female while also seducing his wife, fifteen years ago Border asked for support in busting its cocaine wars in Florida and the agency sent over half the office, he recollected Lewis' depressed acknowledgements over that assignment, his early separation, sending Rhonda to Cuba where only Lewis in those days had authority to enter, his own sense that Lewis and Rhonda were greatly in love, wanting a vacation rental, without any real notion as to the complex emotions lying just below the surface. Hoyt Descartes had conjured Lewis to get to Rhonda, if that was what happened, somewhere in a sequence of short affairs a seduction had been offed and Jones didn't think Lewis had any idea of it, but maybe he had after all, maybe he finally compromised on a hope that Rhonda was bored but not capable of leaving or perhaps it was Lewis who was finally sick of his marriage and had no good replacement and so he drifted emotionally, occasionally very interested again only to feel a familiar tedium a few years later, or the agency asked Lewis to ditch the other agent and Lewis chose instead to foible him. If Rhonda had the first affair, it was possible Lewis wanted her to pay forever; whether Lewis managed his divorce well or badly, it could be he expected Jones to concede to a refusal, especially since Lewis still considered Rhonda his personal wife. Anger motivated Lewis, occasional resentment which had made absolutely no sense at all seemed to derive out of thin air aimed toward any prospective admirer, whether invited or not.

The details of the tasks of abating damage had worn Jones to the mettle, dinner had come and gone with a constant flow of delicious brewed wine, Lewis had convened over a new cocoon of gatherers weaving stories about Bermuda from Hamilton to Harbor Point, the attending ten priests passed a dish of cocaine along with glazed papaya tarts, the pretty female from the kitchen came out to salve the oldest priest's iron-wrung hand for the fingers that washed the canvases, dressed in a tight fitting nearly transparent beige dress of lace, her soft pale red hair hanging free, she massaged his aching head which she pressed against her all too thin body while the others found it difficult not to become aroused and stare, toward the end of dinner she, having produced a soporific sleeping subject, moved to a young priest and leaning on him poured more wine, her place among the brethren uncomfortable to Jones, the young priest while discussing the events of restoring earlier in the day coaxed her onto his lap, ran his hands over her arms, lifted her hair and stroked her back. She ate a bit of the meal, steak strips embellished with green pepper chunks, some salad, a nibble of dessert, as his motions grew in sensual consent, she finished his wine, tipsy and gaily laughing, she flirted at Lewis, permitted her priest to rest a hand over her abdomen, leaned against him, gave the rest a flirtation that included the priest to her right a soft caress about the neck with a kindly peck at his ear lobe, the arousal sufficient Jones discovered oddly to combat any stiffness, removing it altogether. He wondered about their need for her, considered perhaps it wasn't as sexually intentioned as he imagined, and somewhat drowsily detached, watching her place her priest's hand on her thigh, observing his obvious attraction, the other priest's relaxation in stretching his legs, thought their necessity of her was edict far more of survival than even desire. They agreed to more wine, another marijuana pass, three took the dishes in to wash, someone put on a melody, Jones got thoroughly soaked, the girl eventually came over, draped herself on him, and he pulled her down by grabbing her wrists, whispering in her ear she was indeed beautiful. She tested his fingers to which he complained of severe stiffness, in response she led him out of the dinner hall, took him down a corridor to a spa, disrobed him, getting with him into the heated tub, her fully dressed, she kissed him, pressed up against him raising her beige dress over her hips, guided him into her until he was utterly aroused to ejaculation, wordlessly they made love for minutes, the stiff sensation gone in the instant he moaned, her wet hair plastered on his chest, her lace garment drenched leaving small impressions across his skin.

The decision to fly several larger pieces of art varnished beyond discernible recognition by heat in an engine flooding ballast tank room was made by the chief of the colony. Lewis and Jones were taken across the sea to the Virgin Islands, seven emerald, pristine garden wilderness paradise islands bounded by untrammeled sand beaches and vivid aquamarine French blue latitudes, ravine-slashed mountains rising high from multitudes of splendorous, sumptuous green trees, each island more captivating than the last, each a rich density of ultra dark brown roads, a poignant cultivation steeped with paradoxical beauty, for in their cloudless heights they lay without sign of cutting or symptom of crane morphology, a singular house and lawn the sole permissible entry to a complex set of roof-boarded rooms inside which, the strength of daylight not permitted, could provide a cool respite from varnish-vanquished sealant for the first method of restoration to begin a release of stained resin under the lack of civilization's dormant smog. The plane landed in a leafy forest of intrinsic lime and thriving emergent beryl gradation, they followed DiCirn into the Spanish hacienda where wood slat covered art lined the base of the length of walls, their several paintings, so large that each was expected to take an entire wall, carried by two upstairs into the attic, positioned, all windows east closed by wood. Here for slightly under a month the paintings would receive moonlit exposure which would result in retarding any degree of varnish to a previous standard of coloration, then each canvass was hung in story below the attic in sequestered light for as long as it took to establish brilliance, after which time the paintings could be restored by restoring equipment to their basic design, new paint applied overall and documents assessed for replacement costs and rebid.

Jones and Lewis poured cups of tea from their pilot's thermos and took them outside to the lawn where the airplane rested.

"Is it completely over between you and Rhonda?" Jones asked Lewis.

"She wanted it, I signed the papers."

"That isn't what I meant. Do you think you will try to start a relationship with her again?"

"I never intend to. She usually called me. I'm planning to remarry, you know."

"I've asked Rhonda to marry me."

The mood settled between them in a jeopardized filial tension. Jones lit a cigarette and sipped his tea.

Lewis finally said, "She probably won't. She'll return if I permit her to."

Jones controlled an urge to cry. "She told me about Hoyt."

"What about him? He was more or less you, I replaced his depravity with a different instinct. He didn't fall for Rhonda quite the way in which she must have for him. She was prey for him, there are men like that who don't really think deeply about the women they have, Rhonda said she loved him. It went on for twelve years."

"But we see him every day, he doesn't even speak to you."

"He wanted to meet my wife, he said he was all cooped up in the islands, he wanted to know what I went home to. At first it was nothing, one afternoon I fell asleep on the divan and when I awakened I saw him helping her with work, he was all over her, she didn't seem to mind. When I asked him later about what I had witnessed he said he found her irresistible. I didn't really read much into it until I invited him on a vacation and she put on a bikini. In those days she could wear one. He took one look at her, it finished him off. We went out on a boat that evening and I asked her to take off her top, I asked him to be myself, he was quite overcome."

"Why would you even suggest it?"

"Rhonda was like your girl last night to him, she just seemed to enjoy him. It didn't hurt, I knew he looked at her, she is the sort of person who likes to be admired. Why did you?"

"I was stoned, I thought we were kidding around."

"Well, women have a compulsive effect on Hoyt, I told Rhonda I was okay with her sleeping with him, I told him the same thing." Lewis lit a cigarette and took a long inhalation. "Rhonda is complicated, I wanted her to have the one thing I was sure no other woman would ever have."

"I think you were both bored to tears with life."

"Yes, we were. I tire more readily."

"So that's boredom."

"Do you tire easily?"

"I don't know, I've never actually gotten involved with anything other than agency work."

"It shows. I can't say what I think might happen somewhere down the line, Rhonda isn't likely to enter into another marriage."

"I'm sorry I brought it up. I wasn't ready to learn it was Hoyt."

"I would've told you. Hoyt was my age almost, agency life had become unbearable, I didn't think it politically conscionable that our boss gave my ex wife authority over my work."

"I didn't either; did you give Rhonda a divorce for him?"

"I divorced her over evidence determinations."

"Rhonda removed all your photos off evidence."

"I wanted Evidence to see other females, not me by myself."

"Are you still in love?"

Lewis shrugged. "Sometimes. She's fickle, I'm not much better, I like my romances."

The reality was Jones couldn't afford to have fallen for Rhonda.

Lewis caught the tension, and remarked, "I don't worry over you for myself as I think I must have on account of Hoyt, I'm out of her life now. Hoyt couldn't live without Rhonda, she assumed she was ready to leave, the timing is different."

"Were you friends with Hoyt the way you are with me?"

"Right up to the divorce."

"Why didn't she wed him?"

"She lived with him six months. She called me, I wouldn't have contacted her."

"Did you miss her?"

"Yes, it was worse than I anticipated. I suggested we remarry, she's the one holding me at bay."

"If I get her to marry, will you try to win her back?"

"I doubt it, I'm planning a new life."

When Jones thought it over, leaving himself out of Lewis' spousal relationship, aside from Lewis flinging an affair at Rhonda, they had kept their years pretty much to themselves. There was no permanent way to fix Lewis' war injury, whatever impotence it caused him was Lewis' private matter. The incidents that Lewis sought to entertain them both seemed also of a separate nature, not owing to permanence, neither disrespectful nor for a purpose to engender his divorce despite the potential conflictual habitual practices either were willing to engage in. His only prospect at a more societally acceptable life might one day be threatened by Rhonda, a seeming flight of her fancy Jones had not thought to consider, indeed one's

practical living was determined in every respect by a possessive agency that sought to control the results of its inquiries, an
objective he felt entirely justified every last imposed limitation.
He felt negatively sorry for Lewis whose latest gambit could
easily be a saboteur, thought it likely should Lewis discover any
betrayal of the agency, he'd be back to Rhonda at once.

The kitchen girl looked in on him before dinner commenced, smelling faintly of jasmine, her cascading hair tossed
into a large tortoise shell clip, a stark green lace top that showed
her body, a snug woolen skirt to her calves, Jones took her in
his arms and kissed her feverishly asking her if she was real
or a faint hint of ephemeral love, for which she said she was
only as long as he needed her which he understood to indicate
physically at risk. Although he made love to her telling her she
was a need as pained as desire, his loins ached for Rhonda,
for Rhonda's passion, her distilling capability for surrender, her
knowledge as to how great an outpouring of love he required
to feel made whole, as he pressed into her comprehending her
femininity, its exacting nuances, the pulse in her carotid artery,
the light suffusion of sweat on her brow, as he withheld for
a moment, whispered she had beautiful passionate hips, then
pushed again to her height thrilling her with incomprehensible liquid gaze, he thought of Rhonda, the excitement of her
freedom of motion, of her lack of resistance to give herself over
holding back not a part of herself, shuddering in this girl's surrender of tension, telling himself Rhonda was real.

Over dinner whereas she took her place beside Lewis, contented herself with stroking his arm and talking into his ear
between spaghetti and conversation, brandy pouring liberally,
Lewis pausing a moment to run his hand under her skirt, Jones
found himself yet further detached as though his awareness of
the necessity of her passion, once discovered, paled in contrast.
She would have had them all, an adroit creature of enigmatic
purpose, from her fetching clothing to her constraint of hairstyle, how she managed them without their finding themselves
grilled by jealousy was a trick of some sort of attention. The
priest whose lap she had sat was next to her, his hand on her

back, every so often bending to say something that caused her to laugh. It was a shame she was as fair as she was, sensual, creamy, lithe, enticing, for he suspected few could entirely possess her for long. As soon as plates were taken away and apple streudel cut and served with a cherry cordial, the priest loosened her hair allowing a wealth of strands to fall free. She drew Lewis' hand under her skirt and slipping forward barely enough to press against him, while the priest caressed her shoulders, she took Lewis' arm between her hands and rested her chin on him. The dialogue turned to a more serious note, her priest stood to speak, stood in front of her, gave his speech on actual frame lengths required in order to ship, was still talking when it was observed she had gone. When Jones asked Lewis later why he didn't leave with her, Lewis said he hadn't been asked.

El este pensando que las mujeres generalmente estaban delicato para los dias de la semana por muerte, que sus numeras cambiaban en familia, jovenes o saludos; como si, la vida entende para particular instrucciones por unos cuartos. La muchacha, una hija y una tia del suburbios de la ciudad, apparece contenta con los hombres, y asi con el. En la primera dialogo el habia adios al mundo, desire por memoria sentado cerca de ella porque el espere ver siempre hasta tarde como el amor para en la esquina alla, tampoco saliendo o contestando a lloviendo, la lengua no seraba possible formar una frase del amor. Ella hable aceptarse, ella lo responde con despacio y negociante, el estara algun dia ausente, y pues el vera el cielo y el recordara sus montanas y esto ciudad casas blancas con tejados rojos. Cuando el y Luis departan las Virgines, el he sabido que no el volvera al esto punto en este mapa o en verde ventanas. Como un hombre Luis hace mas anos en el amor; el necessita una maestra buena quien hay ir muchas hombres de la vida diaria, por su verdad el apprendido el viajero abre el mundo para principia, el fue una criada cual la vida con permiso. El tejado del pais fue invitar los dibujos del amor principal con todos noches cuando el responde tristemente, aquellos montanas altas al cielo estaban por jarros es artista trabaja. Cualquier la avenida mas hermosa fue siempre sinonimos con embellecer una vida dura, a causa de la extension del territorio, cuando hace frio o cuando en los alrededores las piramides, el vere la gran piramide de la luna – todas apparecere no dejar de ver o reconocer el recreo de la camisa.

The tests to glaze tint of background impressionistic shadows departed normal standards of the five restoration artists. Considerable time and know-how could accompany the arduous task for laying on stirred paint or at best allay even the worst drawn capable over matte design except when it came to wet paintings, the two Avenidas, both sons of a senior master, had taped across lightweight paper while painting in rich yellow ochre, necessitating entire recreations. These five old men were ancient masters having apprenticed in their teenhood long ago, at least forty years when the artist colony was comprised of one building, its slanted red roof of cornice tiles the sole adornment to decorate its hideaway. At least three had begun stripping in the base pinkish pigment atop of which they painted in rose, brown and some embellishment of green, either a darker chartreuse, a lively, if not somewhat spicy peppery pale green, sleeping forested gray-green pastel or splendorous quality-capable damp mint green; their books open to any number of displays as to same color spectrum and shadow contexts. Their principal school of essayist thought drew along the lines that depth made by contrasts of light with dark assisted a better delineation of horizon to distance than more modern inclusion of somber dark colors, among them dark gray, sienna, dash of dark blue to be set into the frame among reds and orange, for typically Cezanne, Renoir or Titian, signed Tijiane. Many studied contrasts depicted within the border of dark seemed almost vivid in clarity as much as a marksmanship of modest red roofs in a haphazard row on deep transgressions of vibrant green abstract pastures or of red outlined boats buoyed in a canal. Lewis by himself captured updated photos, he leaned over their shoulders with a long narrow lens, shot full flash exposures of the Cezanne, gave a kneeling reconnoiter within a wide angle of the other famed classical refurbished properties, not so much as a pose of camera shooting proclivity escaped Jones who after six finger-stiff, thirteen hour days was worn as straight as any celibacy. To observe Lewis in a primer indulgence, despite practiced method and owing to the harmonious blends he would soon procure, Jones knew that Lewis surrendered to an essential series of questions as to what his model new girlfriend Abby anticipated from her own draws, many which filmed the prohibited balconies of one Grenada palace. These long days proved that the endurances of the past continued to be trials of a wicked sort, money flowed from any unexpected source, models and patrol alike sought the finest of life's worthy depictions for which consequences rendered exotic relinquishments, mysterious vanishings, hateful abnegations.

There was one last enjoyment with his young female, a cloistered engagement inside a small room that had a narrow wedged opened window to the red roofing and the mostly stone mountains, wherein he surrendered within her crying out, the sound of his own voice disturbing even to him. It was no minor concession she entirely relieved the distress, nor that her light blue cashmere dress aroused him to a height of anguish, the sense of his own passion fulfilling every aspect of him, her softly pined entreaties experienced by him in rejoice, he crested holding her thighs close against himself, asking himself why she still seemed elusive, wondering whether his only downfall might become an urgent need to have a female smother him, and as though in response to a perceived calling, she turned him loose, wrapped herself about his chest and drew his head toward her, rocking him sweetly, suffocating of him. In an instant he was demanding, in desperation, holding her more tightly than he thought she could bear, an outpouring of urgent repression released, a sob extracted as certain as essential breath. If she were in this place solely to succumb men from otherwise unbearable pain, her place within these priests' lives only to recapitulate away from severe stiffening, he knew he could not find with her a long joy or solace. This girl was unwittingly all his in the moments she arrived to possess him, there was no compatibility to Lewis, no bargain to be dealt out, but there was no honest arrangement either; for him, when life had arrived he was indifferent to human necessities, his work requested no less, indeed he almost had never thought about it, if he tasted acrimonious anger he suppressed it instantly for out of Lewis' incapacities, whether he himself borrowed on love not entirely his to possess, he too discovered an intimacy he had not guessed at and because of his desires, he had come to grow awareness of love.

They flew home to Nassau in an unburdening discussion about the art, the lengthy course of attaching lading bills, storing photos and sending a photo list with costs to the insurer. The islands on the distant ocean lay in unrivaled virgin territory, their sleek mountains as suggestive of a girl's private retreat as anything in nature, once behind them familiar out risings of familiar coastal ports and their towns secured a time-honored sense that the comfort of civilization lay directly ahead. Abby stood on the airstrip, wind blowing her red straw hat and splashes of red and green silk dress like a treatise in the open air, their arrival announced, their descent down the stairs a final relief to return to home base. She greeted Lewis with a tight hug and affectionate kisses and kissed Jones once on the mouth, steering them to her car she recounted her film week up in Toluca, a straight series of evening shots on beaches, a few top nude, many barely clad dress wear showing bare shoulders, one rope sandals, hair set free. They stopped at a roadside restaurant perched over rocks, took an outdoor table with blue umbrella, had served margaritas, salsa and chips, ordered steak and sweet yams mashed. Lewis was all jokes, because the art was destroyed in the tank coming over from Europe, New York customs refused the shipment, the plaster casts were spilled with engine oil, the art undisclosed suffered from every varnish and tear imaginable, the restorations may as well have been dipped in brandy, the days were miserable, not an oyster bar, tennis club or golf link anywhere. Only Jones had dusted, collected chippings, the damage yielded little better than etchings, they smoked, drank, sat in a spa, and worked their fingers to the bone. When reality hit home, while they were too busy to appreciate the artistic works on their benches, they had never-the-less contributed as much as any agent house and would never see the costs nor know when galleries showed. Over dinner Abby massaged Lewis' back, occasionally stroked his neck and head, and courted Jones with her hand on his leg; not until coffee was served did Jones leave to place a telephone call to Rhonda's answering machine that gave a message she was gone on assignment for ten days. From the entry way out of a hall, as he stepped onto the deck, he looked to them, Lewis' hand cupped under her breast, her hand drawing him definitely to her, their mouths touching, she was irresistible. Although Jones would feel the sting of resentment over Rhonda's unscheduled departure, he permitted no direct release of information, picking up the tab, escorting Abby through the densely packed parlor including opening the car door for her, placing Lewis into the rear passenger seat and sliding in beside her.

The evening decided its own contemplation when Jones asked to be taken to his building and surrendered to the definitive idea that they two ought to have their own separate time. Exactly at ten Jones turned on the news, a half hour later he showered, dressed for bed, consulted his E-mail and finding several notes posted by Rhonda including her daily itinerary put through a call to her. He was overjoyed to hear her voice and poured his heart out to her, relieved for her sympathy for she had been to Montserrat prior to meeting Lewis, and she told him it was its own world without inclusion of any reality, the priests were mostly celibate ex officiates whose youth had been given over to fragile compositions of small cleric orders, none realized they would have almost no contact with the world. Because she said she missed him terribly, he went to bed earnestly deserving of sleep.

At dawn Jones went for a stroll to the pool house where he swam fifty laps before going to breakfast for his usual scrambled eggs and salmon fried steak, hash browns, muffin toast with currants, and shot of espresso, he read the morning Herald, consulted the Dow, looked up U.S. Steel. At precisely nine he took a walk through the arbor, meandered across the rolling green, stopping to smoke a Fumar and to admire the aqua emerald inlet, then resolved himself to set about his heels for a brief exchange with Abby, assuming she would have been chased home for Lewis to catch some sleep and step out with their boss for a midnight swim, spa and casino. Running with lit cigarette he traversed the quarter mile to her home in slightly under fifteen minutes. She opened the door, dressed in a long black terrycloth robe, her long hair scraggly from dampness, invited him inside the giant sitting room in which she had three bright station lights, a slide down peach screen, a camcorder positioned onto a couch, red light blinking. She took him by the hand, sat him down on her couch, she disrobed to her partial nudity, removed the plate, the green light came on, and she resumed her filming. She put his face on her breasts, asked him to run a hand along her side, lowered her head toward him until her hair fell over his shoulder, placing a knee between his legs, she pushed him into a reclined posture, all the while conscious primarily of how much of her the camera saw of her, when he reached for her waist she turned half with a put upon pout, then agreed to lie on him, letting him fashion her hair over her shoulders, bringing her hand down to the visible thigh momentarily, then lifting his shirt, another pose, he unbuttoned it, she exposed his chest, when he gazed into her face it was starkly quiet, neither aware not without drama. Despite the fact that he held her to him, she loosened his trousers and gradually she joined to him, her hands guiding him, her body calling to the camera by graceful posturing, she finally captured him as if she had surrendered for the camera at least a hundred times. Afterwards, she got up, walked lithely to the screen and posed, breasts covered by her arm, then went to insert the plate.

She instructed, "While you fix drinks, I'll rewind the tape."

Jones walked behind the bar, fixed two tall glasses with several shots of scotch, soda water, lime juice, and threw a lime slice into each. Abby had deliberately turned down the lights, refocused the camcorder, set it to run the full length of play and sat on one of two armchairs. A good twenty minutes ran during which she posed fully dressed in shirt and jeans, minutes of silent stillness, at one point she removed her shirt, exposing her body, she was preciously beautiful, he had not realized any awareness on his part of what she would look like, she stood and slipped into the dark robe, shook her red semi curly hair so that it cascaded down her robe to her waist, the camera missed none of her suggestive raw sensuality, when she stood before the screen she seemed highlighted somehow, radiant, barely concealed, her face absent of any trace of conflict, a natural. There was a black-out. When the film resumed he was walking to the couch, he showed nothing in the way of suspecting what would occur, she disrobed, the swell of her breast, her position of knee, her strident body without any awkwardness, his sense of being led as if without will, her arched back, a satiny sheen of hair on him, his hand running down her, her placing herself over him. He copied her movements as she sipped from her glass, like an elixir it gave him an immediate response throughout his body to watch her almost undetectable motion, place him within her, although for an inexplicable second he could not recall that he consciously gave in, he remembered when they joined, he had looked at her awaiting some cue; finding a detention of emotion as though someone unseen were present he gave into her. There was something completely indefinable about her, he would have liked her to have been desirous, solicitous, awakening strong passion in him.

She sipped once more and put the drink down on the carpet, while he sipped his, she put an earlier similar tape of herself on, she was more stylishly dressed in a two piece green tweed suit, no blouse, flats, her hair piled into a clip. Her makeup covered her face in white, her mauve lipstick dramatic, no jewelry. She reviewed an instruction book and smiling into the view as if one long wished for had stepped inside her lips parted with anticipation.

"You were learning to sit?"

"Yes. Do you like it?"

"Yes, you are a natural, the camera likes you."

"Because I work for it, thus it films me favorably."

"How did you learn?"

"I was taught my work, to sit still, to look bored, to have no thought, to have no life."

"Who told you to think that way?"

"My original coach, he is convinced the trick of good photography lies in the model's physical attributes."

"How did you come to shoot inside the Grenada palace?"

"We were invited, Lewis asked me the same question, he wanted to know how many islands I have been to."

"What did you say?"

"All but one, I said I had never seen Puerto Rico."

"Have you posed in Grand Island?"

" Not yet. Nor Ventana, Soledad, or Laurenc."

"Who arranged the others?"

"Office of Immigration and Deportation," she replied taking a guess, "of Miami."

"They have no authority outside Florida."

"They determine Gulf Stream."

"I'm sure they don't."

She stood, permitting her robe to easily slide off, and walked behind him and unselfconsciously draped her arm around his neck and kissed him hard enough that he found himself powerfully aroused. He knew he would not stop her, her arm was strong and she was relentless, he knew a woman who took him might keep him. He tried to turn, but she held him there, she spoke to him of her restless caged lust, he was the man she came for, he was hers more than anyone she had known, she insisted he was already turning over his reluctance, already giving her every desire, he appeared always ready. As though he had been sleep walking when he entered, spellbound by his fascination of her passive love too, whereas he knew in moments of questioning he should decide not to lie beneath her, he could not also decide why he shouldn't give in. He gave her no resistance as she kissed him, embraced him, ran her hand as near as she considered advisable, to which he succumbed pleading her to go slower, he gave her power to induct him, at which she tremblingly shed her controlled pose, she shuddered pressing her body against his firm back, she moved into him, her breath was short delivered to the point of breathlessness, she ran her other hand across his head as he began to take brief jolts of ecstatic pleasure, she loved any man who had to have her in the way he did in never ending hunger only of her and caused him to be suddenly aware of her nakedness, across his shoulder creases, his back and side, his arm, pressing hard against him until she reached for him and he trembled to his fate.

He felt he had no other choice when she lay down on the carpet and went to sleep, motion turned on, but to leave. In the wake of a churning storm he walked the width of the green thinking of her as the girl who would eventually marry Lewis. The tossing wind bestowed an unkindness of conflictual driving force in its bent force across the land, reversing direction when it picked up velocity. Jones felt tethered around the legs by its spurning, whipping range, he ran through it feeling himself get battered by drenching spats. At last as he came out of the gale, stepped beneath a cluster of leafy trees, he spied lights at a distance and gave the last three hundred yards a good stride of a run.

The walk was slippery, the hall inside his wing irrepressibly warm. His flat when he finally stepped inside it was cool, a welcome relief to the hampering thickness of heat beyond. He showered, towel dried, shaved and dressed casually in office attire, the oddness of the day plastered on him by a sense of the unreal. As he sat down to his computer at his desk, window open to the salty air, he wondered why he hadn't seen it coming, Abby had been sloshed, she was barely in any mind. He was no longer youth-oriented, he was almost mid sixty, life had long been bland. It hadn't really bothered him if Rhonda wasn't willing to get involved a second time, he could never be Lewis to her, he honestly hadn't thought much about the notion that Rhonda only knew him because of Lewis.

He called Hoyt who answered on the first ring. Jones asked where they could meet, Hoyt thought the library patio was a

private situation usually without staff, other agents or a surveillance deck.

Jones made his way along the cement walk that fronted his
hotel, up a winding road to a small nightclub lounge open to
border agents from ship stays, past a group of cabin quarters in-
habited by all department chiefs up a thin brick wall into a well
sized patio off which was a colonial library building with inlaid
marble statues of Grecian females. Hoyt sat at a table, his late
age having weathered him to a cunning eighty, dark red brown
crewcut, conservative tan and yellow striped suit, stiff collar
pale lemon shirt, dark brown necktie, brim Panamanian hat,
brown stretch socks, light yellow Mocktoes, reading the rating
lists of the Daily Sun. Jones sat on the other side, notepad and
uncapped pen.

"You had a corruption case at Tipside, Cabo Blanco," Jones
said.

"Very complicated, sexy babes at all beaches, all without
men of any age." Hoyt's Puerto Rican accent, clearly Calypso,
was monotone. "We had pictures of moonlight every week for
up to a year, no granted request, mostly of the night sky with
almost no stars. It was the oddest thing, didn't know what anyone was trying to give our systems. I was sent out with other
agents but it didn't amount to much, in fact these females while
explicitly gorgeous were neither friendly nor offhanded. As it
turned out, they were models and Blanco was between seasons."

"With contracts?"

"Everyone. They were paid by six sessions for each manufacturer."

"For season travel?"

"Yes, early to end May. Plenty of nice sun, light ocean
breeze."

"How often in Grenada?"

"One time, that's the mistake. There were two separate
groups, female, male model, partial nudity, separate spreads,
male on a consulate couch. "

"Who arranged the spreads?"

"Some deportation officer out of Bahamas, we checked

him out pretty thoroughly. He resubmitted to the Florida mainland."

"That's a fairly sad state of affairs that it happened."

"Yeah, it had a big upside, I lost a marriage, was nearly stuck in Baja Canal indefinitely, I figured it was best to surrender my badge any way I could. I had more than a few affairs, I'll grant you that."

"Any with Rhonda?"

"I saw it far ahead, but I fell in love with her. Lewis was always on the islands in those days and she was a lonely depressed housewife. She was my sanity for years to come."

"What about a model by the name of Abby? She's the one who was taken into Grenada."

"She's a total knockout but nothing's working right. I'm surprised she's still getting work."

"Maybe she'll retire, Lewis likes her."

"Those models never trade in for a husband. Try a Mississippi model. I had a few I liked. They were soft. They were always in love with me. In my wayward years I kept a girl in my company. I often used to think that if I hadn't taken the detour with Rhonda, that female would have married me. You must know how it goes, sometimes the instinct gets unwound more than you imagine is possible."

"I've seen many variations. Was there any notion that anyone wanted our boys?"

Hoyt said, "The boss thought so, but it wasn't evident to me at any rate. Maybe they had their eye on Lewis and he was nowhere about. Lewis could be someone whose files they'd like to tear apart. I'm not anymore."

"I didn't intend to take this much of your afternoon."

"I'm usually almost always available after three."

Jones could see that the rift that had occurred for Hoyt at any rate had been maneuvered by both sides, Lewis being neither judgmental nor vindictive but decisive. It was odd that nearly twenty years later Lewis was still keying for the camera seeking whatever in his activities a prying eye was trying to quarantine.

He was looking for a way past the elegantly lit walls into those tunnels even though the Grenada situation was long dead.

By the time he returned to his hotel, there was a logotype message on his computer from St. Louis, (UP), "British Virgin Islands, Bermuda and Martinique report climate change despite flurries washing up on track and field penalty box." UPI Arts & Entertainment.

That was the end of the show. Jones returned a four-line story beginning with journalist taboos, "The latter, former and respective 150 words of copy per minute, three and a half minutes of news at thirty seconds a story has tracked sources at the scene of The Masters Tournament but may include a U.S. open, a par 5, dividends rose to 4 on rumors 1 for portfolios."

Jones typed a query to Lewis, "It was a mistake, the photo shoot in Grenada's palace. The deportation officer got resituated somewhere in the Keys. There were two separate filmings, one of yours, also a male model presumably partially exposed seated on a consulate couch. What would you like me to do?"

The return message read, "Come down, I'll give you what I have."

Jones went down the peach carpeted hall to the far end wing. A bleary eyed Lewis answered the door obviously tanked. Jones followed him inside, quick to observe an utter mess of clothing, news articles, unwashed dishes on the counter, stained lipstick on a wine glass, all seven computers on.

Lewis said, as he mixed drinks, brought out bacon and lettuce finger sandwiches along with potato saltines and expensive chive, olive and dill dip, "Abby photo shot entirely nude in the courtyard and at some point toward evening inside surrounded by all that beautiful lacy stone decorous architecture, front shots, no veil, most of every picture in some shadow. One photo only appeared in Elle, since then there have been beach mornings, almost all top nude, hair spritzed up, gloss lips, in a handful of high text magazines, Vogue, Caprice, Island Girl, to mention a few, snippets of those shots. I can't decide, does she get taken to these places, or is she shown preferred scenes?"

Jones took a sip of spiked vodka. "I'm clear she doesn't realize she couldn't be filmed there. Did these magazines request that location?"

"No," Lewis replied, leaving a phone message on her machine, "they choose between shots and poses."

"Someday she'll make a fortune with poses."

"No kidding. Here's what I deduced, she goes to where the photographer arranges. If there is a problem with her for anyone in the agency it is not the fact she is a model."

"Why was she sent here to work?" Jones asked.

"She bought a house here."

"She used to reside in Blanco."

"Then talk to Hoyt. That's his case."

"I've consulted him. He says lots of moonlight photos."

"That's all there is to it."

"Well, what does it mean to you? It doesn't say much to me."

"It says someone entered about ten tunnels filmed in bright lights which resemble moonlight. The connection should be obvious. In these tunnels cargo for shipments were stored between times when actual shipments arrived from ports from where the cargo was shipped."

"That's a relatively old case."

"It comes up in different ways, from time to time we receive photos of new theft of products. For some reason, the groups that heist this stuff decided to take off yet another shipment. Abby doesn't really have anything to do with that."

"The woman of your dreams walks into your life, she takes photos in many islands and for some reason every photo take looks like all the other files of stolen shipments possibly off stolen ships."

Lewis gave a shrug as Abby entered dressed in a black blouse draped across one shoulder and white pants and sandals, her hair wrapped into a white stretch caftan. She hugged Lewis, kissing him, ran her hands down his chest, her back to Jones, sipped from a drink and told Lewis she was so tired she could barely stand. Lewis in a relatively impassioned manner put his hands about her thighs and pressing her against him

French kissed her.

"Say hello to Jones," he commanded.

Liquid gaze, she enveloped Jones, hugged him and told him it was good to see him again. Jones put his hand on her low back kissing her.

"I'm famished. Who's cooking?" she asked.

"No need," Lewis reassured her, "plenty of leftovers." He shoved a plate at her and she ate ravenously, took a handful of chips and another sip of his drink. "She fell asleep last night on the midnight show."

"Was it a comedy?" Jones asked.

"No, we watched a drama, I can't remember what." She gave Lewis another kiss, saying she'd been under the camera all day, slipped the VCR into his hand and told him she had thought about him all day.

Jones was aware that Lewis was trying to elicit inside him the emotions of desire that he should have in himself. Jones knew it was probably over for him with Rhonda. He drew Abby to him giving her a kiss on the cheek and asked Lewis if they could resume their conversation another day, took his cap and left.

He forwarded the fax to Rhonda with his apologies that he could not see her. He was of an indecision, his thought had been to leave the friendship, put in a report. As far as he could determine Lewis should have resolved his case, he had the method in, had placed the officer on ice. Rhonda might not yearn for Lewis but her ties were intrinsically to his reports, she had to know almost as much as he. Jones couldn't in awareness look upon their romance without thinking she would not from time to time see Lewis in him.

Her response was fairly immediate – Darling, I've handled two hundred passports today, only ten family members allowed past the boarding gate, miserable time-consuming detail scrutiny and have literally had no time to grab a bite. With the exception of the pretty model, the photos you've asked for are too shadowy. I've come up with replacements; as you will note the lighting is improved and the corridor is subdued such that there's no competing décor light, the only fault may be the icy moonlight. Let's plan for next Friday, I'll come to you.

The photos she included consisted of a bright light inside a red yellow tunnel filled toward one end with wooden crates of boxes with hundreds of lights, 15 watt, and an apparently moonlit night and a pool of shallow water either under a street possibly inside a covered walk, tunnel like, or as part of a road beneath a garden walk. He created prints so as to determine their state as still-life photographs. The pool seemed resplendent with barely any visibility of the stone covered walk. The road emanating from the garden cast in moonlight held a fresh stark night, but neither told him enough to consult a historical page. From time to time he looked through the files he had taken off Abby's computer trying to match against any image of the two photos finding not a recognizable similarity. He pulled up a 3809 for any photograph ever taken which matched the ones sent – the sets that accompanied were of doors opening to the night sky amass with stars, one inside the palace, all rust color walls with yellow ivory, arches, pillars, layers of drape like stone, a soft stone pink wall of roses, lights inside an arched hall, a long room with wooden doors leading to trellised balconies and a seven tiered golden and rust fountain, seated on the fountain ledge completely naked in moonlight Abby, her hair draped down her body, behind her the male model dressed in a dark satin jacket, his short hair brushed back, his dark tone in stark contrast to hers, a stone wedding ring on her wed finger. Any number of downloads of different angles, all handsome seductions, gave him nothing in the way of discernible information other than they shouldn't have been able to gain entrance.

Jones looked for comparisons in Blanco and Baja Canal. Blanco was filled with the usual scantily clad females with desirable bosoms and curved smooth hips, evening shots gave distance telescope to females caressing one another in suggestive poses meant for men, a house in Baja on the canal, all glass, one story with deck showed the male in a window in bathing hip wear, shadows convened through a hall, on a balcony Abby reclined naked except for a very thin loin cloth, into a bedroom parlor someone had taken green paint and splashed it over walls, a long wall size mirror with writing, Yankee, go home! Jones recoiled, subsequent photos showed the place was barricaded and locked up. Numerous suspicious parlors worth of photos, one a bedroom scene with a young woman such as whom they had met in Florida at the beach house, paint smeared walls, torn drapes open to the wind, a letter on a bureau, the case was over for years, resolved, its lesser components, deck bridges on ships and hillsides, photos of sunny porticos interfaced over blue sea, a sunken ship retrieved, illegal pharmaceutical trade to gain illegal entrance to the States, the last of it copies of original priceless art – over. He typed up a summary attaching the strips of photos, a list of recognition photos as to the illegal ring, names and identifying information from the retrieval file and shot it to his boss. The last of the items included a fountain photograph and a Baja Canal of the two nude models for someone else to piece together for whatever their work lent their investigation.

GRENADA

Jones had had the obscure photo clip of a ship deck for an in distress call on his desk for a day awaiting the completion of a marine cargo assignment to ship satellite cable to San Juan. Despite his request of dateline for complication photographs, none for the week-old incident had been sent. When he finally took to the task of studying the web cam the line feed gave him a one sentence report from the brig:

"Taking in too much water," was the ship captain's final message.

The rail trim was a ship with a high berth. A telescope or coiled rope almost always indicated a ship or a five deck schooner, zodiac deck such as on a research expedition schooner, having one or two lifts, ninety meters, two diesel engine, a long platform forward deck indicated an inside container. Ships went down due to weather that produced big waves, speed, over stacking and grounding, which caused certain vessels to fall right over.

No one could find the identity of the ship. The FB 500 Marine Sat phone with Internet capability displayed no reading, the

V1210 lollitop searched for any ship in distress in waterway operations for containers, ports, canals including lock systems, and last known dry dock for freight handling; there was no match for the type of ship deck for the K series, which were a flat ship, nor for the Atlantic class container ship bearing over 4, 000 TEU capacity, nor the Coast Guard web cutter, no rails on their decks either and many sported high platforms, nor for wrecking ships which removed bridges, piers, moorings, locks or dams.

The station monitor system reported twenty ships in the area above the Puerto Rico line. The number of ships anywhere for all ships worldwide was thirty to forty ships per month. Generally a photograph of the triangular back deck with a surround of railing indicated a fair weather ship; it was the automatic radar plotting system that controlled the position of photo received by other ships at sea or port station houses, the automatic radar plotted the course of the ship in distress, took photographs, and matched weather to course. Each type of vessel was given its designated photo – barges and barge tows were side photo views, fair weather ships were back decks, traffic vessels usually container cargo was a distance photo, and passenger vessels, usually cruise ships, showed the automobile section on the third deck. Once the weather band AIS pulled in the type of ship by photo, then the next task was to look on the schedule to determine what was at sea. Fair weather vessels traditionally carried oil or wet cargo but not gas or dry bulk. Jones called the first coastline station and receiving transmitter ship before he assessed the coordinates as 50, 20 in the vicinity of southernmost Bahamas for the unidentified ship; for Jones the task was to apprise port station command as to whether there was mechanical failure and subsequently were the systems accurately recording, it would not be the eventual query as to why did an insurance carrier receive a picture of a ship it didn't insure. Since the 2004 and 2005 incidents when the Phoenix and Anchorage were thrown by high waves aground and subsequently with the June 8, 2007 disaster when the Pasha Bulker coal and iron ore tanker grounded at Newcastle, Australia and began gushing oil, the entire shipping industry had taken immeasurable safety precautions, especially to safeguard oil tankers, of which Saudi Arabia put twelve to sea a month – one to Puerto Rico, three to United States, two into Guam, four into the Mediterranean, two to Hawaii, ten million dollar corks all. Only OPEC sent United States sixty oil ships a year from Venezuela, each forty million, Saudi Arabia wanted to provide half of all shipments.

The second station to pick up was Havana which thought the distress might be a complication of the mast light when a ship is flooding. An antennae at sea thought the May 16, 2010 oil drilling rig explosion south of Venice, Louisiana in the Gulf of Mexico and the collapse of the Deepwater Horizon rig with the quickly spreading oil slick had destabilized the ocean as far as Bahamas and that despite emergency procedures taken to protect major ports along Chandeleur Sound, Louisiana and Pass Christian, Mississippi all the way to the island chains with Hesco fences in the rivers and on ocean beaches, the potential damage had struck into far ocean channels.

An oil drenched pelican had washed up on the beach of the agency hotel in Nassau early in the morning, some three weeks since the explosion. An army foot patrol along with a veterinarian had emerged with a plastic bag to remove the endangered bird and take it to a wildlife refuge lab where its feathers would be cleaned and it would receive life saving intervention. Other of the army crew had begun a tow line boom in an attempt to preserve the coast from oil washing up turning the otherwise green marine deltas into silver muddy grey chromatic water. As recently as a week ago the lunar tide had deposited massive clay like orange slippery oil off the three mile point and the oozing slick had rocked on the ocean like a shiny patina impervious to the fish that swam there.

Jones took his newspaper under his arm and strolled across the three acres of emerald green lawn that fronted the hotel where he spent most of his days busy in research. The breeze off the ocean lilted catching his pink shirt collar, his heels sank in the still damp tweed of grass, his black linen trousers and grey corduroy jacket a mild windbreaker against an occasional guff of wind. His thoughts as usual were tagged to the job at hand, knowledge that the missing ship had gone astray for reasons unknown begged for interminable pardon, an optimist he told himself it would appear at some island destination, secure if not weather barraged.

Because his mainstay outdoor patio grill was closed this week for repairs, he ambled up broad marble stairs inside the crimson, deep pile cushy carpeted lobby past several boutiques for the ladies passing the men's style salon and spa to the restaurant situated at the end of the hall that overlooked a canopy of white bougainvillea. Inside a striped forest green and burgundy upholstered booth that rested on a upper tier of twelve booths sat Lewis Lewis, his long stiff collared shirt sleeves rolled up to his elbows, comfortable polished cotton tans, brown loafers, a digital computer calculator in his left hand, a pencil hard at work jotting down figures in columns in a legal sized ledger, probably final computations for an insurance collection case. Jones snapped his fingers to snag the waiter's attention and indicated he would start with a soft boiled egg, bacon strips and the usual, glass of fresh orange juice, English sour dough toast buttered on one side and a cup of tepid coffee, fresh off the top, no burner churner's for him. The waiter had his toast, coffee and juice to him within a few minutes.

He showed Lewis his photo of the snippet of deck. "It's no barge tow. It's a ship classification, right?"

Lewis eyed it above the thin gold wire rim of his eye glasses. "Easy, it's most likely the back of a crane ship seen off the mast light. Where did it go down?"

"No way to know. This is all that's available, no corresponding side shot, no ship name, she may as well having been sailing under shroud cover."

"Oh, well, ditch it to the insurance unit."

"I'm under an impression they sent it to us, they've never seen this view, they only deal with what the bridge views."

The soft egg arrived with three strips of medium cooked bacon. Jones cut the egg open over a piece of toast and gave it one shake of salt, two of pepper.

Lewis took a sip of coffee, and studied the photo. "How many fair weather vessels were at sea?"

"Fifteen, I posted for and was sent basic descriptions, number of decks, placement of cabins, forward bar, height of bridge. What makes you think it's a crane ship?"

"Containers stack behind the bridge. Inside bulk cargo may have a high platform, Coast Guard bridge sits all the way at the end, tankards lack rail deck. Cranes are your best idea. What are the mast lights?"

"All are Chesapeake."

"Who registered?"

"Lloyd's Register."

"Well, there you are. Did they conduct safety inspections?"

"All. For vessel safety, bunker and freight."

"Alright; well, I'd look at ships with five lifts, particularly long ships, ton capacity, transportation routes, trade, communication. When does risk want this?"

"I should think preferably prior to file being sent to loss surveyors for replacement costs."

"That should give you a few days, at least."

"It should," Jones answered, finishing the egg, bacon and toast. "I noticed you aren't wearing your wedding band anymore."

"Yeah," Lewis replied with obvious dejection, "I signed the papers. Screw her, Rhonda, she'll make out like a bandit, I threw in her flat. She would've fought for it anyways. I said no to lawyers."

"That's good thinking, it could've become messy."

"It'll probably get messy anyhow, she'll probably want a reunion after a while. She did after the separation."

"That's a separation during the first three years, almost all females have second thoughts."

"We've done four separations, I've always given her an out."

"Why? Does she say something?"

"She says it's getting too cozy."

"Well, what the heck does that mean?"

Lewis set down his pencil, eyed the categories on his financial sheet. "There's no telling why the agency wants another cargo line."

"I didn't know they did."

"Yup, they have decided to add a new port in the Grenadines."

"Because of this rig disaster?"

"No, they've been toying around with the idea awhile, I think they want to add an excursion onto Bermuda trips." He was being candid, but Jones knew as soon as he heard the inflection of his voice he would withdraw and erect another barrier.

Even so, Jones regarded an open speaking Lewis Lewis as at his best and he hung to these rare moments. "The agency has Cabo Rojo and San Juan, can't get any better than that for excellent waterfronts, cruiser yachts or fine dining."

"They want a stop-over to conduct official business while en route, storage under the city for spool, salt, scrap, break bulk. There's nowhere polite to keep a good sizable amount except to reorder, which I don't think they want to do every year."

"Do they find they run low?"

"Well, that's just it, they can't tell. Either the shipments are inconsistent or the demand has declined."

"Could be use is predicated on availability, if it's here, it will be used."

"Yes, it works that way also." His gaze retreated, he looked inscrutable, as he said, "I looked this guy up."

"I didn't realize he's a company man."

"Worse, he's insurance for narrow lens for every British ship."

"Maybe I should talk to him, ask him when the narrow lens throws back a miss."

"What's he going to be able to tell you? He's younger than we are, by half."

"Why did Rhonda pick such a young man? Where did she meet him, again?"

"Work. He's in inspections, he sees everything, not just oil. He's probably the one who encouraged her to take the promotion, she's his boss now."

"You seeing anyone new?"

"I don't have the time."

"How about we throw a party and I invite Rhonda out?"

"Don't do me any favors."

A clap of lightning preceded the roll of thunder just as Jones returned to his hotel flat. The air was warm, a cloud cover advancing over the ocean from one end of the coast to the other, vaporous sheets of rain stemming the start of an ocean spout, suddenly a florid torrential storm of golf sized raindrops hitting the windows with next to no visibility. Jones retreated to his study, opened the file on his computer, downloaded copy on the various ships having the requisite rail. There were nine ships – they carried break bulk, bulk cargo of salt, oil, tallow and scrap, ships with generators, and Midas lifts to take trucks out of the hold. He began the tedious job of review; there were ninety profile files per ship, approximately seven hundred photo shots per Chesapeake, all taken at 9000 9m zoom. The masthead camera did its work, not a single missing ship was unreturned. The first series showed the containers, their safety inspections by function and room, each organized and tidy. The California Luna was promised to San Juan after a stop in Louisiana, Mississippi and up state gulf side Florida; the Berrard barge lines for heavy transport had begun in late May to be used for sulfur transport, the hoisting crane ship with five lifts on deck revealed a high rail deck, wrong width, an industrial unit carried a ball mill to a factory for the eventual manufacture of paper and had been damaged during high waves and was sent back for replacement, a vessel that was to carry bulk cargo – aluminum, grain, or wood chips – was stacked on wood pallets on a stone wharf and lifted by bridge crane to load into the hold, four photographs later, wind turbines were loaded by a bridge crane with an elevator unit, on the tanker ships were three hundred and eighty-four train cargo units, in sixteen rows, stacked three on top of each other, not a foot remaining of unused space, when the high waves hit, the containers fell off the ship, a cargo inspection of twenty ships lined up in Sydney Cove Harbor gave him the impression that the port officer's tasks were consumptive. A big ship with thousands of feet had unloaded sand and gravel on a beach without a pier, correspondence racked in for proof of insurance carrier and thirty pages of questions as to principal carrier, an NVOC issuing their own bills of lading, delays, indemnity for costs arising from an occurrence and photos worth of occurrences consisting of a voluminous black smoke fire on deck behind the bridge, despite an entire ship deck covered by hatches to resemble a basketball court food was contaminated nevertheless, slipping containers, cracked hulls, falling elevators, incorrect readings for compasses, blown engine rooms, refrigerated cargo that had leaked, misplaced trucks with cargo, smashing lifts that heaved at ships, lifts losing timber, U.S. Customs rejections, corrosive damage due to unknown substances; for each photo there were separation claims regarding consequential losses, standardized trading conditions, consignment clauses, transfer of cargo agency agreements, non vessel companies that owned an insurance carrier, a plethora of contracts, loss adjustment and replacement surveys, each with a handful of confirming photographs to be gone through, the shipping industry one of the largest congestive enterprises anywhere. After twenty hours of intensive concentration, having downloaded every proof of paperwork for any situation, matching against any register of photo, batching the particulars for each incident, some of the cargo consignments proofed by indexing for schedules, insurance carrier, ports, product carried, having taken no food other than coffee, no sleep or a morning shave, he threw himself onto his bed and slept, dreamless.

He awoke at five in the afternoon having gotten less than eight hours restive sleep, the sun shining in through the sliding glass doors of the balcony. Jones showered and dressed and called room service, ordering tri-tip steak and mashed summer squash, a garden salad, and a wet martini. When the waiter delivered his tray, there was an addition of cheesecake and coffee, compliments of the chef; Jones ate as though time was of essence, leaving his squash and dessert for later, carrying his martini and coffee to his computer where on the long dresser top he had piled the batched documents beneath each photo of the shots of rail deck similar to his obscure photo.

His first task was to send an E to Rhonda who answered straightaway. Things were grand, she had just returned from a cruise to Grenada where she had taken an agency-directed tour of the arabesque citadel. While there a movie studio filmed several scenes and the nominally trafficked corridors of exquisitely carved stone columns and ceilings came to life under the staging of dramatic light. She was in love again, her beau was a surveyor for island ships, while at the wharf there was a continuous line of instamatic like light on the rooftops, to Jones a certain sign that all blocks of the city were under continual short wave monitoring system. She asked whether he planned a trip into Havana, she would meet him at the airport and take him dining now that she had her freedom; he asked if she might fly into Nassau for a weekend, the idea at which she laughed, her tone gay and unburdened. He signed off with a brief as to his current assignment and she said she would bring him a photo accessory after the fact.

Jones sipped his martini rather leisurely, posting to Lewis' system to save the weekend for better things. Then he looked up her new steady and sure enough found him in nautical surveyors under bridge controls, Stanley Fogturn had made his reputation in navigation bridge visibility for conning position, oddly he was on assignment to the Antilles for seven years and then back to his chair. A ship course admiral, Rhonda was in for a shorter than expected post, something which she very probably knew already, but to Lewis, who had to know as well, her divorce was accepted for some other reason, not to be guessed at by Jones. He could but imagine it was Lewis who had taken another assignation. Jones took his drink to the window and stood overlooking the bay and the fluctuating wind gusting up the water. Life was damnation to a storm catcher, to an analyst the daily news was all one should anticipate. For Admiral Fogturn to have taught when the roughest part of a gale was reached by the storm warning light that came on when the highest wave was traversed made him a popular item for any entry into Grenada, especially if the agency hoped Grenada was to replace Aruba as a secretive entry in winter when the waves were often impassable.

An hour later Jones ate his dessert while watching the ABC news. A whipping whistle wind was on its way in and port authorities were blaming the Deepwater Horizon explosion as a contributing weather complication that could lead to strep throat. The news broadcaster advised as a result of the ongoing crisis shipping carriers select alternate channels to approach the Florida Keys.

Jones' job required absolute, a hundred percent concentration of monotonous work, a flawless ability to memorize seemingly inconsequential detail, scrutiny of problems along with excellent problem solving skill matched in part by any recognition of a major system involving a possible industrial error, instantaneous knowledge of types of ships, parts of each vessel, number of decks, number of cabins, mess, lounge, nautical chart room, use of radio, all bridge functions, steering, contributing cost factors for bulk liquid import and export, damage quote verification costs, and some knowledge of voyage indicators such as compass readings, automatic radar course plotting, GPS receiver equipment, heading control systems and automatic identification of ships system by Saab or other inventor. Thus, like any shipping and receiving clerk, each transaction recorded photos which supplied a ship by vessel name, a carrier, bills of lading by cargo, quantity, assignment number, attachments of correspondence, and any occurrences for which nautical surveyors replaced goods or loss adjusters paid for damaged or lost goods or covered damage to a ship or harbor. There were dozens of profiles for land systems, power plant generators, industrial wind power units, steel rods, timber, or classification sections, bio-medical units, production automation units, HVAC air condition units for commercial businesses and industrial plant operations, X-ray units, and solar units as well as heating and cooling systems, hundreds of photographs of each system, loading and unloading, wharf storage and warehousing handling, transfer from ship to truck, transportation to a building site, and designation.

As he narrowed his search to vessels passing through the Bahamas on their way into or out of the gulf, he focused on combined bulk, after he had exhausted the lift ships convinced he was looking for a smaller vessel in the weight approximation of 14, 790 tons measuring 168.12 meters in length. He studied departure out of Australia for ships carrying industrial chemicals and sulfur up to 22, 000 tons; traveling to Puerto Rico were eight ships per month with unloading stop-overs up to a week. Pictures of wharf buildings, customs and passenger holds and alongside piers and tugboat landings sat the impresario ships, their ramps adequate for any large port, among them Dunedin, Brisbane, Duke Point, Elk Falls, Calliope, Kingston. The tiny rail deck photo played havoc with the high seas, with photos of the Kirkwall Harbors and Union Streets of its mastpoles, the Ashton Coolpix magnifier, Canon EF-S 22 mm wide lens and Short Throw zoom lens coming to the rescue to freeze frame ships passing too closely or bearing down hard closing in the distance. A handful of high waves, disgusting weather, tipping sterns, washed out decks, he looked on V-SAT for din rails and found three, all within the area of his narrow search, one as far north as the Keys, which slowed to accommodate a repair to its barkhead.

At length he considered measuring the shot of the deck from its masthead. Technically he required the ship identification; failing this, he tried with a first, second and third guess at ocean sector by coordinate. He brought up the V2290, copying onto it his photo, to produce the size bridge adequate to the shot. The computer transmitter deployment system gave two distinctly varied shiplines, one, a fair weather with a din rail beneath either a personnel or grain elevator, a bucketladder dredge, thought to be the sturdiest thing on the planet, or a converted scooper post weather bridge marine deep drill ship and second, an expedition reinforced hull capable of cutting a passing zone through solid ice having a medium sized bridge, these two lines showing recent as to month April-May having a knocker and a grounder. The first was an imposing vessel having a slightly reduced speed under thirty knots, a frequent transporter in the islands off San Juan. The other ship was in fact a small size cruise ship, both five decks but this with mostly cabins and telescopes, computers of every type, including cameras installed up deck for observation weather purposes. It was only a matter of time before he found his ship.

The fast runners were put to sea first just prior to the crack of actual light to hit horizon when coastal cutter detection signals received a series of beeping alerts. His fair weather ship had shuddered while on the sea at Point Destination indicating it took a capsize possibly as a result of a box of munitions that could have sparked. Jones radio-telexed the lone port off Bermuda for gale warning information; it was a long shot for a 3208, a fully armed submarine circling in any waters. There were only two such incidents in history – one off the Antarctica directly below the hundsmen, the other outside Puget Basin. Despite its unlikelihood the larger vessel had received two light flashes which placed her right off Grenada to the southern western side of that island, both flashes were ignored, either she rammed ice or was struck. He decided on a hard collision with another vessel or with a pelting, advancing gale front. During a tropical cyclone winds below the common equatorial median bar reached a minimum thirty-two knots, were often reported in at fifty knots or more, battered entire coastlines, bending street lights, discarding roofs, crashing overpasses, shrinking city streets and farmland beneath rising torrential floods, a wreaking fierce hell if ever there were one. It was not out of the question for a ravaging cyclone to produce wind driven oil slicks from the oil spill nor for hail damage to force huge serpents of oil onto land in the form of mud drenched asbestos. Any ship close to landfall would have charted a course upstream if simply to outrun a storm into more sheltered landscape.

He expected a hard swoon to be retrievable from a 2706, a bad weather ream finder. He asked for a transfer to a desk recovery officer and sent a copy to the unit requesting any colliding joint ship, weather beaten or stagnant. Within the hour he had his first set of confirming profiler basin sloggers. These were accompanied by weather observation and positions of AIS vessel traffic. Lloyd's Register had posted a polar ice cap expedition cruiser with seventy days independent operation having been struck by a fast fleet toboggan in early February that had done severe damage to the bulkhead lift; another ship that had found itself slippery locked on a quickly rising oil per muter for two hundred miles had sailed headlong slip speed into a pre-positioning ship loaded with tanks to survey land and jeeps in late May having arrived into Grenada waters after it began losing containers. The rails verified; he photo margined them onto yet another telex broadband satellite communication finding system P-1162, and called it a night.

Rhonda arrived on a 737 at 0420 hours. The first glance found her slender, if not appearing somewhat high strung, her utterly blond hair shortened to her nape, for a fashion which while not unpleasing Jones would not have put on her, a slightly snug fitting grey dress, black square toe heels, a look Jones felt certain could leave Lewis feeling out on the beach. They took the elevator to baggage claim, waited twenty minutes while she chatted about her new job at South End for training, the continual lineup of cruises, deportation at its all time high, immigration denied anyone from the mainland gulf, drugs everywhere, easy to come by, the long hours, the pay incentives, profit sharing, condominium resorts on ten islands, free air travel, an insane number of high lines. When her suitcase whirled on the conveyor, she pointed to it, Jones grabbed it, and off they went to hail an ambassador cab. In the backseat he waited on her words, thinking she had finally shed a backload of antagonism and that alone gave her sparkle and perk, yet as she slid close in on him, he reminded himself not to take sides, for all he knew she was in some amorphous way still relying on her ex husband's leads. He slid an arm around her shoulders, acutely aware she was still seductive physically, her bodice while thin maintained a firm upper torso, bosomy even if the dress concealed her.

Flowering gardens of long estates, many golf courses with ponds, partially secluded gated Italian style, two story apartments whipped past, the day although coming to a close was still overcast with a suggestion of foreboding, she rested a hand on his leg and pecked his cheek. She did the majority of the talking, sharing her ideas in an intimate friendliness he liked in her, telling him, her face close to his ear, who she supervised, he found he knew some of the men, the cost of taking this particular promotion was she had separated from a group of associates she had known for over thirty years. At his hotel he drew her from the back of the cab into his arms as the driver set her bag on the sidewalk, Jones tipped him a fifty, took the suitcase in one hand and his other hand on her back escorted her through the lobby to the elevator down the hall to his suite.

"Fabulous," she said, when he let her pass before him inside his suite, "so much space. Have you been here long?"

"My entire career. Look around, make yourself comfortable." He put her case in the guest bedroom on the dresser and opened the sliders to let in a breeze. "How's Fogturn?"

"Do you know Stan?"

"Never met him, just by reputation. You realize he's with us for a mere seven years?"

"That's what Lewis says."

"What does Stan say?"

"He's been assigned Grenada."

"Because of that ship collision?" he asked, wondering whether his photo wasn't commonplace information among higher-ups.

"There's been trouble for years, the entire place was supposed to be shut out."

"Well, you got in."

"The city there brings in teams of ten every travel itinerary."

"For repairing older parts of the ports?"

"I don't know. The ships dock, young men turn out."

He fixed a glass pitcher of martini, put olives in two long stem glasses with dark yellow rims and poured to the tops. "Cheers, to your new job."

She clinked her glass to his, "So tell me, how're things?"

"I'm well, getting along in my years."

Rhonda sipped half her drink without worrying about her intake and ate the olive. "It doesn't show, I never knew you lived so well, what're you working on these days?"

"I just completed a marine cargo route appraisal."

"Is the work still interesting?"

"Not entirely." He took her to the living room where they sat side by side near a panel of glass walls and wooden balcony looking onto rolling green and a touch of coast and ocean. "It's the way work is after thirty years, it has to be done, I know my limits, that's why I frequently talk with Lewis, he knows everything."

"Did you know he was asked to report on the fortress underground?"

"He hasn't mentioned anything about it to me. What's the problem?"

"He told me years ago if he was put in any position to go back I should get another spouse."

"I think he forgot he said it," Jones said.

"If the agency gave him a consideration, he's probably thinking it over."

"What is it they need?"

"I think they want him to put another shoreline in and direct truck traffic to other port-approved dock facilities. It's not exactly what he's been trained for."

Jones leaned toward her, took her glass setting his also on the glass coffee table, kissing her neck. "You realize how I feel about you. I've thought about nothing else since seeing you."

She relaxed against him, returned his kiss. "I thought about you before I met Stan but you're part of Lewis, there's so much of my life tied up with his that for you to come to Havana to visit me, he'd always know."

There was a duality between them, he was aroused by her, she liked him because he was part of Lewis' seduction to her, he was aware of the tension between them, but with the entry of another man, the tension sprang to life as though his interest was to have some kind of continuity for himself.

He drew her to him and kissed her passionately, his attraction feverish and demanding, she gave into him pressing herself against his body, her length matching his, allowing herself to become motivated by him, as if discarding her self definition in the moment, choosing any course he decided, seeming not to care where it took her. He encircled her in a tight embrace, he thought he might crush her by his incomprehensible indefatigable desire, he needed her and she was wholly compliant, her body went slack, he knew as he had that first day he and Lewis went to see her that she succumbed willingly anything he asked, could he bring himself to ask. He loved her undeniably for himself, wanted to know every aspect of her being, could imagine no other female arousing such profound sense of hunger in him. At some point, the sense of the hour having slipped from any awareness, he watched himself unzip her dress, letting it fall on the floor, in a dream he let her undress him, let her do things to him, his desire became exhilarating, almost potentially excruciating, they made love in exacting cadence, when they were through he felt he could do no more than take her again, this taking consisting of utter rapture, once satiated he possessed no will of his own.

He showered and dressed, comfortable light green khakis and a dark green turtleneck sweater, a bit of cologne tossed in. While he cooked sausage linguini and served a garden salad and chilled white wine, she talked about her regrets over Lewis, her constant sense of an unacknowledged vulnerability, a belief Lewis had walked into an enemy camp and caught off guard, despite being armed, had been tortured in prison. Although he had no visible scars, because he never trusted even her, when he awoke in the middle of the night in a cold sweat, she knew it wasn't his age talking, it was a nightmare. Over dinner, she ran through a list of old worries. There were years when after the disappointment at not having become pregnant by him she believed there was not enough she could ever do to keep his demons away, but those years became replaced by a cynicism that Lewis was heading straight for disaster anyways. Jones told her Lewis was a God to the agency, more so than Fogturn could ever hope to be, Lewis' knowledge ran the flow of information, it was ironic Rhonda had decided to leave when she did.

"No time would have been good," she said. "Invariably something always came up, the work was that way by its nature."

"I can understand that, I've often felt that."

"Well, when two people work for the same agency, there's hundreds of situations that keep them together."

"It isn't as if you've betrayed him."

"I've never thought of myself. With Lewis, his work is the crucial turn, he enlists clues all over his paperwork."

"I considered applying for your old job."

"They will probably look for a female."

He wasn't put off as he thought he could have been. He cleaned up the kitchen, suggested she wear something, she returned to the bedroom, he called Lewis over for a night cap, before she returned fifteen minutes later dressed in grey stretch pants and a hip length white sweater, her hair combed back. Jones put a record of soft jazz on the phonograph, turned on the computer in the dining room to show her his work on the V2210, asked for her ideas, she suggested routing for the post stern once he knew his ship, she was antsy as they sipped coffee to the dregs, he wanted just to watch her.

Lewis Lewis showed up at eleven. He brought his own syrup, gave Rhonda a respectful kiss of acknowledgement on the mouth, asked about Fogturn and when he was getting sent home. She ignored him, poured Lewis a stiff white Portsmouth, poured a Vermouth for Jones and took the syrup herself which turned out to be high bred daiquiri, which was understood to contain licorice Mortimer belladonna, a pint jig in the men's drinks. Jones asked Rhonda to dance and they waltzed about the living room fox trot while Lewis helped himself to Jones' computer to check his work, when the music became slow and melodious Jones turned her over to Lewis who disengaged from the V2910 and fell into step with his ex wife, elegant small turns along the floor near the sliders, one hand on her waist, the other clasped in her hand, Lewis was noble, respectful, distant. Had Lewis thought to confide in him his rationale for throwing her to Jones, Jones could have understood, the sensate emotion was hardly curiosity, it was the enthrallment of watching a beautiful creature he loved in a contained separate partaking, together Rhonda and Lewis danced effortlessly, Jones felt captivated by the fact of her, she represented her separateness of independent measure, Lewis on the other hand was like himself without being himself. In the instant she was her own entity, her thoughts were her own, neither he nor Lewis consumed her with their need for her love, if this was what Lewis meant when he confessed to providing Rhonda with jealousy, jealousy didn't seem to have anything to do with the act, rather Jones' arousal surged forward, able later to be unrestrained. Lewis had drawn her to him, they danced cheek to cheek, Rhonda's face slightly inflamed, Lewis' eyes closed. A slower piece played and Lewis wrapped his arms around her waist, whispering to her, and she wrapped her arms around his neck, Jones walked over to his console and saw that Lewis had requested a mapping, he took another shot of syrup and a bit more relaxed he cut in, pulling Lewis from his partnered position, stepping in.

The music didn't last much longer. They grouped onto the sofa, turned on the television, pulled a blanket over their legs, and sipped their drinks.

"Are you dating?" Rhonda asked Lewis.

"Not a soul, are you?" to which they all laughed.

Jones said, "What's in that stuff anyhow?"

Lewis replied, "Nothing habit forming, although I'm addicted."

"Did you know I was here?" Rhonda asked him.

"Jones told me. I haven't danced in years."

"Would you like more music?"

"I'm fine," Lewis told him, "it'll probably put me to sleep."

The news focused on the weather, the whip wind was due after midnight, snow and hail expected in the interior of Nassau, boats were advised to be locked and motorists to stay indoors.

Rhonda put her head on Lewis' shoulder and fell asleep. Jones suggested they carry her to the guest room, they walked her in both supporting her weight, put her in bed, turned out the light.

"Better check your computer," Lewis advised Jones.

He did. "The army comm. System sent what is essentially a mapping of these two types of ships. These show deck probable damage, potential hazards and wake-producing difficulties."

"There should be on each mapping any communications written by abbreviated industrial language," Lewis said, and came over to take a look. He pointed out a handful of notations. "See? The first comes with a set of tunnels all over Grenada, from a distant photo advance the land covering them looks like, what are these?"

"Looks to me like thousands of white birds on a yellow sand beach," Jones said.

"No, click in – I see that all the time, it's receding water off a basin landform. What was the course set for?"

Jones opened the file. "The set course for this vessel, one time under prior ownership Wilhemsen, was from Aruba through the canal, to Australia, then to Tobaga, and on to Yemen, Bermuda, San Juan and Ponce, to the Grenadines and last stop Costa Rica carrying mostly sand and gravel for stone edifices and landmarks, installation units, and medical center equipment."

Lewis asked to see another file. The next grouping clearly showed that expedition travelers had climbed onto an embankment of ice as the colliding vessel slipped through a funnel blizzard suddenly into ocean view. "Here," he tapped the monitor for a man standing on deck, "a man on port stern where one stands on deck to listen for the sound of any approaching ship, that should give it to you."

"Want to stay over?" Jones asked.

"No, I've got to be going. I'll join you for brunch, shall we say around noon?"

Jones slipped into bed with Rhonda turning her lethargic, sleep induced body to him. She barely came to, the belladonna drug had left her indisposed of, yet she caressed his hip murmuring inaudible words and he nestled next to her as she drifted to sleep. He lay awake for hours perceiving her breath, certain Lewis Lewis had altered the course of his marital engagement to Rhonda, had in fact accepted a new dangerous assignment for which he floated about restless onto a roiling ocean. If Rhonda awakened Jones meant to have her but she slept soundly for hours undisturbed by him or by loud thundering rain as it whipped across the bay, striking against pane and roof for well over an hour. When it subsided, the sliders had been sloshed over with gales of downpour that had eliminated all visibility, she aroused him moving onto him, muttering a few endearments, he came with full emotion, crying in the moment of release, feeling the charge drain out of him, by degrees of tenderness he rocked her body putting her beyond her endurance and gradually she fell to sleep, her hand still against his hip, his mouth to hers. He would think many thoughts including to ask himself his reason for wanting only her, a dim awareness of his learned friend's impotence, of the slayings Lewis must have had to contend with that left him numb, while he had been introduced to their fancy, while he was willing then, while he experienced little evaluative concern for them or himself, after a time he knew he had been solicited. She had become a person who was able to cut through his dead zone, he had never worried that he gave his life to his work, oddly, he, also, was able to be swept away. He had thought he could promise; despite the length of relationship Lewis kept his options available. Jones had thought he could fill the void that possessed Lewis, but here he was, without a desire to be removed.

Perhaps he slept three shabby hours. He was up first at ten, showered, walked around in a robe having prepared fresh coffee, after a half hour he began the brunch meal, buttered rye, eggs d'jardin, French bacon, a liter of champagne. Rhonda awakened just after eleven, showered and dressed in a slinky blue dress that was meant to be eye catching to one naked shoulder, her figure accentuated by the material which every time she walked stressed at her high lifted breasts or slipped over her angled hips and thin thighs. Jones, cigarette in mouth, caught her as she moved past him, the dress caused him momentary pleasure, her body undeniable. He understood Lewis' awakening desires, his obvious fulfillment to her nearness. She kissed him lightly, he scooped her in, his body strained with hers. In his mind he snapped a permanent photo of their liaison, buried his idea of himself as a male who promised her she could forever return to him, remembering then and there she had fallen to sleep with her head on Lewis' shoulder.

Lewis arrived at noon wearing slender black corduroy pants, a double knit Scandinavian turtleneck of black, navy and white colors, loafers with socks, sporting two bottles of ruin rum from Grenada, a bag of baguettes and cream cheese with salmon. He and Rhonda kissed non consequentially. Jones served brunch on the dining room table, opened the sliders a bit, poured coffee into mugs, and set out the champagne into tall narrow glasses iced at the bottom with crushed strawberry glace.

"Chancellor of the House of Commons was on the tele this morning," Lewis said. "Allistair Darling addressed the House regarding his idea of the government's role in the banking crisis policies. I met Andrew Love once in Bermuda, he was all fired up about the need to provide money for green jobs and employment."

Rhonda asked, "Isn't that the item on Lloyd's recapitalization? I think I saw an article about a credit guarantee system for Department of Trade and Industry."

Jones put in his opinion, saying, "John Mann of North Ireland wanted job centers, the dateline came across our computers, they're all asking for introduction of mutuals for mortgage secured loans."

"Well, where the hell's the money going to come from?" Lewis remarked.

"One has to do something," Rhonda replied, glancing at each in turn who sat at opposite ends, "to avoid debt, a micro management system, High Street confidence for building society industry."

"It'll low brush the system for government all over the islands," Jones quipped.

"The ships will stay in dry dock indefinitely until someone raises another interest dollar." Lewis' humor drew a good chuckle.

"Or we'll be issuing out vouchers," was Jones' infinite ability to keep pace.

"It's a definite agreement for repair of fleets," Lewis added. "We'll probably see every older ship brought in through the high dock."

"I couldn't do that estimate finding again," Jones said. "It's the least interesting of our work."

"When have you done costs for traffic?" Rhonda asked Jones.

"In Bermuda, a year ago."

They chatted about the rising number of military suicides in the United States. Senator Ben Nelson of the Armed Services in Nebraska cited causes as extended deployment in Iraq and the recruiting assignments for Department of Defense research and a National Defense task force gave substance abuse as a leading reason, the army had the highest suicides, the marine corp lost twenty-five to suicide in 2006 and forty in 2008. Then there was the AIG scandal, the $80 billion expenditure by the government, the pill bars Zanax pharmacy crimes.

Lewis brought them full circle with, "The question for nationalization of banks that began under Prime Minister Browne has been how to get corporate taxes back into the bank system. My guess is that if there are three million more people since 1999, there's not much point in complaining."

Jones imparted, "A full million ages eighteen to twenty-four that will financially impact education."

Rhonda asked, "Is youth unemployment up?"

"Well," Lewis answered, "it does account for the amount of borrowing."

"Can't cut a way out of a recession," was Jones' wry comment. "Not with interest rates up."

"It's the World Bank overseas problem," Rhonda said, having

eaten a serving of eggs and bacon and now was sipping coffee, saving the champagne dessert for last. "Sri Lanka announced a cease fire, you know, probably to account for lack of munitions."

Sunshine broke through the disappearing clouds. They carried their mugs into the living area. Rhonda sat beside Lewis on the striped black and light green sofa, Jones took the burgundy upholstered chair.

Lewis said, "There was that shelling in Gaza at the embassy."

"All different World Bank expenditure categories," Jones said; "sacking ministers for financial abuses, asbestos in the schools, Bonsley College, I'm up to date on news."

Rhonda laughed. "We are too. It's the early morning agenda from the National Post. By the way," she asked Lewis, "whatever happened to that Dockyard assignment?"

"That's the one. We were out there nearly a month last year," Jones said.

"How did it complete?" she asked.

"We bagged our ship," Lewis said. "It's probably at sea by now."

"I doubt it," she said, having the upper hand. "The documents just got to us."

"What took so long?" Lewis wanted.

"The question of PVs was sent to committee. We had to acquire tests."

"No," Lewis said to contradict her, "we were told to hustle, that the hull was in repair, I myself surveyed it, we were on task round the clock, isn't that right?"

"Yes," Jones said. "We thought maybe a rubber bumper or a change for slip glass."

"No," she was adamant, "it's still waiting."

"Odd," Lewis said.

"We had to examine every photograph for all voyages," she said, finished her cup and set it on the carpet. "She was a sensation in her youth, she transported Winged Victory and Venus, most statues on top philosophy across the English Channel to museums and galleries."

"Probably what she was intended for," Jones told her. "The work was very complicated, demanding, we met with consultants every day."

Lewis got up, collected the wine stem glasses of champagne in hand and distributed them.

"Delicious," she said, after tasting hers.

Lewis agreed.

They sipped, each debating how far to extend the rising argument, Jones recollected clearly Lewis' admonition not to tell Rhonda he had had an affair, Lewis probably had some idea the reason Rhonda wanted to learn what happened there, Jones tossed a question around, was that trip the last time Rhonda was a partner of Lewis, if their divorce wasn't over an office clipboard, if it were personal, why when Lewis and he flew to Bermuda was their separation costly?

"Anyone up for a walk in a while?" she asked.

"Are you?" Jones asked Lewis.

"Sure, I could manage it."

"It's fine by me."

Jones asked Rhonda, "Do you review all nautical losses now?"

Lewis said, sarcasm dripping, "All island loss."

"Does that include edifices, roads, wildlife sanctuaries, yachts?"

"None due to normal wear is on my desk for cost net paperwork."

Jones said, "I didn't realize you transferred to loss adjustment. How do you find the work?"

"It's not bad. My job is with ratings."

Lewis gave his brief summation. "Not like ours, we won't worry over recovery."

"Is Bermuda the problem?" Jones asked Rhonda candidly.

"Well, he wouldn't agree to let me travel with him there."

"We were extremely busy, I can't imagine you would've seen much of us," Jones replied.

Rhonda said, "His point was that he's never married when he's on an island."

Lewis said pointedly to her, "I was incensed when the agency gave that post to you while we still lived on the Baja peninsula."

She retorted, saying, "That's ancient history, for your information I thought it would keep us together."

"You don't comprehend the idea, how would I begin to make sure you were safe? You'd be the one with written complications whenever a problem developed."

"You're usually closing a door on me."

Lewis took a long drink, almost down as far as the glace. "I can't have my whereabouts known when I'm away from the desk, you never want to respect that fact."

"You wouldn't take me up to Dinner Keys either."

"Well, that's stupid, out of the question."

Jones looked askance at Rhonda. "You couldn't go with us for that."

"I would've sunned on the beach."

Jones spoke first. "No females allowed, that's our work, Rhonda."

"I mean," Lewis charged at her, "where would you have put yourself while we were out at night?"

"I would've waited up for you."

"Well, try this, don't put yourself in that position to begin with," Lewis countered.

Jones said, trying to strike a reasonable chord, "Just tell Foghorn good bye."

Before Rhonda could reply, Jones said, "I think it's time for a walk."

The wind had nearly died. The three strolled along the green through the trees toward the beach. Jones walked with an arm around Rhonda's waist while Lewis talked amicably about the early years in the agency, the number of ships entering old San Juan port, the light he left on at the top of stone stairs to his port station flat, a confusion of physicians pouring into each ship that pulled up to a harbor shelf, the number of containers they had to inspect each week. They arrived to a sand embankment, Lewis jumped down, gave his hand to Jones to pull him down to the beach, and helped Rhonda fall onto his shoulder, set her on the beach. There, they walked through the waves, over strands of green seaweed and a smash up of tiny stones and littered shells left by the storm. The air smelled remotely of fish, the fresh salt sea sprayed over rocks jutting from the ocean swells about a hundred feet out.

Lewis said to Rhonda, "I assumed when you transferred off my desk, we could remain friendly, I wasn't trying to hurt you, you just don't understand what you think you want."

Rhonda said, "I would've given up anything. You just took it all."

Lewis said, "The conditions of us necessarily vary, you only want what I can't give you."

Lewis reluctantly drew her toward him, she pulled Jones to her. They stood huddled.

She gazed at Lewis, and said, "Won't you even kiss me?"

He did, as one might a duty, then turned her to face Jones and draped his arms around her. "When did you grow intolerant to me, Honey?"

Jones watched her, the curve of her body, and knew she was beyond his aspiration. She looked as though for an instant she had retrieved a place she thought she needed to be.

"What do you think, Jones?" Lewis asked.

A wave raced up past them and frothy and swirling receded, making the beach damp.

He ought to tell Lewis he was not so lucky, but he held back.

"Oh, Jones, don't fret, he's teasing," Rhonda said, and drew him to her and put her arms around his neck.

"I think you've been at each other too long. It seems she would prefer to believe you can only have her."

Lewis rested his head on her shoulder. "Ask whether she sees him every day."

"Do you?"

"Twice a month."

Lewis said, "Our Fogturn works port, he has to travel about."

"You could visit her twice a month, Puerto Rico is not far

away," Jones suggested.

"I'd have to turn it over, I did agree to the assignment."

"Will it be dangerous?" she asked.

"Can't ask," he said.

"Why haven't you considered applying to our desk?" Jones asked her. He could feel her breathing, he took no risk.

"Come," Lewis said, disengaging, taking her by the hand. "You can drop me off, I'll fix us a drink and send you two on your way."

They started to walk. Lewis asked Jones, "Did you take another look at the file I gave you?"

"I did late last night. It did the trick."

"Good. That's one problematic search to try to find one deck."

Rhonda said, "I told him where to find it."

"He told me. I put on the 2910."

"Had you seen that file before?" she asked.

"No."

"It retrieves any clip that has been stored as part of another file," she explained. "We use it to target bothersome people when a Field agent is reassigned."

"The file has supplied me with tunnels beneath island towns."

"Storage for shipped product," Lewis said. "It's a handy reference as long as you know what to look for."

She hugged Jones to her. "If you complete early you can visit me next weekend."

He laughed at the notion in embarrassment for Lewis. Some unspoken communication between them had gone right past him.

In Lewis' suite they toasted to Rhonda's promotion.

There was a settling of accounts remaining to the divorce and Lewis wound up writing her a check for five thousand dollars. Lewis sliced up leftover hot dogs, cheese and vegetables and placed onion dip on the table with garlic toast and called it dinner. They ate, watched a drama on charting ice floes before Lewis topped off with a spiked brandy, they reviewed the movie, Rhonda agreed there was too much action, too little character, it was entertaining, not like the book.

The day disappeared on them, a shallow nightfall produced a stage set of garden lights that ringed onto the walls. A ship slid across the water in the distance. Lewis put together a care package for Jones, gave Rhonda a peck, said he would call her, and sent them away. Her dejection was obvious, Lewis was over her, she was freer than she realized, Jones was neither in the way nor a pest.

As soon as they returned to Jones' suite, Rhonda said they had made a mistake taking dinner with Lewis, he was working, his mind was else where, she had been aware on the beach he felt intruded upon, she had been wrong to drag up the Bermuda affair, it had bothered her that some ill-minded individual sent her a photo of Lewis having sex with an unknown female, and although she felt Lewis could not have done such a kinky act, she couldn't forget it. She knew she was little prepared for a new romance but she had to assert her rights, her sense of decency. It was all around her, a pervading intrusion, Lewis drank excessively, he was impulsive, rebellious toward her as though she had by her love chained him, she took Jones into a passionate embrace. He held her to him, said he had thought of nothing but her.

Jones took Rhonda for a nine holes game of golf at eight when the shop on the green opened. She was first hand at a swift blow, arching a speedy delivery high into the air for a top rating score, not so poor at a heavy arm swing across a pond. He did his cool even hat best, putting a near ball to a flag six times out of seven. They ran the green, a fairly windy course above the sparkling muddy filling ocean, she taking every stride to capably steer her wind to the farthest find, he aptly succeeded in at least closing in the drive.

He paid the ninety-two bucks on a club tab and they ambled off to brunch at one. A little used patio behind the nightclub, its doors open to gardens in summer, was open since the weather had all but drowned the usual venue. Seated around a smallish glass table, they ordered two tall lattes, croissants and eggs hard. She thanked him for an excellent weekend apologizing for any discourtesy he may have felt because of her. For the duration of an hour until the taxi collecting her bag and ferrying her to the airport arrived, they lingered over the meal discussing her plans. She had to return to her flat in Havana, obtain a briefcase worth of San Juan port files, fly into Puerto Rico to her new station, disseminate task assignments, review status configurations, then out to Bermuda to Hamilton to inspect a cruise ship for deportation problems, verify all passports, contact the U.S. harbors, write up the return bills for re-entering vessels, checking destinations for refrigerated products, arrange warehouse storage, return through San Juan for two inspections, finally she would fly home. Once having ascertained that Fogturn was relegated to Castle to cost a group of paintings, a Donovan, a few Pam Vans, Nance Eckels' House of Sun, Vlad Lepure's Binar, Theo Dapore's vigorous red drippings and would spend a week long inspection in Warwick Long before departing to Great Sound, Jones undertook to arrange a single overnight for Saturday at her invitation. They could tour the governor mansion, go to lunch in the harbor if he liked, view the grand fireworks the city was putting on, get in some swimming, and of course she could arrange to pull the finding file on either ship he had narrowed his search to, he unexpectedly experienced a decisive yearning for her at the idea of being able to handle the actual papers.

When the taxi came to pick her up, he was surprised at his depth of emotion which he experienced as a conflicted letting go. He kissed her lovingly hoping to be able to retain her lingered intimacy, but the minute the black and white vehicle turned out of sight, his longing left. He tossed a fiver on the table for a tip, strolled through the lobby looking for Lewis, discovered him sipping Scotch on the pool lawn having it over with a semi-nude cocktail waitress, lacquered reddish dark hair, gaping cloth omitting ribs to a sparkling blue swimsuit. Jones pulled up a white painted wooden lawn chair, ordered himself a Dubonnet, listened to Lewis' repartee, decided he was playing the field. The female relinquished her hotel suite location and telephone number before she scampered off to get ready for work at two.

Convinced that only Lewis retained Rhonda's address, Jones asked, "Why'd you do a rotten thing like that to Rhonda?"

"Oh, she told you, did she?"

"You're little better than a whipping post."

"It was merely a black and white photograph," Lewis said, rather smugly. "Some day you will see your way to my viewpoint."

The waiter brought Jones' drink with a half brisket sandwich.

Jones took a sip. "You hurt her pride."

Lewis gave a shrug. "She had it coming."

"Is it because of me?"

"Oh, you are nothing to do with it, old fellow. Rhonda sent me a slice of life of the Dinner couple, their refrigerator ransacked, their string of lights inside their living room."

Jones registered shock. "Are you sure it was her?"

"Who but her?"

"I don't think she's capable of that."

"She did it before, she puts herself in a need-to-know. I told myself that was the living end."

"You were infiltrated."

"Well, of course, that's your view now, just wait until you've known her a while, she's not always in a harmless mood." He took a long sip. "She didn't work up here, she worked for Baja for a good amount of time, that's all those boys know, shooting pictures of anyone who steps across the border into Flitty Town, I was lucky, I left first sign of their release of a snow job on an island agent."

"It's nevertheless crass."

"It's crass you want a piece of her ass."

"I did it for you."

"You did it to sign on for good times."

"Something like that."

"You're a young fifty-plus."

"I didn't start this."

Lewis gave him a thorough one-over. "I brought you along because I honestly didn't think you had much experience with women. I have rarely seen you take a female out."

"It hasn't been high on the list. You seem unable to get started without a third party."

"That comes with the territory, you find you live forever as far as anyone is concerned, see it all, have it all, at some point nothing makes for healthy excitement."

"I can't juggle the job to fit a relationship in, that's all. I've had my affairs, those are for when one is youthful. You've never said you wanted to know."

"Fine, I misjudged. She has slimmed, I'll grant her that. Do you like her better than your tennis chum on Bermuda?"

"Yes, that one withheld, you would've liked that more than me, no doubt."

"Don't tell me what my type is, Jones, they're all the same to me."

"There's no comparison, Bermuda was uncommitted, Rhonda is inviting, she doesn't deny."

"Trust me, she'll make you pay if you stay long enough."

"Alright, so now you know."

"Don't worry, she can do whatever she likes."

They nursed their drinks in minor disagreement. The dark red returned in a short white pleated skirt with an extremely low neckline that revealed soft breasts carrying a bar tray and a refresher for Lewis and he began where they left off, asking about why she transferred from town to the hotel, she gave him an amusing answer that she could watch the tables for every player's hand while clerking the change, at which he laughed, the tension dispelled altogether.

"Spice of life," Lewis said. "She's pretty, don't you think?"

"Stunning. Friendly also."

"I agree." He began on his second drink. "I noticed her right off when she climbed out of the pool, a gorgeous beauty, radiant expression."

"She obviously likes you."

"Yup," he said, with a laugh of pleasure.

Jones finished his sherry. "Have the sandwich, I've eaten."

He had spent too long at the pool nursing Lewis' wounded sentiments when he ought to have been studying the new retrievals given him by the V2910 enhancements. He had a sense that in the hour chasing Lewis' blues away time had unreasonably slipped past him, as he found his path into a tunnel of blood red stone and large pipes down the arched overhead ceiling of chipped stone, water flooded a third of the way up, as he checked for an exterior location shot, produced a storm gathering water off the sea of the Grenadines, water and mud having seeped in at calf-deep level, he denied to himself that all Lewis wanted was a good cathartic fight. If Rhonda had degraded Lewis with a sneak shot, she had her reasons, even if the photographs could endanger which Jones considered dubious, he had a hard time seeing any motive for maliciousness, Rhonda after all had sacrificed her career over Lewis. It wasn't as though Lewis had helped his own situation any by acknowledging he had accepted another volatile job, clearly risky, somehow taking him straight into hostile territory, he alone had told Rhonda he was leaving soon. Another tunnel, this one of dark grey stone, the stone sides anchored by thick metal grids to reinforce against an aging edifice, narrow stairs and a flat walk way along the center, an exterior shaper took him to a fortress of thick stone walls and a religious dome, Jones plugged in coordinates and mapped them on a P-1165, producing also a separate file of photos each three by one inch arranged adjacent in a row; a sandstone tunnel set a neat foot and a half above high ground on a beach with translucent eggshell bluish water, he looked for any environmental explanation and found only oceanfront, the tunnel itself followed a half mile of stagnated sand to a rail, where a dummy wooden horse taken off a carousel rested next to an electric breaker system, where directly above were street grates for rain water. A different tunnel of gray clinker stone with a bright torch light a third of the interior route showing against the nearly impenetrable dark like a lit-up room of yellow orange color, a night shot of the same tunnel doused entirely with twinkling starlight lights emanating from the side walls and ceiling, twenty stairs leading from a darkly yellow tunnel wider than the others by about eight feet up to the street, all placed to the southernmost tip of Grenada where there was one town, otherwise the exterior landscape was surrendered to wild lands of dense low trees, a few red or blue flowering plants, herbaceous stalks and prickly pineapples. Candescent glowing yellowish lights in a newer yellow stone tunnel swamped knee-deep with murky oil like dark water; uneven layers of dark yellow, off white, rust, occasional maroon narrow two foot wide passage with concentric arching ceiling stones; a dark bluish grey tunnel framed by blue metal that gave an appearance of windows for possibly three blocks in length with a door wedged open by heavily collecting mud; and a tunnel composed of petrified strata like a stone miners' tunnel. Although he was fairly certain the passages had remained boarded up for decades, he thought possible they led to mansions, warehouses on the stone wharves below the arabesque castle, rooms off the main floor, a few permitted discreet storage along the coasts. He searched for entrances to and from streets but finding none, he looked at old vineyards gone to seed, at their country estates, interior halls, boarded up wine casket cellars, the passages off the coasts appeared to contain no outlet, not even to stone bordered trenches converted to walking paths.

A loud knock on his door shook him from a comfortable session at the computer, glancing at the clock he saw the time was eight-twenty-five, still plenty of daylight streaming inside through the windows. He stood, finding he had grown stiff from sitting, and went to open the door to a slightly tipsy Lewis whose casual dinner wear consisted of black cotton trousers, a starched white, long sleeved shirt, black satin jacket and black Gucci shoes made Lewis appear unusually good looking. He invited Lewis in, showed him the subject of his hours and asked his advice to which Lewis good naturedly typed in a few references and raised captain's houses, medicine rooms and boat houses and adroitly referenced matching coordinates. Lewis had brought his syrup and he administered several drops in brandy and ordered Jones to drink up and then to wash up and dress in appropriate night club garb. Jones took a two minute shower, dried off, chose dark blue corduroys, a blue lace bib shirt, a bright orange bow tie, formal white dining jacket and Gabardines. Lewis hauled him at sunset up the dell to high top cabins, Pompano Beach style deep tan stucco, iron gated, two story, free standing condominiums with long windows, balconies, and patios bounded by the best money could afford. Abby welcomed them inside to a slate covered living room of comfortable dark brown couches, two grey upholstered wing back chairs and a varied assortment of wood tables, a long stylish varnished walnut beneath a large plated mirror, several birch tables for bound books, glass magazine tables, the effect was of a wealthy relation or dead husband who had bequeathed her the joint. She herself wore a plain white sheath, a choker necklace of small white gemstones, a match of bracelets, spiked white heels, and wore her hair down in subdued wavy ringlets to her waist, her eyes kept track with Lewis. Jones excused himself after the first glass of white wine and went to roam the house upstairs, he found her computer in a wood paneled study at the end of the hall, he transferred all files onto several diskettes, then opened a few files surprised to discover she had photographed nude for a semi legal russet market trade in Santiago. She was indeed a winsome pose to a feast, a scene with another female turned him off cold, he scouted around searching for any window of enhancement, Jones found her in confined settings of fresco walls, dim overhead lights, a distant view of a balcony thronged by column statuary, fully dressed in glittering shoulder less gowns, boutique appreciations of deep red under garments, men's trousers without a blouse, on her back, reclined on her side, her hair pinned back, her hair tumbling free. She must have earned a fortune. In one pose she was curled up, knees to chest, not a hint of sexuality; in another pose she wore just a brassiere, whoever photographed her wanted her known for elegance. Jones joined them after an hour, Lewis and Abby sat outside on the patio laughing up local rumors, making their way through a bottle of aged cellar wine, Lewis' hand held hers, her long curls dangling behind her chair, her heels discarded, feet bare. Lewis placed his hand on her nape, drew her to him and kissed her, set his wine on the table and ran his palm over her collar tracing the curve, kneeled in front of her, where upon she covered his face with her body. Uninvited, Jones pulled away from the view, walked into the living room, picked up a book on art, lay on a couch and read.

Glaring lights awakened him, Jones took in the photo shoot gradually. On a rug behind the other couch Abby lay dressed in Lewis' trousers, her chest exposed. She had applied blue eye color, bright purple lip gloss. Her hair fanned upward framing her face. Lewis kneeled on the mat beside her, still wearing his knee shorts, garter, shirt and jacket, filming from a long shot lens. She appeared captivated, she parted her lips, lifted a breast, dipped her finger into a jar of body paint, streaked a line of glittering blue down her firm abdomen. Jones stood, barely inebriated, moved to them, took the camera from Lewis and got six photos of her, two of them in an embrace, Lewis asked Jones to lie beside her, to kiss her mouth and Lewis shot a close up, he suggested Jones kiss her breast, Jones made an act of softly caressing the underside for the camera, of running his fingers over her skin, a motion which caused her to release breath, he moved his mouth slowly over her neck, her collar, pressed his hand against the swell and kissed her, his lips closing in on her nipple, he sensed her hesitancy as Lewis snapped photos quickly of the final kiss and told her as he shot a succession he wanted to take her home to memorize her. Jones perceived a far-off distance come over her, felt her regard Lewis without the slightest barrier, heard the shutter close twice, heard him give her a drop of syrup on the tongue, spill another drop on her other breast, she placed her finger in it and inserted her finger into Jones' mouth, he was instantly heady, without reserve, he moved slightly onto her, tasted the drop, feeding to take it all, Lewis told her to pretend it was him, she brushed her fingers lightly over Jones' head, held him to her, her gaze solely on the camera.

Lewis abandoned the use of the camera, turned off a light. He lay on her opposite side, helped himself to a drink and told her about his job, a few anecdotes, he cupped her breasts, told her she took his breath away, kissed her longingly, asked if she would allow him to undress her. She unbuckled the trousers herself. Lewis freed them from her hips, she turned to face Lewis and just as he entered her, Jones kissed her neck and back, his emotion brimming, he was not quite himself, floating on a euphoric dream, he wanted her to want him too, to feel thrilled when Lewis asked Jones to rest his hand on her hip, move her against him, which he did tenderly, feeling her perfectly shaped backside, confessing she was a dream. Lewis overcame her fast putting her right into Jones, Lewis said she was his best ever, she was so beautiful he had asked himself if he could touch her, he wanted her love forever. Hours later, when they viewed the cam deck, Jones was absolutely struck Abby seemed vivid, looked blushing, her facial quality said she was totally given over to them, she looked as though they had made passionate, sensual love for days.

She walked them to their hotel. On the walk back Lewis talked to her about his innermost desires, there would be weeks when he had to set himself free by traveling on a ship, he always returned to love, he needed that sort of risk taking, he was far past his prime to gamble on affection, he stopped to kiss her, the air flashed, she gave into him, arms about his neck, pressed tightly to him. They walked arm in arm, she in black stretch pants, a zippered tight fitting top and sandals, her head against his shoulder, she careful to include Jones in conversation, drawing him in with a smile, laughter.

Lewis insisted she see his place. She came willingly, in the elevator Lewis said he had looked everywhere for the right female, he couldn't believe his luck. He lifted her hair around her, told her he had fallen completely in love on her rug, she made him feel free. They walked to Lewis' suite, Lewis pushed open the door, held her as she walked inside, told Jones to latch the door. He fixed ginger ale and rum drinks, asked her to make herself at home, suggested Jones get some air circulating about, and while he gave her a tour, Jones slipped the starting diskette into Lewis' computer and the other two he labeled and inserted into his library. They settled to a game of gin rummy around his dining room table with their drinks, Lewis dealt the starting hand, passed to Jones to his left, Abby talked about her recent photo shoot in Jamaica, the grand style hotels, lavish rooms, sweeping staircase; Lewis tossed four cards to Abby, and they began to draw. She put down three, all hearts, in a numerical lineup, and swept the table surface with a card, hoping for an ace of hearts or a joker wild card. Checking her card, she dispatched the joker onto her lineup, said they should play for bonds, and took a throaty sip. Jones told himself she had crossed too great a line over an ocean casino draw that landed her in a hotel room with probably a smuggling patrol agent, for some reason she was tossed out as a non involved participant. Although he thought he could stay over for another party, when Abby toyed with her blouse zipper taking it below her cleavage, he thought it was time to leave, but Lewis sensed his intent and proposed a toast, then cleared the table and brought out leftover pork roast, placing it in the center with several condiments, radish, mustard, sweet pickles, olive paste. Laughing he told Abby she was trapped for the day, which she said was fine since she didn't have to film; they stabbed forks on pieces of meat and dipped into the sauces, took a few bites, and finished off their drinks. Jones thought it through again, this time he said he had dallied long enough and had to be off.

He walked the building length of hall to his suite, relieved to be gone. Lewis had sunk to a depression of the soul, he was fighting a bad demon, neither a religious exultation nor a regimented one, although the depravities of the contained wards of the islands were well known from slavery and falsely applied departure for shipping to overseas storm callings, often of designated inland revised systems for scheduling. Lewis' assignment was of course to be unknown, an indiscernible grouping of cause, complicated by the rapid growth of their large northern neighbor, benefiting the least benign for private secretariats of exploitation. He let himself into his suite, switched on his computer, saved the information he copied off Abby's rolodex onto Lewis' extension and referenced any location for any single complexity. While the tools of industrial standards checked off numerous degrees of latitude, he sent to automated text the entire file, with all summaries restricted Jones would then be able to catalog historical points of interest. He could not begin to make selections until he had carefully considered Lewis' prefect script – they are usually top pay, his girl was Jones', his passion also Jones'; Jones might return to finish up the night if he encountered a reliable methodology, as it were, Abby was not enough like Rhonda, who for Jones was a far better seduction, but placed Lewis in the background. The tangible reality couldn't be the lights in his underground tablet nor the finer materials used in construction nor the blue metallic frames that bordered up old water pipes or the flat walkways that obviously followed a lengthy course, despite his awakening in her flat when at first he saw nothing but the strength of lights. It had to be the illusion of a lit room along a corridor that had no separation of space, if Abby were a sophisticated pro, she wore an unmistakable detection of gold, aside from her spectacular capability there really wasn't anything tangible to go on. Baja had been a real problem, it had eliminated their capture.

Jones had to marvel at the realization, that was the assignment, Lewis had to find any realistic method to disable their further sabotage. Jones had no idea as to how he could provide support, the agency had distributed tasks based upon capability, only Lewis knew what he knew, and Lewis was an enigma. Very possible Lewis had gotten trapped by mortar fire, ran into a room, blasted through a hole in the wall and shoveled a trench to light of day, also possible he had already recovered against any prying eyes to find photos that should never have been taken, if in sending Rhonda negative day exposure he destroyed any find. The question as to intrusive finding was, how much exposure did Baja take, was it leg, possibly, hard to know if they also placed agents on the road. Abby did not join with them as Lewis hoped, her training of posing semi clad had to have prevented it, knowing Lewis, Lewis would no doubt keep her until he had her mostly succumbed. Jones grouped his case under a final category, for complete target as to any recorded dialogue spoken on a rail deck for any ship sighting, then called Lewis and said he was returning in a few minutes.

With counter industrial they were all in the thick until the target was known. Jones assumed Abby worked for Baja, thought it likely that Lewis had asked for a clandestine female object. He shaved, showered, selected casual, tan refined silk, trousers and jacket, a black shirt, dampened his skin with fragrant cologne, his best watch with hidden date, loafers. Abby opened the door, her hair swept up behind her head into a tight coil, wisps set free, her mouth freshly painted, bikini top disposed of, in its place one of Rhonda's grey cashmere sweaters, unbuttoned, Abby's breasts nicely snug against the texture, her stretch pants holding at her hips. Behind her the room was encased in darkness, the only light from a low flame off the insert hearth. Jones drew her toward him, slipped his hands along her skin beneath the sweater, her posture slightly resisting as before, she was still not enticed. He followed her into the living room, noticed Lewis had opened his computer to a string file, remembered Abby didn't have a swimming pool possibly in order to prevent sensual relaxation, technically high rate were models trained as escorts to men or as divinations for females, often youthful actresses. Jones didn't think she had ever worked that limousine. Lewis prepared him a drink and Jones handed it to Abby to taste, she earned a peculiar distracted inadvertent gaze from Lewis to her expression when, barely sipping, she decided it was heavy on sauce; Jones took it from her, asked whether they had slept off the earlier potion, she indicated they lay in front of the hearth to talk, he tasted his drink and assented, it was strong. Jones suggested they sit on the balcony, they made their way out into the chill evening air, sat on stiff shipboard chairs, drinks in hand, whereupon Jones asked about her trips to other islands, she said she had posed in Bermuda, at Boaz, in Grenada at the Sheraton Loes, and in northwest Carrol Island for the wild refuge estate, all shots under minimum exposure, breast-bare, no lower cloth removal, makeup in three eye shadows, shades of moist liptone, sometimes beige wrap, usually fine apparel, two toned heels, shadowy trees barely eclipsed, a male photographer, always heterosexual, often consoling, any itinerary, all nude photos at one hour past dawn for liquid color. Her play time gave her any secluded palatial bedroom but could not use a balcony, ramp or jetty, beach photos were taken midday after one and before three for the lack of shadow, almost never an evening display, never at night. Of course she had men from the set, they were youthful but definitely aging, each affirming, no city travel or caves, no ice events or swimming, she had never worked Clairol or Mademoiselle or any travel club. Her sole attention was to the camera, she had no inability to work escort, except it required voyeur sex with at least two females. Her undoing was to prefer any desire given by an older man of exceptional position, she told Jones she had been accompanied by a gentleman who asked her to dinner at an all male club and her arrival caused an immense flap, he then brought her to his grandmother's sixth husband where she was asked to disrobe for him, her gentleman and he proceeded to toast to health during which she was permitted to approach the older man and let him touch her. He was deeply affected by her, her skin was very soft, she asked him to rest his hand on her upper arm and she pressed to him while caressing his head. Jones replied that was a beautiful tender tale, at which she touched his hand, and held it inside both hers. The sweater opened, he became infused with a misguided passion, a breeze blew across her chilling her skin. He told her Lewis worried that at his age Jones had not been privileged to know many females because of their work, Lewis said – four females in his adult life – for which she took his hand and placed it on the inner swell of her cleavage and said he was young yet;

she said in college she had discovered one afternoon that her roommate had kept her boyfriend late until she returned from work and when she took her shower they had joined her, he was mature and creative whereas her roommate was possessive, Jones asked whether she had ever taught love to a man, she cupped her palm to the side of his face and said she usually only fell for them. He said it was cold, they went inside, Lewis turned the flame up and they settled onto the floor, Abby with her head on Lewis' side, Jones lay against hers. They watched the fire, Jones described the drink as having worked him over, Abby said it had left her peaceful, Lewis exposed her, covered her left breast with his hand, said she was more beautiful than anyone, he only wanted her to know every facet of their lives, she ran two fingers between Jones' lips, Jones tasted them, the drink rising up in him as an unquenchable fire, but he waited, she tracked his chin, neck, chest, her breath subduing as Lewis pushed her breast to one side and back again, telling her he was captured, he could caress her all night, she ran her fingers through Jones' hair, let her gaze go drowsy, Jones asked her not to stop. Lewis leaned over to kiss her, he did so longingly, she strained herself to him, breast beneath his chest, her fingers grasped Jones' hair, releasing him, she encircled Lewis' neck while she held the back of his head, when he pulled back to look upon her, she arched once, Lewis urged her to him, she repositioned herself partially onto him, Jones matched his length to hers comfortably aligned, removing his shirt, slipped his hand inside her stretch pants surprised to find with aching need the lining was silk and she wore no under garment, her skin smooth, her muscles resilient, no longer trained taut, she relaxed against him, the sensation of finding her responsive to his touch released surging pleasure, he allowed the cashmere sweater to sweep over his flesh, Lewis placed a hand beneath her pants, his fingers inside her, moving in and out of her until she thrust against Jones, demanded Lewis, his mouth covered her breast, and as he sucked her nipple, she came, suddenly moist, crying out, shuddering hard.

Lewis removed her pants, loosened her hair to her waist,

admired her backside, he asked if she were sleepy, she said
not yet, he told Jones to finish. Jones undid his trousers to the
knees, raised onto Abby's back, erect he entered between her
legs, dipped into her moist silky body gliding easily, her body
offering not any resistance, her slender proportion exquisite,
sensational, indescribable, perfect, he fit perfectly inside her,
joined, she was made for love, his heart melting, she was so
beautiful, so fine, her shoulders, full mane, those full sensuous
breasts, only him, he loved her, she closed her legs slightly, she
was so fine, oh Abby, Abby, he rushed at her, burning with
ultimate desire for her, spellbound, thinking he would fly, it
was almost unbearable, sublime, his passion all consuming, she
flooded, he wrapped himself around her. Lewis caressed her
head of hair, lifting it, letting it fall, again then again, saying
Jones was radiant, ecstatic, brimming, consummated, it was
her infallible beauty, he himself was surrendered, felt fated to
her, he wanted her for every need; Jones fell onto his back, she
turned over, her hair wild beneath her, she caressed Lewis' face,
they fell into bed, Lewis on the verge, his body pressed close
to her, Jones' hand on her other thigh. Lewis lit a weed, she
took several puffs, Jones took a hit, it was sweetly herbaceous,
he perceived intense yearning, a craving to be taken, he let his
hand travel up, she appeared as though she might have a moment of indecision, Lewis braced her with his leg observing her
without attempting to involve her, Jones held her in his hand,
kissed her face long enough for her to decide to kiss him if she
had wanted, he ran his hand over her breasts letting her firm-
ness excite him, he felt her nipples harden, watched her breathing pulse, pushed up on them from under, sleek flesh arousing
in him an agony he hadn't known could exist, caressed each
slowly and deliberately mesmerized by his growing desire, his
own breath becoming labored, his body pinned to hers, wanting her to be one who could abandon, all thought converging
on a single miraculous expenditure, desire threatening to burst
from him, Jones felt a rush, a thorough rapture, peak gratifica-
tion coming for him, she nudged him down her body saying,
hurry, he kissed her ribs, abdomen, her legs, as she pressed his

face to her, putting a finger into his mouth, he spent himself. They were transfixed, steeped with sex, unable to move for half the hour. Jones traced the contours of her body as he emerged, when she had him where she wanted him nestled against her breasts, she wrapped her legs around his body, he knew he had discovered a magic Lewis needed him to discover, she said she thought he liked her a good deal, he murmured it was Lewis' best favor. When at last she gave him permission to touch her again, she reminded him he had not wanted her to stop, and she knew she hadn't wanted to, lying on her pressing tightly against her, she told him to let himself go, anything was okay, she hadn't had her fill, she ran her hands through his hair, said he could still lose himself, she reclined a leg on Lewis, wet his ear with her tongue, faster, faster, he whispered the moment he slipped inside her, oh Jesus, Abby, where did you come from.

When Jones survived the night, they were sitting up talking, Lewis behind her, Abby filing her nails. She explained she required her separate residence for her business arrangements including for mail. Lewis snuggled her resting his chin on her shoulder. Couldn't she reside with him midweek, return four days, he'd arrange transportation.

Abby gazed over to Jones. "How did you sleep?"

"Dead to the world."

"Don't you agree, darling, we all slept an excellent night?"

His hands cupped her breasts. "I was done in."

"I fell asleep on Jones."

Jones said, "Do you take off soon?"

"In a month, the crew returns to Panama for a two week itinerary. I'm told lots of sand and rocks, no nightclub photos, at least a crowded street with fire hydrant, a day on the boat into border canal, they've asked me to tan."

"Border canal is gorgeous, it leaks with excitement," Jones said, fully awake, conscious of Lewis' not so subtle push against her breasts, of his encompassing her body, Jones' rising passion no longer a distraction, a dim reality that in all long term live-ins he could not wed a female who worked as a spy to their company and thinking this Jones wondered how this ménage began with Rhonda, was he someone in Baja, or in the agency, Jones ran a smooth hand along her inner leg, Lewis lit a joint weed, pushed it to Abby's lips after he had inhaled a shocking three continuous halations, she thought to absorb an equal number, then Lewis fed the remaining to Jones, Lewis uncapped a brewer's tin, took a sip, advised Abby for two, Jones should take one.

When Jones opened his eyes, Abby and Lewis were locked into a passionate embrace, Lewis soaring, trembling with her, if sleep called so insistently for him, Jones had no choice but to submit, an hour later he aroused to her copulating him, he rushed to an ejaculation, the wind and weather had abated, he was shaken out of sleep to Lewis breathing hard beneath Abby, her hips revolving on his without end, Jones became hard as she spent him to breathless gasps, Lewis whispered Abby, oh! Oh, God, Ab-by! It's delirious! Take! My ! breath!

Unable to resist sleep Jones left, he was unaware of having dreams, scarcely aware as to how he came to be kissing her, she was craving, demanding, her lotioned body was exiguous on his, restlessly mercurial, excitable, Jones could scarcely repress his stunning exhilaration, he conformed to her, resonant, cohesive, until he could no longer conceal his convergence, his emotion stirred, the necessity of her stimulus a statute, she possessed an elasticity, the fact that she didn't seem to relinquish herself to the extent of lack of self composure caused him to feel continually desirous, he had to say if this was what Lewis did to create urgent adherence in Rhonda to his effervescent libidinous contemplations, then had she long ago relaxed a possessive tendency, if Lewis himself had been dormant as he had, the pursuit of desire had induced a suggestive attention that unequivocally captivated..

BORDER

Chapter One

FEDERAL EMERGENCY MANAGEMENT AID
    Federal Court
    US Court of Appeals
    US District Courts
    US Court of Claims
    US Court of Patent Appeals

DADE COUNTY
    Commission
    The federal courthouse
    A jury of seven men and five women
    Census 2010

AJACCIO, Corsica (UPI) –
    Army, division, a tactical corps
    U.S. Air Force, propjets

LAWS PERTINENT TO OFF-SHORE INDUSTRY
    4 laws, off-shore betting on a ship
    Selection of army corp. industrialization center
    Communication satellite
    Computer electronic recording in satellite perimeter
MERRELL LABORATORIES PAPERS
    Cayey, Puerto Rico
    Vaporized chemical, methane

11/20/10
The file sat tucked away beneath a dozen or more status reports
wanting terminations of billing completion, photo itineraries,
primary suspect identifications, DOA morgue status, and any
of a number of risk fulfillment releases. Lewis was not at all
happy with what the file called for. To begin with, he had to
relocate out of the Cabo Rojo up to Miami or somewhere close
by, and for another he had to take a unit with him of field retirees each taken off a different file which he felt could leave
them all wide open to exposure; better to derive a new unit
entirely of locals trained for border elimination or court administered to port status. As it was he was assigned to manager
in charge of 144,000 condos with ocean views for sale, 62,000
actually sold, and a schedule of actual related costs that had
to be reviewed daily before the new revised market opened.
His ten men might work the baggie line-up, a twelve hour a
day job at the border of the Keys for inspection trucks driving through customs packed with drugs which were usually
hid inside panels, a 2nd group monitors crew to sit high on
mountain verandas or off to the shoulder on boulevards waiting for taxis – it was not uncommon for taxis to be loaded with
cocaine, marijuana, or drivers to line their bodies. In addition,
chief muckimucks wanted another set of eyes on Immigration
& Customs in Caribbean, when Patrol followed over bridge off
the island, tram mid air, track illegal immigrants with convic-
tions, any record for burglary, possession. Hundreds of illegals
flooded through the Keys driving north off the long span on
the ocean. A thousand miles south of Miami in Puerto Rico –

this was sensitive area for large quantities of drugs, USCG had to obtain custody orders for Panama because smugglers wanted to close distance of drug contraband. Already it was estimated a ton of coke a year crossed into the U.S.

Old San Juan had DEA and Police ICE (Customs) Officers found suspicious material while on board a large yacht when they dismantled a section of wall and squeezed through a narrow passage, the highest amount of crime in the Atlantic was Miami Beach and it was a small city, port stations had been Puerto Rico, Bermuda and Antilles on Actriz, areas of concern involved daylight drama, news, some chase if it went through many jurisdictions and some psychological, first rank – public; other rank – legal. There were worse happenstances than tired files, files scattered throughout the bulk of mundane folders. Lewis would be twenty thousand files into the assignment before he identified a single misplaced section, he wouldn't know where the research could lead until he spotted the irregulars, what with the photo release of the bombing of the Edgewater he thought maybe the agency had enlisted the fact that the condo high rise was fifty percent owned for time-shares made the crime conspiratorial. Because that condo file exceeded four hundred thousand photos, it might be a half year before he encountered a misfiled World Trade Center or some such photo.

The scenarios for drug raids included a top row of photos on the first sheet of the file, access to St. Francis and Chinatown, an espionage movie depicting a chase on foot through a fortune cookie factory and down the street to a restaurant kitchen as a foreign crisis looming beneath the bay bridge, a scene of the Legion of Honor in which art came wrapped up, never as a collection, the new luminescent MOMA, a Meckha display featuring ceramic art on canvas paintings, a photograph of the Museum of Modern Art in Ft. Worth – all glass, one story, looked like a gold block that was situated on a reflecting pond, and across from the Kimball Art Museum designed by Louis Kahn, a one story, elongated building white columns topped with clear glass, photo-voltaic cells, LED lighting; the New York Art Museum – light gray building comprised of three potentially toppling blocks at end of street, grey white concrete, a Kala creation of two young damsels coming down stairwell at opera, Modern Art, loose squiggly lines pink, orange, peach, yellow, white; oil images – all red, yellow, white horizontal with pink, plum, orange dabs, vertical blue, light blue, left corner blues, oil paintings of bombs bursting in air, a wet look, white on yellow, both on red which was imposed on green and teal; lines of vibrant purple, teal, brown, orange, yellow, pink, white, blue with thin black and green lines for art therapy healing; Renoir – young girls reclining on sofa with mom, black and white dog on rug, an entirely different set of paintings, (1) a yellow crescent on teal, beneath it black, red line intersected by bold yellow watercolor; (2) four panels of the setting sun, (3) Scarface – an experiment in perspective of a man shooting water pistol from other side of painting of sunset; and (4) Limited shelf life. For still life paintings by perspective artists, everything as though from a third story viewfinder the successive photos ran unpredictably with Max Hornak – red powdery clumps thrown onto white;

Lagasse Gallery – one wall painting mounted, yellow with some red, black; thick white middle, bottom purple blue with pink; a Garaughty – blue and white broad brush strokes on tan; a dark abstract of branches hanging over a lake drafted in low hues of grey, green, black and white; and then period work between 1990 – 2010. South American Art – vivid pink tinged abstract by Neville Longmore, no use of white; a vivid portrayal of a man smoking on bed in narrow room, contrast wine against tan, a panel light blue gave an overall shadow; a painting of twin girls, blond, blue-eyed, representative of the illegal baby trade of predominantly babies born with major deficits, legal blindness, partial limbs, severe hearing disorder, any former life threatening disease; an altogether calming, unusually restorative Joel Beckwith – man in a bar of tables covered with pink tablecloths, black/white tile on the walls and muted pink ceilings. With the sole exception of the twins which Lewis viewed entirely as hardcore, these sheets in the section of four hundred and eighty photos were straight modern, nothing political nor sentimental.

Across town inside what used to be an old Spaghetti Factory were the still steel framed political art, most of it partially wrapped but each piece uncovered from its waterproof plastic covering; a minimum of six hundred paintings of various neglect, few absolutely ready to be viewed, a high up gallery a quasi-look of authentic oil and obscura. There were six (6) Baptiste Debonbourg, the most sensational the Trane Cul Surprise pale treatment watercolor of stunt cars rescued from scrap, drivers raced front halves of cars, pastel blue, yellow, pink; Derek Boshier, City, oil on canvas, myriad of city lights on dark and deep yellow hills, a dismal depressive work; Deborah Butterfield sculpture of a horse titled Horse, sitting, made of tin, metal, wood, tire; seven (7) by Paul Chan, simple depiction made to resemble actual photography of sunlight window on dark gray floor with gray walls, looked identical to a skylight image; these considered political because they referenced first takes removed as each of seven aircraft descended to crash; (8) Two boys shadow prints in room with rust wall of eight frame windows that appeared first in "Art-forum Chicago Magazine"; a Peter Graham – Yachts from Monaco, pastel ochre buildings, shimmering reflections enjoyed by filter network photo editor as Milan's 0410 Philippine Air came down over Istanbul, together with nine (9) Derrick Hare – Into the Blue, always with his it was a question of restoration but with these he was residing in Fez Parlor in central Istanbul and he painted all in blue to signify all first takes were archived on ice, tide flowing from a beach, soft almost deniable waves, all blue beach; another grouping but not a series, ten (10) Hung Liu, Trophy, dark tan boys dressed in white stiff shirts and tan trousers carry a two seater airplane that had crashed; Michael Andrews, a Canadian out of Winnipeg, commented on for purple, blue and black crossroads on red, a Hans Paus of beige beach, red sky; a style page of art at the Northern Gallery for Contemporary

Art – oil yellow, green, blue, orange, red, brown, purple, pink –
migrations of color; Taetzsch giclee prints on canvas, also two
pieces hung side by side as diptychs, yellow, red diagonal, red
upper left quadrant, and pink lower half of a brokerage firm's
solicitation in the hour; and finally a Wartenberg famous for
color only, no white or mixed beige, she was Israeli whose exhibit was flown to Bucharest, Romania and Haifa.

Twelve photos were released on tags; (12) inside two factories in Ankara, Turkey; F-111 if armed, full alert, a crash in
Turkey, stocked full, men who were detained were transported
to prison were Bulgarians; a side shot of the plane, a third shell
blue with gold stars hauled to England from Tehran; shuttle
cargo transporter determined to be either Romanian or Swiss,
two photos very distant, plane was painted over grey with blue
wavy stamp in Fez 1979.

By the time he was completed through ten thousand photos
and co-notation released information, he had contained an
entire file on IMPRESSION ART – (3) Jeff Ward, Macchu
Pichu, all blue, specks of color, gazing upward; red Grapes oil
on gessoe, artistic realism by Faith Fe; also Orange; a Julia
Carson abstract intense red crimson on jet black, some red on
left; she did traffic in rain well, the blurs were convincing as
wet night streets; Joe Sick, cursive on palate blue/pink/red,
smeared brown, yellow dabs, white paste line, all on orange;
(14) Paul Sinus, Traffic I, on gesso, red on left, tan in middle,
aqua on lower right through window; Michelle Keck – Sink or
Swim, rust, aqua, brown with dripping shiny black belt, looked
like a steamship on fire; Andy Hahn, yellow coming through
dark red; Dafen oil, curve of white wave on blue ocean dip-
tych; Harry Ivan Day, slabs of drab light yellow with sketchy
trees; Keith Garrow white wave and sandy hill against red sky
painted with ocaso-rojo gesso; several George Birrell all which
could not be restored, possible his Blue Art was retitled due to
painting being too saturated; Six Thirty A.M. and Stone Shed
were his famed; and then the wanton abstract color-capable
overlays, first a Zamira Hindez of jazzy squiggles of French

female in ballroom gown with tight see-through bodice, one shot purple, lots of violet, bronze and teal; a j. Lancefield – Blue Saturation; in a comment margin the previous reader noted, "On color repair – why do artists portray air and ocean in one painting?" A profiler had attached some sort of rationale;

Issues for color –

1. Art is non-preserving; does this include all abstract art? This is a debate.

2. Much of the colors used in works cited above are new – it is not known if any of these has been approved; issue is how much loss would occur in water?

3. From Fleckenstein, question for color is introduced

4. Early modern – look for progression of style

5. Different expression of mood created by bright color or primary color, clashes, depth vs shallow, placement of lines, mood vs. political

6. Artistic realism – is this style or era

Chapter Two

A small plane from the Yukon territories in Alaska loaded with seventy-two prints flew out under the banner of KNSA radio Unakleet, battling against the weather which was >40; it was an ERA Alaska because the 180 which carried passengers and freight was a prop unable to fly high above the ground and descend fast in hail sleet condition nose draft downwind once it reached the coast and peaceful river, houses dotted all over, as many as possibly 250 houses. Heavy rain and low visibility for a mile was legal, flying equipment to gravel bar, low visibility which was presumed to have killed Senator Stevens, narrow landing at Nulato Hills, 90 miles N, landed on a ridge top which technically posed a crash site but they came out alright, this area was below freezing 324 days a year, fuel was about to run out at Barrow which conducted about $12,000 a day flying business, fuel needed to get to Deadhorse from Kavik was 250 gallons, and at Kavik it was all uninhabited tundra except for one post that monitors seismic, gas and oil in below 5 weather in September. Any runway 500 ft increased the risk of crash, it was the barge transport that carried 2,000 gallon fuel from Unalaska into Alaska, transferring in Borrow to purchase fuel took up to a third of expenses, the problem of water in the fuel and frozen water killed engines; Ground crew answered phones, loaded weight, marshaled planes in, managed the take-off ramp. Despite a well-trained staff and plenty of them, a plane flew into giant fog bank – control flight into terrain; many a pilot became disoriented and crashed due to spatial disorientation which caused a pilot to attempt to fly beneath fog and hit the ground at full speed, tossing passengers out the doors if they were lucky; if not, the plane crumpled squeezing them inside the seats. Dense flying weaving over blind valleys at high altitude meant less air, less lift; in these circumstances even having filed the crucial flight plan with passenger and route and coordination, they were dead meat. Leaving Kavik and flying over deep blind valleys to Deadhorse as the sun was beginning to set at 8:40pm in Barrow they'd arrive in Fairbanks when it was already night, a sure sign of risk by itself, but the pilot thought he knew his barometer and anticipated no difficulties.

When the crash crew finally hauled in the wreckage they had six categories of art work. In columns which read like college second year master's program, they were listed by label, tags, metal affixation with artist name, and postcard photo, most of these partially destroyed requiring new offsets:

ABSTRACT REALISM

DeLudi – bright yellow, orange in street buildings, silhouettes of people, cars with front lights abstract like carnation roses;

Chinese girl with umbrella at night in teal silk coat, small neon-like color around her red, yellow;

Sally Trace – lots of color for a museum card, bright light teal, dark teal, red, pink, forest green, tad yellow, scrimp of blue, dab orange and peach;

Colored pencil façade of ornate stone building and cornice with complicated windows – Kripgans;

(19) Fine Art Appraisals – painting mist-like charcoal with traces of dark green blossom tree by Qian Shoutie, called "Plum Blossom";

(20) Loel Barr – two views in shadow of country road in ochre, some orange;

(21) Evolution of graffiti into street art – trend;

Grey sky and pond, pencil line horizon, red dabs, white hint of yellow arc rainbow into air;

Scottish Art – man dressed in black jacket, tan work pants with young son in red with shovel on his back and small white flowers on ground;

(22) White sky blue moon – artist unknown;

(23) Blue, red, white overlay, Arabic letters in scrawl

TURKISH CONTEMPORARY ART

(24) Worn strips of paper with Turkish writing on plum grayish painting titled *Skylife* by Saut Akdemir;

(25) *By Abdurrahuan – blue and black slats, red and pink smoke at center top; suggestive of aircraft wings vibrating to crash titled Oztoprak;*

(26) Radio map – by Jodice Sao Paulo titled Static; portraying the Skypiper crash over No palo with a notation as to, did the altimeter fail?

(27) *Turkish Museum set up in 2001 for international art, the Elgiz Museum of Contemporary Art in Instanbul – airplane went down over Saudi Arabia, had left Milan in 1972 at 4:10am and crashed at 8:20am with 110 passengers on board, bomb on board in cabin;*

(28) Whitish very light tan metal with line of eight bullet holes;

(29) Istanbul exhibition "The Little Land Fish" 17 artists from Turkey and Greek Cyprus. Tension with Germany's Merkel;

(30) *Hurriyet Daily News – Media 3 Washington Post – Uzi's*

on display, blur of tall thin Turkish male in black;

(31) *Gulf news by Oran Ahmet – appearance like pieces of paper taped together or panels of metal; in actuality blue and rust painting color between light tan paper;*

A mention in the Art Section that pirates hijacked a carrier ship off Muscat coast of Oman in Gulf of Aden transporting the following: An abstract of orange background with dripping red brushed square, 1977, by Mubin Orhon; a window at top of hallways each with black walls of hieroglyphics per floor; oil painting by the magazine Artodisiac – pinkish vibrant color flowing from airplane window turning to aqua as cover for Contemp Art magazine 09; and two by Nejad Melah Devrim – soaked red torn part of gray panel roped off as in a theatre, looking like an airplane door blew off.

Then there were – the notorious Japanese crash painted by Sairn Erken, an oil eruption on rocky hill, airplane crash; Rob Garrett, gym floor with children's black jackets hanging with video of two young boys; Alley café; cooked fish on a cart; back streets of Tunel district of Istanbul, streets drenched in very bright sun – paintings; Yamanote train line in Tokyo of the same Japan Air Lines 747 on fire which took a crash in 1979 when the plane dove right into train station. There were Paul Chan – Dream House video installation of floating rice paper with written symbol in black; the Sara Baruch – another painting in Skylife collection; all tan floor and walls, colored pencil etchings in predominantly light blue, rust, brown, white of two large holes in metal due to a bomb; were these sketches turned over for the insurance?

Some analyst had gone bonkers with wilderness scenes of Turkey's Salt Lake, second largest lake, wet rail of box cars through lake took salt out of lake to cities; salt flats, crystalline salt quartz; a lake of salt mud, hardened and marshy, in middle of salt in a white sea; under the lake tiny streams whereas on surface salt was tilled into rows, excessive evaporation even as salt turned into water; an important breeding ground for flamingoes, all running through water their petticoats lifted, and the modern museum resembling a salt scraper of six stories, lots of cubes, with central arc, building.

Scottish artists – Moy Mackay, Ian Elliot, MC Tears, Elena Kousenkova, James Orr - who was himself very influenced by co-lourists or Glasgow Boys, Cadell and Peploe, and Seago – who did painting of dredged bay and marooned boat on damp bottom soil?

COLORISTS
Color wash –
Colors of gray, by Mary Ahern, also vivid color landscape, restoration in new color;
Julie Hanson – <u>Twin Boats</u> on violet and crimson;
Bob Otaro, known for blue paintings, horizontal layers for color separation, all palate, tan, white, red, yellow;
William McLane – blue meadow, green pastel;
Richard Lang Chandler – ice on canal;
Lan Pitts – <u>Winter Is Coming,</u> seen forest through glass slats of house like the crashing airplane slats in red at the Philadelphia Art Museum on water in the parthenon building;
Kelingrove Museum – floating heads inside museum at ceiling level;
Hunterian Museum – castle with high tower, preview Chinese girl with hair up by George Henry;
Of Scottish Contemporary artists – painting reality without moral judgments – leisurely nap in grass, landscapes, woman in yard, lots of red.

1/25/11
Jones was in the Miami airport when he encountered the journalist team Evari. Maximized tolerant, buggy sensible, tight yardlings, trust worthy duster, they had arrived from overseas OAS, newspaper under their elbow, the Taylor & Bradstreet quarter a dubious gain. Interviews spooled to the 437 tapes on the 0600 news, then to Cairo, Dubais, El Sorbqi Guzat, two tablespoons chizchat and diced pepper together with fried garlic prawns and gin for the midnight sun twenty-four hours on snow tundra,, silky sheen black horses running through water,

a thousand droplets in their midst. A spicy caviar into a jungle for a look at foraging a river into Sudan when the city flooded up to three stories. All flowers conjured up scents jangled with crème or wisteria as if secrets drifted on the wind.

For Jones, assigned to personally escort the Nakano oil paintings to Sable, Florida, it was onto Alaska, a helicopter to Anchorage and Fairbanks, 70 miles from any part of the civilized world. By dawn he was over a thousand campers in the rugged snow capped wilderness piled into winnebagos for zero degree weather, no clue as to what showdown might take place, mobile command posted by midnight with staff from the wildlife and oil floes units, all views of the stage from a post of X20.6 Intel inside a secure RV, to insure against drunkenness, drug sales, intravenous deaths, and then there were the obvious steerage to fill in and maintain against slope and crevice erosion. Despite a line-up of a hundred tents of twenty pound bags of combined mulch dirt and rock debris to pour along a new crevice line, an Arctic Ski event plied for forty-eight hours, day and night with torches, to watch skiers get towed a hundred and fifty miles per hour by sleds down snow luminescent terrain. On the third day as campers drove toward the bridge to follow the creek downstream, the Intel operation tracked through miles of bush as men on hunts got stuck, ran out of fuel or food, very isolated, worst case scenario a shoot-out in a kill zone, lay in wait on unpredictable behavior of bears.

He had to contend with 4,975 images of flashy long-established art including – Fog & Ice – parking lot, vivid light blue, purple, red, yellow; Suijan Czopor – flowers decoupage sections, ice snow, slanting blue, ice at ocean; Abstract flower in vase – yellow rose, blue, white lily against white wall;

Nick Shupletsov – abstract flowers made with light palate; Robinson – wildflowers on sommerset velvet

K Joan Russell – poppies; before he found the art he was looking for on Page 6, 654, 37 frames – modern art flower paintings of Tokyo – bright light cast to sky revealed stacked grey blocks six stories tall; there were the Tokyo train – sunken building in ocean near beach; the train station midair in neon purple; Hotel Everland – green striped hotel room like train compartment; on roof of Palais de Tokyo, a Grecian looking front with columns and statuary; Dream like dance studio – clear doors in gym with dreamy white building compartment in misty background and light blue space bubble Java Hockey Arena by Coll- Barrev.

NAKANO
(40) Nakano jungle – subway overgrown, tattered train station plane beneath turf
Black man walked amidst ruins
Train bridge
Slanted section of city blue and green with rays of light
Multi-media projection on wall inside studio
(42) Pink door in blue air beneath awning of light tubes at ceiling like subway grate reminiscent of 'artodisiac' – vibrant pink light very surreal flowing out of window that was turning aqua for Beyoglu Constantinople
(44) Giant fish circling over city
Torn page – ink art in three splayed books
Clear picture of painting of fish tail below midline and its square head protruding above water surface which was like thick ice
Sariev, Bulgaria MOMA, curator Iliyanja Nedkova; Varna, very abstract – many abstracts of females on dock or on beach, this one of top naked youngish female on beach, another female dressed in blue dress lying on beach near sea
Many buildings displayed as varying blocks, windmill – no use of white, minimal yellow, mostly green, blue, pink, brown, red
Abstract painting of 6 females on bench in museum with oil in background on wall, crimson, yellow, tan
Cylindrical container ends on railroad track yellow, blue, green, brown
Purple mountain with rice field, cherry blossom tree in foreground
(52) *Big Arco pipe that said 'Art' in large red letters resembles airplane without side windows; "first search removed", probably about hijack 1982 out of Bulgaria*

Light green tank inside all white room with ceiling in look-
alike shards
#16 plane wing beside hangar
The write-up in three photo frames told of *Troy McMullen, foreign correspondent, who covered hijack of plane that was cleared for
take – off through Customs in Ligeia – LATIMES photo of show
by G.R. Iranna of Asian men crouching behind white line on wood
floor each with black cloth over their heads;*
Varna – oldest large find of gold artifacts off coast
*Ian Pollock – Rolex, news correspondent, best most persuasive use of
color H. Emile Matisse of Afghanistan stamp, pastel oils pink, light
blue, light green*
Photo shot of moon titled Messenger Dances by Matisse

An analyst had scribbled, How many landing sites were
ill advised? What was final read when 1972 went off the air?
Machine gave very close read of landing site; What do pictures
indicate as to a coastline?

It was Tangier in blue, where he spent summers as a college student studying an artist curriculum in preparation for
the service. Any artist repainting or restoring art worthy pre-
appraised art had to possess the skills as follows: Skilled any
style with brush including Neo classic, Romanesque, Dutch
– light; American – mostly outdoors; Modern – color, dabs;
Abstract and also knowledge of variations of color, limitations
upon color – white palate faded to yellow and yellow darkens
in two + years, trade craft – 40 years minimum and recovery
with a general understanding of extent of damage to art object.
While in school Jones learned learned to identify from pieces
of color Bhagdad bus explosions, car bombs, art gauze masked
faces – eyes only – were these radiation-exposed citizens alive,
what could they say about bombings? As well as curly cues of
cloth in oil abstracts suggestive of drag, abstract portrait face
lines shown in abstract color art, and use of Abstract pencil
color wheel. Here he was in his identity, the knowledge of the
world that gave him his edge, all of terrorism bespoke through
the fine embellishments of the brush, through a cage of dead
zone houses and nightmarish garish trickery. Instinct caused

him to glance ahead to the two sections he had immersed himself at twenty.

LEBANON CONTEMPORARY ART
(203) Beirut – 1982 tan swings and their reflections, artists
Nicholas Zory, Georgi Andonov, Paul Guiragossian – Damascus, piece of tan metal airplane;
(302) Korea Annette Messager of casino red silk resembling
blood and hanging icons;
(557) Narangkar – watercolor blue wind on square paper beige
sail;

COLOR ABSTRACT SURREALISM ART
Primary color abstracts – red, blue, and green
Castelli
(431) Andre Dluhos – all basic color, tree path, abstract expressionism;
Sam Francis – red on yellow;
(229) Gehard Richter – swimming colors blue, thick gray overhead;
George Canon Photography – painting color on water;
Albers – all teal squares in water color with vertical light green
at center;
(48) Airplane below apartment buildings behind wall of housing development intended as entry road; and
Folded umbrellas in dark on night beach, Istanbul.

Chapter Three

Saudi Arabia, 1972, hijack preceded by lively radio contact
of 3 seconds duration after being in air twenty minutes that
was abruptly cut off, never followed by resumed contact; no
masked gunmen, airplane flew off course and off screen. It
took Ground nine full minutes to realize contact with cockpit
had been severed.

How did this disruption occur? Investigators believed telephone line were cut. When plane was finally recuperated there was no telephone wire anywhere either in steward quarter or in cockpit.

Did pilots hijack their own plane?

Was art ever secretly transported out of a country that had a hostile threat?

Art contained at airport in locked security room fully wrapped; 971 articles of the Koran Bible in a separate hangar close to Customs office in a coastal port – Singapore; delivered September 1971 wrapped in bluish pink inside which was green with gold speckled raw paper; Turkish Customs agents were sent in and they conducted five-week investigation including chemical testing paper of bibles; results were sent to Cairo mosque; they were laid out on shag carpet before being boxed up and shag was admitted to laboratory for testing for trace of explosive; these results were kept in China; black log never recovered; it took two days and two nights to find destination of arrival in mountains east of India at a tiny landing; airplane was repainted in Arabic scrawl in dark red.

No camera contact; it was assumed cameras were dislodged somehow, question by ground because although airplane could be found it was possible this was conducted by radar. Numerous art was in the wrong city or aisle docket – actual photographs were painted immediately and offered as display in foreign country. Did hijacks occur prior to bombings – was there any rationale the hijackers wanted to understand first? For example how to get the cameras turned off during flight?

These people wanted to reduce incidence of typhoid in remote places. Scribbled photo was for first insurance; area where there were six seats which on a VIP tour was removed; this occured around the time tiny Israel was hit every week for weeks by tear gas at her main airport. Possibly this was the reason Saudi can't fly there for protection. Almost all hijackers were Lebanese; many were jailed in Tiberias or central eastern China for blowing up embassies and once released joined a sect; these were all considered Islamic. It would be pointless to look in different countries for similar complexion or type because countries mixed up photos usually on purpose but he looked regardless in tourist and time-share photos. He would have thought Indian or Monk.

Germany 1972 following Olympic Games – players robbed stadium and returned to private owned airplane where they were killed by officials. Their bodies were taken by helio-craft to an undisclosed area and sent somewhere.

Maybe their plane was intended to be their getaway for a Saudi rendezvous.

Someone thought that situation aroused a lot of curiosity. Were any of these players on Saudi military duty? Was flying into seldom-used airports a privilege of the rich? This was the more likely explanation.

Problem on the computer was without coordinates or sectors sandstorms resemble snowstorms tinged beige.

This could be a big item that the agency would run and look at – a possibility that the destinations were chosen for this look. You wouldn't know whether you were still in Germany or Saudi or northern Iran. What was the last landing policy once the FAA declared landing sites undesirable due to air crashes?

Small plastic bag, log tossed aside in cockpit, navigator manuals removed with driver, plane left in parking stall, inquiry started.

02/02/11

Ian Pollock, news correspondent and son of Sydney Pollack artist, window of color. Ian researched why the 1972 airplane went off the charts, flew to Saudi, conducted live coverage against a night sky of grey smoke and red bursts.

His standard communiqué was a photo strip along a cigarette pack Marlboro with a grey stamp to denote where on wall of historically restored Nairobi text pipe is. The artist reviewed is Ruicke whose idea Fragile Art looked at the Islamic word as art.

Ian's hangout with a female correspondent friend there was at the Katmandu 29 Club in central Tehran, Iran, where every day was a new dialogue and every night is a bloody vodka.

A noteworthy artist known to the Silk Road Gallery was Broujerdy whose square houses in a blue twilight valley was at the back dark blue, Prussian blue, teal, yellow, red and gold like sky city.

Basic language was Farsi, frequent photo were of young blond females in veils on bus.

From Tehran he flew into old Cairo coast and on to Bulgaria to examine the hijack airplane, the metal color which was goldish tan.

Thereafter basic standard metal changed to light silver.

PER FILE

Once information was categorized into presumably one organized readable file, he would need to request an assessment of damage,

Determine precisely what had happened, for example had 1972 flown off course per problem in panel instrumentation,

Did airplane fly into a hangar and thus disappear from sight?

Then arrange to replace part or entire structure of airplane,

Billing of each 1 frame for loss along with history of that particular airplane,

Last analyze what was inferred plan for implementation of hijack

Providing a detailed oil painting along with renumerable list of replacement or restoration that showed various list

Could be abstract purple with white streak

Purple lit station for passenger train that imbued snow as gray tinged

Discernment of grey and/or beige tan snow which actually might be sand for obvious determination as to location

Blue would make snow look actual color, grey itself did not obscure sand until distinguished from cement which resembled water, yellow distorted many landscapes but never sand, and green under most situations was friendly, however, purple did not permit non glare thus diminishing source color and greatly intensifying brightness

Use of color wheel for transparency for useful adaptation over art and photo

The rate adjusters knew a lot, most damage pertained to cars. When were dents created, under what circumstance c a smashed vehicle be driven, what type of steering column locked in after a crash, how many vehicles did it take in one accident to be considered still accidental when passengers were uninjured.

appraisal files for approvals to add, subtract or restore to likeness

test strip on lower left bottom to edge to absorb color to test paint

watercolor for reflections, oils for billing

0208 completed – issues in stolen art, color mixture, separation, likeness to realism

had color been approved for registry for appraisals?

previous research on fine arts, abstract realism, is color approved for registry, appraisals

Chapter Four

The Gulf Crisis was still on, the mammoth Deepwater Horizon having inked the ocean with indelible hankerings, none of the flumes nor oil-drenched reeds any equation of durability, billows of smoke finally deplorably salted the marshes, coasts and shallow wash basins a chimera-type dripping entropy. Jones was the news reporter assigned in charge of the gulf crisis, having thrown on a striped grey and Kelly shirt over his undershirt, light green trousers, black socks and tan loafers, a voice piece clipped to his shirt, a tape recorder on the tray, from Washington Bureau – Cabo Rojo, taking an initial-look-see a year after the devastating swamp manifestations of cardigan presses of oil, burnt smoldering remains, destitute weeds, unforgiving ropes like oil lassos floating on a high wind to land.

His newest task was to identify and incorporate as complete files as he was able for the subject that the files focused upon, whatever that turned out to be, a wall of a hundred thousand micro-dots about all sorts of brandy, among them foreign art, fine art, modern art, galleries and museums, high rise condos, expensive boating real estate, ambassadors, drugs, border customs, Nextel, Intel, I-spy, food, books, newspapers, diamonds, bank cartels, a vast resource of information known the world over. He had gone through ten to thirty thousand pix taking the time to write notes or look up an index when he came across any noteworthy photos, of which usually there were few. From time to time he went as long as three weeks before he came upon a suggestive photo. By and large these files were anything but revealed, specific assignments, those were closed having been assigned into a series of separation photos and archived. These sporadic photos were the product of having secured information at random to any of a myriad of thousands of analysts who as they poured over their sections periodically withdrew the photos for comparative assessment, to evaluate as to time status since the removal of the first takes, to review all labs, billings, inoculations, and then to restore in terms of investigative authorizations. Lewis expected one to five photos per section of ten thousand junkets, a likely conversion any field operative ought to look about to. However, at this rate of an air disaster photo per thousand as it was turning out to be, he figured he would be knee-deep in out-takes by the end of the first twelve months; and because an estimable analysis could not begin until around three years into a file, he surmised therefore there had to be as many as five hundred photos that altogether told a convincing byline on terrorist activity as to fewer than four groups.

The new agency under Lewis was lately comprised of ten men at seven locations, all revolving timeshares between field and port command, the Racquet Club Resort on Sanibel Island, three inter-connected eight story condominium complexes that sat nestled in low Monterey brush with footpaths through white sand to the beach and ocean, each condo flat with master bedroom and living room on balcony overlooking Oceanside, swimming pools, tennis, restaurants, boutiques, scuba diving stores and a dock and gas load-up for boats, the ocean still toxically infiltrated by the gulf crisis. Most of the seven office timeshares included waterskiing, scuba sports, boating, fishing on the gulf stream, marinas and nine-hole golf. Van Idol worked all site listings from his penthouse at The Surf Club on San Marco Island where a square pool and sixty lounge chairs occupied beachfront white sand beside a beach lifeguard house. He organized the annual activities of the agent group, making lists of anyone who owned a timeshare, including personal and corporate income and travel or spouse arrangement, any match as to correspondence registered through computer, telephone, newspapers or parallel processing; once the names were matched to any person seen at any site of a crime, all photographs were batched and sent to Special Task. Then the field was wide open for selection of agent groups to maintain surveillance, queries and resolution of the crime.

At Loreto Bay, the Nopolo emerald triangular mountains emerging from the bay with a lone road between the two bodies of sea on which kayakers drifted over clear aquamarine waters was the site of batching and coordinating all information once resolution had begun. The Field agent, in operations for forty years predominantly at La Paz in the Sea of Cortez, traveled occasionally to Escondido and Islas Carmen and Montserrat to relieve art canopies for forensic inspection and rationale as to why it was shorn off an original.

The five-story condo with balconies on every floor and flat at South Padre and the Ixtapa Tesoro with screen doors leading to ocean waves and sand were staffed by an agent each, the Riverfront condos at Cancun on a singular strip of sand and Siesta studied all technological reinventions including upgraded camera especially for Intel operatives and sent copies of photos to chief engineering for immediate photo processing. Since the advent of World Trade Center decimations, there was the necessity of information on vulnerable high rises.

He'd maxed out on mid-life doing every form of endurance he could think of, swimming, walking, chess, writing; by the time he was in his early seventies he had wound up retired, although still feeling life had taken too much, that his personal identity was too demanded of, whereupon he left the world as he knew it and went everywhere in two short years in the Americas, hiked, wandered onto gigantic fields of snow tundra with a mush sled, left them to climb a more challenging mountain, holed up for a winter inside a cabin dug into snow which in the dead of blizzards turned into an avalanche, and then finally returned to the islands to comfortably lose his identity.

Lewis left his expansionist comfortable quarters for a lazy stroll on the beach to take in the late morning air and salty breeze. He rode the elevator with sights of the plaza and seashore coast down eight stories and exited into finite warmth amidst a rolling green and avenue of restaurants, lounges and polo and tennis shops. Without an already precedent boat slip he could hardly make a claim to invention; however, as an agent he had access to the tennis club, the golfing green, the private spas and library and a fleet of yachts which ferried to the gulf stream weekly avoiding hurricane weather. Although he was to be seen regularly on the patio or the green, he received circumspect discretion in the company of associates. The day was shaping up to be a westerly, and he needed the time to think through the latest communication on his desk. He had received image on a male suspect Field had been following for four years. Despite an altered identity at two of seven condos he frequented, all other identifiers were consistent – face shape, eyes, nose, mouth, chin, ears as well as location of scars and tattoo, and worse, voice print matched. However, the man emerged just as the Carlos files were being made known and as a matter of course, no one was being looked at as a solitary operative even if he was captured alone on film. Someone like him had worked for less than a year aboard the KLM. Because the plane burst through its hull leaving a hole the size of the door, crash analysts awaited the release of the detail of spectrometry. The emission line on the flame photometer seldom gave an incorrect read; the going theory for what was tested was that a bomb, cyanide ejection, had been placed beneath the wall three feet to the window adjacent to the start of the wing and passed smoke detection. Patients with extreme proximity to the explosion were found to suffer from an encephalopathy syndrome characterized by weakness, lethargy, fever, confusion, extra pyramidal symptoms, and white blood cells, followed by irreversible brain damage.

Chapter Five

The letter express arrived in the mid morning batch along with its corresponding completed framed final picture which gave a bright yellow and chalk bluff and a darkly blue mysterious shrouded sky. Backing the express were cardboard prints of the gallery in the Botticelli Rooms at the degli Uffiza in Florence, a promenade plaza of grey and blue glass, with da Vinci, Raphael, Velazquez and Dutch oil painters. Each place had received a separate corresponding letter which delineated one set of gateway photographs. Diego Velazquez had painted off a photograph of a front airplane window the small left wind spark of a camera and light medium dark blue rays streaming out exactly immediately prior to the catapult. The file was represented by eight A's with an offset of five vowels and letters and two numerals which represented an air crash. The smaller photos showed loose voice to ground connectors which went to Grenada from a military plane in Egypt, another, a 747 cockpit having been designated as lost world. London Underground responded with their copy of the final picture, a crazy Ivan conning tower, a steep green ground roll-out, obviously a tiny plane, securing the tests. Inspection conducted its ground and readiness perfections, X-rays over seats and all interior parts of both planes, Geiger counter measurements above refraction, light beam which showed yellow, nothing to say there was a bomb aboard, dark black indicating a bomb, on a large airliner it was losing fuel, which signified either it was struck or blown, it was thought to have a wing fracture above the far aileron, its camera showed it went nose down losing buoyancy, second frame was not yet analyzed. Artists had not yet determined the foundation of the blue color of the window.

He spent an on-week weekend between collaborative evaluations watching movies – The Bodyguard, Jimi Hendrix, Masque of The Red Death and Tomb of Ligeia, meanwhile studying under appraiser lens art on ceilings, seasons of art, practical masters, a handful of popular bills and retouched Roman art attesting to darker wines and sunnier whites. In all probability the problems were similar, a false rip into the cockpit, a flight mission photo-demarcation without the national boundaries, for which that airline was shutdown indefinitely, a worthy collection of celestial paintings of the night sky, a photograph of the crater side of the moon tossed in titled Moon Landing, another last sky of dark blue over the cockpit. Life was fleetingly horrific, those poor men, all in their eighties, no collision, nor twilight, he didn't know how once spotting the land below and preparing for descent, all that was possible was spatial disorientation, a crash in fourteen minutes, oddly these were stealth panels, the planes were military recons, they could never leave the land for an ocean draft. The noticeable lack of cities together with the darkish blue made flying across the Alps likely, departure and ETA on schedule, the schedule flight-on-time board an absolute necessity to assessing in which geographical section the crash occurred, the merest suggestion as to implication being a schoolmaster required extensive time with cancellations.

He was still searching for his crazy Ivan and its sequel. The crack of light in the sky hit another light dead center. Immediately he looked for a nearby ship draw and secured the masthead of a large vessel with a distinctive blue stack. He thought perhaps because of the all blue sea it was in the Indian Oceans barely discernible except in a dual bath image of a thrust reverser on fire in a dark red sky. To find this crimson sky, the document that read "first live feed/ten seconds in disguise/no search allowed" made any red-ink inaccessible. It was important to have found the airplane was not picked up on numerous conning dishes, that the few that tuned in satellite faced all directions.

To be absolutely accurate he had to distinguish the color strata of those waters which could be anywhere by separations distinguishing utterly still sapphire from variations all the way to peacock marine. For two days he stripped blue color to define the variations the curl of metal burst out over. Archipelago blue, bright blue, navy, slate blue, iris, gray blue, hyacinth, dark wine blue, pike blue, cyanosis, cornflower, pneumatic blue, somewhat at yellow, cambium blue, crank blue tinged with moderately opaque creatin, violet, dahlia, Prussian, frost, heron, royal, dolphin, dolomite, aborealis, dye, turquoise, cashmere, soda blue, serpentine, Siamese blue, glacial blue, indigo, retiring bluish, filmy, mystic, and pastel. It was tedious desultory work but he knew he had a bad case on his hands. A match in bright blue gave him outdoor plaza cafes, birdcage style lamps on exotic salmon navy colored Damascus rugs, silk floor lamps made of ceramic lace yellow and blue and white china; the Baraka Silk Road by camel through the wandering sands of Asia initially entered on the China Orient Express, the sapphire seas like Israel or the light blue sands of the Gulf Stream of the Antilles despite the archive closet rendering only the fig-gold dome of Jerusalem and the black and white with red mosque weeping distress walls of the Duomo of Tuscany as though the two sites alone constellated the overlying hills of the windy breeze bearing sea that figured prominently below either flight. Not to mention the silk road was the product of Katmandu, the Farsi languages of Iran borrowed by Saudi Arabia, attractive females in veils on a bus weaving up the fortress walls which from a distance gave no indication of chalk but staggered the onlooker by its thunderous curtain of waterfalls and appreciative greenery, flowering cantaloupe, the silk road accessible only by train. The houses in the valley were blue, yellow, rust sienna and fading red diminishing to golden ochre, a host of tranquil Bedouin modern flats, prayer in libraries of antiquity with rising elevators to a parapet, even the slightest illusion being of towers within rows of prisons.

He would be devastated not to capture a real-time photograph that took into account a non destruct sky with blue sky and a plain of tilled land, and sought for a reliable source of information, origin from which a place or person correlated to a finding; possibly placed in a gazette, periodical, publication, sheet, instrument, file, dossier; under any terminology. He searched for, Soaring, fly high, reach high level, ascending, rising, not to be confused with spiraling, putting clouds far below, sun also below, entering atmosphere;

He walked through laborious definitions, anything metaphysical or seasonal or altered to do with red sky. It could be anything symbolic, color of blood, warning light, red colored glass.

Distinct phases of the moon or a planet according to the amount of illumination at night to shoot out a consistent trajectory, proceed past the planet into chilling desolate lack of light, overtake the final perimeter of light spectrum along the coastlines;

A small bomb used to blast a window accompanied by fireworks; was this the correct blast?

A piece of film, exposed too long, the film ultra black; at the point the trajectory would become defined as a bullet, the negative showed as a glinting side of a Piper, as in the movie Bullitt.

Strategic art had come through the Art Institute of Chicago for draftsman art which included figure drawing, anatomy, drawing the human head and forensic art, a sparse few airplane demonstrations were of smoke and electricity, dark amber background, dark crimson almost navy ground represented by Land Images. No release was assigned for value rights managed imagery, photographer or collection although in secured accounts some of the run could be had for a few moments observation under another heading. An archeological illustrator Carl Davis, with scientific knowledge of industry through predominantly Yale and Los Angeles exhibits at the Exile and Downtown Artistic Development Abbey, or DADA, had covered graphics, color prints and density of color so as to develop a coordinative computer for producing matches of a color in a second. The problem with digital computerized comparisons were that to distinguish images of actual ocean from images of color form the computer, laser-rite technological electronics based computers showed rinses as compositions of puddles of water depicted by weight, encasement depth and dimness. Also, once the puddle was produced, these machines drafted color, usually green, to fit the dilutions of so-called fertilizer-enhanced-turf necessary to absorb the indoctrinated liquid originally created for bringing quenching liquid to weary, thirsty travelers lost in a parched desert of sun-bearing radiance of a hundred and twelve degree heat.

There was no reason to suspect that the several photographs in the quarter offered any semblance of real off-shooting of photography stored in the semblance of emblematic theme. Whereas there were plenty of suggestive thematic art, the most noteworthy of course taking up various subject matter such as Dead Sea scrolls, Egyptian museum art, glass from the Israel peninsula, or Nefertitti on the Aswan, the little known fact that all origins referenced the Nile anyway was instructive or at least scientific. Sand accounted for immediate disbursements, withered and reductionism exaggerations, and tours of the lost world by camel described the very first homage from a city through the Negev. He found himself looking at splashes and screenshots, at the unforgivable, a series of curling metal ripping away from the sun, the glare dense and stormy, a fallacy of indecency although difficult to identify, a curling ash in an inferno removed from the spying eye and secured to a far-off sector of remote life, took a second read for thirty-eight miles off shore, the speed of a plane moving at approximately forty knots an hour. The sand dial showed no pronouncement, the windy weather thrashed and scurried and sent chairs and car roofs flying, everything was seasonal, art showed nowhere, no one had any idea what the day or hour was, elsewhere the easterlies were floating through the aquamarine waters of the sandy coastline of the Caribbean, the equatorial zones were pools of

warm ocean surface water, at night were casino currency viola-
tions, drug trade for heroin or green jade, deliberate evasion
or peonage, the annoying problem being that before Customs
could retrace yacht lines out of Puerto Rico into island zones to
look for fugitives, they had to classify all radio to land contact.
This took up at San Juan fortress, displayed graveyard crypts
and crosses on the Intel, zeroed in on ocean liners, on narrow
streets and three-story blue, yellow and pink resort cabins, an
occasional yacht pier, a palm or two bending in a calypso wind.

The Diego Rivera set arrived by day air shipment. It was
comprised of three large paintings and two small facsimiles
describing abstract depictions of a great deal of brown and
black, small amounts of dark yellow, orange, blue, dark deep
violet, gray and seldom green. Jones prepared several litho-
graphs of parts of the small pictographs and marked them as
for an exhibit series, referencing them to film that would cross
germinate for any chronology of form easily misplaced, the primary being red-ink photography or tint sky. Onto these foci
older canvas actual photographs placed, with a history of the
airplane in evidence of the special finding. Most people stood
and walked off after a bomb; even so, for living and deceased
alike, possessions in small white containers were usually advanced to a holding place where an investigative unit awaited.
Only where decided by an administrative chief were depository
personal itemized dockets retained as proof of travel through
foreign customs, luggage was given first rating, thereafter billing permanently sealed all industrial transactions. Despite evidentiary placement, if the prosecutorial conveyances could be
rated, even international courts were unable to obtain proofs.
Singular benefit returned from any source including air freight
and could be grouped by colored stain dipsticks, tag weights,
identification listings or tiny striped parasols.

Color was an inconsistent barrier, if used for restorative
reasons, the art often assumed a shallow nomenclature of average browns, light blue, pinkish ochre or clear to light green
stain. Collection of photos where order was not determined
were lined up film drying style with a numerology distinctive

as to method of transportation, at any point where an evaluator
had to determine the existence of a certain crime, a warrant
had to be sent containing language or revised language, unless
the reference was a physician note for which there were no revi-
sions. All other descriptions were given standard and usual address, strips beneath top frame over painting with artist number, name consisting of show name last, initial and first, and
date first shipped. If painting has been restored to appearance
of original value, it requires an additional strip of adhesive under back frame with color hue type and distribution sampling
if artist prepared blemish. For determination of ecclesiastical
remunerative historical type, the canvas is swept with clear
developing rinse, a light scraping is taken, and the dispersion
of granules is contrasted to any known sampling by a color-
ist. In order to assess aggregate storage wear, syndromes must
be completed on any prevailing scientific principle, the most
noteworthy today being non-boundary geology strata for up to
a measurable distance of a thousand miles. Some clay, sand,
powder legends utilize the appearance of read-allow mapping
as persuasive indicia pertaining to satellite imagery.

The fact that the possessions obtained from the Nakano
disaster were described solely by color indicators for each of ten
total billings conferred upon logic to suggest the crew were air
travel staff returning from a series of standbys and for reasons
unknown returned with less than a full tank. Although landing policy was altered slightly, it was the Air Everland traveling over Baghdad that exploded in air above the government's
parliament that was reclassified as a blimp with wings. If Nakano jungle décor-ist painted speed for predominantly gray and
green, his museum-renown paintings described the fatal crash
that occurred, however he placed a plane beneath turf, presumably plastics nitro-fertilizer placed into a wing or stored inside
a refrigerator until it matured, and gave prominence to a black
man walking in the ruins. The slanted section of city which he
became known for convinced no less than the oddly humorous
attempt on a Maryland hydro-propelled jet brought in from
studies and tests from significant desert ports no one had heard

of, the neon glitzy art of one James Corkell of a bright electric pink door in light radiant blue air beneath a street grate of warm pink nano-grow light tubes. A file of some six thousand one hundred modern art flower paintings took evidence findings as to density.

Therefore the radio chatters for land to air instrumentation which was Cape Canaveral resonant went suddenly dead at three seconds without resumed contact taking Ground a good nine minutes to become aware that contact was severed. Aerials of red sky in the Sudan near the coast above Eritrea showed a red dust cloud pouring in over the oases bending palm trees in a choking wind. The mountainous Libyan Desert in its limitless boundary of red yellow meanderings and crisscrossed ranges, illusory blue sky, a permanent film of atmospheric brightness dissolving its coast to the raised mountains of Tobruk stymied the vast Atlas Ranges of Tripoli, dust storms dissipating all sound into empires of antiquity, the columnar marble of the Mediterranean tablets the last sight before ruination. News correspondent for ITC Lura Mordalles showed in thunderous static, her Egyptian appearance belied by modernism in broom-style hairdo, short sleeved bright usually soft yellow or off orange blouses beneath jumpers of lined trousergarb, pushups and bare backed low heels. Presumably in her thirties, mother of two, she covered the coast-littered poorest Muslim sector for airplane crashes, plastics manufacture and He-ite veiled Corcoran's seeking independence from Pakistan.

He poured over the mysterious erupting fumes during which the Intel 330 showed the roaring wind and heat momentarily expanding the dark blue steel KLM shell into abrupt tan squares at the height of the Turkish parliament spire tower, bursting presumably from the luggage boxlike helm as though from a highly flammable explosive such as radical detonated TNT, in its primary state as artificial as any Constable reflecting stillness river, in a vial it looked to be clear, light blue with a tint rust like oddly dried old paint or oil from a crankcase. The other air explosion involved the 1982 Lebanon Saudi Arabia 747 which on removed first takes showed a dark azure click of camera closing immediately prior to the dense bright blue rays of the explosion blasting like a river dam above the right wing, just as the toilet emptied out a shelf of suppressant, the recognizable trademark of the spark of blast producing an identical rip out of the steel sub placement. Miraculously the airplane kept coming down without brake use or control, a swift unalleviated descent onto sand. They already knew the original causes of other airplane disasters, the air ground altimeter dial that in the tiny chopper cutters gave buoyancy and wind turbulence while suddenly eliminating airspeed, logistics analysts chalking long airplanes to the front rudder on the wing side busting and the floor elevator that operated the throttle mechanism releasing to the floor like a lowering canal-lock system when the tray moved toward dock and had to be relocated by steamship. The only cause Jones knew of to alter altimeter was the iffy till, rear steerage usually found on moderate size big boats for which bringing up balloons out of the water after spilling gravel or lowering through a movable river or canal till created back-pumping. Such incidents were decreasing with the advent of the Sudan government which regularly monitored along the Oman coast side of Arabia. Not infrequently fractures on the other wing side created sudden loss of wind and similar to ice wind, two airplanes losing compass fell nose-plummet into the dark inky ocean, throttle unlocking when the inflatable stairs released. The question parlayed about the racquetball club was, how come if an airplane flew bags of Arab wheat, those airplanes blew up?

It wasn't a simple answer; the moment Jones had a cause of fatality he would push the loss evaluation across town to the fund drawer to have the cause findings selected out for comparative analysis and begin assurance as to possible bomb inducement. Little matter to determine the sepia in stone masonry to conventionalize where right on the ocean with boats the hostel matched any house along Nags Head, North Carolina where the likeness to those beaches on which the mechanics lived overlooking golf courses determined turbulence draw for state-of-the-art flight mechanical control. In time the analyst divisions under any one chief head grouper would call in Lewis Lewis for his typical assessment. Only the depreciation schedule could give any insight into which services these thugs had invested, the Wyndam in Iraq had been bombed Beirut-style, the Sun Terrace in Eritrea had lost a plantation at sea when a thirty-one-seater had crashed nose down after a failure in wind-draft presumed to have a front tilly jammed in a failure to release, a bobbin on a sliding pole caught between its groove, known within the industry as a bare-assed flapper. Unlike its competitors, the Westgate was all bobbin talk, a wide veranda populated with clustered café tables and wood chairs, slightly turned army-green umbrellas, tall frosted glasses of rum minty tea and steeped cinnamon-corn cafes, several ballroom lobbies with large carpet of swirling crimson on light tan background, over dark green grouted tile, brocade couches two facing, another group behind, four accompaniments in all, a bronze gold centerpiece of floral elegance consisting of flamboyant pussy reeds, birds of paradise, calla lilies, and deep purple iris with powdery stain-capable stamens. By anyone's standards the bobbins had it, wire-encased plastic from the floor where the pedals rested, up a thin steering maneuvering shift on which the bobbin maintained flexible control for flight speed. Two-bobbin-maximum tied together like locked-in bees kept the feed from catching inside the groove which was the most frequent complaint that pilots said they experienced when making a steep, short platform dive for computer-telescoped far ground such as was in the Sudan valleys. Although the device was bendable for maximum catastrophic disasters, if it bent as the rudders were increasing, there was a belief that in lashing storms when the airplane experienced unstable fuel content, there had been a blow to the main-hook-line that kept the fuel feed constant.

Jones catalogued all damage to parts before he affixed the first take to the description. The computer print readout reduced all parts to facilitative language. Trainer landing wheels beneath the cockpit became squealor traffic load, high speed wheels were chase runway slow landings, door nearest the pilot stage was the interior folding collapse, far door for a long Fiji with two ramps was coded as a slipper stair to ground. All other look-bout's including wire antennae lining the nose were straight wire with microscopic light lens chips for distinguishing between frequencies, the ambi-attachment straight hose unplugged to its screw-top, the cords that dropped out of industrial airplanes for rope landings that restrained speed lay often untouched inside closed compartments which upon sufficient turbulence for no known reason jostled the front tape computer to report on status markings including, wind speed, fuel, altitude, course consistency, parachute openings. The emit tank flask containing the blue ice on an older 737 occasionally slipped during steep climbs; otherwise the envelope opening as it was nicknamed was relied upon to offset turbulence that increased cabin pressure. Except for a locking brake on the wing side the front far steer column not connected to the throttle gave an airplane its total maneuver once it was blinded in stinging snow at twenty wind or greater if any damage succumbed a banging flotation which controlled rudder right. Jacket availability stored in the tail should a flight need to take a crash in the ocean often was impossible to open anyway, but dramatic crescendos of thunder could cause the jackets to fall through a panel used to offset recon during lightning, in partially submerged ocean the can as ground crew termed the component of the tail could view for landing and the heavy rudder was then used for deplaning.

Chapter Six

There was good radio reception when the airplane destined for a three hour flight to Sidney flew over a radio station air tower. Sacramento came in very clear, also Salt Lake, but neither Cheyenne nor Denver came in. Red Lodge picked up faint air chatter, so the presumption was the flight was still on course.

A bomb had just detonated. It rocked the airplane back for what seems like a second before the airplane nose up began too rapid a descent. It took about twenty seconds to completely go off. Everything went soundless, the clock stopped moving, they called to local air tower, only the sounds of their voices returned.

It was icy chilly.

They were like in a capsule captured in suspension.

It was impossible ground control instructed course for landing.

They assessed from the speed that the airplane lacked control. Conrad or Terry were closest. On the airplane radio returned full blare for several seconds, talking clearly heard, before it then went blank again. The voice on the tape echoed back in a weak decibel having picked up the telephone and talked into it while the phone was arranged but no one was connected. It was a situation of first man on the moon during which the Watergate airplane lost contact with Dulles air traffic control frequency in South Dakota which vanished. This was a dual recording system that talked to its direction. The computer showed a blur to the direction course bouncing it around. Map on a database installed on the computer controlled by worldwide television, landing gear switch was pushed forward. Landing had been engaged; at first there was a release like a second stage separation and non moving drifting, then utterly no sound. There was a sense of becoming cut off from the world, of being in spacesuits with air tight helmets, of being in slow motion; there was space, the glow of blue over the earth, dotted surface lights. No one had memory, everything in the cockpit had gone.

The flight lost all radio somewhere near Gillette after which it floated drifting over water for the duration of up to one half gasoline tank until it crashed near Terry. These airplanes could fly five hours eighteen minutes before they were one half hour to empty and had to re-fuel. Blast caused airplane to sway tremendously, there was loss of gravity as wind rushed through cabin, bodies were thrown through air, some were pulled out with the explosion, the temperature was icy freezing, all dead;

Rush of wind at some point ceased to the blue of black night. There were thirty-seven seconds from blast to crash.

The file summary read, No billings.

First take photos: Big explosion of fire billowing clouds erupted into three fireballs. Three latches took some sort of explosives device. This device was believed to be valve releases in a hydraulic system below the compartment where the food was. In those situations for which records for billings were necessary, the files included final take analyses, column amounts and presumed particles.

For this crash which actually made it all the way to St. Paul, analysts finally made a determination that there was trouble inside the luggage.

The news section reported backward vest gave out where a ship was going and where it beached; they weren't certain they had the correct mastheads, the ocean they were sure was not in the Indian but off the Gulf of Baja. The rags stated a parliament representative and divorce took holiday abroad during an Armistead conference cited sale of airplanes capable of continuous alert to interior of government;

The shipping industry was in some way surrendering loss of product to eventual commerce with air that was previously the exclusive control of land-based transports; a second concern was some radical left third-wing group had paid to leak confidential docs to public about illegal military exercises at religious covenants at which nuclear arms were sold just prior to explosion; in addition to the flight disasters there was the Lockerbie tragedy in northern Scotland when a rail going about ninety miles an hour collided into a nuclear plant and caused the immediate disruption of chemical explosives reaming trains along the outbound lanes of the stockyard.

The group whose responsibility it was to find the airplane path of descent just prior to crash had relocated from West Virginia to the Atlantic Ocean side of northern Florida and had decided to adopt a German-oriented program consisting of accumulating high sky rise penthouses as conviction-proof for design or implementation of bomb/crash occurrence, departing for good a former selection of both cemetery together with job site allocation. Out of the 149,000 condos for sale including penthouses on the top shelf of the Indian River junket, 59,000 had closed-out with hundreds more selling every few weeks. The Keys group headed by Lewis Lewis was a tight group, the agents resided predominantly in the seven Keys, he and Jones and a few of the Nassau top brass lived on Longboat, a few men spent winters on Emerald, Perdido and Siesta Keys to escape the rain and humidity elsewhere, and without exception they kept a strict adherence to the seven to five-thirty, coffee filled, half sandwich with diet coke at noon every day, the cases were everything, they lived to bring in any goddamned iota of a bust and sat round the clock eyes glued to the telex with pen and pad scrutinizing the fast board for any detail that might round out a piecemeal situation, Haiti, empty alleys, street corridors ward off poverty-enmeshed teens, schooled orphans, every so often the governor's office asked for applicants to work the bake programs and a van filled with meat and potatoes for adults and fortified leche for babies would move slowly through the church quarters and slum areas stopping at each gate to ad-minister service. Despite the belief Lewis thought he had left this all behind when he divorced Abby, he sat on top of the world with a lamp lit awaiting night fall and candescent tin lamps dotting the sand beach from one end to the other. Life was refined, even without the hooplah he was making out bet-ter than the average turtle, any agent in his seventies with the horrors of the world packed into a dozen cases could say living out of a hotel beat bum city in the Keys on the beach, check-ing the restaurants, conversing with shore to island dispatch operatives, hey hey to the beach patrol cops, the dead and sorry DEA and border drugs. Even with the retirees close by enough to drop in every few months, he had his chores on a sched-ule – he dropped in on the three hundred and eighty churches twice a year, stopped in at search red cross operations in his area weekly, and contacted either by telephone, computer or hedgemony crop fund network old cronies every three months like clockwork, spooning off necessary work in any amount they might be able to work in on an average of year output.

He awakened at dawn, usually four in the summer, to see an absolutely perfect still ocean with shallow sandy recesses and coral reef depths of sapphire and utter indigo. Taking in a cup of fresh coffee, he reclined on the deck and smoked a reefer. Afterwards he showered and dressed, and began his computer contacts which took about two or three hours; then he was ready for beach patrol and after talking to project leaders and ministers he dropped into lunch, often at eleven twenty for tuna in mango or fried plantains and corn arroyo, following this he strolled hands in pockets to the wharf road and looked in on medical patrons, many with sickly jaundiced skin and other feeble disorders of mild rheumatism, all on their way to being cured by natural hot springs, medicine and improved, medically-sponsored diet. Always he was back at his tiny study in the wide hall taking orders for medicinals from islanders, then telexing these to a local populare pharmacy run by an island physician in his late fifties. By four he was sipping hot rum, ready for an early bath, a maid into prepare dinner, often flat bread with hot sauce and drops of cooked lentils with lamb, available to show an apartment flat for lease between six and eight, in the hot tub by eight-thirty, on the green every weekend early morning, some boating in the Gulf Stream, some fishing from any of fifty docks.

He had decided in his early seventies he was too old to put up with a sassy chick for long, he indulged a few long term relationships in the good weather, sometimes went to visit Abby or stopped in on Jones. More often than not he was alone taking in peace and quiet without the taxing rumination of his middle years, the quiet feasting sight of the ocean from the eighth floor the most comfortable enjoyment of forty-eight years in the field. He ran through ten novels a season, did some watercolor painting, and took in a boating expedition to Rio every few years. The task for his agents was straight forward once he encountered an non completed file sitting in the midst of liberal subjects enjoyed by Keys residents, art, theatre, condominium rentals, shore fishing and boating, grounded transportation, missing persons, scheduled expeditions, medical technological advances, new marketplaces, parish markets – the tasks they each had to administer to were, how much blood was on clothing of injured in a crash or grounded aircraft? Then for each traveling tourist, photo from the ticket counter, Department of Motor Vehicles driver's license or identification card, thumbprint, matching prints, address, telephone and family members listed on agency workplace, medical record or household insurance; and from luggage, were there medicine, prosthetics, eye glasses or prescriptions?

His own task was a bit more complicated – he had to verify with actual documents if obtaining these items were possible, whether pictures were taken of the crash, was the shell or plane sections hauled into an appropriate warehouse for further inspection and evaluation, were photos taken of the wreck inside the hangar, had lab tested against the interior for spatter, blood wastes, tissue or residue; had explosives experts been brought in and consulted with; had analysts identified where the device was placed and what type of device it was, and had spatter marks been looked at for who the injured party was?

For the two big Boeings, he had sent for an inquiry as to whether street lights took pictures of the two exploding planes over parliament and coming down swiftly over the coiled fence and airfield. He had also requested clearer sound tapes of the loss of communication with each successive geographical air tower and length of disconnect. NAVAIR had sent by shipping express one landing tape by sequence of Turkey Air Lines which he had to deliver to each agent on his team before he ran it through his simulator.

Chapter Seven

From the vast arid red sand landscape of the Atlas Mountains of Fez came the blurred excitement of reporters portrayed on a film strip of cosmopolitan narrow cobble alleys which switchbacked through the festive city with the night sky in the background lit bright red with canisters of aerosol smoke and bursting ramparts. Again the vessel with a blue smokestack appeared on the Indian Ocean, its hefty bridge categorizing it as a large ocean-going liner. Jones sent Lewis a request to bid for the actual ship with a trail-fender or a hook on the alleged date of sail.

Lewis began with his news service in the Fez clubhouses. The Rasht 29 Club was in full swing; it was like a party every night at the Fez palace, a restaurant-bar-hotel that catered to diplomats and upper class businessmen. Lewis' contact was a language-historical restorer of ancient Nairobi text, a small Coptic Muslim from Cairo who traveled monthly to ten middle eastern nations to report on husbandry practices among outcasts. Most noteworthy was the Prashnanti who staffed a silk road gallery with Turkish and Farsi jugs, oriental rugs, gold plated copper and spice that arrived by camel through sand by the China Orient-Express bringing on occasion birdcage style lamps, silk floor lamps comprised of bone ceramics with yellow lace and sapphire washed, four-foot high gesso pottery from the gold dome Arabic quarter. While two Farsi men hired as workmen skilled with blueprint plans, concrete, wood and tile for approximately ninety seven hundred lira a year built Coptic cellars, seven houses, all with upstairs to every stall for three vans, nine sheep to herd or graze, seventeen outdoor poured concrete roofless shelf-rooms from which to sell prepared meals such as cooked lentils, couscous, Ramadan flatbread, lamb steak and a multitude of sacks of flour, bulgar, cayenne, anise seed, lemon rind with pepper, jointers, and stuffing soup bases.

Modern houses were garnished out of white clay ochre material and fully furnished platter kitchen of a long counter, yellow flagstone tile throughout, a living room overlooking the sea, a downstairs bedroom and bath, and three upstairs bedrooms, each with rudimentary vanity, toilette and shower.

The language-historian had pushed several notes into a small traveler companion guide contained remarks – "Blossoming flowers, predominantly white, choking the port with billowing, flyby swirls like tufted perennial grasses, a floating dock that is partly submerged to allow dockage of a small ship, Turkish container with side rafts, and raised dock to keep the ship high." Parachute capability to manipulate an airplane so as to bring its longitudinal axis parallel with the ground evident lying about the docks. In an unrelated photo pix he obtained geese flying in a flock recorded during emergency landing into a marshy field beside floating dry dock, numerous air cargo delayed because of poor weather conditions. Forward compartment in some airplanes, empennage or tail instability remarked upon, elevation, medical worthy notation as to lungs, Jones as usual had been meticulous; files of art very assiduously took him through no less than fifty files for a narrow lined total some sixty thousand photos. He had given the hallmark archived prints for ten minute sketches, decimated window panels, glass saturated by deep impact bloods, reflections of queer foliage lit brown resembling instantaneous moth-eaten white tinged fabric, splashes of blue fading through and through, which he circled and shot back with a query, "any other 3-second light prints?"

But overall, excellent! Jones remained true to his touted reputation, he was the most thorough investigator Lewis had ever come across.

Thinking ahead to an abundance of immediate-status tasks, Lewis knew he would have to examine the landscape of reflective surfaces of buildings, lakes and vehicle windows for images of the throttled airplanes, he would have to figure on estimated exploding blasts, darkened shadows for descending dispersions of pellets, rate of solar wind, atmospheric and climate changes, and blood spatter on far walls, chairs, the essential formidable links recreated in sequential Mylai rooms corresponding to the great sea and destitute deserts that ravaged the crash and burning shell. It struck him that the complication of the photographs he was seeking were suppressed in favor of an enormous section containing about a hundred files, each approximately a thousand to fifteen hundred pictures, there being over two million, four thousand photo-files.

The list Jones had exhausted began with abstract art surfaced to include Malibu ocean front, Vermeer, Renoir, Picasso, Monet, Oil images, Modern Art, political art, fine art, Museums of Modern Art, Legion of Honor, Catholic Art, Naiads, as many as thirty files, numerous ones subscribed to colorists out of Glasgow, others artists who painted primarily in blue, or in yellow, or red, or brown, only ocean, solely pasture, weary city workers, hikers, students, families; draftsmen whose expertise captured head and shoulders, profiles in exacting symmetry, muscles, miniscule details of limbs in motion, all of the landscape color photographers, an abundance of some twenty thousand photos, series of frames consisting of warm mediums of factual data for crimes, archives that offered photo-likeness for any tragedy which any insurance corporation might have had to track down the moment of a hijack, crash or unlikely death.

The accompanying static-file he had been given consisted of the following statistics listed under the heading,

Murders:
820 in California
1 in Rhode Island
3 in Alabama
80 in New York
1115 in Chicago Ill.

For which he interpreted 8:20 departure, chief justice for the state of Rhode Island temporarily missing, three buildings down in Alabama, Highway 80 to New York, ETA into Chicago 11:15. Who knew what terrorist activity this notation pointed to? The second World Trade Centers had an ETA as 9:11 in the morning. If the Illinois reference lay in the pile of art it was for an unknown descriptive with any single realizable variation.

The back file reviewed by one Public Safety Mathematician showed the dilution rate as 1:26. It took twenty-six seconds for one person to get killed. He re-assessed Jones' subsequent listings: at Al Azhar Mosque & University, to the Egyptian

Museum and at the pyramids where one had to be capable of walking forever to view the pharaoh graves and Coptic temple. A standard abbreviation attached on a long ruled sheet folded twice gave the Beirut landing as a score of six innings with a print read-out 2 RBI, 3 ARF which signified Aerial Reading Fahrenheit; this seemed pertinent to the World Trade Centers disaster if only because Beirut suffered the loss of a single misplaced 747 Boeing. During the four days potential hijack Egyptian and Nairobi agents swarmed into the Egyptian hotels along the African coast consisted of Azure Cove, Three Nile Palms, The Cairo Dan, Egyptian Bazaar, The Memphis and The Nobles Palace, and to the salt beaches of the World Mark Club seeking any tip from any far crow's call as far north as Lisbon, a Scottish castle on the coast with dungeon room for a prisoner, Lisboan Plaza through the arc entrance to the main calle of hotels and shops and docimentos, the two bell tower cathedral staffed by French flutists, Graca Tram trolley porters, to the Estremadura and snow covered peaks of Alma Enrique to listen to phonografia linguists while they sampled tapas at the Wine Bar, tasted Moroccan food at Flor da Laranja and Portuguese tobasco-smothered fish.

Jones had made fotolia notations as to churches everywhere, an independent source catalogued under proteccion d'aire.com, security bonifacio desks at luxury villas in Capri referenced through Palazzo Al Velabro and Via di Marco in Tivoli, each overlooking an expansive velvet greenery known to all Italy as Marco Simone. From terraced stone compartments on River Arno in Florence to St. Croce in boats right on the ocean, Jones had taken down televised warnings of imminent endangerment as the compass began a spin-stall and the airplane began losing altitude as far as a confirmed entry at Nags Head, North Carolina signifying the pilots had captured a valley located high above known life designated in the Alps, both pilots electing to ignore everything but what was on the ground, unable to get in yet to any Alpha station broadcast, a final photo-dict frame showing a temple above the ocean on a hill with intricate carving in rock with stairs, followed by a cool gulf stream Magnolia Bay at Cocoa Beach. And then Jones' relief grouping, agents stationed for several months to years at top rate timeshares, one-half floor with balcony or an entire floor, two shelf, average costs affiliated through Lewis himself now that he had become accepted for security status research document analysis on a customary case by status basis, for the islands, typical fare being $30,000 to $75,000, on the beach, with velveteen golf courses, twelve pools, three miles of shops, veranda restaurants, chauffeur-driven sports coupes, mini-vans and beach carts, complete medical on site, outdoor movies, boating tours, cooking classes, wineries and museums. He circled the Magnolia Bay resort and ocean for an inside-notation release.

The drogue route was made of marijuana, cocaine and her-oin and worked its way through every cranny and cabinet nook where couples of all ages showed under a presumption of seeking cool shades of condo flats in big art deco buildings at garden plazas or river bank beaches. Within a few months Lewis would have compiled the analytical findings, grouped the medicals separately, photo-picts returned to archival de-posits and compilings regrouped. Manufacturers in Nether, bromide concentrate in sufficient quantity may lead to expired air, inhalation stress, put into soil 12-24 feet to deforest crop plant, tissue concentrations, distribution, epidemiologist, en-vironmental hazards, quoted from Morbidity Weekly Report, CDC, Atlanta, GA. Lewis Lewis had twenty-five separate photographs of airline incidents and crashes, the first being the airplane that exploded over the parliament of Istanbul which the rear of the aircraft caught on fire. The airplane landed two minutes later relatively unscathed despite passengers feel-ing shaken and requiring weeks of services in order to acquire calm latitude. In addition he had reports as to air speed at the time of occurrence, destination fall time, microscopic floating fragments, conjugal liberty, and an index of other criterion that would later be used to discern cause and possibly disruption of contract. For one, the billing period was in lapse because the communication to the airplane did not lapse right away; for another, there was already a billing portfolio on file for a crash and the screaming down airplane resembled its predecessor for several seconds; also when the craft landed the door opened halfway and got stuck keeping people with body weight in a fixed hold hostage. Although the vans rode right out along with the hose cart which began spraying the craft immediately, the ground to air contact recorded a series of failures with indication rising to suggest the craft had lost cabin gauge at least once during its descent. Photographs which read for all sorts of codes had corresponding photo rationales such as a dark side of the moon, which meant instantaneous death and combined spatter on window or wall attributed for each one hundred windows of a wall panel, evidence already for M-109, a Gruder motor, flying from Germany into Nether and winding up redirected to Amsterdam; another evidence remark for a MM202, a Nether-made shorter passenger airplane created for flights lasting less than two hours, the airplane having lost control tower and drifted through the reaches of coldest night headed for a harbor descending rapidly, billows of parachute silk issuing from its holds, the pull of the ropes perceived dimly as a fastener, bright lights from the ground having been sufficiently lit up to give the descending plane ready ground.

The various files for resorts along highly trafficked coasts near their large city industrialized sectors gave one no forbidding sense as to the photographs that showed individual incidents, a series of three smaller airplanes with forty windows on each side, the rip from the exploding device leaving aperture-ripped door opposite stairs side at three before wing, presumably creating such severe wind force these crashed. Jones had posited otherwise. The airplane was already flying low, reduction in altitude brought the small craft down below advisories, the cockpit cabin door was jammed, the controls were set for any body of water which produced a river close to a train station, the speed was adjusted for long rate descent and thus the plane taxied onto rough hilly terrain where it jaunted along until it succumbed to the width of the river, the pilot being able to lock in flight control to the ground.

He kept an updated listing of crashes ranging in severity. The Milan flight for the Istanbul's Turkish Airlines, combustion to the rear, spreading fire beneath the hull welding permanently closed the electrical control systems; and Japan Airplanes, clobbered descent at 2100 feet without cockpit control, even though communications were intact throughout. Lewis added off the list of another agent formerly situated in Ferrotown for the KLM which once the camera explosion penetrated its protective sheeting it too plummeted, crashing in under ten minutes, leaving everyone alive except the seven passengers nearest the chair that cracked. The airplane was presumed to have been losing fuel, it was either blown or fractured, nose down, steering gone, it flew into equatorial sun, altimeter in a stall-spin, compass off its axis, map control too dark to accurately determine course, all point-course readings eradicated. Top Agency controllers would want to know whether two – the KLM and Turkish Airlines – might have been designed by one group.

Lewis routed a form for requisition of information back to Jones with an additional proviso across the top; were there more than one inspection conducted after each required activity performed? He made a list which he included in his note to his agent:

Turkish Airlines, left Milan 0410 headed for arrival in Baghdad at 0720, crashed with few fatalities; Japan, left northern Tokyo 0340pm headed for arrival into Lima at 0650pm, crashed upon explosive; Nether, left Sorney 1100 headed for arrival Turkey at 2200, was redirected onto Jordan coast with no fatalities.

When Jones consulted a file for Lebanon irregular landings he came across the airstrip where the KLM airplane landed, the two countries' coast port small airports were often confused; it was a frequented airport midweek especially for businessmen traveling from any north shore port along northern Africa because the British often closed flights during windy

seasons for any number of reasons; as well as for beverage vendors, stage groups, students commuting between the countries
between summer and fall when businesses reopened for both
work and special season tourism; Lebanon had redacted her
airstrips for any type of emergency landing especially during
monsoon weather, in fair weather aircraft stayed on the cement
in full view of a nearby harbor, when it hailed the airplane was
eventually tented so passengers when needed could exit into a
van which carried them to hotels; stone harbor with long two
story building, dockside walkway, office buildings on estuary;
despite this the paper file that pertained to the index with the
photograph contained a rather unusual notation; harbor, broken rocks embankments, grade forty feet, shallow end ten feet,
extend to one half mile, green light at entrance to docks, red
light at buoy, at sea cruise liners predominantly. During low
wind passengers are escorted onto wharf for yachts to travel
to Sudan; methyl bromide utilized to cultivate access to sand
without terminal; a question was, were these military airplanes
to Egypt? No one thought they were but the question had to be
considered, flights to and from Afghanistan were represented
in a category of lost world; caverns displayed the brightness of
light blue rays emanating from windows of planes created for
image intensity by Diego Maneta; at least one stone fortress on
the ocean was a graveyard with crypts, crosses, small managed
cottages, narrow streets, three-story blue, yellow, pink stucco;
Policia Ciudad, a telephone call had reported in as dead, three
seconds, before static began; unforgiving desert for a thousand
miles, dust vapors, dark dark blue oceans, smoke and electric, yellow canary background, dark crimson getty images;
and agents monitored for weapons, complete inspections. On
Omaha 423 radio from a Blackhawk helicopter he had an outfit
scouring banks with Border Swat Teams, who make up second line of defense, the mountains a primary dead zone out
of which almost no one survived, searching for where airplane
came down, control units sent out, band units also deployed,
previously there had been occasional incidents of illegal fertil-
ization when incidences of smuggling were high.

Lewis had located a lost world alaporte which had their own courts, paranormal training, computer interfiled data systems, that include telephones, all call out social cases, transfer information through billing, offices, enter churches sometimes, rent patrol vehicles; these started in US and get deported, no one bothered them, they looked real, all law enforcement was required to report to work daily, technically none could leave the US mainland for any reason, could not obtain permits for anything, lacked driver's licenses but had pistols, forgers sometimes to get them in. He had first break with television contact, airplane descending overly quickly, then falling, contact resumed an extended fifty minutes before darkness eliminated view. Then – there it was, the ship in a second photo, blue stack, wide bridge, all black body down to its low water gray line. He grabbed it.

He called Wanda, a frizzy dyed blond who wore tight sharkskin pants and a snug fitting sleeveless white camper shirt in her late sixties, at the Blue Design Art Museum for lunch, they ate at a stone kitchen off a side street, parked car, walked four blocks, ordered noodles with vegetable salad, a side of calamari steak, topped off with pie, a salty dog including key lime, frothy on top, and tea. Afterwards they walked ten blocks, from Veradero out to palm trees to take in sultry, warm windy evening. Lewis talked to her about the ship he'd spent a day reading for, it was just frigging huge, seven decks, all windows, a wane-mate's cabin on every deck, one would have to be blind to miss it, but no idea of its name let alone which ocean it sailed into and absolutely no indicator, the ocean recorded was beautiful light blue island deep-water. Wanda's suggestion was a ream stack of every ocean known to a camera.

Lewis had numerous light frames for penetration of depth of metal with camera matched color of blue – burst corn blue, archipelago blue, bright blue, navy, cohash blue, navy, gray blue, hyacinth, purplish, pike blue, cyanotic, pneumatic at yellow, cambrium, violet, dahlia, sapphire, Prussian, frost, heron, dolphin, aborealis, soda blue, serpentine, Siamese, indigo, retir-

ing, opalescent, agate, mystic, pastel and murine, each variation a necessity before the blow itself was assessed and with it,
body count. Tens of photographs of beige sand, hills of wind
shaped sand, hundreds of miles of shadow over nude visages
of the Sahara, wind patterns rippling over sand, high point of
intense bright sunlight and then the airplane its ceiling ripped
open, two flaps opening to midnight blue, glacial cold, a cradle
of hell spitting with temporary fire,

The night resumed under holiday festive lights with beer
and o'deurves to midnight, Lewis called Wanda for an after-
midnight nightcap to which she agreed; trying to determine
questions with which to request supportive documentation
from the picture gallery once he had obtained a final picture
of the crash sight, he made a note to himself to find out if any
pictures showed a device that was planted on a plane? Had
staff run X-rays over seats and interior, and what did Geiger
counter readings show? What did the light beam test show?
Blue was negative for an explosive as was light grey or yellow; Did test show at fifteen minutes for any of eleven locations in the aircraft a positive result? In any photograph were
there pictures of ancient men standing beside staff and tired
dog like a sentinel standing at the periphery of the dead? For
glacial blue and retiring blush were the typical revelations like
unfolding scrolls so dark it was impossible to decipher brown-
red stain of dripped blood and waste from blue grey purple?
Most near dusk photos were marine blue, certainly the fading
twilight of much fuchsia gave way to the surrendering belief
that life had been abruptly negated, disregarded by a grandiose
faceless presence. The subject matter was tiring, his emotional
state resisted any acknowledgement that there was death about,
that life had disappeared and he had to find it and regroup it;
this was no easy assessment; the further he looked the more
exhausted he grew until he had to pull away, surrender to the
finality of a descending orbit, not fully knowing what to expect
once the agencies responsible for finding recapitulated knowledge as to who each body was. Time was essential, life was unpredictable, and certainties were unknown. Any crash wreaked

almost as much a wrecking crunch as the bright impact of whatever had occurred in space. Inside of ten weeks he would complain of aches and low grade fever, his mind would take an exaggerated toll too. A floating dock than can be submerged to permit entry of a ship and be raised to keep the ship high and dry, creation of close airstrip made by cement containing an anesthesia asphyxiating chemical, schedule for first agent in charge of inspecting all industry logs as follows, 0800 open all windows and doors prior to wind which starts up at 1000, go down for coffee, 0950 pick up two sandwiches, 1100 see mailed tapes regarding skirmish and bombs in Bahgdad, send e abroad with details of shootings, 1800 break for dinner with reporter from embassy for dinner on terrace, talk about movies, 1900 write notes, 2100 go to sleep. Marshland along water is crest-ed wheatgrass, cotton salt rises above waters of temperature floods, in processing becomes gas, dogwood Cornus, used pre-dominantly for drogue where parachutists de-accelerate an as-tronaut capsule, or for pulling a larger parachute out of storage; measurements of solar wind, atmospheric and climate changes, blood spatter on far adjacent window at 10,000 pictures, nota-tion one airplane, it was a bad circumstance that took it.

Desk references, twelve notations among them modern art as to meandering river amidst thirst quenchers, irrigating canals drying up, Rochelle Gallery, Ireland, test velocity and wind in desert for TGV and cockpit for tears through metal, question how were tears made? Photograph of NASA Sendai Tsunami low lying cumulus at ocean level, land black, olive, teal with wisps at four miles per hour, Halley's comet, photo of Jiyyah oil spill dark blue on ice. File Lost in Space, explosive has slammed impact at individuals in seats nearest explosion, France, exhaust tail after aircraft in question blew as a gas gusher, replaced that year by military industrial jets with open exhaust tails coined Mirage 2000, reported in Star Telegram, London, communiqué revealed no response by telex, closed on computer, picture of incident a mere decal, still a problem; sent report to Corsica. A newer 727 came highly recommended as a good flight, relatively risk free, a Thompson, exterior teal with pink letters, rides seventy-two people, had twin engine, good flight under three hours. An N52 plane crash on land bucking for the ocean, tiny two seater, brothers dead, hauled out, no smoke. Top rate for timeshares, 1 shelf or 2 in glass highrise Florida buyer for first 5 years cheapy $1120/month for ½ floor with one balcony, $2800/month total floor with two balconies with $60,000 down up to $75,000 total, if tourist wants to live in these, costs and square footage retail varies, average cost included rare crestview $175,000, on beach with golf course, twelve pools, three miles of shops, best of romantic idylls, natural stone studios in a Capri setting, toward the end of the coastline a St. Croce harbor of small painted boats bobbing peacefully, ski heavenly type flats of nothing but tiny window front houses with small porches and sandstone piazzas, vineyard processing tank cellars everywhere, wine bars, pleasant strolls along a corridor of trees, luxury villas with museums to write home about, not to mention Jaco Beach, Costa Rico, salient ocean views, private terraces with spas, comfortable balconies with large living rooms and modern kitchens with views of a footpath through gardens to the sparkling sea, grass parks of Panama City, if he Lewis Lewis had to denote galleries, post schedules, release color charts and maintain communiqués, he had the subjects, such as they were, apartments reserved, villas and office half a hillside from cathedrals, wine cellars, docimientos, hotels and church rectories, and villas of Mysterie. Normally a retired agent who had requested ten to fifteen years in Europa asked for Italy for Lucca or Assisi simply because of classically profiled archives, a measurement of thirty languages cross-permitted to gigantic orifices of crimes, many crime waves, notorious as likely as war-faring. But he had hoped to stay put, in the islands of his enduring years, entering a sole archival registry that held him to Haiti for any similar sort of profile. Thus, timeshare rentals were a choice commodity as were nursery and station. This was his most convenient lounge in the sun, plenty of golf, idling on the outdoor patio, pretty females, casual introductions, tennis, one-person volleyball, fishing, snorkeling, and running. The fact that the dirty files contained partially destroyed files on military use of aircraft capable of low, water-surface flying or hovering for special recon photograph capability was about as standard as the method by which cases were assigned; just because investigative files lacked the objective presence of these in working files was besides any reality. Since he no longer had an agent command, now that he was looking at where on the horizon these situations generated saboteur-sabotage, he had the seemingly beneficent lifestyle to match industrial expectations.

He had aced it. Not only did he have the analyst tape on the shot-down Billings airplane as comparison to Fez, he also had Fez and Japan, dive-bomb rushers, mega-capsule driven airplanes whose photos showed ground debris focus while on the screen in Montana homing control the airplane free-fell for minutes before it sprung a parachute and blocks hung like python talons from where the wheels were coming down. Japan had gone into the ground full gear, her rear on fire already, spinning like a candle out of control aiming for the river nearest the train station, thought to have been tampered with by city roof lasers, landing without any ability to pull up on the throttle, here and there other landing fiascos, airplanes on fire, hulls smashed on land having descended over a river, wings smashed, cockpits crushed, tails shorn off, collisions in fog, air turns too late, two photo- negative captures of the two 747s identical with a flaring camera-bright followed by an apparently atom-splitting device which blew an elongated hole in the metal possibly from the below compartment. Were there any similarities in description files or would he have to open his own files on consultants? Had Policy changed landing protocols or recreated airplane design? Jones should have first right to index, then return with notations if any could be described or outfitted, and he Lewis would mail a section to NSA.

Much later still-lifes of brilliant oils would be slaked over the canvas, drawn and grouped at warehouses to provide draughtsmen artists with ochre color that might house injured burn victims for months to years; the stunning oils were yellow mustards of wildflowers, each stem visible as a moving hair in a turbulent wind, bluish water through a tract of green and brown farmland all the way to the snow-capped Sierra foothills, snow slogged fields along a dried-up river where willow trees hung low at the edge of a farm fence, watercolor of deep ore-rich mountains and glass-cut blue shining water above which along the coast a muddy avalanche covers the narrow, two-lane road, vineyards as far as the eye can see covering the entire 20"x24" canvas sloping as hills in yellow, blue, purple and faint russet. After 2.4 million images, twenty files per peeled back sheet, eight hundred and eighty pictures per average size file, three thousand photographs per file, now up to forty-five thousand photographs, the industrial field agent had long retired, even if he continued to spend fulltime developing judicious outcomes on previously incomplete folders, he himself having sought a more enticing comfort from which to analyze the reductions of a lifetime spent successfully on numerous industry-era accounts. In the news Pete Anslow, reporter, had discussed a slide that closed a major thoroughfare at Half Moon Bay, the anchor showed a considerable tear in the pavement, a walkway in front of a house connecting the entrance with driveway, and national news for a drug cartel busted by the FBI in Washington, DC, drug trafficking, immigration crimes, bribery violation of the Hobbs Act, near a train muni track the camera picked up lights cracked like a propeller, the town of Santorini crowded with bright colored mansions each sitting atop a windy hill overlooking the pristine blue sea, wildflowers swaying in a breeze, almost no vehicles except two deck buses making the steep climb up the island past iron gates of churches twice a day, finishing up the evening news with Nicholas Brendt on oil expenses in the Far East.

He thought by now the multitude of investigations which had plagued the Damage Control Office would have filtered down in yet assailable procurements but it was all a clean slate, the massive drug growing fields a distant issue, the numerous political assassinations throughout the Middle East dead and buried and gone, none of the smoke remained for what it had been. On one weekend every five years he flew into Tangiers and was taken by ship to the nomadic jungle of cottonweed and sand and filtrates, drenched oil that fed weeds along the great Algiers River standing inside a hydrofoil boat or hydroplane waiting for any sign of an airplane landing in the desert near a shallow water port. There had been overexposure to toxic medical toxicants used historically as industrial fire retardants and to fumigate agricultural commodities, grain bins, mills, ships and greenhouses during those epochs including narcosis and naptha. The British had come into tag every new minesweeper, a device for removing and neutralizing mines by dragging; in addition methyl chemicals known to cause temporary blindness were being receded as the once-previously hostile environment took on grasses and shrubs that could detoxify soil. He was no analyst but the eliminations were in miniscule amounts and he had visited the sanitariums and clinics seeking any evidence of inhalation problems. He was out of his settlement expertise, thrown into clandestine treacherous robust training for fifteen occasions, a sharpy whose knowledge of box camera, binary and Antarctica Sea compared with equal knowledge as to examination and inpatient descriptions, having spent several years in passage, mariner and battleship, on his way to Special Forces to evaluating undisclosed material.

Due to tightened security measures over the Sudan, a handful of bomb messiahs had shaken the Saudi Air Lines manufacturers when the plane burst into non caustic flames, due to greatly lowered salaries and numerous ongoing layoffs thirty rebellious Nakano ground crew obscured landing by disruption caused by cut communications while flying, and the final problem making a perfectly excellent super stellar 747 aircraft resemble a time capsule drifting in outer space over the rugged desert of Saudi Arabia before it dropped like a canister earth-bound. Nakano became to be known as a last supper sort of thing, a scene in classical art, seven men sitting in the final hour, bags ready, tickets stamped for transfer to an underground which would usher them far to a labyrinth to a museum where they would take sandwiches and beverage amidst Degas, Cezanne and Gauguin.

Dan Simmons BBS foreign scene reporter for News 3 KCRA sporting an open collared striped shirt reported three men in an investigation of Saudi Airlines with a congressional leak of information, secret meetings viewed on film, the same old usual 5-story condominium in the Gulf just prior to the oil crisis, the Cairo sun, private dock, grass, trees to the waterfront, joined by Colin Baker from Thames News, reporting on series of first takes per plane, documented 120-134. Welding sparks striking from the aircraft after a clear-for-takeoff inspection showed all series were sub-arranged matching drawings for comparative analysis. Often with nothing to keep busy Lewis opened his files for checks on mechanical parts working with a checklist including tightening bolts, running engine on computer, checking accelerator, oil, temperature, compass, other safety nose cone, rudder and steering, luggage and brakes.

Someone had noted an absence in the lights under a window, the appropriate dated file brought a mechanic for lights. A rolling chair on the ramp for the stewardess on the wing, after it got stuck it was returned for belt carpet; a six hour job usually with a catch clasp, verifying photographs in the first takes removed had a receipt with photo fingerprints and two badges. A stowaway under visor of luggage rack had filmed a lean male riding up on the garment shelf, scrawny, dark haired, presumably destination port, overalls and blue mechanic's shirt. The question of course was, how did a chair get accessed for removal; this one leaned too far forward and did not come to upright position, the extension broke, thirty chairs a week had to be repaired off site due to the unheard of reason that three thousand people sat on them a month. Then there were the brooms inside seen by outside hangar employees brushing off upholstery and exterior mops scrubbing dirt with industrial foam and jets of spray, any of whom might have access to the plane interior while it was standing off to the side awaiting final inspections.

The air shuttle contained ramp mounted guns that fired to the rear and three-barrel nose turrets for clearing hostile landing zones showing Mission Mercury, flight on which passengers froze to death after encountering a space station in north western U.S., the big question was a dedicated plane preserved in a gigantic warehouse in Aberdeen Mood, Scotland for over nineteen years as forensic analysts poured over the remnants of a really bad wreckage. A reconstruction of the crash scene showed the side without stairs, the entire top pulled up, one of the worst crashes known, a bar in the executive quarters with plexi-glass through which a car traveled like air cargo until the touchdown, a quarter mile still in the air putting down over a fence with coiled wire when the initial blast blew.

Following that explosion there were plenty of crashes to complete any deadly listing of small and moderate size airplanes, in Alaska the crash body planes numbered for disorientation to new sites and adverse weather – DC-6, Piper PA-14 and -32, Cessna 150 and 172RG, Caravan 208, Bell Jet 206, DD-28D-1, Piper Tomahawk, Cessna 206, and a de Havilland, each situated either in reeds downstream or against the turn of wind on a steep hillside, parachutes and rudder stick seriously damaged. No way out meant unlikely to come back. The crash of 1988 left three survivors, pilot sobriety and travel stay-over for sleep examined unsuccessfully; the crash was also not the result of high winds, ice on the wing or landing gear problems, it was due to a bomb, same style as other Boeings which had been manufactured train compartment with 737s lined up for manufacture, at the end of the line an air capsule for missile launch ready to be attached to 737, the type of explosion to the window several windows further back from the pilot section was conjectured as typical car bomb because of where it blew up on the plane, the explosion a swift blue radiant streak before a nebulae-looking gas cloud emanated sharply swaying the airplane causing it to descend rapidly as though the pilots were aware of a sudden forward thrust jettisoning fire.

An industrial trajectory corporation normally issuing equipment to the Army was selling guns for hire to overseas BOAS businessmen accommodating them for massive thunder velocity-muzzle weapons, high tech torpedo stingers, loaded wagon capable of firing strategic fire, and Cobra-efficient small radiator, high product, efficiency yield, Class 2 auto-coach; manufacturing time was under two months and were compatible for transporting inside the sleeve of a Zenith, this was a guess by any normative standards.

The most misleading element was the resulting rip the bomb left in the metal – no car bomb left it on a car, it blew the car lock to smithereens – and therefore although the rip occurred in three planes seeming to suggest the same calculating monster had made all three, the actual probable cause eluded him. It was a nose dive, a downwind hairpin steep stall which left the pilot no other method to pull out, a fatal kiss-off, certainly made by the weight of pressure on the plane, designated to be substantive.

The Nacional Journado Vive reported that border control depended upon area size and threat and availability of technology, urban problematic conjestion, rural high brush swamp low brush, mobile surveillance system, name and information, Xray inspection, Saudi coast had grown dramatically in last six to eight years since the hijackers of the Saudi Airlines Airbus 222 were caught and condemned. The worst problem facing Oman were oil was required to be mixed with ethanol on the way home and loaded oil had grounded ten ships that spring causing the toll in ship cemeteries to rise, many a beached container or Pasha Bulker or Western Sahara rusted tanker or cargo ship were beached purposefully taken to a ship-breaking yard to a reserved plot where authority was given for dismantling a waste ship, especially when crews could no longer send a ship to India or to Bangladesh.

An independent commission that gave clearance for anchoring, beaching and breaking also provided separate permits for how to transport waste to other carriers and avoid spillage to the sea of hazardous substances, the three cities in which ships were scrapped for their useful metal were Bangladesh, Alang Harbor and Suisun Bay, all hired two hundred and fifty people per duty required sometimes totaling over twenty two hundred fulltime employed personnel year long to dismantle and sink, attempting to put to work the little more than six percent unemployed, despite being outstripped in industrial creativity and technology by the top two European nations Switzerland and Finland, both which would take in through trade imports industries nearly thirty percent unemployed from the Mediterranean. What was good for business often didn't amount to soap by the time the shipping industry had run its course for twenty years of trade, five years to denigrate fifteen great bin ships, another to burn and sink, a last several months for photography to shoot the final resting places and coral nesting beds.

The analyst whose task it was to correspond airline accidents to coastal demarcations of ships going down wrote a final obit, "while there are no correlations for wingtips or left wing fires, we are at a standstill as to how a tank room meets its demise, with a firecracker barrel shrapnel lit candle solidly tied in wax attached to the plank side of the steel structure. It often sizzled through a wall an inch thick leaving a gigantic tear approximately twenty feet long, could be as many as four feet wide, a debt drawn on the calculation that a swift opening meant quicker reduction." No matter the declared ash from gas leakage to a cargo ship, by the time the tower and ship rails were removed, a shipyard crew still had to contend with hulls that seldom rocked, swayed or tipped after it was placed in its plot at its dock.

Magnolia Bay tested the ripped part of the Saudi aircraft agreeing it had been made by a device not unlike a door hanger which blew out a hundred feet per three seconds, fast, lighting a minor nebulae of exploding gasses filmed pink, blue, yellow. Their coast dog aviation experts determined it was the chair crew who had set the bomb inside the lower wall of the plane just prior to a repaired chair being re-installed.

They further hammered out a scenario which held that seven German boys in 1972 stole an aircraft, flew it without radio, landed somewhere outside Lebanon, picked up petrol and took off for Saudi Arabia vanishing into the windy sand.

In 1983 a Mexican 747 disappeared from southern Spain

and although it was tracked by interior communications to India, it was reported as missing due to an alleged wind storm presumably in old capital Arabia.

As recently as 1993 the seven emerged in commando clothing outfitted with guns, supercharge radio troposcatter, pinpoint trajectory, Taka narrow money, Argentinean pesos, and Peruvian new sol, photographs having confirmed a Pravesh Banque, India bombing and a suspected unilateral air tragedy over the Atlantic, Boeing 443 leaving Cairo, parachutists descending at night through smoke and shooting fireworks onto the Vitava River of Prague.

The investigation checklist included pilot drunkenness, adverse weather and spatial disorientation, the plane attacked by an unmanned aerial plane shot off the desert landscape caused the in-flight 777 wing to burst into flames, all passengers accounted for by name, matching fingerprints, up-to-date addresses, telephones, vehicle ownership by vehicle license registration number, photo clearing through customs, all in less than a half day. First take photographs of the crash with passengers filing through the doors were removed, inside the awaiting vans there at the site to transport them to a dead zone hotel, the living five people received minimum detection for fracture and hematomas in those who were unable to walk, for those two who could, it was routine blood pressure, eye examinations, hearing evaluations, and simple eye chart recognition.

The plane itself was tested for residue, blood and tissue wastes, and deplorable general damage.

An explosives expert was released to the crash to complete initial paperwork; after the wreckage was hauled to a warehouse, analysts poured over the hull examining for where the torpedoes hit and the extent of the damage which was considerably less than would have been anticipated.

The photo bucket showed a series of ground to air torpedoes, some ten skinnies, aiming for various sides, the tail, and a wing, and miraculously the air ship survived, most of its body and entire cockpit intact.

When the pre-boarding analysts reviewed points of interest where planners took their idea for deadly force, they wound up with a hodge-podge of five businessmen who had combined perspectives from a photographer of Ivan Corsa street art, an artist of a popular Monte Carlo summer beach scene of naked males lying beneath parasols of swirling blue and white, nine photographers of a father with a child on the back of his bike and a female in crimson seated at a table in an outdoor café, at a modern art museum in Poitiers.

It also showed a Florida hurricane raging winds of a hundred miles an hour, blowing sand, the chaser eye giving relief, a false sense of security, the eye wall most severe, everything flying, trees and buildings splitting apart.

Out of these evaluations, the crash team compiled their evaluations within a few days, all subsequent trafficking determinations were posted to a file and closed out, a psychiatrist having noted that the surviving pilots consumed larger amounts of liquor to produce the same effect, they were experiencing persistent vulnerability combined with cross tolerance after a year using different drugs as sedatives, all had developed a physical dependence produced by repeated use, upon cessation of prescribed drugs they experienced noteworthy withdrawal symptoms, leaving nearly 20% drank daily to alleviate severe anxiety.

Nothing remained to extrapolate other than the fact that once a crash was survived personnel were almost never returned to travel. The resulting depression became so all-pervasive that the general tendency was to want to give up before they were faced with doing a task, procrastination while unpleasant permitted a person to avoid something altogether, most succumbed to relapse from a higher independence.

Hospitalization was common, major depression and bipolar anxiety or cardiovascular difficulty in combination with diabetes required year-long inpatient bed stays with adherence to medications and regular supportive psychotherapy with resulting strong therapeutic alliance over minimal two to three years.

Peter Lewinsohn talked about the collaborative teamwork between severely depressed patient and resonating, empathic therapist as a condition of competent guided discovery.

Archeology became the essential language – spoken and non verbal.

The patients found their way to a psychiatrist who wrote out prescriptions all day and who put them in a spacious sanitarium overlooking gardens, a patio and indoor spa pool supervised by nurses.

That ended all necessary documentation except for new programs which could bring enhanced relief, patients painting walls with oil fresco and applying portions of scrolls created on parchment; ultra large rooms painted to replicate the desert through which one could wander for at least an hour; or throwing pails of oil paint at wall size canvases for hours until exhaustion was released.

The day began as cloudy and windy, a fierce summer breeze that had taken the gulf stream during the night capitulating giant droplets of rain and by the early hours toward dawn had ended. Lewis strolled out onto the nines by six, played three hours teeing off at a mean ninety, and showered and towel-dried in time for the waiter pushing the breakfast cart to arrive. He sipped whiskey and egg cream well into the hour, peppered his easy-over-medium eggs with toasted wheat spread with butter and mint jelly. The news bombarded the background with more tidbits on the Hilton-Panda buyout by Anniston, the news breaking story having run throughout the evening since yesterday's five o'clock hour – Jersey business had secured an operation in northeastern Ireland, another hundred acres on southern Bermuda's resort district, currently they were negotiating a lounge and cabins in Waialua Hawaii. He called Jones on the ticker tape inviting him to a game of tennis at half past three, a look at the reports and then a walk down to dinner on the beach. Jones would have spied out the inconsistencies by now, despite Lewis' having studied the number of people who had become hospitalized and who were suffering depression, Jones would be calculating the number of air assaults measuring off against military exposure not to mention junked, overused debacles.

By one o'clock he was restless, he had put aside a new novel by Clancy and had answered the first queries in a batch of a hundred from island parish priests. Two whiskies and a slab of tuna-macaroni salad on a rather significant dollop of crab cream cheese on cinnamon toast later, weary of awaiting the Telex, he took a short nap in the full sun on the deck for a refreshing hour.

The flat in the tropics contained a sloping jade green lawn to the sparkling aquamarine sea, trimmed bougainvillea, rose bushes and tortuous leaning trees, and easily half a dozen patio restaurants and a dozen pools, tennis courts, backgammon, bicycle paths. This was a redux of Sayan, a stratified terra meandering creek with large platforms of waterfalls spilling into a shallow tile littered with gold and ancient silver bronze coin. Nearest his studio were a black and gold trim tiled pool, a black and white marble patio and loose stone pavers, giant ferns and yoga center. He was a million years from his grounded ship with pier tower, the crew had long ago disembarked, the funnel bar anchor sat in sand, the base of the ship rested on the incline of a beach in southern Melbourne amongst hordes of big bosomed, silvery blondes with bangles and a strip of cover cloth, the fascination of youth and tight skin. With the plank bridge having fallen over, the steamship couldn't go through the canal, it had to take the long way around, marooned it would eventually be craned out of the water, winch snapped and hacked like any sea-bearing octopus worth its flagellum. Report in hand, Lewis wandered about, sipping a whiskey crème, feeling the tipsy effects of the sought-after emotional distance preferable to any prescription drug taken to combat the periodic war wound in his foot. The Saudi airplane which was originally considered a hijack dropped off surface, the yellow blip closing onto the equator at high noon as if producing its own vanishing shadow, the tell-tale reassertion of the solar cheeseboard moving at angles to signal more air traffic. The fact that the plane was thought to have landed in another jurisdiction did not dissuade controllers who switching to an in-range signaling frequency picked up the craft for all of seven seconds. A radio context to the ship in Yemen waters gave strategic air base coordinates and inside of an hour fourteen jets had been sent out; all in all the measured corresponding size and description produced a singular plane which in its descent crashed its right-wing and located the wing part in a vast marsh and the plane below rock on a large section of terra nova desert. By the end of the day while the equatorial hamsiin winds were raging a path of destruction and mental instability, the door cracked open and the first moon men walked the planet. It wouldn't even be a week after the aircraft disappeared. When it next went airbourne it flew directly into the sun and before everyone's eyes exploded.

He hadn't believed it. That damned plane was still on the ground. The Saudi government sent in a command unit to torch it and instead two men wound up dead, tied to a railroad track, muzzled. It was a bad situation until Lebanon paid a pilot to infiltrate and fly the seven bandits anywhere they wanted. It wasn't his call, in all probability wasn't anyone's call, a short stop ideally when agents came across them, it was shoot to kill, empty all rounds into their fatigues.

The 747 bound for Mexico was scheduled for United States but no one, himself included, thought the airplane would enter U.S. boundaries. It was more than likely it would make an attempt to enter below the eastern bloc in through Romania or undeclared southern Austria. Whereas all broad bands were on alert for an incoming pigeon the beliefs were dour that any detection system was capable of flagging them with a landing panel replaced or a radio tuned for static.

When Jones stopped by, Lewis was settled into his fifth, no more happy to have just sold a single timeshare for August through February considered by the real estate offices to be a complete sale, and a small flat on the seventh floor of a slightly older building. Although he had made a pass at the buyer, a young girl with impossibly skinny legs, he was not impressed with the fact that to walk the two blocks he had to pass six buildings, each with eight condos, only two buildings which were seasonal rentals and if he could fill them by cash down, he'd take a cheaper sale first, because who wanted to be chained to evenings every month doing nothing but showing space?

The weather report was in, it was hailstones in Budapest, clam diggers in Bratislava, pasty dirt shells in Dubrovnik, no airplane would risk getting pounded, maybe it would aim for Innsbruck or Salzburg. It definitely wouldn't return to Munich, forever German officials would be armed and on the lookout; but for some inexplicable reason they had made one attempt to aim for central Europe and thus it was presumed these men had a powerful connection they couldn't be without for long. Munich's Old City spired gothic churches were rumored to have trained every last Munich officer who knew the boys well enough to identify them and gave these inhabitants tickets throughout the Hapsburg region awaiting their spelled descent. The Germans were tragic in their beliefs of human folly, Lewis thought it entirely possible the hijackers once free would travel just about anywhere.

"The loss adjusters will only rate injury," Jones said. "They have strict orders. It's not the same as a grounder."

Lewis handed him an egg crème with tequila. "It depends where they emerge. They blew up a port, wasted a ship. No way will they hide in Antarctica the way those other fools did. You want to buy a condo?"

"I might. How much?"

"I have one for sixty, one for twenty-five."

"Sure, either."

"Let's walk over."

They left their glasses on the dark blue formica and rode the elevator.

"How's Rhonda?" Lewis inquired politely.

"She left me for a younger sailor."

"Too bad."

"I'm making out alright, I've been seeing this lady for a little less than a year. Whatever happened to your model?"

"You can never keep one, they aren't truly there with you; they belong only to the camera."

They chatted about the ladies, the islands, the Virgins

had proved the most relaxing; the condos the finest beachfront property anywhere even if the lawns were a bit plucked. The twenty-five came with an entry hall, a small kitchen bar and stools, a living room to exile oneself in with a long balcony and view of the ocean and a bedroom, full bath and sauna, and laundry. Jones wrote him a check for eight grand.

Over dinner they discussed the terrorist situation, Lewis had been given an Interpol position on account of the fiasco in the Oriental East including India, and he had been on his assignment all of five weeks digging through pictures of collapsed structures once an advancing army moved on. The world had a distinctly expensive diversity, a stiff pedantic conversationality that attracted fine art along with patron joinings.

Analysis: what insurance was cuff to ankle? First it was a different type of airplane, could be similar to Lockerbie 103, gold cuff link and trousers most likely referred colloquially as a Giorgio Armani; Gabbana had pushed boundaries of dress and luggage with stand-up roller; why then a sign-off at an insurance corporation for cars? Could be insurance paid out first, brother is the insurance pro; cleaning upholstery on seats or overheads could damage levers by either foam or crude assembly and pays out approximately cost plus up to 25% for redesign. It is $6,000 per overhead with up to $1800. It went without saying that bomb blast design reviewed how tight welders seamed overlays; air vent operatives who came a dime a dozen were infrequently known to have tied a net line to a cork and blown it out of a jar timing each occurrence. Technically a stall which was the most common problem during flight was in truth a fuel line-feed problem in which the fuel did not make it entirely through the engine. There was no known reason for this and mechanics who opened up the fuselage would comment that there were either obstacles consisting of rusted oil can sludge or a crack had sufficiently put enough pressure on the system delivery that slight loss possibly due to evaporation or leakage was thought to exist.

Cuff or mild hat-do; column-maker such as coffee maker, this is either a bathroom, a cockpit communication out or a panel out; a wing shear is referred to as a wall-sorted magnifier. If one knew one's items well enough, one could predict the entire request. Investigators estimated that a cuff uninsured meant a definite Lockerbie with a bomb inside luggage, cove access referred to refrigeration which suggested a wall out, a column-maker to take out communication was probable, unless what was wanted was on the ground, lights out in the tower for a touch-down after dark.

Ian Ferguson, reporter, first reported as Malta Air to Frankfurt, was subsequently confirmed as Pan Am 103 in which suspect Al Megrahi placed bomb wrapped up in clothing in suitcase, which caused airplane to explode over Lockerbie, Scotland, killing 259 on plane and 11 on ground on Dec. 21, 1988. It was assessed that a door to baggage was tampered with. Tripoli Airport closed during this time; in other news Libya accused of having hired the suspect in airport operations sent Scuds back. Pix identified acts of malfeasance including female who placed suitcase on conveyor from inside luggage terminal up to wreckage.

In another ongoing investigation Ian covered the strategic where-abouts of one female Saudi Lodesta Umbragia, thin, off tan skin color, reddish short hair, a capable tinkerer, thought to have admirable skill at stepping up the timeshared release of a typical trunk bomb blast.

His desk partner Adam Jewett put forth a belief that the Lodestar actually owed its exceptional blast magnitude to the rate at which moderate size motors could fly up a very steep incline. In an article that would revolutionize news reporting Jewett ran a column on small aircraft crashes. In 1983 a small airplane D3-1721 was determined to have been lost over the mountain top of Machu Picchu, prevailing winds having scuttled it afar of Lima to Cusco, ice having accumulated in the fuel tank blamed as reason wing almost sheared off losing power forcing airplane into narrow descent through drizzling mist that shrouded the snow peaks of Mt. Huascaran making for scarce visibility and plenty of questionable spatial disorientation. Immediately agents were dispatched from the new

Museo de la Nacion, of the Callao Plaza, 2 bell tower yellow, two-story building adorned by thin white line of stone, ornate stone heavy wooden door, adjacent a long yellow two-story building with white stone around arc 3 door entry, a bell tower at the end, iron rail on the roof, pink and yellow three-story apartment buildings all along narrow pedestrian/small vehicle Calle Colusa, and boarded a train that would usher them in five hours up the mountain peaks to emerald studded peaks to wind-driven spellbinding Picchu. Forgetting markets with bags of cilantro, red peppers and huacatay, teams of rock climb-ers threw on their cameras, ropes and picks and took a plane to the Lost City of the Incas, through flowing descending strands of wet mist that left droplets on the windows, to grass covered stairs, stone walls without roofs, dozens of Anasazi-type dwell-ings tiered to the top to the air crash site to help agents evaluate the wreckage. It would be almost a week before they would discover a piece of wreckage had toppled into a lake-filled gorge amidst cacti at midnight of a moonlight-bright sky and sank into the shaded bay where they dredged from a catamaran yacht and several fishing boats and a dozen kayakers. Through the thick fog remnants of a collision with a tanker leaking jet fuel was finally getting moved to a bay warehouse where the body of the aircraft would also get stored until air accident in-vestigators arrived from Nicaragua; the motion tracking zoom high resolution and optical zoom lay in the wreckage still at-tached to the non fractured left wing – it also had a 30X digital zoom, a handsome feature intended to detect any problem in flying over steep terrain. The pilot, it was said, was a dare-devil, up for anything at least once, often flew in demanding weather, through lightning storms, surfaced crash-style into snow avalanches, charted rainy pelts upside down, had lived a bombastic, queer sort of existence in defiance of nature as though life were not precious enough and a walk on the wild side of the bizarre somehow awakened him to his mortality in a way nothing else did. Not much older than Jones, the crash pilot had flown the steepest mountains of the world, angling his tiny aircraft by comparison up the desperate slender angles of Mt. Everest, the Alps, Andean Patagonia and its icy aqua blue ice fields, to Los Amates Mountains towering above Rio de Janeiro, gravel peaks sliding down to the absolutely still see-through aquamarine waters of Botany Bay, and hiking in after flying the unending cliffs of the Ancash.

Through the capitulated cliffs of the jagged Amates the lineup of fifty windows of three pieces of salvaged metal of the airplane that exploded on July 17, 1996 off Long Island's sky way hung in the snow embankments of a wilderness ex-pedition, no longer posed on a steel ramp of enmeshed wires nor detached from its cockpit that held secreted into the over-head panel an envelope of explosive FTX, a newer chemical manufactured in Florida for the purpose of detecting its metal powder on X-ray. Originally utilized by C-2 explosive analysts for detection in glacial ice fields, it had recently been tested by upholstery during a simulated air trauma descent for recovery. This would make the sixth photograph evident in a non related file, this being vacant empirical wilderness treks, not altogether unrelated to condominium timeshares although he'd have to prove a far more governable link or to classical and modern structures of buildings. Jones downloaded the single draw while he also searched for laminates, prosthetics, grafts and billings, the muscle of the Mission files. While it was presumed the plane left Malta headed to Frankfurt and then put down in Paris with an hour and a half to fly to New York, there could be no viable explanation as to why the airplane was report-ed having gone down in a plume of fiery gaseous smoke over Scotland, except that in separate clips an Indonesian-looking female falling with luggage down the shute was assigned first to San Francisco and next – presumably accurately – to Paris.

This was the file. Air crash experts, all thirty of them, were still toiling over the wreckage, pulling at the release tabs of the communication mesh, examining how many colors cor-rectly remained intact and where the lines were truncated when they split apart. There would be no completion probably for up to ten years once each compartment was rebuilt and final last-minute instructions and turns received and documented. This was the airplane which when it blew sent a spectronometer's worth of aviation glitter predominantly red, silver and blue whirling through the cabin and into the air as the plane descended as quickly as it was able. It was the same accident that when it crashed into the Atlantic, spirals of oil shot out seemingly of the vents mixing with glitter; from a televised distance the gushing liquid resembled thrashing prawns on several skillets. As it was consumed on its one side the outer sheeting fell away from the cabin and to sea, while the shooting stratagems of oil exuded like firefighter jets aimed at a burning wall.

Jones lined up three out-takes, the prawns in gushers, the falling wall, and crash. He sent for receipts on each compartment, transcripts of any final communications to JFK tower, any photograph showing an individual or individuals with access to the body of the plane. Within the hour he received an indexed copy of a final communication – one of the pilot's had called the tower, discussed the problem of how to keep the runway on the computer on the panel, and was given instructions to receive on another channel at which point all technical computer data vanished. At that very moment two streams of misachieved fuel broke through the plane releasing the outside wall on the right wing side.

Jones awakened at five fifteen in time to witness a first sunrise, the bright orb poured over the eastern exposure and scintillated on the placid water, steamed coffee with a dash of cayenne and cinnamon piqued his alert curiosity and he drank sparingly on his balcony taking note of the mildly warm jet stream breeze. Had he given any real thought to the fact he was no longer residing in the Puerto Rico Islands amidst pastel stucco colorful three-story Spaniard style houses, he would have placated curiosity with a slow boat to the reef followed by eggs and fish before seven and a stop into the tourist agency to find out the activities of the week, he was a crab fisherman at end summer preferring to catch the placid sea before hurricane squalls were unleashed, the frenzy of fall storms made life restrictive, lights doused on and off all season, flooding washed up onto verandas and plazas bending trees and punching holes in rooftops, the females disappeared for months, and the cruise ship industry left for New Foundland and better, more mild weather.

But he had not prepared for either weather or surroundings. He had to miss a course on the transportation industry for Customs which he was slightly resentful of. Despite a list of bugaboos including the fact he didn't have Rhonda's telephone for the Keys, he was only put out by too few trousers, shirts and shaving cologne and lotion. The rest he could subsist on – a batch of coffee filters, tray of fresh cut fruit, several pre-made sandwiches, all the room service he could want, a spa and sauna and a closet-full of fresh white towels, and a seductive view of endless aqua blue ocean that tore him away from an all-too-small desk filled with policy manuals facing a wall. He set about to resume his year-long assignment transposing all raw data off his lap top onto Lewis' household computer, an IBM United Press International page-master with significant dateline data that popped up on a miniature template. So far he had slogged through slightly less than twenty thousand photo images of a file he estimated was approximately a hundred thousand images, all first photo-takes from crimes as well as from damage assessment evaluations, billings per one frame, spool-tape talk, religious imagery, condos worldwide used by traveling salesmen, beach shots, a hodge-podge of stylized art, Giclee prints, chase scenes, drama and news, some museums and their modern files, poets of Elegos, and assorted border inspections for the United States and Panama DEA and Customs international police. Lewis had warned him in advance: the file while simply of photographs could take several years to document-proof; it was unknown the state of each file and whether it was adequately described. However, once he opened it he realized eventually that it contained all sorts of control items; he could be at the profile computer for hours every day merely sorting through what was there and making sure each photo file was complete. He had gotten overly absorbed on Miami Beach, collected row after row of beach and road images for customs, opened each as a file and looked up banking and crime scenes, adding injury photos, and determining whether individual people remained in Miami.

Now that he had come across various airline crash photos, some certain to be first takes, most he presumed had already been removed to dusty archives, he had to index them, his first task was to evaluate the assessments of damage that had already been categorized, then determine what analysts thought had occurred and whether chief evaluators had noticed lacking permissions, communications, summary narratives, tower advisories, and so on, in the final closure of a paper trail he expected there was always a plethora of photos, reports, crash inspection narratives, articles and billings; sometimes an analysis for implementation of billing and did the loss reveal what had occurred. Someone had tossed in under commentary to request analysis on motion-tracking devices, another person had asked for first takes of Bahgdad. Of the twenty thousand files he had already reviewed at the rate of fifteen pages per hour and fifty pages a day ideally four hundred photos a day. Jones was one of the fastest readers and even faster a critical-factor analyst, but he had almost reached the end of the condo file and he now had to reduce a spectrum of on-sight witness accounts to a matching cross-archival system of frequent names that wound up in different cities upon certain seasons.

Reasons for crashes varied, dust and sandstorms not to mention thunder and lightning, freezing rain, fog, cloud height, visibility or wind, could have to do with extremely low visibility, not enough ground, a spin, a stall, sudden loss of height because a wing sputtered or an engine lost power, which happened all the time, but the more experienced the pilot the less potential of a burn to the potato. Jones ran his usual checklist for loss cost – the computer that controlled airspeed factor, the pressure altitude, with plotter, compass and rotation, essential for being up in the air, deviation and variation, wind triangle, ADF, engine, weight and balance of baggage, marginal visibility, fuel consumption, turn indicators, oil pressure dial, and rudders. After listing each plane's structural deficits as a result of each failure, his monetary hit list looked no more no less a bid on an adjuster's aeronautical rebuild, as follows:

PART	NAME	USE	COST TO RETROFIT
Cockpit panel	Lambert conic projector	Plot course to destinat'n	$200 million
Wind triangle	Bendix stabilizers	Control turbulence	$ 40 million
ADF	Automated	Direction finder	$ 1.2 million
Radio beacon	VHF	2-way radio	$ 15 million
VOR REC	Morse	Code capable	$ .1 million
Engine	Boeing/other		$300 million
Turn indicators	Incl. coordinator	Change direction	$ .3 million
Elevators	TAF	Control airspeed	$ 10.2 million

The written notation on the Billings, Montana disaster read Class B struck by 4.5 hit a flaps-up which in pilot-jargon, Jones decided as he arrived to his office subdivision on the belt behind the golf green and casino, maximum turn pilot could control was too seriously affected by a sudden power-decreasing stall with a steep turn at 70 degrees of bank, a fucking shotgun of a situation, pilot was already too low to touchdown when the problem occurred. His estimation was wrong luggage in the utility for weight and balance which threw off center of gravity; thus, he went looking for any listing in the loss arena for a notation as to "auxillary load" since sometimes the smaller aircraft carried that demarcation after a bad crash.

By the time he had dug up the incomplete listing for the Macchu Picchu crash which listed wing icing and practice for an upcoming medical search and rescue, maintanence records that showed too rich fuel mixture at high elevations, heavy rain in fog with poor visibility, Jones decided his pilot was a bored student, the final notation complained of recent inspection required having exceeded four hundred flights in a history of six thousand flights, unmarked emergency exits, unappropriate boom attachment for a fork truck, obviously used in the oil spill gulf crisis, and unmarked lifting slings. It was the final item he took a neck-prickling reaction to, so he shot it by late afternoon FAX "for your eyes only" to Lewis Lewis at his new stag density timeshare in southern Pensecola in which he requested any similarity.

The James Edgay file turned up on a clerk's desk after apparently much debate as to why an engineer had gone on board the 123 prior to its departure from Oakland; the mechanic named James Edgay resided on Heggenberger Road north of the airport and worked driving stairs to the TWA airplanes and when airport staff was low he worked gas, TWA was the sole airline flying passenger flights until 1971 in the United States, this was a first in the industry to delay a flight to San Francisco as a result of a load balance problem below the luggage rack which was checked twice, ties having been carefully appraised for shifting proportions, fluids carried on board being the potential problem, taking upward of a half hour longer than usual causing a boarding delay. The mechanic hand carried a box of instruments to the plane from the far hangar on the field and then deposited it at the stairs to the cockpit, meanwhile at the opposite end of the staging area a runway control flag-man had extended a barometer tape over the pavement to time take-off procedure, inside the tower a rating man read off runway line-up as each aircraft drove to the starting gate, flight number 123 which was scheduled ahead of two other planes had to wait while a 737 destined for Mexico and a Southwest plane took the lead and were granted express-air status.

Sometime later in 1996 James Edgay mechanic file would turn up situated appropriately in the worst airline disaster in U.S., the KLM-TWA off Long Island in which he was suspected of having deliberately placed a honing beacon constructed either from a clip-on radio on a jacket in a suitcase, Jones had what he suspected were incomplete photos of numerous fatal disasters for KLM-Pan Am to San Diego, TWA landing in the Atlantic Ocean with entire plane submerged, red writing above windows showing; the Japan Air Lines tail-gasoline gusher, which Jones was convinced that the gas mechanic had designed this one, Jones needed a radio expert who could build a beacon that a tracker on the surface could track a wake-up call utility that snoozed for a minute and came back again while by satellite transmission eyeing a line of travel made by a spinning motion imparted to a ball in tennis, perhaps a microphone specialist would suffice, that would have been the TWA nightmare, it looked like at least one person had to call the job right on the spot, first injury was man's ear ruptured and bled, second was man standing who was returning from bathroom was pushed onto people seated who grabbed onto him as underside of plane was smashed inward.

There was a saying that all bombers knew of one another but his gut feeling was that this guy worked solo and was an unknown, Philippine Air crash was one of many false landings which did not prove fatal, when wheels did not descend caused its pilot to land in trees, many a soft crash due to too much fog or fog at night and no way to decide where land was in a mountainous terrain as in Guatemala, Alaska or Wyoming; but these couldn't compete with the tragedies; San Diego in 1979 was the really bad one because it was unable to stop or get airborne again in time to not trample three hundred and forty houses, the Tomcat airplane over Poland shooting a fully industrialized airplane gutting it by fire in 1987 and then Lockerbie Scotland 1992 was horrific with fireballs streaming out everywhere, and finally Istanbul crashed burning after it exploded over its own parliament analysts thought carrying a car that blew up on board. Each required thorough review to assess completion, each might have a thousand photos or ten depending upon perceived severity of each crime.

The Wyoming crash was the most thorough but without photos. Otherwise data was in place, the cockpit communication, loss of response, drifting, static recorded by a distant station, as far as Jones was able to make out absolutely horrific, those poor, poor people, the windless silence, brutal injuries recorded from some phenomenal capability on board, presumably they were dead even while the plane harnessed by parachute drifted across a river into another state.

Lewis documented the fax from Jones attaching it to his newer photos of ballerinas practicing pleas before a long mirror, each girl dressed in pink short chiffon skirts, dark pink ribbons laced across their feet. He separated the billing and placed each cost with a loss appraisal with its photograph of the artist's work, these being painted by a well-known abstract Polish Tworkov in a collection wrapped and shipped in four works titled "Pink Bresk," each appraisal when finally completed would accompany a red head young verushka taking a bow in a short white densely chiffon skirt, white toe shoes, or an African melanchova attired in a satiny pink chiffon long dress, her bow hiding her satin toes. He tossed in an Andrej painting photo of women wearing masks, the presumption being that at least a suspect had tripped an alarm provoking a store owner or knowledgable archival to release his government photograph. The Villa Fleur Museum in Plac Wolnica which had previously that same year showed an exhibit of Avant Garde featuring of the Wojewodztwo Maloposki the celebrated Jan Matejko's The King Jester dressed all in likable red would send that painting to Two, or Doe as it was pronounced. Whereas the affiliated costs enumerated into the millions and Warsaw village, its market square of tan, white and apricot three-story dwellings so remarkably similar to the Left Bank, specially requested to be patron, the costs would nevertheless get attributed anyway to Bernardo Belloto paintings of views of Warsaw from the terrace of the royal castle. His paintings had often served as models for recognition of buildings and sections of the city reminiscent of older eras. Poland was steeped in a belief promulgated by many of her artist medicine fellowes of drowning in a past of earnest civility while surrendering to a hopeless bleak, gray inwardly surreal contemplation of borrowed zeal. At 41 Florianska Street paintings of King Campo Gillette utopia as a deranged asylum gave a life sentence to the society that gave prominence to da Vinci, Rembrandt and the Flemish artists of tainted indoor light, because of the funding foundation the museums were boycotted on account that Gillette manufactured razors.

No doubt, he e-mailed a letter to Jones whom he could glimpse sitting on his balcony laptop on his lap, apart from her pessimism over her militant Mocak who had all but one mailed death to a sightless producer of destruction, there had been an unending series of adjudications aimed at ending this modern type of abduction, Poland's artistic symbols approach Latin America in Beksinki of a dark man with torch to the sky and bird of salvation trapped in cloth like release, colors rich if not poignant, her airplanes ripped apart at the roof by heinous foul acts, art becoming the object of protest set by Eva Partum of Lodz for whom every birth was already demise. Lewis instructed Jones to contact the agency's air transportation consultant for two courses of direction, the first to identify at any point reference to weapon and upon paid receipt of loss billing to resurrect all photos of plates of blood burst and conjointly refer them to the conceptual artist Anka Lesniak whose stunningly captivating painting "Fading Traces" had earned her world celebrity status.

Since this was the worst piece to any continuing investigation, agents had to make sure when they took breaks they were sufficiently able to rid themselves of the haunting scent of mortal death which if it hung on too long caused good men to err in fallible ways. Blood burst contained no real way to discern where a flying body was when life terminated, when the blast ripped through the metal under-sheeting had it snagged a limb or when it peeled open the roof like a can opener did it create a circumcision in a man's skull? Each plate was carefully studied based upon wind airspeed of objects in the plane, on how thoroughly absorbing the amount of blood rendered was, the proximity of stain-imprinting sometimes gave invaluable data as to scene, mal-exposure, instantaneity, and so on and so forth until all life and extinguishment comparative analyses were known to the satisfaction of team of medical evaluators. When the last remaining report was completed, the billing was detached, ditched in a drawer with hundreds of thousands of capable oversight, and closed leaving behind hundreds of photographs, most of which had been used to denote calculations as to time, place of occurrence, size of damage, weather factors especially frost which often killed even when proximity to flash did not, length of injury by centimeter and physical description, flask amount of blood, or symptoms. In rare cases all that was known were dollar amounts, no photos, first takes were entirely removed, listings appeared as blank empty headline boards; and taped recordings were eliminated, typically as a realizable occurrence of resounding echoes combatively sounding off on equipment at any station in the path-arc. Lewis ended his correspondence with Morse code last contact on the Wyoming savagery of the canopy shooting over Flamingo-West, the vertical geography, whistling wind, fifty-five degrees, ten miles per hour wind; if he were to become ambitious Jones could use loss of turbo-crop as an echo chamber in an effort to seize upon a cracker-jack prize buried in some pigeon's bin. Boop-boop-hah, boop-boop-bah, boop-hah, boop-boop, then a sizzle, a loud thumping on all walls like someone looking for the way out, and finally frightening tearing sounds. The horror was they couldn't escape, even he, no stranger to the perdue of sudden abrupt cessation, was unable to shrug off that unmistakable nausea, that further numbness, the culminating sorrow that life was about to end, a final fleeting realization of irrevocable loss.

Once many years ago someone sent Lewis a picture of a jazz man playing a trumpet-horn, eleven separate colors flying at his face and torso, otherwise the man's body was entirely dark navy. Lewis had sent the picture out to be enlarged and it was taped to the inside of a closet inside which dozens of manuals had come home to a final burial, yet stashed for each relocation that promised to last longer than four years. Every so often he opened the door and the larger-than-life poster which faced at his desk looked as though the color was sudden, a goop flung across a room. Sometimes at twilight he dimmed the light such that his jazz man appeared to return from a great distance. The image took the tension out of an already anxious alert as to date and time provided in any of sixteen formats and all languages including computer ASKI, until the van crew punched in their alarm upon leaving to the site, medical OR's went on stand-by, designated police and county sheriff and Haz-Mat took down coordinates in preparation for rescue.

All rescue units had responded at each crash, it was methodical and sweeping, not any detail overlooked, in the dismal hour it was so he knew he didn't have to count up the vehicles, ambulances, and staff; once he requested a billing each station would be listed by number.

When the numbers came in they were not of lost aircraft but yet of more play listings of art, none of the eastern bloc, nearly all of frequently listed blue beach umbrellas, recliner lounge chairs, average size yachts and cabin cruisers, likely to be found in the Cambridge, MD series #s 1-18. Lewis knew the ranks by memory – yachts lined up along walking dock on Biscayne Bay, choppy blue water, nice harbor with pole lights, floating kayaks at marina block club, palms, tour boats, 900 Bay Drive, green water creek, patio dock on river; he still wanted and had never found a photo reference to go with an overlay of light blue ocean on a door of a new condo in a 4-story condo with balcony, walk to the dock, post lights, ship at far dock, no. 82 for the Gulf Stream. Enclosed with his listings were a straight off the strand for weather forecasting severe storms over the next few days in Mansfield, Eyewitness news live mega Doppler 7000, and Nexrad Towers as an additional contact when lost in a storm, all of it suggested a weather-beaten down CDC without any real way to either alert Search or send a helicopter. He perused the attached billing coding and selected out at random a mild breather expecting it to consist of photographs of the Machu Picchu aircraft in flight strung by TWA 800 and Pan Am 109; matter of factly he raised American art, six stunning vivid photographs: the first Georgia O'Keefe Ballet Skirt, all white dabs with tinge of grey at the edging, like a plume of feathers; a second eleven females in long white spritely chiffon skirts for the San Antonio Metropolitan Ballet; a stage full of ballerinas in white, satin breast top, chiffon poise, yellow, green and white flowers crimping buns, a pastoral from the auction box art; fourth, young solo dressed in bright yellow satin and cuff; and last four girls in long blue dress by Degas. Whereas the stage bows almost always went to a ship in distress in a pouring gale, the advance weather had to be derived by an air crash of some sort.

Near fatalities were sent from the Sarat region having been collected with the Tretyakov Gallery from Moscow for works shown at the State Art Museum of Abramtsevo, two works titled A Game of Preference 1879 and Pond in Arktyrjka 1880, along with popular Vasnetsov off auction out of Olga's Gallery, a young female in silver headdress, a Van Gogh church, a maiden in white sitting in a powder blue interior and view at dusk of a mountain slaved with fresh snow, all to discuss worthy notation on the subject of othorexia nervosa, a disease of which diet limited to a few foods perceived to be highly nutritious and extreme social isolation follows an apocalypse of unintended catastrophe. Apart from the obvious, too few people getting out of a collapsible plane and walking to safety, sightings of horrific landings were segregated into a loose leaf artist briefcase with a title stamped across the top, Views from a High Balcony, and a ream of photos, each vivid, stark, color bluish, warmth of sunshine, sand beach and ocean off Florida; mountains, rock, valley and town; desert sagebrush roiling loose over red soil; a narrow high-up glimpse of pool lights; red tile rooftop gardens at a lake, ice arena music extravaganza with ice skaters; snow mountains; yacht harbor amidst palms; city views real estate of Lima, Peru; high dynamic range (HDR) opera house; neon signs on main boulevard similar to New York City 42nd Street; small living room tile floor and balcony, room ten feet width by twenty feet long in Mar Del; Taj Mahal lacy studio, and view from the bridge of a large ship and cresting ocean. But for a 414 flying and lodging into snow on a mountain top, Bobby Allison's crash at Miller High Life and Natz Peters at Pelican Hill in Newport, California, approximately 3,698 photos were taken of the September 4th, 2008 Qantas collision in Sydney, the other material in the thin portable document folder (PDF) of the Air France Airbus #447 crash because the airplane lost its ability to fly at high nose up during lightning and bad weather, a continuous hunt made for the black box, a list of terrorism that went on for pages.

A list of museums was attached, some eccentric and eso-teric as any listing could be, all to look at the minute shredding that occurred in backrooms by chemists and artists, sixteen each had a different flank, Spy Museum made of red clinker brick, Philadelphia Art Museum, 2004 Bremerhaven U-Boot Submarine Museum, MOMA, New York City, Cleveland Crawford Museum, Echo Studio in Chicago, European Art Gallery in Chicago, Miriam and Ira D. Wallach Art Gallery of Columbia University of New York, the King Tut project at the New York Metropolitan Art Museum, The Modern Wing of the Art Institute at Griffin Court, Kansas Atrium at Over-land Park, Taubman Museum comprised of blue glass in Vir-ginia, the new minimalism introduced by architect Steven Holl whose emphasis on simplicity and light created a white box ice look at the Nelson Atkins Museum contrasted to the empirical lines of the six Ionic column one story stucco building reflected on calm water; the Rich Feizer glass art – bright glutinous yel-low base with teal and lemon chiffon wisps at top – at Morse Museum of Glass in Orlando, Florida; and at the Joshua Mill-burn for lines in art and design. On a see-through transpar-ency marked for Ethel Carrick Fox's girls in an garden mart of flowers and the Immortal Prophet Bird of a king and queen on a throne in dark brown, bronze, mustard and faded orange be-neath which an additional playlisting included the spire abbey Doll/Toy Museum in southwest Brooklyn; the modern whale-color Milwaukee Art Museum, a gray temple-like height with light blue pool-like floor situated on Lake Michigan featuring Rangel and at the Met Museum of Art on Ellis Island a host of archival monograph catalogs, among them litigation compa-nies to pressure the government to release various portions of crashed aircraft for study included John Su; Marquis Residence in Florida City of photography and lab site; Broward Art Gal-lery; St. Petersburg Museum of Fine Arts; Dauphin Island, comprised of three mile long highrise bridge; Azzurra Marina del Rey; Highway 43; and Thorne Cliff Park, groupings of galleries located within offices of one another on the Florida Panhandle, the Interior Corridor; Orlando Museum of Art red white arc with high peeking windows and long glass door-style windows, Tampa Museum of Art; Tehran Arjantan mosque domes a top teal and brown glass, and the Norton Museum of Art in ceramic shiny corporeal blue, white and gold.

Jones' furniture arrived by United Federal Express, he put against the far wall in the living room he set his Oriental rug of floral black background with pink flowers and a lone bronze with pink flowers in front of the glass wall and sliding door to the balcony, a narrow, square walnut dining table with seven chairs opposite the island inside the kitchen along with nine candle candelabra. By week's end he hoped his selection from the village portico would have been transported, a wall-size gigantic canvas painting of the ocean and an upholstered brown and green tweed couch chair and ottoman for the living room set. All was fair in love and war, the entire shelf listing of ten pages with five shots preserved in sequence across each page for a complete wall listing of up to thirty photos gave him the total grouping necessary for the type of crime being forwarded for coding by list and manufacturer. There it was in clear radiant Nikon, a main floor of nine hundred and sixty square feet, the entrance open, the reflection of swimming ocean actually sky, an overlay of darker blue giving an impression of a lengthy backyard pool, the immediate successive photo from the interior of what he assumed was the same house, a cubicle of a thing. He clipped the two with a crimson clip and sent the page to the photography lab. The real pudding was to be found on the final page, a ten-four alert as the chief metabolic pathologist might refer to it, and in this case the police silent alarm swathing shocks of red light over the street was for a hijack of a pilot to make an air escape into the Caribbean. Ever after law enforcement including Customs, Federals, Boat, Contraband and sea to shore poured into the islands, set up resorts, opened bingo parlors, ran numbers aboard cruise ships round the clock, a string of shimmering lights wavering in the inky waters under moonlight month after month. Within a few years thousands of agents from fourteen countries had purchased timeshares and traded in a Florida high rise office for a gabardine on the boardwalk. A vast grid of Sahara from the Atlas Mountains of Fez to the towns of Tobruk, Tripoli or Jerba might contain aerials of red sky over the Eritrea, an air wing pilot flying at low altitude through a dust cloud, because of the time it took any station on the ground to identify horizon the industry changed basic standard metal airplane to light silver. The familiar stuff was also listed here and there, however from an analyst's point of reference all photos were essential, Shawn McNulty's Epic in Red; Messenger by Matisse; his best, most persuasive use of color in Still Life; and Ruicke's Fragile Art. A notation on coding that read, "to manipulate an airplane so as to bring its longitudinal axis parallel with the ground;" another revelation for someone – "delayed because of poor weather conditions, could have been geese flying in a flock; too much wind, too much surface." And there was, "flying too soon, the tar on the roof wasn't yet dry, even a dark bird could by repetition take up a flap;" numerous remarks seemed to indicate a good deal of attention for details concerned with landing, airport identifica-tion, transfers made that same day.

In the Caribbean the big event of the day was a gas tank of petrol the length of an airplane exploded as a 737 set in for a landing, the band unit reported that the landing plane took a tail burn which presumably left no survivors; however, morning came and saw not a throttle ding nor an Omaha 423 radio ditch; a week later the Department of National Security claimed that a 777 plane carrying human cargo made an illegal entry on Highway 19 descending fast from dust clouds into a thousand miles of arid, blistering, tortuous desert without so much as a shoreline or water-hole. All of this sent the Internal Affairs Division looking for illegal response units, the problem much greater than anyone realized, helicopter-airborne units lurked at dusk in forested terrains for unfriendly smugglers who had crossed the desert and marsh wilderness on foot. Usually in uniform they claimed to be Air and Marine Assault who entered Love Canal from Nogales to El Paso, Texas in torpedo boats and heralded themselves as Home Base agents, either way the U.S. Customs had no such unit as an air assault or infantry rifle or a home anything, chances were someone who worked for magazines overseas brought in talent which they then set up in an art gallery, rented the semblance of patrol vehicles and gradually brought in pornography, medical billing and set up offices, no one bothered them, they looked real.

When he went back to slot in the actual photos for the final release into his file with matching first sheet he was surprised to receive another unidentified picture gallery to which the corresponding numbers went as follows: photo reference no. 18, picture 200; no. 20, picture 239; no. 26, picture 341; and no. 28, picture 385. Within the series the prints made sense, removed from the order of significance it was the different angle of a similar photo that each of the final showed. He faxed the set over to Lewis who said he had vegetable and chicken skewers on the grill and chilled beer in the fridge.

The image against the back wall of Lewis' glass enclosed nine hundred feet top penthouse of a female with heavily purple lidded eyes was typical Swardrovski, the rust striped tan carpet City Lights, the only furniture in a gigantic four hundred foot sitting room a couch upholstered in tiny crimson and brown square glossy satin by Lipstick, and the ultra modern kitchen Snaidero with aluminum stainless steel appliances and island all the way to the glass. At one time Lewis was said to dwarf the perennial agent with his sense of scrutiny; today he housed magazine interests for the agent who never left his flat, who with twenty to thirty dateline bylines had to produce tea club news for any type of barefoot-loose agent looking for the caged cushion. As promised the grill was going on a patio of sorts with a pool and lounge chairs, the city of four and five highrise resorts, galleries and custom border offices making for a glitzy idea of modern wealth day or night just below.

Jones inquired, "Any idea where you'd go to obtain a referral to a company that outfitted a gallery?"

"Oh, sure, small restaurant and jazzy lounge with brown glass candles covered by fishnet." Lewis was off-handed in his good natured reply, pouring two beers into tall blue glasses, handing Jones one as they walked onto the patio and went to stand at the rail for a look at the rising city.

"Would this have been local to Florida?"

"No, this was out in California off the beach boardwalk on the coast. It was a long time ago, maybe as long as 1991. Janella wasn't married yet, she was living in Venice right off the boardwalk, she threw a big party for us the evening we arrived at a café with a few courses, steak and lemon leaves in a bowl, red curry chunks, lamb and mint sprig with basmati, mango lassies for everyone, topped the dinner off with chai and cream; early the next day Janey took us for breakfast at a small Puerto-riqueno place overlooking the waves and we were served hot oats, brown rice and Asian jelly clear noodles with spicy dried meats; and Levami took me to a copy place for my teaching class and after we dropped into this hole in the wall, Tibetan food, a real dive for three bucks but the food, simple as it was, tasted excellent, fried pork, string beans, rice and dipped apple baked slices served with chilled tea. I don't know where Levami came across this place first but he was known to the family who operated the lounge."

"It sounds you'd have to obtain drugs to get listed."

"Probably that's true."

"Not as easy as it looks, is it?"

"Well, it's always in the background snoring off a dozer, contacted inside a section of ship or in interior walls of a moderate sized cocaine plane was plastic banded crystal, stuff which after tested failed to turn white, not really crystal but some chemical which as it steeped in the whiffer turned soggy and eventually turned yellowish amber, it took a good long week to get it there but once there was potent jelly, smoked it was stronger than hashish oil, it would make any working clerk selling suntan oil completely sogged. It was placed inside tins and resembled resin matter, the only way to dump the stuff was to burn it, sinking it didn't do the trick, divers who went down could break the stone off. The high rises seemed to attract the drugs in gigantic numbers, the storage for the penthouse galleries had to be watched constantly. What the penthouses couldn't achieve were tossed out in a bid for insurance for a weather-busted plane."

Lewis was enjoying the upturned wind despite the late evening and the fact he had been looking up indexes all night, he was having a good time drinking a cerveza.

He told Jones that he had taken off the afternoon to see a bunch of flicks, Rendezvous, a real film terce noir, Carlos in subtitles about a despot who tried to seize power by exploding car bombs near embassies, Secretariat, the horse that could run title championships, and Deception, of a female who murdered call-girl Johns; he did some reading, rare for him, John D. MacDonald and Aletha Linley, cooked chef style, chopped salad, prepared consommé, gave it a dash of red wine. No laundry, no chores, he was between showing apartments, Homeland Security had set up an office with Panamanian DEA and were running spools and a wire tap, he could see it through his telescope Intel, a 280X, the newest in close-up available with court order; since they entered he had ditched eating out, the high view of any vacation he decided was to enjoy the air and view of the ocean and every night to get plenty of sleep. It was five years minimum for a crash investigator who had to walk through the crash scene to determine how the crime got started, who had called the shot, who needed to be hired through which particular insurance agency, what the minimum item line had to read to get the high rise started, who would obtain the bid, out of which hangar the aircraft would come from.

Jones said he'd heard the fence was looking for a lakeside cuff bow, he had checked against refrigeration and two big cocaine planes were out of the yard from Merida, the castration was planned for San Diego for the Tailor and he sent for authorization that everything involving cargo had to be nixed; he ended the evening with a splitting headache and Andy Garcia in The Mean Season also starring Mariel Hemingway and Kurt Russell at the Miami Journal tracking the shooting of a teen.

"Where did the problem tip-off originate, any idea?"

"I heard a rumor it was from a ship entering through High Bridge, who had left the trade winds in the tropics following the easterlies from the Sandpiper Hotel off the Farallon Islands."

"A number of ill tidings accompany the waste barrel although where the motivation lies is a guess."

"Did you get my call?"

"When it came through the telephone rang a half ring and when the recording clicked on, the message was already going."

"Where does that leave us on the till?"

"Boats aren't subjected to the exact same standards as small aircraft are."

Lewis ran it down. At the inspection dock on the wharf, if the artist's party was suspected of having committed a crime, they were detained but not deported; even if the art buyer lived outside the U.S., ICE checked for paint, color still had to be on the market, cool water print analysts analyzed for intent to dilute original color and finally files, old and brand new, were opened. If color adhesive was practically speaking to be altered for an airplane exterior as it had been in the Yucatan 2007 airliner industrial component in-frequency broadcasting crash, the entire operation had to be shut down, turned immediately into a component-radio testing site and automobiles shipped in for loudspeaker installations and then those cars crated and sent anywhere overseas until an actual car was determined to be used by the circle in question.

Jones knew how that went. He was downtown driving to and from the dock every three hours, checking off bills of lading, looking up any pertinent carrier, questioning goods, stripping down chipping paint for lead, tele-tron checking for hidden compartments, sending the customs crew in daily to remove walls and break down floors.

Yeah, it was a mess, not only did the procedural activity slow down moving medical supplies where they were needed in Central America, canvases were ripped to shreds, bills were returned as undeliverable, storage stations when filled remained closed for a year, analysts were borrowed to compare to trafficking offenses, the paperwork was endless, it was a plethora of print-outs stacked in offices by the crateful. He knew they were in for bad news when there were no numbers on the standing placement bills and the crap could be shipped any-where into any unseen alley off an undesignated port. Canvas was used as watered-down paste for inferior banding on inside walls to prevent cracks, diluted color in cans now hardened was emptied straight into the ocean shore with gravel and over time became easy shedding for boats requiring repair to be loaded onto. Already Border had its hands full just shutting down il-legal doorways and removing itinerants to repair shipyards and corporate control yards.

A chill wind had started up and they moved inside. Lewis put marinated steak on the kitchen grill and diced mango and chutney and served dinner on square dark brown plates with cold soaked cucumbers, green horseradish and grilled garlic bread. Over chilled sake wine they kibitzed about recent crash landings of many a DC9, those owned by the Sinloa Cartel and others purchased by U.S. Agency spies rounding up pounds of heroin crossing the border at sensitive junctions, man-made roads, Omaha 423 roundups, inside fire and forget, illegal weap-onry, agents who had walked the boundary with sniffing drugs for twenty years finding themselves suddenly in an un-enviable position of having to track anti-tank systems for infantry.

Jones thought the entire problem entering the border could be chalked up to illegal money; currency had to come in with product containers, art, or houses. Boats coming through the Port aux Basques area were stripped apart, especially the fuel tank; same in small craft.

"Only thing we have to do is figure out how these dealers have access." He himself had looked at packaging for transpor-tation, at the anabolic or lumpy market, anything capable of hiding other product, and these days the dopers were getting aggressive; either that, or they were too rich to give a damn.

"It's keeping the Coast Guard busy."

"Yes, that was a million in federated exchange for cocaine seized in gulf."

"There were several tons of coke in that DC9 crash."

"Director of Civil Aviation was assassinated on his way to

work." Jones interjected.

"Yeah, I had to fly in, take a look."

"It didn't look so great on the type-pad."

"Really upsetting, I was shown to a hide-out in the mountains fortified like an above-ground tunnel so I knew something got out of control fast. He had notes on day-night integrated sight on target in adverse weather against enemy advisories, I couldn't image what took him into such clandestine operations but we scoured the area with everything possible and posted eighty stations over a forty-five hundred mile terrain. We tore the place apart for months at night just to compare with any enemy satellite photographs."

"It's infiltration into U.S. is what it is. The availability of cars is what it is."

"Small foreign cars and boats and docking permits, latest craze, fucking nightmare." Lewis said, and poured more sake. The night turned into a philosophical banter, wine pouring freely, a bit of dry Vermouth chasers, the lights of the city sparkling in all directions, natural disaster missions going awry, transportation into the jungle almost as popular as resorts on the coasts, coding gone berserk, news from Reuters all too infrequent, it was like waiting for the bus after midnight, they finally lapsed into a discussion of the roof bomb on the 737, it wouldn't happen on a 747 so policy had decided it was time to pull the favorite horse off the line-up which quite expectedly would push up costs, and they drank through two bottles of dry Vermouth talking about what sort of mechanic had built a roof job, the talk around the border inspection stations was it was a female who worked tar. When Lewis' new girlfriend arrived, Jones left. It was already after one in the morning.

The day made not a sound, it was one of those erudite mornings when even with the fan on, nothing from outside escaped in, just a sense of oppression of nothing going on in the moment. Within the hour he'd leave on board a fishing rig and boat up to Daytona Beach where the shrimp trawlers that went out every morning at three would be getting in. They made up a hundred trawlers in all, and any bringing haul got weighed, checked and registered; the slightest mishap brought the Customs out to investigate every inch of the rig.

The wharf was agog with five fire vessels, men in red plastic jackets running amuck shouting orders on half a dozen vessels, doors pulled open, ship grain elevators exposed, decks raised masts hanging with nets, ship hands with mop brushes scrubbing the aft. Rumor had it a man had gone out after contraband, but no one with a weekly pay wanted to be involved with the chase. Firemen had flushed every hand from inside onto the deck, hands clasped behind their heads, patted them down, emptied pockets, while another brigade ran inside the cabins, around the decks, flinging open cabinets, compartments, rubber boats. When the poop was drained there it sat, a square package the size of a small dot matrix computer all bundled up, even with brine washed away, the poop still stank like hell. Jones figured he'd be there all day, possibly into night, the dislocations were synchronized with two computers, tension was high for two hours until the printout was locked in, the fluid was in thin vials, on the street it sold for a thousand per half, the stuff was popular in Biscayne Bay where the spark plugs were see-through with light green skinny vials inside, anyone tuning a wideband could get in, the fluid when soaked on heroin made a happy fellow into a walking dead in hours, no one who walked away after removing the oil from the gear shaft was any decent to work for months, their nerves were frayed, mentality boxed.

Sometime before three a Wisconsin wing was ferried in on board a stern, the aerostar crew was already talking nose dive as probable cause. It was compared straight off to the Hesa Iran Aircraft 767 without windows calling it like an unmanned aerial plane on too small an airstrip, yellow smoke trailing the touchdown into the desert, it blew up while landing. The investigation was handled by the Alaska Injury Law Group, who followed transportation up to Wild Horse to assure food delivery. The wing would be situated inside a marina storage boathouse for umpteen tests to be run, there'd be photographs,

files, each file might contain two hundred pertinent files, target radius might bottom at six thousand photos. Jones would
end having compiled the majority of the network; it could be
months before he completed one question, what photographs
were taken immediately prior to the offset, probably a good
dozen, but it'd be a long week before they would be advanced
to his computer by air-tech.

Public opinion held that for any skyscraper art forum seated in
the center of a city if it were too high up perhaps over twelve
floors it presented a serious hazard for airplanes attempting to
land in the same city sector, if in addition to height and width
the art could be magnetized. The idea that high realistic art ex-
hibited possibly inside glass a reflecting light by other buildings
or in and of itself was an ignominious belief, not to be worthy in
either blueprint nor foundation breechclout. Neither a holmium
compound nor field hockey would send such a hunting out of
the pictorama of the skies as for instance a helicopter sought to
descend onto a narrow high landing angling away from bridges, other buildings, roof walls. Lewis had begun his computer
work that morning before dawn when most apartments were
still asleep and thus the ability to work on comparable static sky
files was above average. He took a vue at each horizon point for
three eastern coastal cities, being Cape Fear, Atlanta and Fort
Lauderdale, for the sky, honing in on clear day captures and
re-opening already worked files for U.S. airline disasters and
Turkey air explosions, of which there were the Istanbul crisis
and an-over-sea fire, and let the computer run a log per point
for as many minutes as it took to withdraw a single image of
the first frontal file for any explosion. The tool bar readjusted
as it exacted for bright clear day skies; the computer was trailing in and out of twenties of photos at a time, spooling through
archived or shortened versions of files which had been entered
by agents and agencies worldwide in compiling first-moment
histories. It took about forty-five minutes to trace files and hook
a lead, but what the computer put out was a ferry top and interior all wood deck and harbor shallow ocean posts in the bay to

match the ship they were searching for at sea.

Lewis Lewis would say many occasions, necktie and shirt-less, borrowed indiscriminate and reluctant admirer, that after forty-two years with the Bureau he left in 2007, entered semi-retirement, the sole task by this stage of the game was to iden-tify a perpetrator, all of an unknown identity left to guessing, the likelihood according to news sources was the Middle East, India, Yemen, or upper reaches of Pakistan. His 702 airplane schedule that he followed over the world and accompanied at every waking hour that he still to this hour awoke at six, walked a mile for a cup of deepwater coffee, when he returned sat in his terrace and checked the daily star, after a half hour review sat down at his computer to analyze another batch of two hun-dred to a thousand photo texts, all indexed by the media of the local domain, every now and then he took his café in hand to the city desk for rapt discussion as to who was seeking whom in the field of cross-territory-domain. Everyone knew the de-lete-stored files were too dangerous to look inside, all involved sources were analysts but the danger rested with analysts who gave approvals on pre-industry for how insurance was paid out. Law, religion, technological-medical contributions as well as technological inventions, high-street finances, Dow-Jones, de-encryption and deception coding gave VIP Art its latitude over the horizontal accounting. The screen gems in Fine Arts had the latest celebratory art on display for where rave was going, the scarlet elevator for example of the Sperone Westwater Gal-ley, a four-story Lower Manhattan glass slinky building built by Foster & Partners. Into the trim gallery that had stairs in a gar-den of grass and wisteria with a lounge-summery table and two fabric chairs, a romantic long pool with lit jets, interior made of an elongated kitchen with stainless steel and modern appliances separated by stone wall between living room and kitchenette, then through high retail doors into a full room display featuring the chief suspects themselves, an ultra thin female in Roberto Coin, all of seventeen, wearing tiny pearls in gold weave neck-lace by Barocco to fight Youth-Aids; a stunning brunette who in coiled bun posing for the Mandarin Fan group worked as a ballerina in pink chiffon and shiny pink toe shoes modeled sitting on crimson black-speckled stairs, having first displayed on Eight King Street, St. James for a sale of six hundred lots, then onto a Palm Beach gallery built airy box style, John Barman high up vane, for the immediacy of the ocean just beyond the pool; other featured talent associated to the good lookers included Clive Christian residing in all gray and pink wood walls with a water-shower-like chandelier for his "Book of Rooms," Derry Moore on very stark, French chateaux Marquis de Sade placement of period-piece recliners; where is the world? And Lalla Essaydi of three females, two who were gathering cloth to a lone veiled female whose face is evident, and a photo of seven veiled females wearing the same cloth, originally at the Museum of Photographic Arts in San Diego; and last a David Yurman photo of a sexy blond with a to-the-waist-long necklace of pearls and links, naked to the shoulders.

He worked each look-alike photo until boredom spat out a drunken summer and mindless waste of work, blowzy weather and refractory days had lent themselves to neckties and bikinis up and down the beach strip, the necessities aside a bit of boating, roller-blading, gallery hopping, reefer clubs, card playing under an umbrella, taking a course over at city college, bowling or evening matinee at the movies, weekend church was about all there was, unless the person was over the age of fifty and then there was nothing except an occasional stroll on the beach at five. The usual list of suspects took in a cabin cruiser with a party full of young girls and geezers for a hundred bucks every weekend and after a season had enough to rent a small cottage fully furnished, four hundred and twenty square feet, a big long kitchen with patio doors, outside a patio that wrapped around to the living room, a tiny living room large enough for a loveseat and two chairs and low glass table and lamp, and a bedroom and bath, two twin beds, a shower, toilette, some cupboards for towels. The luxury of living, rarely matched by a boo-boufant etiquette, for the emerald-bay sort of crime-evaluative agent handed out two certain privileges – one's own byline, researched and secured by trace-accurate information and the candor of dealing often solely with one's professional classification. Once one had dealt with earning a wage and trimming a lifestyle down to the knickers, bodkin and woolen scarf, the remaining vestige could include a barroom flat, a sweet surrender of any age, and a stove worth skillets of souf-flés. Better workers lived on less.

Probably Lewis would say of Jones that what it took for Jones to make it down any long road was getting the sole piece of information to break and bust a crime ring; and for that Jones paid dearly, more so than Lewis who at the very least got laid once every so often. Jones sat stuffed in an apartment, but one only with a relinquished-for ocean view, or in a rare time and place on top of a mountain squelching a too-long divorce with no interests other than mist hanging low over a bough-studded quintessential dramatic ravine. A rare agent would say they had done much contemplation of this nature, but to return from the wilds, the Bora-boras of the treacherous story-seeking was a seldom quieted pursuit. So Jones had the deser-tion complex whereas Lewis had the coveted personality of the bachelor-urban decoder, none really desiring the fish-stings his reaches of traverse brought them to. Neither did they pursue a Susan Czoper-type whose decoupage sections breathed awe into ice snow slanting blue ice floating at ocean surface, al-though the image was sought-after as much as the air crash in the Nepal wilds. A soda and lime downed with a sliver of blackened spiced snapper on a crisp cracker was just as work-able for a meal as well-done burger topped with onions and beans when the going was on, intense-driven by dateline or Milkweed. Jones who couldn't adjust without his laptop had to have Lewis' ear; although Lewis might suffer the isolation of thinking through the ubiquity when it was time to drink he did both, drank and took a gal home until he thought he might make it semi-permanent.

These deletion files as to what sort of suspect was filmed in a workday were departure from the first strips; a twenty photo all rooms was a Baghdad situation, a single line row was a heist of frightful money but no advantage, and a line-up of five plus one was a bad row. Even minus collaborative files the photos of Fine Art and Modern Art surrendered no recognizable identity of any individual with airport industrial contracts simply because most corporations for upholstery or repair of seats, overheads, carpet or wall sections were run by local firms managed by women, and the charting for females tended to be more cumbersome, the least favorable that to obtain clear thumbnail pix of a female with the correct scars, marks and tattoos required a lengthy court document. Thousands of inmate photos were evaluated, any male who ran a shipboard dance parlor, any flight risk, bonded or otherwise, female mug shot line-ups, all proved useless because no two photographs could cross match for motive, opportunity and access. Photo pages were unavailable even where clearance was granted. Lewis downloaded every single page onto separate loading zones, a process that took hours through the night into the next day before he was able to catch the verifiable splice.

At Lewis' instigation Jones began with beachfront properties with pools, patios, decks, recliner beach chairs, umbrellas, state-of-the-art computers, links to twenty or more, and links to metal flap bracing and access to hangar and airplane manufacture or repair. The residences whether they were used for on-shore station communiqués released a cross-pollination for computer text as to any of several crash causalities, interference with flight maneuvers, descent, wind pressure, weather such as lightning, spatial disorientation, engine failure, loss of cabin pressure, human error or intended error or an explosive. Once a suspect was listed, indexed on-site tabulations were pulled; for example another analyst working in recorded conversation text had matched thumbnails in four countries and found an index to 1973 with a Charleston train accident during which the train railroaded a nuclear power plant. The one demarcation to suggest all texts could link to a crash was read at Daytona Beach while the Bronze Cup was being won by Stereo Six had an aerodynamic engineer query about entertainment systems and after a cursory check that went through a checklist of any interior – aero-medical interior, cabin, galleys, washrooms, insulation, components and fittings, fit-outs and completions, furnishings and floorings, lighting, signs, refurbishing and repair, security – landing gear and engines CF6 and JT8D, thrust reversers, anti ice shields and fan exit guide vanes. Aside from these conversed vulnerabilities, presumed areas of interest were the avionics of the cockpit such as display, nose and bearings; wings including guides; components and interiors such as sections, tray tables and overhead bins. This then constituted a gallery of issues, each as worrisome as every other, the exception being to non owner lines, among them the strident cockpit-leveled Boeing originally and non-indestructibly built by NOMAD. Thereafter surgical mechanisms replaced fairwidth industrial applications for obvious neglectful rationale. Thus, as dictated obtrusions came to light on text language nets it became apparent there were at least several groups in the vicinity of the Carolinas who planned an airline crash.

A female who walked the wall to the tower gate who slept with a double-barrel Uzi to test whether soldiers could fall asleep while holding one unlatched came up for an immediate. Without her grey-green duty wear, she was typical Coin, all chest and shoulders; in the right light at seven in the evening in warm summer chintz barely garbed standing on a balcony she was at her most revealing but photographed with a pilot beside his fighter jet locked the image into the bier. The Panama Drug Enforcement Agency had her in a raid of a warehouse in Mexico grabbing forty-three tons of heroin and five tons of coke off a DC9 just prior to the day that the Dr. Romano Romero, Aviation Director of Medical Supplies was assassinated along with his secretary and her aide. When their bodies were found riddled with blood and proof of spray gunfire on an infrequently traveled red mud road in the midst of the jungle, the U.S. shut down its Acapulco station inside two days and left words with the Mexican Narcotics Divisions of the Drug Enforcement Agency, Federal Bureau of International Investigation, Immigrations and Customs Enforcement, Panama Canal, Homeland Security, collaborators with the U.S. Government, and put out an All Points Bulletin looking for an Alain Guzman and any information as to infiltration into the U.S. at the casinos where one could live on a hundred a month especially for weapons, the Javelin, known as a fire and forget weapon; an anti-tank system for infantry with day/night sight integrated for target use in hailstorms; weather maps, electronic surveillance, and small transportation vans for natural disaster missions in the jungle. In addition a million in cocaine in dark bags was seized in boats crossing the Port aux Basques along with safes and metal doors which contained money that had been shipped to a real bank when it was intercepted. Graphics had scribbled a note that a Coast Guard chopper picked up that a Roberto who walked sentry for a little less than half a wall was being sought for in the assassination. Somewhere in the fray the weapon was picked up having been discarded presumably after the shooting. It was unknown manufacture, a sacristy item labeled much like a double wire inside a radio.

Father Romero was a god to the non government towns who survived on surplus brought in by pickup vans. Not only food, he was a botanist running batch tests on generic penicillin, bottled mold to combat botulism and fungi, and on vitamin injections. Every so often he sent a loaded syringe into the mud caked tiendas for bent-back laborers. He had erected a supply industry to the town of Praia which he sectioned three blocks east to west and two blocks north to south and in it stood two two-story buildings a block each with a parking lot large enough to turn around inside. Rooms that kept canvas-bagged beans, rice, nuts, dried milk, cans of soup, and endless stacks of Coca-Cola also stored marijuana, cocaine, frost, toe-rooks, sliced trim, and bags of bum and wink, coffee, and rolled rice. Inside three buildings on mats in twelve by thirty foot offices, home to fifteen newspaper reporters and printers consisted of single beds, desks, computers with plug blocks, a tall closet and draped windows to prevent smoky sunlight from yellowing the objects of those offices facing one of two rivers and pulp mill.

There they slaved, four men went door to door to determine sanitation, water and food while an equal size team built outdoor toilets, and indoors, kitchens with cupboards and coolers, and erected ceiling fans and rudimentary tile floors. Inside a large garage was a single engine ski-plane used for taking men fishing and distributing medicine. By the day his life ended, it was obvious he was there to spy on the weapon-stash, look for methods for bringing it in disguised and who the bandits were.

Aviation had no method to target locate an airplane the way a train could locate any transportation inside its three radii. Therefore the pilot had to be the one to report his visuals as he was flying along, once the pilot had flown over the government's accepted boundary of the country there were no radio-signal barrier designations, and for that reason looking for an airplane, not so for aircraft, was no longer a relational discovery-bound capability. In order that an airplane was located including when it was shelter-protected required a visual land-mine sweeper and that was the problem for industrial espionage, no device could make contact with a mine sweeper because the sweeper fixed every station it found. Therefore finding the particular Guzman wearing dark sunglasses who appeared relatively tall and so thin as to be emaciated could also fix anyone he regularly did verifiable business with as a result of matching dial imprints and cell phone networks. In the case of Father Romero who chose not to conform to running a parish as a result of two ordained priests being killed some ten years earlier inside their own Catholic rectory, the establishment of the order as an industry set was successful for ten years until aircraft trajectory pins picked up his ski-plane motor when he flew over the entire jungle and was followed upon return at night by a light source. The dense tops of grayish walnut looking teak trees shone with bright yellow light giving off an appearance of entrusted delegates of impenetrable crowded foliage. The air filtered downwind drifting lazily past strata of iron pyrite and wild jasmine toward the river while below unforeseen forces hidden in the cranium of the blue haze of forest waited, chains mortared until miners finished slaughter of baby elephants which were used to carry once younger elephants were raised. The airplane motor could be heard long after it stopped being seen, fluctuating in the distance, a casual drone, dropping into the bowl of the planet at the outer perimeter of the port.

This time when Jones withdrew the art files and selected out photo pix of all rudimentary yellow oil paintings for the film negatives they preserved and the red oils for ink preservations he labeled each photo by its drawer number and separation code and placed them in order by row, select and look-aboo, number with letters written over them, 001-213-VXZDEYPLH. The yellow oils out of these pix numbered about five and showed under microscopic dark lens corners of a first look photo specifically of an airplane descending fast, nose down, wings busting up with vibrating pressure. City horizon buildings appeared upside down, unfriendly plaza corridors opening onto the sky. Jones removed an appraiser lens to study the abstractions looking for unusual indicators of sky, ground or signs of loss of control. The deciding factor for the negatives was location for one sky rise, a grouping or proximity to other high rise apartments. Of all imperative factors which typically included location within the city determined by city block coordinates and highways, views that could be seen at each flat, surrounding grass or waterfront, lights inside buildings, lobby size and décor, presence of a restaurant, and available services. Normally whatever condos were needed for – hanging overpasses, urban streets, and ambiguous reflections – usually it wasn't for a nose down neither with coursing wind stream, nor for a swaying building, but for an air vent on fire. The bulk of condo apartments for sale appeared in voluminous page sheets only because architecture gave rare exactitudes from country to country.

Any standard of an upper class which proliferated in a densely urban center was recognized instantly for its metropolitan sophistication, packed-in and radiant, clanging and juxtaposed but at ease. A desire to subtract, to put on the market place or to stand selfishly opposed to the soiled conclave of a multitudinous nomenclature placed the sheets of photo text in mass geometry. The subculture of pix identified glass monoliths where on the outside a man climbed glass by squirting a spinneret pulley to give him a trail of tenacity. The big red couch elevator of the World Trade Center represented a layouts finder, a window space to put all one's shit into, for an incident already passed the only representative photo was of a text width. Other values consisted of high rises on book jackets which indicated that one's stock portfolio was locked into irreversible stocks and thus couldn't be exchanged; glass mansions lit brightly on any cover meant that a person usually a man had left his stock market option to a close friend; and an editor's choice very simply indicated that a national corporation had dwindled in their market value. Thus, to locate a man of zenith strength for which the profile pix gave a sensational nightly-lit stone mansion, two-storied, glass on the coast side with pool and deck, situated on a beachfront, whose pastimes included Martinique, Cannes, San Sebastian, Cairo and most seasons North Carolina starting from Cape Fear suggested to any well-seasoned journalist either business or family connections to the preferred cities; devout Catholicism and expensive ancient dark sapphire rosary beads woven into macramé trim, papal consignors who blessed the Rosicrucian confessor with sacred water, the one known item was the vehicle fan that was also an office fan without lights was made the operative mechanism for an explosive. Although the belief was the man was black, an overhead camera pix showed him to look white, large golden Bronx curly ringlets in some pix while in others dark prescription sunglasses, dark golden hair, excellent physique but slowing down, no longer sprite, picked up in a dark green or black sedan driven by a curly blonde, daughter or wife, he wore a plastic purple raincoat, in one picture he wore an all black matching velour casual gymnasium attire with white bunny lapel that in a photo resembled a small microphone.

He went weeks back to the question as to whether the tasks of itemization from the most recent crash were completed – pix were taken of the Japan nose dive and removed to permanent archives only to be restored in one of two situations, another same outcome within a month or a photo taken of the rapid air descent from any condo flat worldwide; the wreckage was hauled into an air hangar for complete forensic makeover; more pix taken especially of the burnt interior; the entire airplane was tested for residues, blood wastes and skin pieces; and when these tasks were printed, only then were the explosives teams asked to conduct an air path shroud investigation. As usual they wanted to answer whether there was a single device construction used.

Only Lockerbie had a black box that wasn't destroyed. Whereas it produced in the first few seconds prior to exhaust emitting into the cabin and there was a piercing, shrilly audible squeal followed by shrieks and terror and after a few seconds feed the cabin and cockpit became an unmanned exploratory spacecraft; compared to Japan the receiving air station at the train depot at Nakano recorded repeated queries by the pilots as to where they could land in a field saying the airplane's rear was producing gushing gasoline and a runway landing was impossible unless they could land on the ocean. The dashboard downloaded into Ivan Corsa street art, Monte Carlo glicee prints, a painting of a male dressed in a green silk suit with rust colored Spanish ruffles shirt standing at a bar with drink on the counter, sculpture on the Rue Maison of couples in embraces, Notre Dame lit at night, father with male child on back of a bicycle and cave art. So this Nakano airplane destroyer who had placed a device somewhere on board was a family man, a frequenter of unusual beauty in classical art, familiar with local avant-garde exhibits as well as with the alleys of Paris by night. Jones cut out a photo in the last row on page 21, image 264 of a man in a short van traveling the cramped streets in Poitiers.

In this one circumstance the discovery of a father-son identity of a squad team did not follow the typical syndrome for discovery which for any sort of explosive – airplane, building and street – began on page fourteen, a crisis of hearts or at least one heart and was understood as love, for a device implanter did very little else with his life. Love, as it was contemplated, proceeded to heights of wild ecstasy, was devoured, a brain child, an avowal of commitment, a broken promise feigned to. In the subsequent pages twenty-two to thirty with some one hundred and thirty images, reduced in a half day, he found a few dead-on certain profiles which he selected out and taped across blank photo-image positions and routed to a Design agent. These were numbers 283, 301, 314, 390 and 412 and were a rooftop apartment at the Bairro Alto Hotel terrace in Portugal in Lisbon, wicker chairs, wall sofa and long table in a patio on Praca Luis over a warehouse by the harbor in Bica do Sopato; a shot of climbing a mountain ensconced in snow above the clouds; cottage garden bungalows in Avalon on historic lands; a dinner in a midtown neighborhood in a cosmopolitan wine bar next to a church, pistachio and tangerine walls, equal amount of air as water for a waterfront view, modern design by Le Corbusier, meal of roasted black cod with fennel, steak tartare, rosemary crumble cake, chilled white wine, and whipped cream and cit-rus blancmange parfait. Once he photo printed the five references he cross-referred them and laid out new images consisting of a Ralph Lauren light blonde, dressed mostly in choker of square silver medallion and silver beads, web lace, loose draped fabric with chest and collar bone exposed; sedan at curb, dashboard light evident, and the door handles were invisible, inside a dimly lit room a pile of Larson textile burlap, seamed and bark and a Ralph Pucci chair, the room in a narrow three-story warehouse on the lower west side, all glass, largely kitchen, green Breccia marble top, at the end of the block the Palazzo Barberni containing the National Gallery of Ancient Art that featured Todd Eberle's Empire of Space, all black squares well above the city, several chipped.

Jones compared this photo series to other series in stock, spending hours, examining any target that left fingerprints on a counter, and by the end of the day feeling he had studied literally every can available on Bica do Sopato for any traveler since that street was constructed, he drew up a list to ask where this male had gone on board any of the airplanes in the file – was he with airline stewards, any pilots, bags who tossed the trash, straightened the magazines or replaced the barf bags or searched the rows of seats and closets with a scan-tron; did he have business with air compression inside the cabin or with the mechanic? Whereas he, Jones, was interested in who came up on showroom coming and leaving, Lewis Lewis would want the proof as to what gave the identity over to an Implementation category. To do this, Jones had to produce eyeballs on the street, either Intels or Maxguards, cell phones or carry-ons, Liviards, Bixby's, Leisor's and Beltrans.

There were lots of circumstantial settings to find witnesses to. Although the person seen on camera leaving the suite where the computer had been slapped onto the glass was Caucasian male, the identifiable prints were for a black male. One was a gas & electric man. Witnesses on the air field glanced up and saw a black male pull a sticker off and slap small pad device onto window; another witness bumped into his shoulder as he came off the airplane designated for Japan and apologized and voice recorded subject's response; car pulled up to entrance as he came out. When security was turned off, camera somewhere else continued to record dispatching fingerprint on worldwide telex of person who disconnected it. Camera photos of every room were taken, names matched to who registered, referenced to fingerprints on file through DMV and criminals pulled including permits for firearms; all light bulbs vaporized and burst in every hallway and room entry; X-ray crystallography identified gasoline, fuel oil, minute quantities of perfume and thinner, each based on chalk color distillation, light obscure purple, light teal, green, bright flare orange; this recorded like a band of light streak. At these other points of reference he wore surgeon gloves to obscure latent fingerprints, all parts of body were covered, and he never spoke; clothing was not purchased locally, no weapons; however on database keys small black print type was seen on upper top of key, man who appeared naked to the belt was seen on other keys; voice imprint was parallel-processed in distribution of sounds geographically in a day and identity known in a week; task-rate identification listed nine air disasters in all with proof of direct

sightings including a misplaced smoking gun report for a federal building; air liquidation staff took from the assault scene
witnesses who saw the criminal draped in a tan drape wearing
it like a hood attach a device the size of a telephone book to
the window with streamers flying from it like a fan-operated
heater; airplane went down, and law deputies arrived for bodies, took pix, looked for black box, and sent pix to lab, and lab
sent findings for analysis.

All in all the photos showed the Milan departure at 0410
with ETA in Istanbul at 0814 for which fuel compartment
blew up flying in over Turkey; Singapore 1201 headed for Japan with ETA 1323 took a flare in the tail causing a nose down
and crash in the country, and it was these flight disturbance
photos that revealed a hooded man walking through the rubble
and debris allegedly located in Nakano; was this the Seattle
2118 scheduled to land in St. Louis at 2428 which took a bomb
set by a female which lost all communication at 4:38 pm in the
afternoon flying over Terry and drifted almost an hour over the
Missouri crashing finally at St. Cloud where among the wreckage was the flight control console as well as the black box which
was still recording incoming station queries?

Overlapping taped evidence for Istanbul were two eventful
disasters, Lockerbie, originally recorded at Yemen which also
active-recorded Baghdad bomb, secured under SAFE, another
distress electric mishap to food compartment; and Brazil 0202
destined to arrive in Texas 0820 during which its window ig-
nited bright pink while flying over Antilles, the gutting tear
created a charge like a waterfall over rock similar to Yellow-
stone, the same identical flare as for San Diego 704 which once
detonated the pilots could not keep control over the airplane's
course; all future tests indicated both bomb design and lead
install were the same people for these two disasters. After first
takes there was a string of photographers of rooms, the very
best, Michael Moran, Gordon Ball and prize winners take all
– Derry Moore and John M. Hall whose light quality was itself
the obsession, and then inadmissible polygraphs for the Convention Center at Dodger Stadium – why does an employee set

up a soundtrack? But after that day everyone starts doing it –
and Trade Winds, before one sees a car with light blue tinted
glass parked in front of tall grass which on first glance looks
like broken glass smashed like glass that has splintered; the
closest image that month was the micro-cosmic glass break-
age of a 747, scarcely the red rug with bluish wheat sideways at
one end to three-quarters gap by The Oriental Carpet, entirely
polyester and silk.

It rained hard, through the morning the after sound of
dripping off the roof gutters like a persistent reminder, pools
forming on the grass, reflecting towers upward, an aimless
day, nothing to think about or do, except stare at the placid
ocean, wish for balmy weather, an end to listless, tired, pernicious wastrel afternoon, vacant thoughts, dismal, obscure and
obscuring sameness. Despite his reluctance to proceed or perhaps owing to the fact the images were more graphic, more
suggestive of dire absolute death, Jones grouped the photos by
scene, each similar building and foundation categorized, all
identifications batched into a line-up, missing links circled,
same month explosions placed in a file with its description
written in ink, until after an hour he had a certain chronology
and could determine where the design perpetrator might have
gone and the people who set the device inside a structure. His
agency didn't handle buildings which he tied into a single real
estate listing and mailed it off to a south pacific address on an
isle, and although the analyst might have enough to surround
a house or regular restaurant, it wouldn't be any of their groups
that proceeded; only the aircraft with manufacturing failure
although technically they had to give another evaluation as to
cause for the fire on board the thrust reversers of the Boeing
10 which allowably, per the notes of a communications park
and forest analyst had the airplane floating well past Terry over
the Missouri down toward St. Cloud, radar picking up signal
staging for the panels in the gear shaft, no one answering any
inquiry, the receiver as silent as though the plane was manned
by an interdict voice database, a considerable length of almost
an hour before it began to descend. An analyst had suggested

a pretty crazy idea, that the Boeings were tragically most of them given over to lack of adequate response capability, both Japan and Alaska as accelerator-blown as the Machu Picchu nose dive into crystalline waters despite having the ample landing displayed on the adjudicator. So it was as Jones removed the binding off the essential file, the pertinence of the disaster written at the top of the first page of a seventy-eight page document, he marked his own information sheet and unofficially registered the cause as tail-weight. Four hours by train from Grand Key to a coast hotel, swaying palms, flat land by placid grass, beach white sand, slight incline, lapping waves blue horizon, rock straits, green across state, tall swamp grasses and lithe trees, wheat as low green leafy rows, separating by row as the train picked up speed, water canals, liquid farms, paddle width canals of choppy blue gray water, five city blocks by one half, beige brown sand with sugary sand on top, moving warehouses, stations for firehouse, library, train, police. On the high river a park and cemetery – dark inky water flowing almost like a flood plain barely controlled by the two banks ushering it upstream, as rural as any gulf city, most similar to Appalachia, flowers each vivid color an attraction to imbued intensity a single strip seven blocks long inside a cucumber plantation, nutmeg, violet, lavender, magenta, rust, peach, salmon, pink, cherry, crimson, blood red, black, teal, light green, light yellow, canary lemon, intense mustard, deep yellow, cornflower blue, and mad blue; just about everyone gets out in Miami, lines of passengers awaiting boarding cruise ships, a checking off by port officers, two blocks stores inlaid toward the freighters.

Jones stepped out, body stiff, on the sidewalk fronting the round station in Hollywood, and made his way across the lawn to a cab to whose driver he gave directions to a beach house fifty blocks on the coast. The rental was a cute but small husband-weekend cottage with fry kitchen, closet lunchroom, sitting hearth and short hall into the bedroom through which was a small deck with cloth lounge. A mixed beverage of lime soda and vodka removed the damp heat. The sole question prior to losing ground was, "Can you see us? Are we still in the sky?" to which St. Paul replied, "Aye, Mon, see you clear as warm weather."

The small 727 out of Ogden, Utah was picked up on all station frequencies, not any difficulty until it crossed the next intended flight plan of Sea Tac Watergate 774, when it glided into crackling stars and turbulent weather, when it came out, the station at Raider Pass asked, "Where is this one?" to satellite intending any station east of Pine Hills to transmit a responder.

Not until the answer came through did any scout master assess how far off course the plane had drifted, elusively almost an hour passed before St. Cloud placing a finder to five northeastern radios said they had the plane on the satellite dish. When the plane crash landed, she was reported with air ground coordinates of St. Cloud. Analysts advised against computerized cockpit saying that the radio permitted communication during the entire episode even after death was reported because it was isometric. For the 410 on satellite flying over the Yugoslav mountains in 1978 at 0541 having flown from Milan with an ETA into Istanbul by 0719, when coming in for a landing it circled over the Turkish parliament elevation 1750 feet, left turn stable, trees, lake, plaza and medical in rapid succession, nothing more than standard maintenance needed to prepare it for its next flight when it taxied to its stall. It rested two and a half hours between flights, mechanics came out to check the weather gear panel stabilizer, the low rudder adjustments, and the engine timing fuel center. At 1202 the plane began departure procedures, at 1220 the plane pulled out of the stall and proceeded to the gate, and at 1237 took off down the runway, following a flight path east west, rising nine stories to 1674 feet into the air, turned right over trees, the lake, and as it moved above the zenith of the parliament buildings, its center fuel tank exploded, fuel and metal bursting at six hundred feet per minute. Estimated death toll figured in at 119 people.

Originally analysts considered this to have been an altimeter bomb timed to detonate when the plane reached a certain altitude. The finding was that the internal rudders failed to connect the fuel through the engine. This was based on direct observation after partial reconstruction that the center fuel feed was obstructed during detonation causing severe leakage which caught on fire. Cause was not due to human error. Cause was listed as not human error; a bomb device of unknown construction.

Mechanics reviewed the Japan Airlines disaster, and determined a small detonate device was placed in the food compartment.

Basic situation-crisis facts, preventive maintenance was performed on airplane 410, for this a detailed description of work done was recorded in the air-ready logbook for flight conduction; along with date the work was completed, name of mechanic performing the work entered in the civil and engine maintenance book; as well as initials, certification and certificate type held by all approvals for the work performed. On the wall was a pilot certificate with a written approval showing recent annual flight review and up-to-date expertise and the renewed medical certificate. A pilot who holds a type rating is required to have operated an aircraft having a total weight of 12,500 pounds as opposed to one involved in training flights or test flights. The pilot in command carried a full load of passengers had made three take-offs and three landings within ninety days in an aircraft of the same category and class. This criterion was completed at night during the time period one hour after sunset to one hour before sunrise. For the 410 Istanbul city law precludes rising above 1,800 feet ceiling within the first minute. The explosion occurred at 900 feet above ground for which the parliament building directly underneath was under four hundred feet. Other criterion verified included whether the 410 had normal cruising speed with adverse wind conditions with a magnetic course of 185, was sufficiently either below or above clouds with three miles flight visibility and one thousand foot ceiling, Was an alteration or repair that could affect operation in flight made? Was the 410 test flown and approved for return to service? Forces that affect equilibrium of flight include when the aircraft is accelerating. Problem occurred between wing chord line and relative wind, and involved propeller blade descending on the right producing more thrust than the ascending blade on the left. The airplane weighed approximately 2,200 pounds, during a 60 banked turn while maintaining altitude it was required to support 2,200 pounds of weight. Previous pilot noted engine roughness that grew worse during the carburetor heat check.

Cause of loss of power was initially subscribed to excessively high engine temperature by excessive oil consumption and possible permanent internal engine damage. The satellite map of the city showed the runway and across the straits the low offices amidst grass, there were Salk maps of the beach some thirty miles away, roads and ships, a satellite image of something, plane, land form or a ship, and a NASA map of the mountains. From the airplane it was only what one could see out the window. Despite the truism that the weather depiction chart gave surface analysis to the pilot on the AM radio, station 76, the sky cover for all three planes listed sky cover as overcast and weather as haze, drizzle, ice and snow. In spite of these advisories visibility was expected to become uneven, no telling what the sky could have reformed to in the four minutes it took the plane to begin climbing to ceiling. Thus, prevailing visibility gave turbulence, ice and cloud to low ceiling of three hundred as probable. Even with the alleged twisted center fuel tank, given a most recent fuel pump inspection, shortly after the airplane set down on ground although there were no signs of a spawl or vaporizing missile, there had been recorded static electric as evidenced by frayed wires and charred fuel lines, everywhere else the airplane's body was in neat shape without need of repair and alteration, the fact that the Japan Airlines plane 720 was seen advancing on the water in a fireball, spraying red pieces of metal, a methane gas cloud spewing in its path, placed the wreckage on the platform of the underground subway station. Especially her nose down, she couldn't come up, her pilot had to make a distress dash into the ocean or determine how to get the six passengers inside the cabin onto the ground before the plane blew up, which he did whether or not they lived. So, Lewis realized taping the six or more photographs together and dropping them into a cloth bag, Istanbul and Nakano were identical; no fuel explosions, probably committed by the same fuel mainline addict described on the Net as lanky, medium brown. No one baled out in any of these three, not from the quiet drifter, nor from the burning center or the speeding rocket. They took injuries to the ground.

The man flying through space dressed in trims, socks, brown trousers, green shirt and black tie fell from something and landed directly onto a small 727 going about a hundred miles an hour, giving the two pilots near-death palpations.

It was as unlike the black male who fell into the ocean who when he was saved reported an airplane losing jet speed and turning onto its wing.

Had Jones to know who he was dealing with, to have selected out one or two tourists who arrived every winter for either the Olympics or the movie festivals at Cannes, he might have a business man to alert airports to, but chances were the speculation had been referred for comparison evaluation and no one would ever learn anything further. Otherwise, the cause given for the Turkish explosion over parliament in Istanbul, although the explosion struck from the center gas manifold below the cabin, was officially assessed as due to incorrect feed controls of the internal starboard, and the nut-so ludicrous report stated that in Milan also where the 410 had departed, there was not a mechanic with internal rudder-testing expertise in Italy or in Turkey.

Why the Ogden plane flew over Billings, Montana encountered severe thunderstorm over Grand Forks landed nicely in St. Cloud made no sense after reviewing the transcriptions; seems it ought to have burned up or run into a land form. Recorder dialogue and radio gave a sketchy picture.

"Conditions rain cloud over the horizon, red skies craft warning for AGIS system for small boats; one-half hour ago it was hail. Don't approach – get out a look."

Then there was the radio at Lander, Wyoming – "I see you FA 219 clear as day." Over Billings, Montana – "How's the weather out of Ogden, hear you had a few dust storms;" and over West Fargo, North Dakota, point of last contact, "you're flying fine, 219. There's a bit of stormy weather up ahead near Lower Road."

The FA-219 flew into storm clouds and direct turbulence. Ten minutes later it was found drifting over Terry, the pilot's final entreaty, "Can you see us? Are we in the sky?"

The cockpit analysis gave schedule and plot. At the time of the final communication they were charted at six hundred ceiling, seven stories above tree tops. The interior rudders were not engaged, only the elevators had any steering capability. Elevation off runway with substantial time allowable was clearly indicated on flight mission control card. Center of gravity moment was where it should be, fuel capacity was fine, baggage or passenger on child seats should have been alright, standard maximum moment was listed at 2200 – Jones found the load average but he noted on the average sheet that an overage showed and he thought it was for maximum usable fuel.

When he received both cockpit and flight control, Lewis remained mystified. All dead signified a bomb, but with all functions still intact a hundred and ten minutes later then it was conceivable damage and body count was due to a chemical release of some sort. He'd be damned if he knew what to look at, whether it was the same as Turkey, if it in any way pertained to Nakano, could be a wing problem, a spill in the congested motor. Twelve pounds less at -0.1 Moment. He recognized that the flaps were lowered although there was zero wind, but the runway was not yet in sight. Headwind read in at five knots per half-hour with an approach speed of sixty knots. The pilot did a superb job if technically there was no way to land. Same as Turkey, no way to get the plane onto the ground. Yet both pilots got their airplanes down fast in under a minute once they were struck, Turkey pushed in its throttle.

The emission line found a month ago proved correct. The photometer turned in a color of white, dark brown and green said that Turkey was fuel load. Weight of baggage was within limits, condensation in the fuel tanks was unproven. Despite appearance of damage made by each device, all planes were subjected to similar conditions. Constant speed was interfered with, something inside the fuel made an explosion, two out of three were unable to land, and the third once driven at speed was unable to be released from target.

Lewis was on the sweat, off the sauce, for the week it took to fly to the various warehouses on the eastern seaboard to see the restitution restoration of the three airplanes. He was certain he could detect what the crimes were that had taken each plane; no mistaking it, at each air field it was a big dose of reality. Of all the junk in the warehouse from which the reconstruction had begun, men dressed in white coveralls repairing the interior between luggage and upper video compartments, the VCR having with a light source blown up the ear phones headsets of almost every passenger on board. This was the stirring debate for the seven analysts for the airline were originally uncertain as to the sort of device that could kill everyone on board without in any way affecting the discernible functioning of the craft. The question arose in reference to land to craft multitudinous relays; a million arias a decade, every symphony concert attended, every acoustics panel outfitted with state-of-the-art Dolby; sound better than ever fetching its best, most convincing transponder-station interpretation with the use of flight plan simulation. There was the picture on screen and the sound communicated as if from remote plateaus, signaling through the night, a radiant light high up in the midst of nowhere, who or what could get that far up without creating resounding status of static, what other than a convergence of infinite dew drops might affect an intra-stellar trip, the mechanics also agreed that the induced sleep was unlikely to be a mechanical device approximating mass devastation; the problem arose from a chemical induction or a commonly held experience other than flight itself.

There were twelve analyses submitted during the final stages of reconstruction on an Islamic wave of incorrigibility which took thirteen trains out of their yards onto levy lines and surrendered them through brick cell houses into watersheds. Each of the twelve referenced the Lockerbie nuclear power plant shutdown and although the first absorption sheets were solely French trains out of Paris, a media blackout denied any actual discussion while having renamed every incident. Thus the largest items got the majority of press; the steaming pink glass key of industrial ceiling to floor neon art was relegated to the lobby incident of two House buy-outs, the first being a group of dogs on leashes chasing a thief at a police station into an empty pool at a men's station house in Birmingham where if the bays wanted a bobby killed chances were pretty decent an ale or pool house would surrender the cord the same damn way one might do in a bobby in the country beneath a basement. Throughout northern France the train was the sole nighttime transportation to the Loire; in the winter with snows six feet deep the tracks stood clear as rail bars and the trains rushed through, great light blaring, whistle stinging the cold, no other vehicles quite as effective or on time including across the bridge. Thus, once the first take shows were archived, the twelve sheets, labeled with tiny photos and stamped with both court roll call and batch and row identifiers, became the official print-bag which a federal games plan officer referred to.

In the end a telex read, Franc Cinderella's Coach – off main bridge Petit Palais, twelve art galleries. The batch department compiled one and a half rows to number six in the first row and to number three in the second consisting of the crash site in Missouri designated by a yellow band, the Japan Air Lines window number nine designated by red and black band, and Istanbul, a hydrogen explosive that blew in a minute but took fifteen minutes to resolve, noted by a pink band. Of the various categories that proved circumstantial as to suspect were a man on the airfield near the Milan airplane before take-off to final destination, an inspection analyst who gave the same airplane its approval to fly, and repair personnel who placed repaired articles on the Japan airplane, and a print on a counter at an airport shop of a dark Latin male in his seventies buying film. A first network perusal revealed a blonde white man depositing a suitcase filled with hundred dollar bills in the interior departure inside ramp a year in advance of the JAL disaster. When Lewis-Lewis finally put together his response, he omitted any weather as this sort of analysis was considered strictly baseline communication, and instead relayed with an overlay of mountains any flight mission, all relevant pix and all billing.

With receipts on the queue, their assignment wore on indefinitely, by now Lewis' moodiness brandished itself on occasion like a weapon; despite this, he was established in nature, still active, swimming and playing tennis at the No polo Club, an erudite landscape for a weather lab as ever there was one, aqua crystalline waters beneath the kayak, moon rock gardens from the laboratory down to the cliffs that circled the bay. If he was still generous in giving, long standing with unlimited authority, he nevertheless encouraged his men to behave agreeably, comfortable in their perch, to adhere to traditional beliefs, be linear in thinking, low key in temperament, but never weaned off the agency, loyalty first before all other dispositions.
Jones himself was a mouthbreeder sort, a long weathered chap who carried eggs of future revelations in his mouth, yet a practiced correspondent agent who considered neutrality the first pledge of liaisons.

The two men walked across the plaza, a faint wind stirring about making the painstaking job of editing mountains of photo-editorials a burdensome task. They wore tan trousers and dark green shirts, the military garb of the hour, nylon stretch socks and dark tan leather shoes, a trim cap that stood on their heads front to back dark green and tan. Lewis had completed a range of fifty thousand one page photo stills on a recent series of airplane crashes and was discussing the succinct points of analysis with the younger Jones. Lewis at seventy-nine made it his letter to pull all edits instantly from the line-up of stills which might pass over the networks the younger agent, sixty-four, would cross-file on for reference notations.

"The medical brought in standard billings on the JAP and the 402," said Lewis, as he held the glass door of the twenty-four hour hotel coffee shop open for Jones to pass through.

"Ophthalmology, dermatology and balance. We're comparing charting in every county throughout the country."

"Supposing this perp doesn't go for testing?" Jones inquired.

"We're placing our bets on a man with military training."

"Parachutist, maybe?"

"Someone whose been to Riyadh, sure."

They were seated facing down a steep glade of pebbly gravel to beautiful, see-through crystalline waters on which two kayakers lazily drifted. The waitress came, a soft looking blonde with dreamy hazel eyes, and poured coffee and took their orders.

"Any possibility he was a physician himself when he trained?" Jones asked, giving the weather station scenery an appreciable gaze. There were no porpoises in the waters this season; even the usually crowded harbor ramp was almost empty of boats, kayaks and paddle boats.

"Everything is being considered. We're taking into account the smaller aircraft go down descending at pitch downturn speed without a pilot in the cockpit, so someone has to know a thing or two about automatic release."

"Walking on the chalk line, so to speak?"

"Well, you know the Machu Picchu was another Everland with the wing busting up in smoke causing it to descend too fast," Lewis replied.

"How was the flight scheme determined?"

"There was a man in services who was essential to boarding staff."

"Upholstery? Boarding? Stairs?"

"Not those services because they can't tell which airplane they've got. This would have to have been air condition; mechanic had to rip out main haulage and replace with oxygen in preparation for high range second landing above the sixteen thousand plain."

Jones asked, sipping his coffee black the way he liked it on mornings when he was hard at work typically inside the lab upstairs running the parallel processor computer for cities and hotel registrations, "How many overseas stayaways?"

"Three, each locale beside the air towers, no receipts, cash or card."

"Three errors – we should be able to find them if we have some idea as to who the search narrows down to."

"They all vanish off the screen. When all is said and done, we will maintain a complete file on a person who matches most tourists of the season; it's likely we have one of them with the top of the marquis flat."

Lewis had come from world cities of ancient civilizations mixed with stone capitals and modern glass with stylized patio walkways overlooking classical waterways, a dozen boats tied up to a stone harbor, dark olive intermezzos bordered by thin silver leafed trees, citrus, kiwi, an abundance of fertile soil and fruity wine cellars. He might as well have slept for years, a soiree of food too rich on the palate ever-present in the senses, each final journey of exhaustion advanced through a period of reckoning, decided upon seemingly by chance that the best life took in views of stunning landmarks, surrounded a tourist in a glance with the Eiffel, the Grand Palais, Notre Dame or the birdcage glass museum; then a swim on a fifth floor, a martini and early evening nap. Usually at the labs he stayed at the pub from five to midnight nursing a brandy, chatted with the lab coats waiting out the heat with a frozen margarita and chilled smoked salmon, at seven he went downstairs to gamble on board a lit yacht and listen to talk on their private Riviera that tuna boats were going out and it was excellent pay for the strong of back-enduring fishing nets to spear squid at two in the morning.

The torches were already lit, lights of slices of fruit twinkled on a strand below the ceiling in the bar. All evening the salty air circulated in a whipped up breeze, the parking lot adjacent to the entrance had a line of cars with their tops down moving through to let men out. By nine o'clock the Gulf Stream would be calm, not a ripple on the water. The boats with jet skis would come out by ten just as the outside decks of the two restaurants were packing in, the oyster catchers would be getting in with their loads from a mile beyond the bay. The waitress brought a margarita pitcher and salt rimmed, tall frosted bright blue glasses, a plate of crab meat on half hot garlic bread and an ample side of marinated cucumbers.

They unwound from the intensity of the day talking about the latest equipment of software that could compile any presumed image off a un-secure network of travelers. It was being touted as state-of-the-art, this unusual identification kit revue of various reported personal features; Jones expressed worry there could be too many bogus suspects, some real good footwork overlooked, a handful of sloppy outcomes. Lewis thought of the advancement like any recent stride – DNA saliva matching, recombinants in blood, fractionalism wherein a glutinous halogen-like image could transform into another known image.

By midnight when they returned to their suites, Lewis found on his database that his method for GPA zeroing in on webcams proved insanely productive; it gave him fifty photo shots, assembly shots for disasters, withdrawing any photographer's work that gave him additional proofs. An ad that said, Robb & Stuckey tweed sofa; also Snowdon 2007 bone thin female wearing a dress skirt red-white stripe giving a lecture at the Guggenheim; by comparison a Fans ad, photographed in front of the new all glass San Francisco Museum of Modern Art in the gift shop below a clock in dabs of red, 920. Across the top of the negative strip were seven images, each vivid, crisp – News 3am of an ocean beach scintillating water on sand, rust-orange, brown, teal, light blue sky; Artist Gallery, pears wrapped in white paper by Bruce Katz; Pipeline art, Australian art and ocean showing at Fort Mason by Jeff Clark, photographer; Venetian Red at the Corcoran of 12 showing duels between two naked men in window; Lee Miller's photograph made in silver gelatin print titled Drowning man, of a dead SS soldier at Dachau; and a stone angel on 12 dark tint panels titled "Fragmentation" by photographer Hedi Slimane. Run together, images spliced and blurred, the red and white in an instant a fan turning overhead, dabs falling like gigantic debris of blood, the blue horizon line atop glistening sand, another candid instant of light golden pears in utter white wrapping becoming a pipeline and blood flowing into dueling men, with silver gelatin stain became reduced to a narrow strip of colors – crimson dark rust red, light blue-teal, white, silver and black along an edge – the telltale sign of hydrogen. And only one man known for that type of glass-blown, pipe sealed vial, a neurotic clandestine camera watchmaker of such renown, he made watches for government-regulation cameras.

FEAR OF DROWNING

Everywhere in Copenhagen the water was a menace – a menasch, a drab dark blue. It crashed in covering land, and pooled; then suppressed land.

The dens knew everything about land – they barkkened it and there it sat – boken-bloged. Shlakken-haggin rose bushes were put into water upside-down to group the mud, and from everywhere mud would attach gradually to form soggy land. Eventually shlakken-heggen raised land to a height of a hilly high road. Only blogg put bacchin on the ground. Bacchin, in fragments of taither, or canvass cloth made of sails, dried the land.

The Irish ken-milled marshes, dredging land with root – often it would bog a full ten years, rowers trapped all at once. Hoof boken stomped the flood dry, squeezing an ironic amount of bay water into a depression, blakely – if water rose, in went boats, motors on, sputtering the water back to the drying mud flats. Botchel-botch dutch cravin stooped, meaning the Dutch next door poured stairs into the depressions for the foothold; above in grey blue skies came hokens, or trees, branches flapping like witches on brooms. Jagin hoof, horses in fear of drowning moved soil into rifts creating natural irrigation. These jagin were wind gonnars – as an advancing net, terrified, they charged, literally plowing horses, trees, fields.

Sheilah and I went back just forever, we knew each other as dens by arrangement of our studies in Belgium when toward the end of the platinum era, we were assigned to a shop as the only nickel plate artists whose scrutiny could scrape shavings of nickel off tamer metals, the commodities of the day lavished with silver lead, a new envy termed chocolate tarnish, actually a bronze, and silver iron, a shinier bluish metal. Sheilah was tall for an abstract female, vibrant straw black hair, her hawkish posture an aged result of standing for long hours over action art whose exacting embraces gave the observer a permanence of that very notion that discipline must be demanding. Once I had received my own commendations the dependency for which I kept a firm towline dissipated with its guarded anxiety that spelled my own concentration with a knifing tension. In those days slavish reductionism tolerated no quaint fawning appeals; one had to be discerning, restorative and above all likeable.

The home belonged to Sheilah and then gallery owner of a posh one room museo John Ogivile, the oblong interior of high walls with glass at the top pronounced with her sublimated canvasses of treacherous darkish purple and rectangle of crimson, each a different placement. Into a great hall of expansive maple flooring, floor to ceiling glass, a large square of emerald green grass in the yard surrounded by a cement border, inside modern furniture, bamboo wood, vinyl cushions bright green, yellow, tan. A mezzanine with more wall sized paintings, same motif, crimson rectangles on brown backgrounds. Looking down upon a crowded room, one had an impression of huge open space.

Her work was tight, abbreviated. I created studies of contrasts, mostly gates. Each made up an entire painting with a look of adhering chrome, lead plate, bronze calculate, silver alloy; still others were ornate gold, a tinge of wrought stained chip. In sunlight the combined taints took on properties of glass – a greenish leaden look, or water-ruined blue. On a rare occasion deeply red embellishment adorned aged silver. At shows each was hung over raw wood from the ceiling, mercurial silver framing within frames superimposed of rods. A small studio and kitchenette in a stone warehouse along the oceanfront retained an outdoor shed of paint drippings and despite fairly good earnings, I chose to live nowhere else.

Originally when I moved from Europe to America, I trained with a master. Blond and stalwartly, Dutch to his essence, Rhuga was entering his sixties when I found him, a single syllable conversationalist whose invention was to combine driftwood and light weight metals welding them into petrified objects for table art. He knew everything about the torch – how to get an icy look, ways to create texture, objects to attach, raising images, raising veins. He knew other things too – about females, how to age well, scrap to hang onto, philosophy. Every evening he took a cool bath, donned a robe, ate raw fish, drank a sour. He periodically dined with the same intimate, a woman who ran an art college in West Beach below Los Angeles. He would tell me about her, she had turned him onto Spinoza and Liebowitz, she was in her fifties but lived for the immediacy of the day. Everything he said I adapted.

I dropped in daily, after class, at one. He wrote a letter to my school saying I was an apprentice. He was the only male I confided in. Being alone in a new country, I regarded him as a parent figure.

I will only say in retrospect that dependency is itself a self recriminating object for it instructs as to the very nature of regret of fulfillment it composes. We were strolling downtown after an evening of Mahjong at the YMCA, Rhuga discussing the merits of learning to out think an opponent, proposing that perhaps an objective of winning held certain fascination because it relied upon mathematical superiority rather than upon endurance, as art did. A mathematical mind viewed the game as a maze, the fundamental achievement based upon an ability to look far past a moment of repartee. I asked him whether it was better to achieve for oneself, to which he answered that for an expert the comprehension of opening moves relied intrinsically on a certainty that past a certain play outcome diminished to few options. Twenty years of knowledge of the game confronted by fifty.

Rhuga himself being past his prime had early in life sat his youth on a distant shore overlooking a vaster ocean than a canvas and leaving that place was joined by good friends with whom he corresponded for many a bleak moon who abided by beach articles rather than by paints. The driftwood already shaped by forces of nature required only reminders of civilization whereas color, even one dimensional imagery, consented to degradations of parity and therefore was to be avoided. To be pure, color ought not to persuade by use of shadow; contrast ought to astound, there should be no perspective, neither of spatial distance nor by measure of comparison. Thus the utilization of black was shunned, white ignored, depths of one color such as tones of blue to signify subconscious derivation discouraged. Objects of art would ideally represent their materials alone; the observer had to be made aware that the material as much as the art accounted strictly for itself.

I would stray – minimally, by painting objects, gates. Immensity, not volume; life-size, not spacious, neither opening nor stopping. Nearly a ruin of one's upbringing to practice such a principle, for each color used had a suggestibility, if for no other reason than one's society taught it. Despite Rhuga, or because of him – because it is innate to want to paint oceans, deserts, forests – the yearnings to provide some distillation no matter how slight were often prominent. Dominant colors, flat texture like paint on walls took on minute glistening ochre, a dab of chrome, peppery purple-bronze because purple almost never qualified for a relational contrast. The art was an idiom unto itself, only what one saw, the interpretation was one's freedom, the metallic colors contained equal resonance, were only surface, the whole painting gated, there was no way to possess the representation. No way to acquire, become laden with, to take privilege over it. One was to be instructed by the art itself as one painted.

Sheilah and I dated for the two years when she separated from her husband. I thought we hit it off smashingly, we knew each other notoriously well. Because she stayed with me winters during the off-season rental of a rehearsing room, I watched her canvasses take shape. She began with a thin red, selected a corner for the rectangle, rinsed the rest of the canvass with purple, applied dark purple and black drippings, went through periods of depression, barely ate, wouldn't undress out of her workmen's overalls, left the bulb on throughout the night. Weeks later, on went the dark inveigh of purple, like a slash on a roller, over her careful drippings, in both directions. After it dried, she took to it once more, applying thick spreads of color until the painting began to lose dimension; then worked in the red covering it with crimson. In the last, she mixed in a gloss and atrophied whatever contrast had held.

My art would take on her style in these years. A brilliant yellow green, a thin brownish tea rose line just above center, slightly greener yellow below; a struggle to prevent the line from receding into a horizon. A rust green with a sun of olive, the green not quite right until finally I took her advice and flung rust repeatedly onto the canvass, then washed it with light green, gradually applied more and prior to it taking permanence put in the sun. For two colors, she was the artist. The moment I understood how Sheilah thought was the moment I had left the alliance with Rhuga. I had no awareness of the fact at the time, the shift was subtle, that there was a necessity for stirrings beneath imperceptible solid color was elusive, but as I achieved the adamant strident drama in color, I was abstract, no longer snagged in the realism of metal. I went to substantive xanthic vitelline; when I achieved citreous yellow, I applied a topazine ball, definition given to titian shadings. An amber line above center disparaged realism, I had left the familiar in favor of the metaphysical.

Invaribly Sheilah returned to her husband. If I ought to have given thought to keeping her, it didn't occur to me. It would be months before I realized I missed her, months longer before I asked her to mentor me and she refused. She withdrew from the art scene, took a sponge in Vienne for a half year, my letters returned unmarked. As usual Rhuga advised me to leave her in my mind, to inform myself she was seasonal, she possibly took a lover every so often when her husband traveled. Women weren't meant to be had, any of them, in their hearts they were all traitors.

I mourned my loss privately. Rhuga was in a mobile phase, stringing together petrified wood with torched parts of heavy buckets and engine parts. On impulse I dropped in on his art instructor. Mavis' studio was stylish with an immense kitchen counter of black formica and glass cabinets, a dark stained wood floor, studio lights and hall. She told me Rhuga was her inspiration, led me down her hall to a dozen locked storage cabinets out of which she pulled mounted canvasses of early works of his students, all dens, which she believed had stymied his creativity. The paintings were exquisite barely perceptible lines of varying greens, of an opalescent iridescence, soothing. I took one with me.

I suppose in some sense we don't give ourselves away easily. We are a people that won't return home any time soon. The gotchen, or blustery ill winds, may spill rain, we won't be there to see it. We will pretend we are new ghavin – masters of fate – always leaving – jaxloch, imbued with hues of sturdy planks; able to get away.

The green lines seemed the embodiment of a high wave. It had the Danish mentality all over it. The den needed no direction. As dens we weren't neutral. We were a breed forever fighting a future we won't hold.

Water was an essential domain, but water was not an only enemy; the enemy was being encroached upon. Technically water was not a high wave; it poured in. The tides hit Denmark from all sides. Germany provided spekkel-lacha, small winter homes for dens until the tides went out.

It was intolerable a den would have painted this, what many Americans could have found relaxing. Rhuga might have found it disturbing.

One day I asked him where he found the patience to instruct his dens. He said dens, more than most, lived for the simplicity of what can be seen. I asked about his student of the green lines. He answered grouchily that a new kamer to art was disguised in the fairy form of a female with shrieking black hair who as she mastered the untamable of the den pre-conscious creativity learned to release only the element with which mankind shrinks behind a façade with others knowing something quite menacing lurks. His real fear for his interning artist was her inability toward control – during her creating stage she herself was often tortured, if about the preternatural need of a culture that remained fenced in by inevitability, because without it, this shamen aspect of trying to raise as if from a dark inclination a solidifying passion, she could have behaved with greater awareness. He, of course, recommended symbolic color as an art form advising she leave the hildreth qualities of art to others. I ought to have told him I knew her and that she was a brilliant artist. I knew though he liked a closer representation to the absolute, a truism that confounded the pacified ambivalence of menasch, stopped the honest horror of engulfments, gave the mind a new language of kashtamika, dutch for the unending horizon.

HIBERNATION

The light of winter's day receded into the ethereal quintessinal sky leaving but a hint of sparkling brevity. In this most northerly abstract the combination of crystallizing ice with clairvoyant ocean was a tinkling far off sound as when giant ice-packed snow cliffs calved and descended retaining the reverberating echo of a roar upon which absolute stillness dominated. The effect of coming upon this phenomenon filled one with utter humility; of seeing magnificent ice cascades shower into the sea over a thin misted veil of freezing water through which hills of ice rising out of the depths were visible. The ice wilderness so unlike any paradise gave off pristine magnitudes of ice flocks amidst unparalleled mountains of pinkly imbued sunsets and blue sunrises. The winter neither placid nor contemplative agreed only with peculiar skies amassing with torrential gusts settling in high peaks where a chafe wind never quite ceased. Absent of birds or creatures, borrowed drifts carved passages through centuries of aging wild lands, undiscovered, unpolluted, bilious, unheralded majesties. Every year first late spring, third week in June, breaking the enormous quietude, a small airplane could be heard before it was seen some ten minutes later to scatter a pack of mules.

I entered this plateau knowing little of climate or completely untrammeled space, sent for a half year to shoot photographs, write preservation, collect data on trails and lakes, interest only, intending to secure a city editorial desk, having served on state contracts and funds; life had abandoned my closest friend to working sixty hours in a four and a half week, time relegated to swim barracuda workouts, an occasional meal, comparison of film in the dark room. The living situation was a mess and twice divorced with stay away injunctions, remarried spouses accusing her of parental alienation, after advising the oldest to leave her father for freedom from his tendency to over employ her; and unpaid support. Long adjusted to embittered telephone combat over two girls, ages twelve and seventeen, whose new mothers brought youngsters of their own, she refused to relinquish advice or consent. I was typically harried myself between flute recitals, textbooks, martyred weekends, constrained budgets, her girls sent to her two weekends a month and spring and winter breaks without their clothing, make up, homework or special diets. Long days prescribed a caretaker – enjoyment retained for swim meets, Olympics and Sunday brunches with study groups. Honest male friends from Front Page or Sports came and went for right or wrong reasons, ex husbands duking out a new undesired dyad.

First camera shots found high ground from which I telescoped lens stymied a series of fluttering snow in the Adirondack National Park, ice slippered mountains, non fathomable skies, reflecting peaks in grassy marshes, isolated switchback courses, glaciated windless troves, no sign of people. In order to appreciate the absence of mankind, one had to become accustomed to an essential ability, to look far beyond the needs of self, to accept what is, to allow to release from oneself the vagaries of the human plight – desires, lust of nature, envy over what isn't, marginal desperations, selfish house tending, barometers both for wandering or for hibernating – to legitimately strive for an as uncomplicated an existence as a passive observer. The depths of the human soul find in its least complexity an inability to immediately divest of layers of citified living, if only the images that one holds as dear that produce our livelihoods for the schedules we must adhere to day to day are what keep contained that very same inner voice that longs to cry out to be set free of restraint. Controls on the apparent harmony of the totality of demands carves our instinct into fine tasks of each shallow and deep breathing and herein rests that imperial machination of the genius of civilized creative denouncements, the all-too-clairvoyant of destitute callings comes to perceive our stored up anomalies of productivity, to call us into some sort of wilderness, to tear us apart from arrogance, pride, deafened soul numbness; every so often the magnitude of our carefully charted weekly solicitations thrusts itself upon us, whether we are feisty and aware or disheartened and close to breaking. Thus, the distractions in the forms of desire for stimulation, a bit of TV as darkened masses of clouds thundered across the plateau, a bit of melancholy baby tapes where there were no outlets, the shower bitingly cold, nothing to calm one's unsettled sense of too much foreboding; without these to alleviate twinges of distress, the cloying pervasive detachment one longs for in such a setting would prove days away, remote, remissive.

Passivity makes for no pretenses. Honest taking in requires lack of ambition, a sober submission replete with non aggression; of the unspoiled wilderness the observer beholds a private solitude, a collection of unadulterated expanses, a singular accommodation of all clandestine observations. Like an auscultation, a listening to sounds from the lungs, the briefest echoic tranquility, undisputed authenticity, peace, a long sought after separateness. Astute destiny an archetype – a monotheism, sovereign austerity. Alert or hypnopompic, the quest for the soul is deference to pious origins. Vital essence, profound psyche, unclaimable lands, ennobled prolixities. The solitude of the territories lies in what is written of the imagination of desolation; in blizzard regions of descending chilling bice snow, navitivity and papal conjugation. Lakes conjure a permanent reflection of stilled towns and high towers except in winter when they freeze.

The glistening of day crinkled, blue undefined; the sky for each hour resonated a steely eggshell blue, French blue, hyacinth, wisteria, marine, pavonian, likewise tributaries from the upper ocean translucently flowed into the Great Slave where worship of the immortal eternal, of endless life held forever in blue, majestic of colors, indescribable, intangible, nearly invisible from any distance, a shimmering silvery faint blue, barely perceived, inviolable, inherent image, dilute tint, a shade of reverent iridescence, soon to fade.

Between bowls of miso soup made with cold tap water, I inveighed my thinking with a twinge of acknowledgement, of another journalist I invited to join me – he was easy to become dependent upon, during my first year of divorce her attempts to protect herself against dishonesty took me to him. I was asleep, an ice storm having shoveled a heap of snow into the doorway, the window panes in locked embrace with a world in which distinctions were given over to layers of snow; in a somewhat alienated state, wearing trousers, a red and black flannel shirt and suspenders, and black woolen regulation socks, I scarcely perceived his kiss on my brow, neither sexual nor withholding, curious in its arousal. A monastic depiction of celibacy, watching for shadow, length of sunlight, clarity or stippled sky, to discover the effect another person could induce. By the time I came to, he had left the room; I treaded through the pine hallway to find him in the living room at the large window gazing at the sole sight, at frozen curling waves of the lake, perceptible through a myriad of dense pines.

"How's Margo?"

"Margo is Margo," Grigorio answered with slight impatience as if acknowledging that minus the constraints of working and insufferable boredom he considered his other world tiring. "You?"

"Deplorable. No one really stays for long."

"Well, yours was a straightforward divorce. Mine is different. The last time I asked for a separation, she cut her wrists and the hospital telephoned me. I would as soon pack her off to her mother's but she calls, demanding and sobbing. In the last year alone I've had three affairs."

"Women from work?"

"No, from the photo workshop. I deduced after I entered my forties I might never obtain a divorce because she will never agree and technically there's no cause. There's no children either but despite that an attorney I consulted says I'm not likely to get an agreement."

"Montana's laws are strict on the idealism of marriage."

He said, "It's a bind which reduces me from all freedoms, I feel I must always be summoned by her at an instant, and I can't not respond when it is life-threatening."

"I had no idea, I've often considered you two a happy couple."

"I don't have the unkindness to stand her up, although these days I am rarely to be found at home. It's far less complicated than it sounds, we were young when we married, her father counseled me as to the fact of a personal frailty but I did not see it; she is, as you know, slight in stature, lithe to hold, emotionally dependent in a fashion I once found alluring, we talked about everything, she had to have my opinion, my most private thoughts, and I suppose I credit her with helping me discover my true, most constant nature. For years I couldn't look at any situation without discussing the aspects of the assignment with her until all possible perspectives were exhausted."

"How did the dissatisfaction begin?"

"I began to realize when I needed to be alone that she could not tolerate this. She would come find me, want to know what I was thinking right then and there; after not too long she began to accuse me of hiding from her or of being evasive."

"If you couldn't restore yourself, couldn't be alone even some of the time – " I tried to piece together the abhorant description with any memory I could find for my observation of her, she was small in stature, a dark blonde, conversational, a girl on the arm of a handsome man, seemingly reserved, reticent, a catch by any male standard of convention.

I questioned his sense of his own life, the presumptions he

had to have started with, his original pride over his young wife, his attraction to the pristine wilderness, the perfect reflection of quiet waters, the thunderous skies, the scaling mountains of Canada, each still essentially detracted from its setting, his wife immaculate in the photographs he took, breathlessly preserved, contemplative. "She doesn't impress an observer as confining, or a nag."

He smiled, a trace of ironic sadness clawing at his expression. "When I met her she wore a silvery satin, her body smooth beneath the fabric, a large bow of black and silver ribbon material at the back, her small shoulders elegant, a perfect posture. She clasped my hand and at once I was struck by her gestational magic, a barely tangible adoration as though in spite of a room full of guests, for her I was the sole person to whom she could relate."

"You enjoy being captivated."

"That's youth. I was twenty-nine."

"Margo has never struck me as a clinging person."

"It's a front, she is polished, exquisitely so, not innocent or with conceit, she is schooled, has one close friend, but underneath she is incapable of letting go in the sense of having her own life interests, she insists we are part of the same entity, we have to eat together every meal, if I am developing photos she has to have me appear at regular times, if I plan to attend a staffing and there's no way to include her, she invents an illness so I can't leave her side. After thirty-some odd years it's an imposition."

"Shall we take the conversation outside, go for a walk? I'm feeling a bit cooped up. I think some fresh air would do us both some good."

We put on coats, boots and trapping shoes, mittens, stocking caps, took our cameras. Outside the chilling air braced us, breath froze like crystallization, my eyes smarted. We slogged the way over impossible snow to the lake, the waning sun also frozen, tall pine unaltered by the climate as though the forest lacked capability of being flocked or drenched. Through the turning path between rock the lake awaited, a singular expanse of dark blue, of such a depth one might palpate one's internal anxiety of a place where an unanticipated stumble could render death. We stood on the shore as inevitable visitors, gloved hands almost touching, until he removed the camera from his neck, adjusted the zoom and shot a round of eight scenes of lake, piled snow, trees, and several of me. I pressed against him, kissed him, he snapped a photo of my face, unbuttoned my coat, returned the kiss to my neck.

"Will the photo turn out well?"

He smiled. "You will be amazed, I promise."

The sky surrendered us in darkness. He led the way back, taking my hand, as if I were his youthful charge, through the bone white glistening snow, the shadows of the trees supernatural, the atmosphere stingingly bitter, a sense of time shrinking, the snow drifts descending from remote hills as though they contained trapped houses, a stillborn sort of life.

Inside the darkroom he prepped the phosphorescent paper and poured in fixer. In the several minutes it would take to develop the frame, he examined the film he would subsequently bathe, clipping it by a close pin to a narrow rope which ran the width of the bathroom, keeping me beside him, every now and again indicating me to watch the salts. The picture of myself became clear, unmistakably a focused concentration with black cropped curls, I drew the photo out, placing it under a sun aperture window; a next picture in an adjoining salt of the lake having captured flecks of snow and formative ice, distinctive to produce the tiniest sound of tinctured breaking, a startling awareness of consciousness. My senses were alive to him, I was so familiar with the surface of the lake, my own lens infraction were to telescope snow as it fell, I could not have seen that sharding of ice had I known to look for it. As ice formed it made a sound which conveyed to the seeking hiker that once the spellbinding vista was discovered, fracturing ice would become a brief panorama of descending particles, once played, gone, eradicated. In daylight, if disintegrating formation caught the sun, it echoed back as darkness. It was a perception of hearing, in the very instant of detection, it was non existent yet startlingly vivid, inspirational, to contain it for any eventual awareness, hauntingly elusive. I placed my hands against his back, he turned slowly to me, I was instinctually drawn into his view of the natural world, with a sudden jolt of ecstatic fever caught by something I knew I might never understand. He kissed me longingly, the connection between us fierce, an embodiment of the ever ephemeral, distinctive, releasing in me a fertile, fervent desire to be longed for, removed from every normative dyad, to be transcended. I was simultaneously without will or definition, borrowing of any intent he would devise, rash or careless, yet unwilling.

I was young again, unknowable even to myself, hungry for each new, unfamiliar arousal to awaken my sensations. An intrinsic reforming of impressions, constructs, idiom. The first comprehension one has of love is of giving into the will of another, a later age pulls in a deciding agreement to combine personality, tolerance, and over time ambivalences. At sixty there was no acceptance of incompletion of experience, one had reintegrated living with the gradually softening belief that not all aspects of living of a popular culture were necessarily desirable, if accessible. We relaxed about the cabin, Gregorio scrambled eggs and bacon, we sipped tepid coffee on a snow covered porch, nibbled at broiled Danish and grapefruit, shot pictures off the roof top and avoided an obvious growing attraction. For his final evening we spread out our photos for comparison – his concluded a collage of weathering trees, cold water with the hint of a ripple, a strata of snow bank, one of myself seated on the roof deck taking a photo; mine as usual saw the last ray of day, a flock of snow under a moonlit midnight sky, the vast clouds and their reflection. When he left squealing down the road in a black Lexus sports coupe I was surprised to find rolls of film hanging in the darkroom, the developer tray washing over his ripple, the lens refractor with a photo of the mountains with trails down the side. Oddly our afternoon conversation came back with crisp clarity.

"It's called child domicile," he had said, saying he had consulted a psychiatric attorney who specialized in cases like his. "These are females who enter marriage as underage youth, they are fourteen or fifteen, sometimes younger, rarely older. They all manifest the same type of survival behavior, cannot express real feelings, do not explore their own identity, exhibit no ability to psychologically separate. I asked him what legal recourse I had; he didn't think there was any."

"What will returning home be like?"

"I will give her written descriptions of areas I've been to over the years, label the photos, send them into my desk finder, complete index cards and try to avoid the complicating queries of the trip. I'll tell myself it's as though she is seized by depression, she has a rarely understood disorder and because she is unwilling to enter a treatment placement, I must remain patient with her.

"I offered her alimony some ten years ago but she wouldn't hear of it, nearly hyperventilated. She's an extortionist of the human soul, I told you about the early phase; it does proceed to repugnance, eventually takes on avoidance and eventually is worse than endurance; it is disgust. I am in slavery."

One would caution oneself, think twice about leaving, count the cost, perhaps let well enough alone, hope the desperation was a phase or that the individual could actually grow up and tire of them. But these were mental children who did not learn from their exposure to worldly experience, permanently stuck within a rigid composure trained possibly by terror or its antecedent horror of a world gone madly awry by Nether bombings, displacements of social order, children abandoned to parent themselves without financial capability or without having been reared combined with family heads of households to live the role of a young child despite their limitations of soon to be adulthood. I would stay by a lit hearth in the dead of night, sip cold cocoa, snack on a garden salad with tossed-in pimento olives, crisp squares of pumpernickel, a slice of avocado, orange, a meatball dipped in cheese, reviewing pictures, lining

them across the long dining room table, studying them for suggested currents, rain patterns, slowly extending shadows, sequences of moonlight, the typical fanfare of a communications
bureau. No telling that Gregorio who worked the magazine
affiliate kept extremely close to his index a handsome portfolio
that caused a good many feature and also required a negation
of abridgement. If his idea of what was possible relied upon a
society that created a relational allusion that was too threatening to be interacted with, it reduced his stunning photos to the
necessity of also creating images impossible to retain.

TRANSPARENCY

In the grey and brown stone house gallery situated atop Montparnasse between two churches which clock towers rose above the narrow alleys of the packed in, densely crowded city, dark and light red ribbon appearing through a partially made loom work shawl of lemon and mustard yellow weave sprinted with lime gave an impression of buds curling through seeded trellis. At a distance seen from down a long hall the red color seemed at once like cinnamon peppered onto a smooth skein until up close one saw individual yarn poking through as stiff short bristles. An oils artist whose notoriety made him a knife expert in grey, magenta and sepia, Luc had long been taken with the effervescence of hue since childhood, particularly of red, of ruddy sunsets, crimson peonies, the conundrum stealth of incarnadine, of gaudy pensive cerise. Luc himself was tall, in his forties, bony, thin across the shoulders, jet black straight hair cut above the ears, his grandmother Fuchsine's fancy, for it was she who raised him from age six when a motorcycle accident claimed both teenage parents abroad in some desolate corridor of Cairo. She had earned her five hundred hours in ten years studying Indian orpiment and Claude tint and produced gigantic canvases of a lean knife of crocus, saffron fields, London fogs, bowls of quince, rarely straying from her deafening mastery of gamboges. Despite this intensely inward consumption, she nevertheless pointed the youthful Luc onto stages of more mature persuasion, with a coal pencil, next a raven oil base, gradually permitting the neutrals. With a built-in antennae for reds, he was engaged by discordant, intransigent lines; suggestive garnet, Venetian, cochineal; all cadaverous, distant, ecru. It would take a dispelling imposition to pull away from those lively warm carmine buds to enter the adjacent room to view the nocturnal blue-black canvas barely glimpsed when he approached the weave that had attracted him.

Slashes of chiaroscuro punctuated by grisaille and nut brown assailed him, somber silver or garter-blue would have been a better choice to create the obscure, a grey cold tarnish. Although raised on European movies, on classic black and white, big cities, the snobbery of expensive chateau art, he was long at war with adults, their rigid structure, schedule constraints, need for correctness, politeness; he had entered his mid twenties when he seemed to notice stark color distinctions and tried to fix them to his canvas. He would have traveled into rooms of aniline and puce and indigo and cyanic blue before he came suddenly upon his own painting, a floor to ceiling work rendered in stains of vermillion, crimson, and rose rust tinted with reddish brown, knifed in copper and steel, a controlled tertiary opacity. Beside it, his most recent work, a personal confrontation of sorts, a small picture washed out in cinnabar, applied by palate in overlapping sections of terra rose, red ink, muslin of crude brown. After painting twenty years he would tell himself he had replaced the penalties of worry with stolid annulments of passive endurance.

As usual he played possum to Fuchsine's energetic enthusiasm as she unloaded canvases and paint, his silence neither agitation nor dejection, his room upstairs on the third floor overlooking a small roof garden a tornado of trousers, shirts and neckties, his chore day not yet until the end of the week. Luc sipped hot toddy doused sufficiently with peppermint tea, hot garlic bread with anchovy paste on a Spode china plate, a wedge of lettuce with a dollop of mayonnaise.

"Has the mail arrived yet?" he inquired, when she was done separating the load into his and hers.

"It hasn't come in two days. Are you expecting a letter?"

"A notice for a girl's art college."

"What did you apply for?"

"A post as art instructor in Paris."

"Can't hurt. What does it pay?"

"Three thousand francs, good sum, if I do say."

"For a year?"

"I'll return home for summers."

"I'll tie a bow for you. When did they say they would tell you?"

"This month, shouldn't be long."

He felt a traitor to not have discussed it with her first before applying, but she said, as though a pained expression revealed his thinking, "Ah, don't fuss, Luc, it will give me a chance to air out that musty smell in the studio."

"You'll miss me, won't you?"

She tussled his head with a fond gaze. "I'll make out just fine. Don't you worry."

"I'll write you once a week."

"Of course you will."

His mother had written letters while she and his father were stationed in Egypt. Fuchsine had a box full, photographs as well. Gaza, the pyramids, the Nile, the pharaoh's tombs. They were all Luc knew of them as worldly people. His mother, a tall dark haired winsome bride with his dad, a tall lack luster reddish blond who when Luc was a toddler carried him about or rode him on his shoulders. All he knew was his mum, they had lived here.

"You can visit, I'll send you by train," he said.

The college consisted of five buildings, all French King Louis

Versailles style with opulent gardens, private tutorial patios, some with enclosed hedges and sun dials, others with roses, small lakes, and untrammeled rolling greens as far as the eye could see. Twelve females attended art school for three years before each would be turned loose into the Parisian marketplace as sculptors, artists, interior designers, musee curators, and the like. Luc was given a studio and bedroom overlooking the grounds, the interior which was ochre fresco, tellurium, and sunroom. He began with basic instruction in one color oil painting. His students sat smocked to draftsman tables, brush and blotter with red paint, straight backed as though at lyres plucking ricochets of layered color. Each week over four months he made them paint mucky, muddy, smeared, stained, tainted, tarnished until red took on in dried proportion harmonious and complex impressions; he proceeded to transparent color, then to fog, frost, to shades, coloration, glow, and daub, then to enhancements with other colors, grey for somber, orange for warm, black for grief, ivory for cold Chinese whiting.

Red had its own language, a philosophy and a colloquial set of presumptions. For most it could be described as assurance, augmentative, abstract, answerable, avowal, attribute, hearten, sanctioned, power, denunciation, flagrant, infernal, battle, crusade, sin, kiss, impact, reverberate, impassioned, responsive, decisive, reaction, bleed, bludgeon, throb, potency, promise, ancestor, safeguard, nation, unadulterated, moral, coagulate, forbidden, reliable, robust. Each adjective became a painting, fierce champion red, stillborn compromising red, sweet delirious possessive red, shocking gory brutality red, scarlet letter sin red, a nation of crusading red, throbbing potent ecstatic red, red kisses, red umbrellas, russet plains red, red harbor lights, reds.

Into the palate of reds came love in the form of an erudite scholar of paints, a long legged beauty of willowy candor, wine raven curly hair worn free to her waist, soulful brown eyes, a crescent shaped mouth, comfortably attired in an A-line woolen skirt, grey cashmere sweater, black and white saddle shoes American style, a strand of pearls.

Luc had finished grading mid term papers, was lugging his satchel to the administrator's office, when behind him a lilting reed of a voice queried,

"Como se llama?"

He turned to face her. "Luc d'Jardin. Y tu?"

"Maria Consuelo."

"Es espana?"

"Si, por supuesto. Tu es professor del arte?"

"Es verdad, mi primer ano aqui. Puedo comprar un café?"

"Bueno."

"Estudiando?"

"Estoy clases para continuar mi doctorate en los colores. Es mi cinco ano."

He made love to her that afternoon, a light rain tapping against the pane above his wrought iron bed, their sleek bodies glistening with the hard won effort of virtue, a splendorous giddy dizziness having asserted itself into fascination. She would become the one portrait he would paint, a soft ebullient contrast of purple, lilac and wine, her mass of curls each a study in themselves. The nights took on an ardor of discreet adoration, they slept, he with his arms about her shoulders, awakened to her breath at his cheek. He returned afternoons to find her comparing dye manufacturers – Claude, Venetian, Prussian, French – and like any chemist she measured off against time testing each dab from its tube against small canvases already grouped with paint, summarizing ingredient and description for decade, solubility, quasi pigment, combination of color by category, red, green, yellow, black, white, tensile grade, or how quickly the color dried, her dominant interest to determine groupings of paint that dried the same no matter when they were used ten to fifty years after release. He became accustomed to her character as the most true of true.

His grandmother visited following spring quarter. They took her to the Petit and Grand Palace squares for bon appetit, through the warehousing stores for unusual yellow, to the museums, the churches, to the top of the Eiffel, then to the college for a stroll around the grounds, lite fare at the college restaurant near a duck pond, to a lecture, a few artistic movies on Picasso, Monet and a modern Per Svensson for his jazzy use of yellow in abstract expressionism. While she stayed over, Luc asked her to review art slides of his students, generate a commentary page, Maria mixed color for Fuchsine to take home, and they hoarded hours in the studio drinking coffee, supping freshly prepared mashed red skin potatoes and garlic clove, and painting into the wee hours. Fuchsine drew a Paris of boulevards of six story stone apartment flats interspersed with flower gardens and outdoor sidewalk cafes, the Arc d'Triomphe, and tour buses in varying yellows, hints of brown, bronze, white. On her last day they took the Metro to an exhibit on transparency, an inconsistent curtain of white rain, by Wyn-Lyn Tan, a Finnish palate artist showing with Valerie Ng, broad slashes, palate smears, hints of blue emerging through white, cubes of yellow. Tan was illusive, Fuchsine, who had resided in an artist colony in the Blue at Copenhagen, said at a nine-thirty dinner before the midnight train arrived, for the land humans lived on could be right at your feet but one would see only ocean in three directions. The elusive was always preconceived for a coastal Finn or Cope, whether art could be eventually made tangible, the central dilemma was the amount of surface water which even from the air engulfed the tireless efforts of a population that sandbagged the thinnest shoulder of land. They left a sandbox of half stubbed out cigarettes at the train station in Paris when they saw Fuchsine board the train on the upper deck to depart for Montparnasse.

The very next day after his three classes were over, Luc strayed into an arbor enclosed by twelve foot high hedges to enjoy the solitude over a cigarette, a demitasse in a paper cup and a piece of meringue pie purchased at the campus restaurant. The sun crossed overhead leaving in its wake a shadow of himself looming over the sand colored grains of tile pebbles, the sound of a fountain nearby awakening in him his refined sense of having been orphaned too early in life. Individual leaves escaping the wire netting struck him as primordially vivid, the scent of Maria's bathing salts sweetly compensating, the twelve red and brown canvases dramatic in their stages of creation, life too precious to be taken for granted approaching him as a declaration, the instant of his parents' death keenly recollected, unbroken in intensity, preserved, perfect, intransmutable, inviolate. Tears sprung to his eyes. In a moment of intense awareness he shed his cosmopolitan desolation; as he savored the meringue, sipped the coffee, as each taste aroused a finite flavor he felt infused with a conspicuous vivacity, a clear sense that he had lived deserted, estranged, sequestered and now like a naked man entering a baptism was unconcealed, received.

When he returned home for a month at the end of spring he found awaiting him a letter from the gallery saying his small painting had placed first prize.

AN IMPALPABLE TONALITY

The black train shot out of the tunnel under pre-dawn grey skies, the yellow light the only color in the darkness. Periodically the lights inside the compartments flashed on. In a flat overlooking the tracks a telephone rang, its shrill unanswered yet perceived by workers awaiting the oncoming train calling forth a collective subconscious reminder of all types of outcomes to shrill rings, the distinct presence of someone there who won't speak, the sound of the call connecting, the dial tone of a hang-up; as little to do with absence or with failed connection. Michelle Canttry, procurer, at fifty a curly reddish brunette who had spent most of her adult life on the drying creek of the Grande in Tesuque, was at the gallery on the Prince Albert docks having opened the blinds of the windows overlooking the street at brick two story buildings, each a compliment to natural views without ornamentation; across an ash wood floor of two hundred and sixty feet on brick walls hung the ten exhibits – two of each artist, Tom Burton's black cross on blue background and blue cross, Bob Otero's restive blue building beneath a purple sky, pink building, Sabin Cornelio Buraga's blue neon and green signature electric colors, Gus Cummins' blue light against bluer hue with copper, Jeff Hayes lifelike blue bottle, his brutally honest red paints and silver brushes and translucent mirror; each work reminiscent of picturesque Latin village spirituality. She had intended to find mostly black oil paintings for show, but black as a single demonstration was nearly impossible and she settled on predominantly black with iridescent blue. The dungeon of city life, its morose time-consuming fatigue, barely breathable dank air, churches along every alley, the narrow corridor of a murky muddy river like a scourge on an otherwise clean but sooty stone environment, all produced a sense that one aged young and when no longer young, if bereft of husband or close friends, one resided in shadow. No one would cross Winterhaven, whose lack of mind relieving color created the conscience of black oils, no matter city's long dismal rails of blackened steel, dark brown factories, rising cropped black apartments, loss of teenage innocence, past the border to the putrefying bog land of love canal into which every chemical salt was trenched to eventually raise new land. Because the gallery although tiny was situated off the railways in the warehouse section close to industrial offices, crate and cargo plants, the remaining sludge steel yards, approximately seventy men daily walked in at lunch and closing, picking up a cup of coffee at the entrance, mulling about. She never saw them at any of the markets, out and about with wives and children, nor on the rail docks; their lives were private seclusions which if they entered bars to rid themselves of a lurking oppressive incongruence they did so without notice, for her fiancée took her to each of thirty-three bars every weekend Friday and Saturday late nights. Her gallery was the one spot of color to hundreds of men whose routine, mechanical, clandestine lives were marred by lifetimes of piteous, rank treachery.

She would show these five male artists for two months before she ordered in prints to archive in the back fifty foot room from which her patrons would order limited editions. Then she would bring in a new set of displays, once a year a sculptor, anything that reformed repressive themes into an elegance of brightness, any somewhat soothing counter to the cultural miasma that governed life in the industrial factories. Her patrons were seldom expressive, deadened faces well past their thirties who gave nine hours a day, five days a week to an assembly line to produce for the cog and wheel in weather conditions of chill biting cold, a month of pleasant breezy saltine spring, a fortitude of sweaty, sticky, stultifying heat. They were neither political, angry rebels who thought America was knee-deep in persuasive corruption nor were they country desert transplants who would someday strike outward to the sun cities of retirement in Arizona or New Mexico to bask in open windy wilderness beneath vast snow capped peaks or salmon red pinnacles of canyon land stone monuments; these men spoke of no ambition, they were a passive, unformative, inarticulate species by the dozens. Yet, in they walked, in groups of two and eight, inquisitive, seemingly brooding, polite subjects, often repeaters of earlier exhibits, helping themselves to a glass of hot coffee, recalcitrant in their observant contemplation, some spending up to an hour studying the works.

"Hey, girlie girl, are you at home?"

Michelle climbed out of bed, went to the half opened window and looked below at Miguel, her fiancée, standing on the stair with a crated package leaning against the post column of the porch.

"Be right there," she shouted, and threw a knee-length Scandinavian red, white and black sweater over her tunic. She ran from the one bedroom, a huge two hundred square foot room with exposed stone, down oak stairs to the portiere of the three room landing and unlocked the beveled door for him, greeting him with a dry kiss. "What have you brought me today?"

He was full blooded Santa Fe Hispanic, dark wavy hair, angelic round face, coal black eyes, thin boned through the shoulders and arms, washed out tan, educated in mining at Tucson, a pigment expert, the first son of a mining silver weight expert and an only daughter of the last Ashi Spaniard from border Texas.

"Just arrived off the freight ship into San Lucas harbor, I'm told a strident prefecture work."

Michelle poured two glasses of ice water and orange pulp and mixed them while Manuel stripped the packaging off the crate and slid the framed fifty inch wide by sixty feet tall painting and propped it against her one accent dark tan wall in the kitchen dominated by a ceiling rack with copper pots, ample vivid dark green tile counters, stone dark brown floor tiles, and stainless steel sinks and refrigerators, a cherry wood circular table with six chairs. The painting was dark blue with a lighter opalescent blue ledge, approximately seven feet, which radiated in varying sections over the entire canvas. From the distance Michelle backed up to the opposite end of the room, sipped her usual morning drink, the ledge became resonant producing a hypnotic inducement.

"Very workable," she said, at last. "How did you find this?"

"She's a local to interior Baja, she's known as D'Raja, paints usually only with raw color, this is her first variation."

"Can she give us a few others?"

"She only is allowed to sell four a year to U.S. I'd have to check into it. I may have to send a boat in."

"Offer her twelve hundred, whatever she has. Inquire if she will paint in one additional color variation in eight years, three more for a thousand."

"Then if a museum purchases her, it's an easy twenty thousand with a commission of two to you."

"That's life, the only way an artist outside U.S. achieves."

They sat to breakfast, cold kippers, the previous evening's green pepper and olive pimento soufflé, a side of marinated orange squares, cups of demitasse. They talked for over an hour about the current Otero exhibit, the reception that the well trafficked warehouse public was giving it. Michelle thought that prints could sell out by summer, he wanted a Buraga for his office downtown.

Love making acquired its usual depletive syncopation,

Manuel being a creative soft caress, Michelle a willing embrace, silent as she took him to her suggestive depths, a lover who made no further demands. When he finally left, she remembered it was this Sunday he had to take his young son to the carousel and park. Most would say this was the ideal that life had to offer anyone from a dingy town.

Michelle had lived for a year in London where she took courses studying Dorothy Parker, John Donne, Robert Frost, Thomas McGrath and Earnest Hemingway, Islands in the Stream, whereupon she took a taxi one night, the moon squinted like a wish catcher, tree leaves a demarcation of intricate creases across a full moon, utter dark making the leaves appear dark bronze brown. Light from a constable station the same color as the silvery white moon threw a pale square on precise grass. That night toward morning had brought dense black clouds descending to earth, a nightmare of black cloaked wind which she had never forgotten. Coping sentimentality arrived in a jigger slopped with rum, a dash of cayenne, a vacation equivalent to a floating deck on the Thames, where in a port downwind a half hour east of the twin parliaments sat a turntable on a cross, yachts with a vacillating magnetic steerage. Days then and again spent walking down narrow lanes between three story London flats, past exchange banks, shops, all the way by cab to the red and white striped Westminster Tower, up to Buckingham Palace with its elegant parks, fountains and statuary and Changing of the Guard dressed in crimson trousers, black top coats and helmets with black feathers, with muskets, mounted on black horses, then to a Bath church replete with ivory bone trees to the stained glass ceiling, red velvet pews, private stairs to priest quarters, a coffee shop lunch on the square, a stop to Brown's for drinks, off to a Roman Bath tour underground, tan stone building blocks, warm blue green mineral water, an old English town with the Avon river running beneath a bridge, hanging ivy, Roman colonnaded banks, meandering cobble streets crammed with corner pubs, tiny shops, bakeries, galleries, an abundance of art and artful gardens for a mile in any direction. On her return she stopped into the Consell des arts et des lettres du Labrador to make arrangements to have one small exhibit shipped to Winterhaven, Arizona, U.S.

Years had crept as weary lines around her eyes, nose and mouth, she had found it difficult to retain much weight, cold and damp weather produced its own infrequent immobility, occasional exhaustion or short temperedness. In her youth she taught lighting for stage, her passions were little known oil art and from time to time decoupage mixed media. Once she was caught in a storm when the skies churned as solid black and whipped over the plateau catching an occasional spark of lightning recalling that summer day on the Thames when black sky descended like a wicked heaven repealing the damned. When she finally decided she would follow artistic observation, it was to the artists of black oils she sought a pronouncement of the declaration of vivid suppression. Black was the most poignant of the mysterious, its bifidity was as nocturnally inky as water, distinct as ebony as trees during a storm, raven as with cawing birds of prey in a thunderous whirlwind, the depth of stain in chronic mourning, an antithesis of clarity and light heartedness; a profound sin. She who had lost no one, who knew nothing of bitterness or death, whose knowledge of despair was nothing about organic causality brought upon by continual exposure to color derangement, yearned in all respects to confine the definition suggested by utter darkness, impalpable tonality. There was no other color which no matter how dark it became was ever black.

The rain had taken on a grayish gauze semblance. It appeared to dwarf the buildings in the street, to humble the sky. Inside the heat of the gallery thirty men in their late years walked about pausing to consider a painting, like numerous men in days before this they were without comment, in abated observation they found the nature of vivid contrast mesmerizing, true, florescent, as to the paintings of deepening blue they too stood quiet, riveted to the palpably obscure, often Michelle sensed the moods of men as somehow similar in a nod of acceptance, a brevity of study, a flicker of recognition of a sense of what might be visible. She moved from her unseen perch, descending six stairs to the floor, walked to the darkest painting, a Burton, his black cross and asked the group of four men whether they liked it.

"Obscure, too much shade."

"Oh, I wouldn't say that," his friend replied, "it's more to a leaning of being deaf – turning a deaf ear, bad sign for a priest hood."

A member of the group said, "No friar's lantern here."

"And you?" she asked the last man.

He was thoughtful as he answered. "The sky is ultra blue but the cross is darkly black, unfathomable. It doesn't seem to represent a knowable God, possibly the absoluteness of the Almighty, perhaps it is an image representing faith of blind men, hard to tell. The cross itself is not illuminated, it's entirely shaded, eclipsed as though the essence of the cross or the integrity of worship itself has entered a sphere of immoral or unreasonable or just unknowable darkness. What does this artist say to you?"

Michelle said, "For me it represents walking down an unknown path."

The first respondent said, "It has a deeply religious overbearing."

"Yes, I quite agree," she said.

They separated from her leaving her alone. The paintings as they had the day she mounted them whispered to her, they were indefatigable segments of Mexican skies, the colors boldly carmine, blue, neon, the buildings, slabs of thrown paint, the crosses all symbolic of a prejudicial culture out of which a multitude of families found their cross bearings, their finite representations for truth, education, journey and vision. Within the hour as soon as the last patron departed, she locked up and headed the two blocks to the train station.

Obsession neither resides necessarily with disease nor desire but finds its secure hold in foreboding, in an inexorable determination to exact the contemplative with a relentless craving of finding a single special truth. Into the hollows of repetitive yearning to learn that which derives unadulterated essence, emergent in madness or in possessive arousal, obsession follows no practical dictum, but its own spillway course. As the train sped from an entanglement of buildings into mountain divulging plateaus, it shot along a concrete morass of tinted windows, despotic ravines flying with the speed of steel, a grayish series of compartments destined for a stone tunnel at the long end which lay a concentric suburb, box houses, willow trees, knurled oak, codependent succulents, partially submerged rows of cropland, frontage roads with cable and electricity going into enriched land, rusted cars, barns cracking with disuse. A coal heap from which the shovels scooped generous portions of rural heat fuel would inside a month flow on a barge through chemical, gnat-infested, stagnant waters held in place by tons of refuse and coal-produced asphalt and choking grasses. Through a myriad of trees these cesspools would burn the slow gliding junkets surrendering burnt ash leaving clumps of small hills to be barge-rolled into flat jetties. An older, more primitive society would abandon the shovel – this culture described its toils by a language of protest in art, as though no earthly individual would comprehend why the air reeked for decades and birds abandoned former habitats. When at last she arrived at Manuel's town, dozens of brick buildings dotting a solemn canal which the planks were actively rotting, a population of a hundred all who worked asphalt and rail, seven black turning shovels lined the delta unearthing soil from a pit and flinging it across the high levy into bog. There was no church here, no soup kitchen or homeless shelter when the two industries shut down in winter, only ten hour education centers where time to time a young migrant was to be found retired on a bedroll in a bathroom stall. Michelle took the alley to the small square block in the center of which stood a fountain and alabaster angels, three holding up the top tier of a bowl over which water cascaded into a smaller bowl and brimming descended into a pool where children tossed dimes, nickels and half dollars. From here on all sides of four blocks rose the ice and rain stained metallic and bronze stucco apartments in which Manuel had a top flat, five hundred feet of interior exposed stone, a small kitchen, sitting room and bedroom overlooking the jagged mountains tethered by ravines, cutaways and gravel yards. He had said this was the closest he had come to escaping the torturous desert of Baja and since he was old enough to jump freight trains he had planned where he would find work so he never had to go back.

In her dreams Manuel was a man who knew the world at an early age, he recognized slag from cauldron, pistol metal from rod iron, he knew patina black from soldiered grey, vibrating bars from pitch pipes, the underground beneath one's feet from the solid virginals which although they could be overheard were impossible to be felt, concrete being the obstacle to the strum. When she listened for his breath as she liked to do when she spent her days off there, she saw rather than heard or sensed his wrestling with the conflicts of his youth, the demands of a family, the height of sandstone pillars, the stark blue tile houses south of the Corpus border, the moon angling between two giant slabs of irradiated rock pinnacles, the train's compartment lights flickering through a field of wheat like continuous light reflected on a canal.

They dined inside his dining hall at a walnut table with eaves overlooking the train station and platform, rows of new tiny condominiums all glass facing the new park with mallard geese and rushes. White flavorful white, chocolate cheese fondue in a pot on the table, a garden salad mixed with black and purple peonies, crusted hot garlic bread sticks and hot sticky caramel sauce for the fondue; they discussed the placement of their next exhibit for which she wanted to open the office to place the purples. Manuel consumed as usual a half bottle before he engaged in the subjective art of juxtaposition, requiring a dialogue with the expressionism of the abstract. These new displays were minimalists, not the gobs and layers of thick paints applied over months – two, three streaks or thrown paint onto a stark unrequited background that invited almost no response. Michelle wanted a bold, impersonal, non ambitious profile; their selected artists were ultimate consummates in black/white contrast, some in black, gray and white. The absence of color reminded one of a city of snow piling up everywhere, no sky to be viewed, nor ground to be measured except for track. They would have to place the Alison Cowan, of wooden dock pilings and reflective chemicals on shoreline pools elsewhere because it was vivid form, brown shadow, white snow on every post. Art Donovan's superlative abstract of white, black, terra burnt sienna and stark fleshy beige had too much color to fit an impersonal obscurity although Donovan was an irrepressible favorite. They settled on a direct look to the panel opposite the entrance of Robert Burridge, all a discombobulated arrangement of black, gray and white, no blending; on the right exposed brick "Binar," a Vlad Lepure, thick white slashed on black, beside his a Franz Kline, a black dominant abstract with black, white and gray, minimal blending; beside Kline a Theo Dapore, a thin red dripped vertical line over white angular lines on black, the white thrown in a triptych; the next, a Sharon Smith titled "White on Black," a nebula of white spills on black, and at the end of the wall, "Warszawa," by Alyse Radenovic, accent black line near a row of black houses on thick white, the lines of the palate knife in evidence. Across the room on white drywall a Sandy Low, her piece "Low Tide," all color black and white of boats at pier resting on water created from inky black and white oils taking up the entire wall. Michelle wanted inside the interior wall leading to the tiny archive room containing prints a Tom Brown, eggshell, yolk, and runny translucent whites on a dark grey skillet beside the Shawn McNulty, "Cranberry," a palate of scraped white with red squares, blue and black light impression separated at the center by red, the lower division a yellowish brown; on the inside room wall the large Mark Rothko titled "Red Brown Black 1958" of a flat red rose background with a block of black succeeded by a red block below it and a terra brown block in the lower third; three paintings opposite the door to the tiny patio, the Cowan pier pilings and J. Wayne

Lewis' New Mexican vibrant art of a shattered pane over a gold mustard yellow background shared by a vivid blue, as opaque and transcendent as any blue, and his snow on light wood seen at sections of angles.

It was the idea they would clear out the office and refashion it for six paintings of vital opalescence that Manuel objected to. For the trade-off he would have to give her a large closet as a bookkeeping office for supplies, lights, sales, and even though he was adamant she shouldn't establish the tedious details at her apartment, he believed the transfer would in time become restrictive. She said, four broad wood stairs into the tiny oblong office could be justified for the lucent, more garish displays; for this upcoming show a Shannon Willis, dripped brown over red on orange on a wall, on the partially exposed brick an Angelina Cornidez, the strident shapes of black and brown with two smears of light orange suggesting a cave; over the ten foot high, bronze sculpture of a male ballerina, Renee Reezer Zelnick's "Strappy Sandals and Little Black Dress" Ziegler girl on purple background with false eyelashes and purple lips, and crammed onto a small wall that led as a narrow balcony often toned with lights over the larger gallery showroom Ken Browneart's yellow ochre sky over brown earth, Nancy Eckels' "House of the Sun" with its persuasive red corner and squares at the base of white, red and purple palate, Marina Broere's "Inner Sanctum" brown background, muted blue, icy bright yellow slab, a softly imbued pink circle on bluish brown, and last Zachary Brown's "Deluge Abstract," of a purple stain extending on top of dark blue and aquamarine with a bright red halo in the sky, the best of the bunch of his art.

They finally agreed as they topped off their meal with bitter Java demitasse and heavy whipped cream along with two lines of cocaine and a liquid chaser of a spoon worth of heroin that the office would stay as it was, the six color artists would occupy the drywall and print room. Manuel charted the exhibit by slide photos, marking location on the walls by represented tags, creating his standard two page brochure by painting and artist bio to be reproduced for the opening in three weeks under the title, "Obscura." This done, they completed the night with desired displays for a fall season exhibit which she relinquished that he decide would feature brown, bronze, images of dusk, murky contrasts, gloom, shade, silhouette, midnight and umbra, for which he would recommend the tints, tones, gloss, and sheens, leaving her to work on a year-end holiday of lights in oils. His production would qualitatively define shadows of shade, pale, gloam, daybreak, sunset; hers would focus on afterglow, reflective glimmers, phosphorescence, ghostly beams, glare. They talked over themes, use of paper on board and discounted it in favor of oils on canvas, no wood, cardboard or porcelain or clay objects, they made notes, copious descriptions, canceled some out, talked about the tasks their public worked on seasonally, what art could be meaningful, when at last Michelle said she wanted to obtain at least one train oil, none photographic, of the silver streak running over a bridge reflected in moonlight water, a shaded serpent sooty coal blending into the river's brush, pounding forward into the maze of the city, the sole light in the entire landscape the yellow flickering light emanating from the train's exterior cabin, the best she could think of was Vangobot's "Train pulling into Station," all tones and shades of dark drab olive green, lighter shades of army green, liquid light green with dashes of white, the scene of the train at the end of a tunnel, its light a whitish green, a suitable opening for an exhibit featuring shades which at a distance resembled black. Manuel thought Bob Dornberg's black train interior with bright yellow and beige faces ought to be preferred for the common class of working man, or Vicki Shuck's "Union Station Afternoon," a colorful interior of pink, brown and faded blue for a man awaiting the arrival of his departure. They couldn't agree and after a while, the darkness descending upon the dim lights of the town square, he turned on the phonograph and they danced cheek to cheek, Manuel holding her tightly against him, she with arms wrapped about his neck pressing her lithe figure rapturously to every protruding angle of his body, the desultory existence of the familiar oppression of boredom and long learned tedium of feeling claustrophobic in a town without awareness or excitement, that itself a quality of psychic starvation, leaving her, replaced by a cool confidence of breezy sentiments of enthrallment, the stifling dull benumbed, the intangible released by feverish inspiration. .

A TANGENTIAL SEASON

The day dripped with ninety degree humidity. The sprinklers had run all morning since about five-thirty giving the arid soil a good drenching soaking the cinnamon and pepper trees and honey suckle vines tied to vine lattice boards by string. Just as the sky lost its early wane, the soakers like their own choir grouping stood in a foot of water, the vapid leached blossomed branches shrouded by mist off the winding canal that escaped into orchards, long tubing of suckers filed along the dirt truck road from its river side down into flattened fields, mostly of cotton and purple thistle. Ranch hands had departed for the weekend on account of the July fourth festivities of which there were to be a decorous float made all of tea roses and later out at the wharf where stepping Penny sold rides on small motor craft canoes a showing of fireworks shooting from canons like gigantic light green, brilliant azure, fiery crimson, and burning yellow and white star bursts into the night sky. Hundreds of light pink carnation corsages for the ladies would be administered to the ladies of all ages after the vendors of hot dogs, grilled hamburgers and meat stew closed due either to a complete sell-out or the eight-twenty hour was reached. The idle had paused on the shooting water system long enough for the hoses to spit water rudely at tree trunks leaving but a spit-eye of darkened crabs seen only up close. The three bedroom, one story house set far back with a wide screened veranda overlooked a road worth of grass mowed daily and sided on its left ten acres of trees and the canal and on the other side through broad palm, sun burnished leaves about a half block six houses, all tiny, each less than four hundred and fifty square feet, a plot of grass and swimming pool to keep the next generation amused. Inside the big Scoffeld house the burly old man named Rufus and his now middle-aged daughter, Pamela, a vivacious skinny blonde were awakening, he had slipped into a long velvet white robe over flannels and went out to the veranda where their man Joseph poured freshly brewed coffee and served buttered rye with apricot marmalade with egg sauce on porcelain bone china, crème colored with a gilded edge of silver. Pamela who during spring and summer rose with first light read the morning post, her hair tied high on her head in cockle bells, workman's jeans, a shirt clipped at the neck with a blue china cameo, and socks and rough shoes. Separating the newspaper she gave her father the sports and business sections which he blocked in in black felt tip to signify the opens from the nickel and dime averages for rising or falling values in stocks.

"What's in the news, Pammy?" Rufus asked, as he took his first sip of coffee.

"That jigsaw puzzle of southern poverty law made a ruling," she replied, eyeing him over the brim of her section. "Judge handed down a verdict of guilty to a French masoneer."

"That the strangulation case of that poor gal?"

"Yes, Sir, Daddy, she wandered past tabacco lands to the wrong part of delta Louisiana bird land, was found with her hands tied wasp cinch behind her back, God's breath sharply disposed of. All of sixteen, her parents posted a high bail weather status for her abduction."

"Must have more than black leather gold etching notes written which were stolen," he said, proof of tall cistern engines rising off his bubbly cheeks. He bit into his two toast allowing for the thick jell to form an instant tarnish of savory taste inside his punchy wide mouth. "Let me think, she wore a pretty green pinafore over a blushing blouse of tiny yellow stitchings of flowers and high dark yellow pedal pushers sort of romp style. Last seen at the mogul station trading stamps toward a fetching set of silverware."

"That may as well be but they say the detectives were baffled by the fact her assailant had stiffed her up to be an old lady in a wig set wrong on top her head and a billowing cape so that she resembled a trench pipe balloon to induce water. No one thought to check on it."

"The train cashier escorted her to the stall room, I think," Rufus declared, and took another round bite chasing it down with steaming coffee. "Does the news report where she attended school?"

"Holy Names on Upper." Pamela handed him the news bulletin page which he exchanged for the sports, usually stingy with the fractions until he was onto his second cup.

"Upper Canal, is that so?" He searched the news column until he found a description. "It reads she was newly a sophomore, hoped to major in ocean marine biology. She would have entered through Teasdale, two years to clear out those entrant courses. Wonder why she didn't take her stamps to Pintur?"

"No idea, don't imagine it says." Pam had moved onto a new report. "Columnist says cost of funeral lanterns decreased. Any notion as to why?"

"Couldn't say, Pammy. Who's making the report?"

"Doesn't say, Sir." She turned to a latter page and ripped it out, setting it between them. "Here's your Holy Names on Upper. See what they write, won't you?"

Rufus Scoffeld, son of Mathew Bourbon Scoffelder, raisin harvest king, had been an attorney in his day to handle two lengthy trials, Pamela at his side as his legal assistant, a hundred and forty words a minute shorthand, one for mining by irrigation, a case which ran the length of his forty year career and

the second, for the banana bight which surrendered growers
to farm banana trees inside tall, three story greenhouses, both
messy litigation covering everything from charlatan witnesses
to unscheduled shipments as a method to protect corporate
earnings to staged confrontations of employee work lines by
boss hired intimidation, all unworthy hassles that hit the front
page of every last newspapers for a dishonest decade of share
cropper's rights and manifestos. After eating a bowl of fresh
fruit consisting of earnest melons – casaba, honeydew and Lau-
rent, a reddish orange succulent shaped like a small eggplant
shipped south all the way from New York's inland orchards –
and a fryer's grape, strawberries and kill-ice winter white berry
with red hairs, Rufus went into the living room, his small sanctuary of Carson couches, Heredon polished woods, and Tafa
oriental rug, red trim, blue, green and gold interior, to consult
his law books on declarations for disposition on teen rough-
necks and their blushing brides, usually share cropper families whose eldest daughters outlived any reasonable Harvard
or Princeton law intern to run off with some ambitious wharf
storage leniency man from the North. The cases were few and
far between, the famous Nathaniel Turner Hopper case in
which a man of his early thirties had assisted with unhitching
a train compartment and sent it off with a boxcar load of stal-
lions to the west coast for palace shows; the Edge croft murder
of a daughter of a wealthy socialite for which two well known
counsel married to each other who gave opening judicial law
against brass knuckles Stevie Clomfer; the Snow White file as
it was referred to and for whose teen daughter, a promising girl
destined for nursing college, was found dead in the snow piled
fields of Pennsylvania's white cucumbers, and the Rosse file
wherein a fourteen year old Negro student attending Baltimore
Cray land High School was discovered dead in a swimming
pool having just won the try-outs for an intercollegiate meet.
These cases were the hallmark fair weather beacon standards,
all miserable scrutiny up to which the typical salvation of excellent preservation of evidence was deemed to have failed. Not
only were witness statements shallow containing very little

merit to try a case, there was a dearth of unkind comments drafted by youth unworthy of tempering the gracious marble halls of future courthouses. Clomfer killed off the prejudice against him; such foul mannered politics for this girl whose plight while not much differing nevertheless held no links to any obvert eradication of knowledge.

By the time the pools of water had drained off leaving the long dirt covered roots protruding from the soil, the morning had debased to a smothering bothersome discomfort. Josephs went through the house setting all the fans, beautiful crystal light stained tulips of glassware hanging in ten cups apiece beneath long rotating oars which as the afternoon proceeded would give off a gas lamp ethereal appearance. Pamela fixed her hair sculpting it bouffant after which, a mere five foot six, she dressed in a bouffant two piece outfit, an aquamarine top with spaghetti straps and a white, knee-length skirt and white patent leather high heels. The remainder of the day would be spent typing a summation that she would then give Rufus for comments. In the middle of the day sometime around three she would steal an hour beneath the fan in the garden room amidst fifty or so pots of crocuses, weeping iris, bunches of purple gladiolas, maiden fern, creeping lilacs, dark red and oriental yellow pansies, charming climbers, salty sea wild grass, a crammed in effect of sleeping tendrils and sturdy carnivores.

The draught of the ice toddy left no surly complexion as its companion drink, a bourbon sweet, would have surrendered her to near discontentment. At five her handsome ex husband, a trial attorney for the sauce corporations on the dock landings of Orleans, came calling. Leonard was arrived at seventy-one, some six years aged about, a stockinet gent of curly black hair, cupid contemplation, usual bib long sleeves and twinkling blue cufflinks, dark yellow linen trousers, and strapped sandals. He accepted his ice tea under a veranda fan, stirring in two brown sucar lumps, a bit of thick crème, and sipping it wanted to know how many continuations for the Durance file.

Rufus was polite, a bit skirmished in the jaw. "It lasted a

week shy of a season, but it shouldn't have gone that long."

Pamela took Daddy's lead. "No southern poverty publisher requires so much time. State bills aren't in requirement of fetching honors."

Leonard had stood in the stall a full day swearing to evidence. "A didactic reasonable persuasion to examine delta water content, bayou dregs, old towel sand bags, the remarkable selection of brick, fry lime, adjacent slough canals, spillovers from deluges and the like."

"Who tried?" Rufus asked.

"Our very fine governor."

"Sluice is mamam's particularity, ever so easy on the choke, ever so lengthy in the recourse."

"Spring rainwater down pile, river always altering course, vanity ship resting out on plantation."

Rufus nodded at his daughter. "What say we turn over stones for a tadpole or craw daddy?"

"Only if the river ails to the muds, Daddy."

"Which corporation was interested to obtain the Door?" Rufus inquired, with a wipe of handkerchief to his perspiring forehead.

"Rotation for water steerage during late season in wild lands," came his son's reply.

"That's a mighty trying matter. We're half in adjudications on those stips alone."

Rufus was eighty-three, Pamela sixty-five, no ill tempered manner flowered between them on account of her accepting young Leonard's proposal; if anything the two mannerly fellows got along famously, it were as if they made up their own table.

Leonard said, "This latest ruling is already given for appeals."

Rufus seemed wearied. "That's trial trot work. Pammy can help with the postings, you of course may use up to five or six hundred tortes a trial, but if Door becomes implicated in this mason's hearings, then you'll see your elbows rolled to the seam."

"Where is the nibble to the crossing?" Pamela asked either.

Her husband answered, "The Marshal prefers to see its case having a queue for the idea that gal entered corporate land and not so much as a road or a light."

"There was no cab drive-up?" she asked.

"Not there, between acre tilled sugar beets. The cabs wait on the tabacco sloughs."

"The rotation has available clear waters," Rufus stated, "making it accommodated to having jurisdictional authority to provide safety. Since that poor gal's life ended up on clear, it goes without saying that if the Durance had already staffed its buildings, it should have at the least sought legal mores against any person wandering through. Because the state has a moral turpitude to gas that filthy mason, he will take the injection, and then there are ten thousand laws that hold to their failure."

Pamela wiped her throat with pretty pink roses on green cloth napkin. "It's so utterly hot today, we should go inside."

Neither gent nor father took the slightest inclination.

She protested, saying, "The ice cubes shall melt in this spell. Won't you, Daddy, persuade yourself?"

"Quit your shushing," Rufus denounced.

She kept on with, "This heat is a repression. It's sapped all my strength. I don't imagine I'll have energy to eat dinner."

Leonard said, "You've never taken the humidity well, Pam. It's the succulents you ought to feel pity on, they'll be wilting."

To Leonard, Rufus recomposed. "It's true enough the flowers this morning sipped up the entire river. We had pools everywhere."

"No one was a witness to that unnatural sight," Leonard said. "It occurred in water spilled into the row that surrounds the slope where the feeders are trenched. New water was released just that pre-dawn."

"Could she slipped and have fallen?" Rufus wondered.

"Coroner gave its report claiming she had removed her shoes which were found beside a bag absent thirty pieces silverware. It was an ungodly abduction."

"What was she strangled by?" Pamela asked her husband.

"No two pair of hands. It was a pull off a pipe."

Rufus asked, "Where about was such a pipe if it is significantly for the tabacco?"

The evening gambled ever so gradually to sunset. Jasmine and pepper released a mixture of sickeningly odor full scent and spicy flavor, pungent enough to bring tears. Off the wharf loud booms shot a dazzling array of descending canon color, brilliant vibrant fireworks, one right after the next, blue, red, yellow, light green, gold, silver, orange, purple, shooting stars, orbs of falling dissipating streaks, overlapping pinpoint starbursts to fill the sky, glaring white rockets, crimson and gold rain, booms of azure, wands of chartreuse and gleaming stars of orange crackling forth, forty minutes of non stop thunderous cascading bursts scintillating across the black night, everglades of light green, warm green and velveteen green, showers sizzling with red, yellow and blue, as the sky filled with a frenzied crescendo to an unheralded excitement of explosions, each spurting forth, gold shooting stars issuing earthbound.

The chandeliers lit up in a gassy misted hue informing the interior of jazz lighted parlors. Rufus and Leonard spent another hour killing the lazy languorous heat exchanging comments that produced at times outrageous laughter with intense laughter. Pamela ordered cold fish in minted gel served on sliced raisin roll brushed up with apple butter. They dined leisurely, wine pouring freely, Rufus finally in good spirits, conversation about old cases providing for the sentiment of a closely affectionate family, the fish a catch of perfection, the raisins as plump as if just picked. The sprinklers went on again and plopping sounds of water sliding off the trees onto the ground could be heard amidst July Fourth smoke poppers and croaking frogs uttered out on the river. Leonard would eventually join Pamela for a nightcap and Rufus would nod off in the high backed rattan chair as wind flapped up above the trees; fireflies lighting about the yard, Josephs would cover Rufus with gloves and a heavy blanket in the event he slept all night on the veranda.

Leonard and Pamela arose at five. In the gallery Rufus smoked his bowl and sipped his weekly espresso while Josephs prepared a crab cake loaf with stewed licorice rubbed onions and garlic speared sweet yams. The interior of the house was salaciously cool, the fans having whirred all night. Josephs poured two patterned square green and black teacups on saucers with espresso and served the couple on the veranda, with a side of toast, sliced blood red oranges and egg cup. The sprinklers shot streams of water at diagonals over the lawn and orchard cavorting rising mist, soaking the grass with an appearance like sparkling dew. They split the Sunday newspaper taking sections of news and sipping coffee lapsed into long practiced comfortable silence, each securing a sense of rare enjoyment at the luxury of the family home.

In Pamela's youth her mother had abandoned her to follow a married man halfway around the world to study the ancient monastic arts. Still in the cradle Pamela had known no one except her father and Josephs and because her father permitted no adult female into his life, Pamela grew up accustomed to the house being her father's solitude. She liked to think she lived in a sheltered cocoon of existence bartered to one time when she brought Leonard home to introduce to her father. It was twenty-two years before Leonard confessed to being homesick for his Battle roots and his mother; although she agreed to divorce, he visited monthly for a week without fail. The two men conversed on the telephone between visits over their cases seeking advice and legal remedy, thus by degrees Rufus borrowed a son for all his fuss and contemplation.

The soil filled up with six inches or so of water presenting the trees in a clear expanse that submerged their thin trunks like any distilled, very shallow bayou from one end of the orchard to the other. Their brown reflections showed gracefully, the evenly measured distances made for a seemingly endless length of water, onto the surface a dragonfly alit occasionally gliding on a circular ripple of its own creation. Except for a nurtured abundance of boughs hovered in proximity, the elegant darkness of the density of brown soil and extent of tree trunks proved existence was its own quietude changing throughout the morning as the sprinklers negated their flow and the saturation diminished, the soil again became damply dark. Seldom appreciated for its fern sprouts and recalcitrant seemingly dormant dimension, it symbolized an intangible tangential season, life not apart from stillness, a serene, relaxed, sedate fulfillment.

An agile, versatile heat rarely rumored by a blousy breeze gave a rout to endurance. From time to time in a boat Pamela could stake the raffish day with perseverance, an absorbing book and chilled tea gave her a similar subservience. With Rufus' retirement in the past year she indulged her indifferences staring out the jalousie in the attic. This sometimes romanticism gave her a refrain from perplexity. When she next glanced up from her half eaten breakfast Leonard was wading into the length of clear water, his trousers to his knees. Pamela abandoned her comfortable retreat walking across the lawn to join him.

"It's cooler, isn't it?" she asked.

"Oh, by much."

"It is nice on the porch."

"I lay in a sweat all night. I forgot how hot it gets out here."

"The heat was defeating last night."

"I didn't imagine you had a hard time once we went to bed. You slept straight through."

"I usually do."

"I went out to see to your daddy."

"What time was he awake?"

"It was around one. I asked his advice on my case."

"What did my father say?"

"It will take years."

"That long?"

"He says no way to file on pipe or cotton clog in any less time."

"What a pity. These deep pockets just keep getting deeper."

"My say-so will of course have to scare up a rile or two depending upon what the court will allow."

"Perhaps you ought to ask for a backwater ditch hearing

to make them tell you which field and rows aren't patrolled for boat except after dark."

"I'd considered that, but there are lit storerooms every third quarter mile."

They walked back to the house, the saucy impatience wearing thin on her, the need to find a mutually compatible understanding was duly choring him. Pamela took her adieu on the porch while Leonard went to speak to Rufus again about the pasture's complaint.

The morning seemed to have taken on a sweltering brilliance, a sunny complexion which allowed neither a shadow nor breeze to stir up contemplation. Despite the fact that she was already aching with drowsiness and reclined on a lounger at the far end of the veranda beneath an advisor of shade, she permitted herself to give the men their undisturbed time to banter. Rufus would in his own good time toss his son-in-law the brief which Pamela spent nearly a day typing and the two would retire to the yard with sprinklers going and sweat out the summer toil with ribaldry of back-and-forth delivery of summation. In the spell of three hours she would read a short novel, Ivan Voinovich, write her notes as she pleased for each chapter, have a cup of chai tea with a small fruit cup, and nap on and off until Josephs had watered the garden room for the week when she would listen to Beethoven and sip iced coffee for an hour. By dinner time when the men nursed their second scotch she would imbibe her startup followed by a lantern glass of absolutely chilled icy coffee and a lathe of cream.

The shrill incessant annoying ring of the telephone bothered her more than she could say.

"Yes?" Pamela picked up in the hall off the entry hospitality cordial.

"Why, Pammy, is that you?" Leonard's mother Winifred chattered in that inarticulate girlie voice of hers meant stiffly for a spring ball of fifty guests. "Leonard said he would bring you home for a week between intra session. You intend to come, don't you?"

Leonard hadn't whispered a word about to her. "It depends on Daddy's Interim. I'm sure Leonard mentioned it. Every summer, I've only yesterday prepared another fourth criterion for mention ables."

"Will Rufus come when he's free?" Winnie was persistent to the day.

Pamela pictured her ex-mother-in-law, a wisp of a blonde. "Of course, we would love to see you, take you a clotted apricot plant or a fragrant blossom."

"When may I expect you?"

"One minute, Nana." She looked in the scullery, went off in search of the two men in the garden room where misted air filled the ceiling rising up from gardenias, ice ferns, leafy arbors, clandestine trellis climbers, a new lemon bush; and found them, shoes and socks off, resting their tired feet in the crick. "Nana wants us at the week end."

"I forgot to ask you," Leonard said.

"Yes, I can see that, but she wants you also Rufus."

"Sure, you tell her we'll come on Friday, two days." Rufus said.

Pamela walked the distance to the hall. "You still about, Nana? The men were outside down near the crick. Rufus says not until Friday and we have to leave Sunday."

"I'll see you Friday, then," Winifred said, insistent and pressing. "You make certain you don't keep me waiting all day."

"We will arrive early, Nana, don't fret."

She rang off. They would put in their annual appearance; invariably Rufus would want to stay longer. Leonard might take Pamela to the craft fair as likely as not depending upon the weather. Nana's large antebellum house was two storied with an enclosed balcony off three bedrooms on the top floor, a grove of magnolias, patio behind the home, a long pier off the river. In her youth she had insisted on living out of the middle bedroom, taking ice tea and spumoni cake roll with Nana who for years doted on her with weekly two hour long motor boat trips into the misty drippings on Battle Creek until Rufus dragged her back to a cyclone of hearings, dispositions and trials.

She wouldn't say a friendship had survived legitimately, Leonard was by rights her only son and Nana insisted he remain to see after her elderly convalescence despite her ability to drive, shop and have her hair and nails done. There wasn't room for two women in her son's life; either occupancy in the house needed no second mistress or her son was not permitted to divide his sentiments on a wife who lived elsewhere. When the army came to wage training, Nana took Leonard to the base to hobnob with military counsel, only they were allowed to her trove, it would be summers and summers to come that Nana oversaw personally to the budding friendships her son became tolerantly forecast.

Pamela returned to the shady spot on the crick where she left the two men sitting with their druthers. Leonard swung from the rope swing tire shouting ship ahoy, and Rufus, leggings rolled up to the knees, was making the most out of a quart of sugar loaf, maple-processed raisin brandy, sobbingly laughing as she rarely witnessed him do over some sharply regretted chapter of history, gnats gliding on the water causing it to dimple.

"Was that Nana's idea?" she shouted at Leonard.

"I forgot," he retorted from his swinging spinning umpire seat. "Nana's without the soul of finer people to amuse her. I honestly didn't think shoring at the house was a vengeful capitulation."

To her father, she said, "I hope you like that old bag. We'd do better to send Josephs," to which he chortled, fiery in his coat of arms.

"You'll not persuade me to lock up Leonard's bastion," Rufus said. "Is it too much to ask, Pammy?"

"She has no air condition there except in the bedrooms," Pamela complained. "I'll just wilt, if I stay in my bedroom she'll accuse me of being bold in the sack as she used to before she chased me from their home. Whatever d'you suppose she meant to suggest, Daddy?"

"We could always ask Leonard. Say, boy, why don't you lower yerself some?"

"One moment, Sir." Leonard calculated even tread ground and jumped falling to his haunches. "What's the complaint, Missy?" he asked of his estranged wife as he wrapped his arms about her neck.

Pamela said, "There's no air units downstairs, I'll be damp all through and through."

"You're not s'posed to rise until late when the mist hangs about the trees over the water."

"My tradition is here, you know that."

"I know that. Don't you worry over two days."

She sat on the lawn chair on the grass while Rufus rejoined in a lively debate on legal remissions as Leonard waded up the creek. The water level was low, many of the sandstone rocks were tarnished by the sun. She handed Rufus what she had pulled up on the computer about prior objections which he firmly patted beside him. In the distance nearest the house Josephs could be heard mowing the rambling green.

Rufus said to Leonard, catching his attention with yet another all day discussion, "What do you think about these tidewater proportions?"

Leonard ambled on over, scooping them up as he put on reading eyeglasses and, perusing the wording for directive diction, he stood to an invented rostrum declaring, "First point, murdered victim snagged by grip off pull-pipe, proven by photograph levered in disposition; second contender as to proof of malaise, one jill joe having applied for and rewarded with day work in the pipes in cotton fields, said marmalade having lived at a houseboat lodge that regularly weekend notes spilled leftover bourbon to the walk-ins from up road to a tune-up, suspect shadowed victim for under three miles. If a person is shown by any means to have either accosted a younger or less endowed persons that ensued in a struggle to the ground overpowering and succumbing them in an area for which bale lights can be shown located at less than an eighth by shouldered shadow, then it will be affirmed the malice became aforethought. Did you put this together yourself, Pam?"

"Yes. You like it? I compile all Rufus' tyings."

"You've more or less fixed the trimmings."

"Read my third contender."

"'Third, and the point to that which a remainder may affix, only three exactly concluding testimony speaks to in conjunction to wit, none property existed prior to the date; none proportioned could be remiss, and only sole victim could attest; thereby any confrontation in the dark helped by any furtherance of baneful wrongdoing, swears by a heretofore condition that states a wandering deceased person enjoins earlier testimony by statements overheard at same proximity as evidence. To wit, the declaring person was alleged to have acknowledged verbally upon receipt (that she, Victim) did receive a farther pound worth for the value of resold silver estimated at a dock half coin.'

"It says she in essence signed for the books she traded in blue chip stamps valued a hundred dollars for sum property."

Rufus said, "Her assailant must have followed her from the trading dock. Any part claim to that?"

"Plenty," Pamela replied, "but law doesn't borrow on any two parcels for fact. The deed was said to have been committed absent of storage and moonlight in a crossing below tillage. The farm market that places a car on the road assumes only that road that lacks visibility. The corporation which owns the other plots and that puts them on retainer for additional productivity has no authoritative responsibility to either string along lights or staff a vehicle."

"I don't think we're looking any at language as to part clock," Rufus said kindly. "What about a telephone that placed her? They have them in the ground all over farms and lonely roads. It would be easy to distinguish between a pipe being choked by water, a clear single syllable, and a human demise. There ought to be a call recording of her being strangled. That's an obvious settlement."

Leonard said, "The point that gets refuted is not that she had her life taken but rather the resale of silver was granted a disposal garnishment meaning the army has to pay. The attorney for the bereaved family won't see it that way. He will argue the obvious arrangement, that the army supports the shops while the state fines the crop land."

Rufus added, instructing with, "The crop evidence will in all likelihood answer if she was heard for even one word, or if her voice was audible, garbled, hushed or muffled, a wheeze, a convulsive catching of breath, or was there a digression overheard?"

"Brevity of resonance, declaration of fact," Leonard summarized Rufus' summary from the Clomfer case.

Rufus remarked, "A tad shy of guilt with overture, the overt statement of Casius Clomfer was, 'if you know me, you've drawn a line to my doorstep.'"

The jingle to Nana's was a dusty windy journey taken at night along the coastal parkway through two states permitting them to arrive ten hours later while the night still weaned. Wearied and made deficient by hazy weakness, they stowed the sham blades at the pier and entered through the swimming pool deck into the garden room alit with gas lamps of ghostly bright white oxide, passed along a gaudy decorous hall of Grecian inlaid female trussed statues and upstairs to a gigantic landing to their bedroom placements. The two bedrooms letting to the same porch identical, azure marble fireplace, ash hardwood floor covered by an oriental, magistrate-demanded deep blue, black bordered, saltine colored edge, magnificent king sized brass bed and screen doors to the wide balcony where French doors thrown open caused a stultifying windless derogation despite an overhead fan of long silvery oars. Seemingly a chilled pitcher of icy water and lemon slices floating at the top was a clear welcome but whereas Leonard took his in a glass on the porch, Pamela wetted a cloth and plastered it over her face and neck.

The interior was miraculously breezy, at half past six the day was already shorn of attitude, not yet a limp handshake, a cool imposing gainsay of wind circulated about, the gallery table inside the kitchen overlooking the river was set with fine clear red china, teacups filled with espresso, a raw sugar cube at the ready, a dish of sliced green melon, buttered croissants, a host bar of jams – Olli berry, strawberry, boysenberry and raise berry – and hot porridge. Nana took her usual place, dressed for the day in white sparkling stretch pants, a sleeveless buttoned pink blouse, cut low, to her hips, white high heels, her blond hair tied at the back of her nape in a braid looking less than eighty-five, sipping her demitasse to Rufus' amused banter. They were hard at conversation for the army's recent entry to wipe an oil spill which had flowed up river turning the naturally blue water a murky tin grey.

"Don't you but look pleasant, you both," Nana said, with a familiar brim of resentment directed toward Pamela who had come to the table in a robe, her son dressed in fetching silk trousers, suspenders, a stiff yellow collared shirt, handsome loafer shoes, his grey streaked brownish blond hair brushed away from apparent thinning temples.

"My, but you've laid a spread," Pamela commented, staving off an ensuing jealousy that was always present. "Will you be invitation inclined?"

"Tomorrow night a small soiree. I hope you packed something appropriate."

"My best high gown."

"Oh, Mother, do not snip so," chided Leonard, his voice somewhat high strung. "I've promised Pammy a ride up river. Is the boat fueled?"

"Ready to go. Rufus, another slice?"

"Certainly, I can do with one other."

Winifred stabbed a melon and pressed it upon his plate. "I've arranged all blue lights on the lawn, a band to play waltz, soufflés of all types, deep dish orange, chocolate, meat and raisin, and a tub of dunking apples."

As usual Pamela would have nothing to say about the rotten snobbery of a game meant to dampen shirts down to the hostilities of garter belts and T-shirts.

"Can't we at least say men are their jovial best at dunking for pleasure?" Nana asked, innocence as a bell rung.

"I slept soundlessly," Pamela said. "It was thoughtful of you to air out the rooms."

"What a bit of appreciation you are."

"Well, Nana, it was a bit sudden."

"Leonard forgot is all," Nana said, her petulance rising. "Won't you take Pammy to the dockside at Battle Creek?" she asked her son. "They've put in a yacht club; there are over a hundred sailboats."

Pamela sipped her espresso, gave a nod of approval, accepted a croissant spread with boysenberry jam, and took a bite. "Excellent," she said.

"Glad you like it," Winifred said ruefully. "It costs a penny to set the table."

"Yes, it does," Pamela replied. "We spend a fortune on breakfast, it's the coffee and cigarettes, you know."

"Well, you're far away, one can't ride downstream for a meal."

"That was college, Nana," Pamela said.

"There are advisors here."

"Undignified ones, I should have imagined," Pamela put in her two cents. "The bachelor who wanted a crayfish affair or the attorney from Dixon who usurped Leonard's time."

Winifred stared Pamela down, the sentiment could not be reasoned with that Nana might actually have preferred a gay attorney from Mississippi to become a partner. "I suppose we are stating a negativity."

Rufus patted Nana's hand. "Little else to do here in the evenings except fan for the heat."

Pamela answered her with, "You were invited to relocate."

"Excepting this home has been mine for the length of my years. Why is that so difficult to understand? Certainly I want my son close to his inheritances. You, of course, can't bear the idea of tearing yourself away."

"I work for Daddy. Leonard doesn't work here."

"Pamela! Winnie!" Leonard cried out. "It's impolite," he said to his wife.

Rufus said to his daughter and son, "Both of you, cease your idle chatter." To Winifred, he said, taking her by the hand, "Let's stroll, shall we Nana, and you tell me all about your son's education."

The river was a saturated monstrosity of lethargy. Pamela measured with an oar to the river bottom and retrieved sticky mud and slime. While Leonard rowed the barely moving motor boat upstream, Pamela contented herself from the stern with looking at dead silver spackle, gossamer threads of moss clinging to bards of week-old oil, trunks of trees normally restive at the river banks gorged by a profusion of gunk and sand, more than one shifting sand bar trenched by algae and stagnant waters. The wind had died down, the occasional splash was neither fish nor current but a falling plant which having been dislodged or slightly uprooted by far flung slithering oil carnage finally gave way; like a quickly dying fish swirling toward a net somewhat below the eddy's surface, the root was caught on a trapped surface into which it eventually surrendered.

"It's a contagion out here," Pamela uttered, and wiped her profusely sweating brow.

"The inlets shall get clogged," Leonard said. "The boat will require a scraping when we're done."

"I didn't realize the spill had come quite so far."

"It seems to have completely infiltrated."

"I don't see any way to make it to base," Pamela retorted. "Perhaps we should return 'lest we get stuck."

Leonard jammed an oar into the stillborn waters, connived to reverse when the boat tipped on an unseen obtrusion. They sat precariously, persuaded to do nothing, the sun shone vengefully upon them, the lack of wind caused an almost intolerable restlessness, but Pamela kept her complaints tied to fearful silence. Toppling into the ashen stream, Leonard dived beneath the boat; within seconds he resurfaced, his hair entirely blanched with mercurial mud. As he struggled to land inside, the boat heaved side to side, a weight of uncontrollable disposition. When he finally winched his body over the rim, he propped the motor untangling a massive amount of rope-like harness which slowly released its capture in gradual spurts of freedom causing the boat to slide forward and then become pinned again to a mysterious root. They lost an hour to this pernicious grasp, the clutch of an oil burdened habitat recalcitrant in its newly deposited shale beds. A sudden swift pulling away through a heavy mud consistency gave distance into the river, the boat making speedy recovery from the sandy bar at three miles an hour, Pamela stifled a release of breath, Leonard jabbed the water with an oar; detecting nothing he reassured Pam they were free.

"Did you ever tell Nana about your advisor?"

"I wouldn't tell her a thing like that."

"Perhaps she had you investigated."

"I'd thought of that."

"Perhaps she paid him off."

He sat gripping both oars looking uncomfortable.

"Why else would she blame me?"

"It's been over a long time, Pammy. It's not as if I've gone back."

"I should have told her it was before we married."

"That's just how Mother is. She doesn't view things the way anyone else does."

"It's not fair to me."

"She wanted you to make your life here."

"I couldn't deal with the society here, what use would I have been? You have your office."

"She wanted you to become more of a daughter."

"Nana only wants to extol her virtues."

"Not much can I say against her."

"Then try telling her what actually happened."

"I can't, she wouldn't understand."

They ferried downstream, a wind accommodating their speed. She kept her back up refusing to talk, the same argument hounding them portending to some wisp of misbegotten fate, the damage between them never restored, Winifred at her whip sorely aggrieving the loss of her son to marriage, the son unable to exact to any type of marriage, without feeling he was complete, finding only a return home gave him a dedication he longed for. Leonard wouldn't deny the brief interlude but he wouldn't concede to it even if to do so removed his mother from their shadow.

Saturday night was aglow with candles in every Japanese lantern. Afoot a folly of southern governing legal counsel played dashboard for a score of two to one, the gentlemen ahead over the ladies, lights rampart in air as shooting star sparklers, a handful of attorneys at the dunking barrel, shy lads on a turnstile, there were festivities on the lawn, the patio and on the pier. Honest baked caramel puffs, chocolate and marshmallows inside bread sticks roasted over an outdoor grill, a large cake lathered with whipping cream opened and a live female in a bikini rose out, champagne poured freely, shouts from the pool sparked interest by a group of young men who jumped in fully dressed amidst astonished female abrogation's. Easily seventy people ran about the place, Winifred conversed with arrivals but the party which had been held annually for the past twenty years needed no directions to put people at ease. By midnight due to a storm warning the party had dissipated, Styrofoam cups strewn about the lawn. While lantern lights flickered in an ensuing breeze off the river punctuated by streaks of lightning, a handful of remaining adults convened inside the living room beneath whirring fans. Outside a storm flashed heavy rain pour which washed the garden in puddles wide enough to lose sight of the grass and patio. Lightning flooded the windows with white sheets of electricity from which damp heat settled oppressively inside the house.

"We can put up anyone who wants to stay over," Leonard announced.

"I'll obtain bedding," Winifred said, and went to see to the task herself.

"I'll bet others get caught on the road."

"Last year we were put to a shed down river when we were in boats having relays."

"Oh, I recall that, we all got swamped. My boat sank."

There was laughter and concerned questions.

"It doesn't matter really," someone said; "it's just fun. We were lucky, we dried off and went home."

Pamela poured night caps for six people in addition to herself and Leonard. Rufus excused himself to go upstairs citing old age and too much excitement. Leonard kept the spirits going with a ghost story interrupted only by Nana who entered with cot mats and bedding. The erratic fun turned to ghastly horror the minute Leonard completed his story-telling and Nana turned on a cassette meant to instill terror from eerie, chilling spine tingling, cacophonous, jarring music, a favorite spook provocation from years past. Leonard had run outside and with a new flash of lightning plastered himself in a skeletal sprawl over a window eliciting horrified gasps from his guests, who pointing yelled, Pamela herself never having adjusted to this talent event reacted by being equally scandalized, equally angered. Owing to a realization that if Leonard didn't show up to their bedroom that night was indeed fine, she stayed with the guests through the storm talking instead about Rufus' famous trials, putting them at ease, warming their fragile energies with leftovers and orange juice.

An absolutely attestable shock, she told Leonard the afternoon of their departure when he awoke; he and Nana were like two big kids who never really had participated fully in a sensitive social grouping, Nana was selfish without any sense of reality, for him to have displayed an intent to psychologically injure their guests went far past any discernible polite behavior.

"The heat did you in, that's all it is," Leonard said. "No one was as miffed as you seem to believe."

"How would you know? You didn't return after that sadistic prank."

"I was sopping. I went upstairs for a change of clothes. Nana came up and we talked nearly an hour."

"You didn't come down to learn what was going on."

"It was well past one-thirty. I assumed everyone would be asleep. I can't stay up here any longer while your father and

Nana are about. Get dressed, won't you, and come downstairs?"

By the time she descended the hour was pushing onward to two, she wore a box pleated navy skirt, a silk sleeveless blouse with a navy bow, and swept her hair into a lacquered do, light blue makeup applied, red lipstick. She found them outside seated on garden chairs taking in the rain-enhanced air sipping iced tea. Her hair laced into an elaborate braid that started high on her head, Nana was dressed in a shimmering silver blouse with see-through sleeves, black stretch pants, and silver high heels. Rufus wore his usual Saturday apparel, dark tan and crème striped silk trousers, a ruffled yellow shirt, a suited silk vest to match, dapper high step shoes with tan socks. Nana was holding court, dismissive of the party except for the creature who stood out of the cake, too many adolescents who threw themselves into the pool, it had taken her two hours to clean the mess, smeared frosting, crushed orchids, tens of champagne glasses, fruit custard flambé in dishes with melted ice cream, small parasol party favors in Shirley Temples, dips and chips on the pier – endless. And then this morning the air went on the blink, she had barely enough time to throw left-overs into a soup, the preparation called for chilling two hours, she wanted their final afternoon to be anything but chaotic, she hadn't expected Pamela to sleep all hours of the day either.

"When did you two put into Battle Creek harbor?" Nana inquired.

Leonard looked sheepishly at her. "We never did, we got stuck on a bar and spent hours getting off it."

"Heavens, Pammy told me something but I didn't catch the entire picture." Nana said, primping her hair. "What is there to get stuck on, for goodness sake?"

"The current has reformed the bottom sand."

"It's been years since you kids took the boat out and you just don't recollect where the drifts are."

"I had to swim under."

"You poor dear!"

"It's nothing, Nana. I've done worse."

"That river is so unpredictable this time of year, that's why

I permit Jonah to row up."

"You've gone to the base?" Rufus asked.

"Oh, regularly, every spring month."

"Is that twice?" he asked teasing her.

"Seven times, I'm old hat on that crick."

"A pro with the oars?"

"Well, some, where the rushes grow, but we motor most of the way." She asked her son, "Did you have a chance to speak to Jonah when they stopped in?"

Pamela said, "Why, goodness, Nana, I'm surprised you invited that Jonah boy."

"It's his papa of whom I am speaking."

"Did you see papa Jonah?" Pamela asked of Leonard.

"I can't rightly recall," he answered. "Where were they at, Nana?"

"Oh, I'm sure they came," she replied gaily. "They helped the band set up, I believe."

"I wasn't paying any attention," Leonard said. "I avoided the band altogether, that Dixie corn, one may as well wave a flag."

"I didn't see papa," Pamela said. "How is his son? A trial on the lewds, I imagine."

Nana ignored her as she sipped her tea. "Papa attached the connections. He's helped for years."

"Isn't that sweet?" Pamela was upset. "Leonard, are you certain you didn't run over Jonah?"

"Oh, Pam, must you?" Leonard's expression was strained.

"Why, Leonard," Nana said, fingers at the straw, "what inscrutable perception have we to say for Jonah? Of course, Pammy means to remind you of the year Jonah, so drunk he couldn't stand, chopped the flower hedges with his mower. Wasn't that a bother? The gardener was dismayed."

Rufus asked, "This is Jonah Blevins, our trial ascot out of the delta?"

"Yes," Nana said; "He's alleged to be a real dandy."

"Nana, must you?"

"For the good Lord's sake, Leonard, it is passion that is

contested," Nana said, making every effort to prevail.

Rufus, determined to view the man's adjudications as honest, said rather forcefully, "Blevin's done wonders for tort law, no sins of omission, no truly ever determined, crimes of passion out of which all conclusions derive a single basis of foundation, he was merited on domestic cruelty wherein the law states a husband can be put to death."

"How realistic can that be?" Nana asked. "If the husband bears a consensual spouse –"

Rufus interrupted saying, "A sin is no less a sin when butchery is a practical blunt instrument delivered to an outcome for bestial injury."

"Whenever shall we hear about invisible injuries that foully dispose a young man to the trials of the flesh?" Nana imposed upon her family.

Hearing no slight intended, Rufus commented, "The sins of the flesh are not any legal deposing, it is a question of property rights of marriage as opposed to personal rights of sanctity. A man injured by sentiment brought on by an unfaithful wife cannot in the eyes of the law attempt to murder his wife. Similarly the man to whom destiny has given the unfaithful wife can neither make a claim against the wife's legitimate spouse."

Nana drank her tea to the jiggers and shaking the ice inside the glass, she announced lunch was sufficiently chilled. Glad to be relieved of a somewhat jousting conversation, the three followed her inside to the spacious kitchen when Leonard having distributed wide porcelain bowls on silver edged plates of the chilled curried chicken, diced apple, raisins and consommé to the dining hall announced he intended to open shop on the Les Strasbourg square with Barrister Johnny Gavert, Esquire.

"How stunning," Nana was pleased. "I didn't realize our Gavert made esquire."

"Yes," Leonard replied, having situated himself at the head of the table, laid his napkin on his lap, and taken the first sip with a nod of approval the soup was indeed chilled, "Johnny has tried every review to arise off the river including the passage of maritime military. He has an excellent enjoiner for the corporate sinister policies burdening the appellate, not to mention the piece work from the reclamation of human use lands."

"Gavert lost on promise, didn't he?" Rufus began a scent for another opener.

"It wasn't a fault case," Leonard said; "The governing matter lay with the fact that the parcel didn't consist of all deeds legally bound to successive generations."

"You couldn't argue on redistricting?" Rufus inquired.

"No, totally wasted effort as it turned out. The jurisdictions don't allow any contention on account of the river changing course."

"How has he completed on sole authority?"

"He's made out alright regarding land owners, but sole is neither elevated nor put to egress even under appeal, making it less perfunctory as a remedy."

"That's enough to formulate a decent basis for private joint law. At some later stage they'll toss in a prison beckoning."

"A circumstantial conviction could be a sugary sport," Leonard said of a postulate retinue. "I've already done any fair standard of dispositions, appeals, arguments and non disclosure of penalty."

Pamela knew Gavert by name through the Battle counsel to be a streamlined, edgy sauce of a biting whip. It wasn't her place to look at Leonard's graces in legal store and remedy; if Nana adapted to the wits of a new office she would soon as overlook the flagrant disposition of the notorious whips.

Leonard said, "I'd as soon become content with all prison, in spite of the fact this state puts away a great many middle class men."

Nana rose to his defense with, "Marriage law incorporates to joint household with all ammunition aimed to the man who raises a second family."

"The sting is to the undeclared heir," Pamela stated.

Rufus rendered, "The wholeness doctrine technically allows one spouse wherein there are children born prior to a marriageable unit. It does not address the event of more than one spouse. I'm not certain it matters until a document is assessed for property. The other part of an injunction describes but the contention that whether sole authority gives proportioned welfare is usually immaterial, a finding made to favor the wife. That is how those conflicts arise."

"Gavert's last trial surrendered in the face of promise on the added argument that although the deeds were originally under one lawful owner they nevertheless had moved through numerous contingencies," Leonard said. "While vacant land was used for cattle hustle and was permitted to become owned, in time with death of sole authority these parts, once use terminated, fell to reversion."

"Context is a querulous creature constituting rarely benevolent assigns," Rufus said. "Every so often the Court accepts a challenge, but modern society has simplified the basic tenets to chart and plat except where the dispute has been farmland forever."

"Florida allows parcels that have been eradicated by a moving flood plain to become sectioned if the remaining land is not within the jurisdictions for farm. Alabama does not agree to restore unless the original basis is farm. Mississippi is the more liberal but their laws hold that land, not a house or building, can be restored within seventy miles of a flood line."

"Well," Rufus asked him, "how likely are you to argue for Mississippi?"

"I did one in concurrence with Gavert on wild lands."

"Sole authority moved into Alabama?"

"Yes, we succeeded in the stipulation. It wouldn't have been accepted for a benefactor of wild lands. We lost on the same proverb for Georgia."

"Georgia is a bear."

"Nowhere like it, the law is impossible to convene."

"I suppose when you come again for your week stay I can give you some points as to challenges established in Georgia that were derived in her neighboring jurisdictions. Train law, for example when shipped goods are lost, gives no forbearance to other states; whereas postal law allows for transportation to be estimated for cost. That's a big one. Then there are the slavery rules – no indentured servitude exists today although if a person works in a domicile capacity and leaves to marry, the order of contract is still considered enforceable if the domicile was hired as one in a group of non English speaking menial labor. That's Georgia for you. Every contested hearing rests on one fact or the other."

"I have a case with a governing principle as to the course of the lower Mississippi which flows past its eastern boundary along the ocean wiping out substantive portions of Alabama sealed land."

"Ah, yes, I told you what I thought about your pious legal remedy. You won't see any interdict for land that periodically sits several feet below ocean until it surfaces as the Mississippi corrects its course. When it does then you have to have it staked again for up to eighteen moon cycles whereupon if all levied land surfaces the penalty can be declared."

"Gavert thinks we can ask for a cool water basin on the premise the land is held intact as an entire tract inside the confines of a basin slop because the depth there is less than comparable ocean shallow migrating waters along its coast and coastal inlet plain."

"Well, let me think," Rufus sipped a hot cup of espresso contemplating the consignments of law which addressed seasonal tides. "You could certainly argue in favor of merit of retention. You could graph some hypothetical relational plateaus as evidentiary. Tertiary land remains the rule. It would take at least an interpretation for use if the state intends to farm rice, salt or bag sand. If the state controller wants irrigated lands, you're out of luck. If the state has traditionally placed migrants in the disputed area, your argument doesn't stand a sifter's chance of standing buildings even in water."

"Even for two and a half feet of water?"

"Well, technically, there's no barrier of reef, levy or land to separate the ocean. It could be reasoned that one day the land will break up and be lost permanently."

"What if an ocean wall is erected surrounding the land?"

"They aren't likely to probate it unless its purpose is for a shallow harbor. The courts won't agree for land to become tract for another use without first showing boats won't become dry beached."

"Gavert says he has photos of previous Mississippi birds that migrate when the land submerges, that the pelican flies there for its winter, the pink ostrich goes for the fall."

"You have to get another endangered species there because only the pelican is at risk; then you can try for a sub-contemporary land use to bring in funds."

"So, that's Gavert for the news."

"A joint practice should endow you with good fresh ideas." Catching Pamela's gaze, Rufus tapped his watch to say it was time to shove off.

Scents of white gardenia and periodic jasmine wafted in the evening off the coastal orchards that lined the highway, a soap fund industry that financed many a bed and breakfast. Pamela drove with the consistent cautious speed of one who knows home is not far away while Rufus, the wind from the slightly open window ruffling his jacket lapel, chatted on at length about his impressions. Overall the visit with Nana had gone well, he thought, even though Nana made a point that Pamela had abandoned a husband in order to pursue her career.

Pamela contradicted him. "Nana wanted me to remain bound to their home despite her son's early affairs."

"She has resentments, you can see that. Leonard's associates won't be suitable in the long run."

"She will make his life unbearable when he stays late at the office."

"My guess is Nana's been trying to fix him up with dates."

"He won't remarry. He's comfortable, he has a decent practice and as long as he doesn't purchase a townhouse, his home life is with her."

"Do you know Barrister Gavert personally?"

"His wife and he separated years ago after he was rumored to have taken a mistress to a hotel."

"Was the mistress female?"

"I assumed so."

"I took Nana to mean he is queer."

She said, "Well, that's not expecting much. That social grouping has wives who are listed on social register, some have obligations of child support; many are said to keep a female in town. Gavert wouldn't step outside the mould."

"I suppose Leonard was ordered to stand in on Gavert's case."

"I rather thought so also. The blue pelican is a rather invented notion."

"You don't imagine Nana introduced them?"

"Not a chance. Nana would just as well commit him."

"I'm not convinced," Rufus remarked. "She invited the old flame."

"But there was never any intercourse. I consented only after Leonard tested negative."

"I don't recall coming across either Jonah, and I spoke to every last person."

"It's a tedious matter, her insistence in meeting Leonard's associates."

"She is a mother, she may have reasons to worry."

"I can't imagine what they could be. Leonard brings test results every so often as proof."

Darkness had fallen, only house lights gave an indication of a town.

Rufus said, "Blevins is a superb trial attorney on the lewds. Everyone who knows him knows he's flamboyant. Gavert can't afford the blue pelican on his Vitae."

"Especially if it wins their case."

"Alabama's not Louisiana. A winning decision for Alabama on her refuge lands will hold everyone's attention forever. Leonard should bring in a consultant for argument."

"I agree. Alabama's the only state to have voted for a flag without any blue. No blue, no ocean."

"Yes, I remember that notion. It would be appropriate to Georgia which has no ocean on the gulf."

"It can't be that Gavert is from Mississippi, can it, to try a case on the strength of wetlands?"

The garden and orchard hung in floral indecision. Josephs had neglected no detail. The trees stood in their foot of water, the lawn still retained its dew, the veranda had been swept free, and the tea glasses were covered by saucers onto which two small almond biscuits rested. Inside, the crystal chandeliers glowed in misted salvation, their stained interiors like bluish fog in their incandescence. The interior kept none of the week's sweltering repression; the garden room was constituted by snapdragons, lacy ferns, bougainvilleas, the flowers regrouped such that one was instantly aware of a cloying restraint. The rattan chair had been left as when Pamela last napped there, the couch untouched by human hand. Eventually she made her way through the kitchen gallery to her bedroom, changed into pedal pushers and a blouse, and returned to the veranda to join Rufus for late night tea. He sat on a white rattan cushioned chair as Josephs trimmed his hair, tea glass in hand, a cigarette to top off the return home.

"The holiday did Daddy a world of good," Pamela told Josephs.

"Glad to hear it," Josephs said. "Nana telephoned. She asked that you call her."

"Is there any report you want me to give her?"

"None," Rufus said.

Pamela went inside to Rufus' study and made the call.

"Is that you, Pamela?" asked Nana, groggy with sleep to be awakened at two. "I asked Josephs to have you ring when you got home. How's your father?"

"Daddy is fine. He says he enjoyed himself immensely. It's the first real party we've been to in a while."

"I'm so relieved you arrived home fine. I was worried about Rufus. He retires early."

"He's aging, Nana. Life wears him down. How's Leonard?"

"He's gone to bed. He wanted to talk to Rufus again about his case."

"Definitely, Daddy shall call. He has to consult his library.

Is the house back to normal, Nana?"

"It feels hectic as though it never will lose the frenzy. I asked my maid to sit with me this week before papa Jonah takes me in the boat."

"That's a wise decision. Give Leonard his freedom."

"Well, he's busy with the case. By summer's end he will have the office to contend with. There's so much to do, wallpaper to hang, carpet to measure, furniture, lamps, we can't let these boys take matters into their own hands, they lack a strong intuition."

"Tell Leonard we arrived home safely, Nana. Tell him he can drive up to see Rufus if he'd like."

"I will, Pammy, I will. Do you mind if I ask what happened on the boat?"

"It's nothing. The heat strained my patience."

"Did my son say anything about my inviting papa Jonah to guide the boat?"

"Not to me, Nana."

"You remember what you said to me that first summer we put you up, Pammy?"

"I was young and very impressionable."

"You said you wanted a man to be a man."

"It was just an expression. Leonard was shy in those days."

"Well, Pammy, he was scarcely twenty-one. Boys are slower to mature than girls."

"I suppose that may be true."

"Did he talk to you about Barrister Johnny Gavert?"

"I heard it when you did."

"I'm having his background and credentials investigated just to be sure. I told your father what I think about a man like that. I told him I was afraid it was starting all over again. These men are like predators."

"You've no reason to say such a thing."

"Don't I though? Haven't you both put me through enough? All that sneaking around makes a person weary to imagine it. Papa Jonah has confided in me all these long endless years."

"I think you should ask papa Jonah why he's under that impression."

"I don't need to, Pam. I was just curious how you could let it go on."

She said her adieu hoping Nana's wickedness did not spring its own epiphany. Too bad Leonard's father had died while fighting a war leaving Nana without a man to raise her son. With no husband to exert influence, they went the way of grieving families, bereft of post, Nana locked herself inside her marital chamber for days to mourn inconsolable battle, no one to feed and clothe her seven year old.

Pamela drank a sleeping draught before she returned to the veranda where the two men laughed over a bit of indecent humor. "Nana sends her love, Rufus."

"Did your call awaken her?"

"Apparently, the entire house had gone to bed. Leonard needs additional advice."

"I'll telephone him soon as I awaken."

"Don't forget to advise him on a trial counsel replacement."

"You be certain to write that down," he requested of Josephs.

"I'm going to bed, Love," Pamela said, giving Rufus a friendly peck. "Don't stay up late."

She entered the hall turning the chandelier light low, passing the kitchen into her room where she pulled back the coverlet and lay down. Leonard was older, nearly thirty-eight years separated his infatuation with Jonah, her belief he sought a companionship to replace his father; he was a modestly retiring attorney, several successes behind him, the partnership with Johnny wouldn't possibly add up to the sassy description by which Jonah in his effrontery persuasion had seduced him. She had learned about it from Leonard himself who feared he might never escape the town's mastery over him, or love her enough, because he faced uncertainty as to who he was as an individual aspiring to law. She thought in retrospect many times it was simply youth asking of maturity in what unforeseen ways did life experience shape a man's fate. For the seasoned lawyer, the delta nightlife with speak easy clubs, cheap bourbon and raisin bread pudding, its decked parlors and piano bars, consumptive crayfish beckoned to fishing boats on the misted waters of Battle Creek, elms dripping with garlands of moss, young counsel living on the tort work offered them by their aged divorced and not so closeted trial experts.

Pamela awoke from a calamity of bitter chill issued in from offshore. Her sense that the men were also awake caused her to want to covet aloneness. Despite momentary selfishness she donned a robe and wandered through the hall outside. From the veranda she saw the water in the orchard had frozen; an ice mantle lay over the ground hiding the roots much like milk fed to dwarfed trees stymied their growth. Walking the distance, beneath her feet, the lawn was a multitude of icy spindles, tree branches glistened in a crystalline sheath. At the orchard the ice penetrated about a half foot, its surface glinted with colorless glitter; she prodded it and discovered it was hard, granular, impalpable, freezing splinters of dripping water immediately below, a lingering retard incapable of slackening, phlegmatic, stubborn, renitent. Like so much of life spent with every anticipation of lasting endurance coupled with stratagems for prosperity or putative resource, the cyclical mooch of depositions governed by evidence and remedy, one moment ephemeral, the next realistic and uncompromising, aggregated for tranquil assembly. There was no haphazard distinction here, she saw Rufus emerge onto the veranda, cup and saucer in hand, and waved, comforted by the constancy of his presence, although in that precise moment the shrill shriek of an egret could be heard coming from the placid canal a half mile in the distance.